THE BIGOT LIST

A J.J. McCall Novel

THE FBI SPY CATCHER SERIES (BOOK 1)
(Previously Published as The Seven Year Itch)

S.D. SKYE

FRANKIE V BOOKS
AN IMPRINT OF LADYLIT PRESS

The Bigot List (A J.J. McCall Novel)
The SpyCatcher Series (Book 1)

Frankie V Books
An Imprint of LadyLit Press
P.O. Box 461
Cheltenham, MD 20623

Publisher's Note:

This is a work of fiction. Names, characters, places, and incidents either are the product of the author's imagination or are used fictitiously, and any resemblance to actual persons, living or dead, business establishments, events, or locales is entirely coincidental.

July 2015

Second Edition

ISBN 978-0-9839202-9-8

William Jr.
William Jr.

And in loving memory of
Francine Vanetta

Acknowledgments

Thank you God. Thank you God. Thank you God. Through whatever challenges I endure, and there have been many, You keep giving me another story to tell and another day to write it. I will be forever grateful for this gift You've given me, and I will tell every story You put in my heart as long as I have breath to breathe.

Thank you to the men and women of the FBI who lay their lives on the line for this country every day. The United States is safer today than ever because of what you do.

Thanks to my beautiful son, William, who is always so supportive on the days I'm stuck in the writing cave. He's the reason I live. He's the reason I breathe. He's the reason I am.

To my Dad, William, who brought me through one of the most difficult years of my life. Without his love and support, I couldn't have brought J.J. McCall this far.

To my dear friends and beta readers Lisa, Carey, Becky, and Jos-Renee, thank you for suffering through my early drafts. It's because of you that this is finally ready for prime time.

Thanks to my cousin and graphic designer RheQuan Robinson for the fantastic book cover. He nailed it on the first try. Thank you to my cousin Kim for having the good sense to marry him.

Thanks to my Facebook readers who helped name one of the series' characters—Grayson "Six" Chance—Keleigh Crigler Hadley (Grayson), Anya Rhamnusia Guillino (Six), Jounay Thomas-Ross (Chance).

And to anyone I've forgotten, my apologies, but my heart says thanks!

Who Is
Special Agent J.J. McCall?

I love mystery/suspense/thriller novels. Probably considered a groupie in some circles. This is despite the fact that I've had a 20+ year analytical career in U.S. Intelligence (over 12 of them spent in the FBI) which too often colors my view in terms of plot believability. Despite my real-world experience, I'm a pretty big fan of authors like John Le Carre, Gayle Lynds, and Daniel Silva. What I find interesting about the genre, and somewhat disappointing, is there isn't much diversity when it comes to the main characters in spy and espionage novels. Not one prominent African American, Asian, or Hispanic main character. Yet, from my own personal experience in working at or with the major three-letter agencies, I've met a number of highly capable, competent (and often exceptionally performing) agents and case officers from a range of ethnicities in the intelligence, counterintelligence, and counterespionage fields.

After leaving the Bureau and pursuing my dream of becoming a writer, I eventually decided that if no one else was going to tell their stories, perhaps I should. So a little more than two years ago, I sought to write a different kind of spy novel with a different kind of character. And because of my vast experience in the field and work with so many agencies supporting a range of missions, it's a story told from a new perspective—one based largely on the realities of counterintelligence work inside the United States.

The heroine of my series, J.J. McCall, is inspired by an African American agent with whom I periodically worked for several years. I remember first seeing her walking through the halls at FBI Headquarters. She was this short, stylish woman in a pin-sharp pantsuit. She looked about 12 years of age (and I wish that was an exaggeration). I assumed she was a new case agent working a temporary duty assignment in the espionage unit. After weeks passed, and I continued to see her, I said to myself, "She's still here?" I later found out she'd been slotted as a supervisor in the counterespionage program. I was in disbelief, couldn't find my jaw for days. After snapping out of the shock, I wondered what drew her to this field that was largely dominated by white males—but I never asked. I figured it was her job, and she was doing it as I was doing mine.

Eventually, we were assigned to an Intelligence Community working group together, and I got a chance to see her in action. Whoa. She had an almost innate ability to walk into a room, command it, and wade through all the white noise to cut to the core of an issue. Surprisingly, she wasn't at all arrogant or bossy, just no-nonsense and very just-the-facts, Jack. I had no inkling of writing a series about her at the time, but the memory of her professionalism and my admiration for her stuck with me.

After writing my first two novels, the name J.J. McCall came to me one night in a random dream. I woke up and couldn't forget it, couldn't shake it. I knew it must be a character name, but I had no idea at that moment which character or what the book would be about. I only had a name. Days later it hit me in a flash. "That's J.J. McCall!"

When creating the J.J. McCall character, I wanted her to be complex and layered. So, I had to create personal and professional issues that are in no way representative of the "real-life" J.J. The fact that she's a highly functional kitchen drinker (a growing problem among women with high stress personal and professional lives) is her fictional personal issue. In terms of her professional life, I wanted to somehow infuse J.J. with the ability to cut through the BS. I wanted her to have a gift—not a super-power—but a gift. To me, the psychic thing had been done a number of times before, and I didn't want to walk that path. So that got me to think about a different route.

Espionage, spying, and intelligence collection is all smoke and mirrors. One of the major challenges counterintelligence agents face, a significant problem, is attempting to discern the truth from lies. When an FBI Agent pitches an officer in a foreign intelligence service, and he refuses to speak with the FBI, does he really mean it? Or is he putting up a front because he's afraid of getting caught by his counterintelligence service? When a new Russian diplomat enters the United States and claims he's legitimate, is he "clean" or is he a spy on a mission to steal U.S. secrets? From operational covers (or legends) to targeting and recruitment, to intelligence collection, the human intelligence world is built around layers of lies. So, just imagine a character who could detect a lie in this world?

Pretty cool, right?

So now J.J. detects lies…but then I immediately wondered if I had made her job too easy. As writers, we can't make anything easy on our characters or it's not fun for the reader. Readers like to see characters that face challenges, characters that suffer before they succeed.

After some thought, I realized the gift was naturally self-limiting. First, J.J. couldn't be everywhere at once or listen to every conversation. Her gift would only be useful if she was speaking to a bad guy at the time they were lying. Secondly, people lie for a multitude of reasons. In addition to attempting to deceive others, we tell lies to protect feelings. We may even lie to protect someone from harm. So, even though J.J. can tell whether someone is lying, she cannot answer the very important question of why without digging a little deeper. So this gives her an "edge" in this spooky world but limits her ability to leverage it.

A reader once made a comment something to this effect. "Well, why doesn't she just ask people if they are the mole? Story over."

I'd love to see J.J. walk into court and say, "Yes, lock him up. I'm a human lie detector, and he made me itch so I know he's lying."

That probably wouldn't go over well…and might get her locked up with the aluminum foil hat people.

And there you have it.

I sincerely hope you enjoy J.J. McCall and the first in this five-book series which lets you follow along on her quests to find American traitors working for Russian Intelligence.

PROLOGUE

"[Swine traitors] can take their 30 pieces of silver, but it will stick in their throats."
Vladimir Putin

Monday Morning in Moscow…

A hulking Mafioso known only as Mashkov hovered over Mikhail Polyakov's mangled corpse. The ax in his massive hand dripped with the blood of a traitor. He would not live to betray his country another day. In the safe house basement of the Soltnsevskaya-owned safe house and death chamber, his remains lay on the concrete floor. A pool of crimson surrounded him, and his flesh had been gashed and hacked beyond visual recognition; death's stench thickened the air. In order to serve its only noble purpose, his right hand, which bore a crescent-shaped birthmark, was left intact.

A sliver of light shone through an undersized window revealing the wicked grin that parted the executioner's cigarette blackened lips. Colonel Anatoliy Golikov. A Russian intelligence officer, he was a member of a cadre of Russian Foreign Intelligence Service—SVR officers—from the First Department. His professional mission—to recruit people who sold U.S. secrets. His personal mission—to kill anyone who betrayed the Motherland.

His skinny eyes, slight frame, and borderline gaunt face colored him weak, but his iron-fisted will and suffocating persona made him a man few crossed. Even fewer had lived to brag about it if they did. The son of a former hardline KGB General who executed Russians spying for the West, he'd filled his father's sadistic shoes well. Left nothing in his wake except a trail of dead American sins against Russia.

Golikov compelled his two most reliable henchmen to observe the murder of their comrade. The gruesome killing would serve as a message to them and make them more effective purveyors of the one they'd soon deliver to their colleagues posted at Russian embassies in the United States—spy for the Americans and your life will come to an abrupt and grim end.

Golikov circled the body at a measured pace, rage ebbing beneath his nerveless exterior. He teetered on the edge of insanity. "We should feed him to the sharks, Mashkov. A fitting end for traitorous pig, wouldn't you say?"

Mashkov nodded as Golikov eyed his cohorts, his unnerving intensity intended to strike fear and warn. "Comrade Vasiliy, your passport is up-to-date, yes?"

Vasiliy nodded. "Mine and that of Comrade Igor." Of the SVR counterintelligence officers working under Golikov, he'd achieved the higher rank—Captain.

"Good. Both of you are traveling to Washington. The Center has authorized funding for two temporary assignments, and they have given me the authority to recall Comrade Viktor Plotnikov."

"Comrade Plotnikov?" Vasiliy said, his surprise obvious.

"Yes, we suspect Viktor may be providing our communications codes to the Americans. Aleksandr Dmitriyev, chief of the counterintelligence operations line, will see him to the airport. My friend here and I will interrogate him accordingly when he returns," Golikov said, nodding to gesture Mashkov. "While I hope we've found the last of J.J. McCall's traitors, I must take active measures to neutralize any that remain. You are my most reliable officers. I trust you to carry out this mission." His gaze shifted between the two.

Vasiliy and Igor both nodded; everyone knew their respect for Golikov was born from fear rather than admiration. "For how long? My wife, she—"

"180 days minimum. But I'll extend it as long as necessary to clean out the riff-raff," Golikov replied, his expression affirming there would be no negotiation. "I would go myself but Washington is not the only residency with this problem."

"Yes," Vasiliy said. He and Igor both appeared anxious to leave. "Will that be all, Comrade Golikov? We should be getting back to the Center."

"Not quite," Golikov said, his every move, every expression, spilled with evil. "Please, take a seat. I need you to pay a visit to the U.S. Embassy here. We have a gift for the new Chief of Station." He turned to the murderer for hire. "Mashkov? Will you do the honors?"

Mashkov lifted the ax blade above his head and slammed it to the ground, slashing through the wrist bone like butter, his force strong enough to sever the appendage with one blow. Igor and Vasiliy cringed and pressed their eyelids together. They turned away as Mashkov lifted the hand from the unforgiving concrete floor. He placed the appendage in a steel ice-filled box specially designed to leave its contents undetected under embassy security scrutiny. After sealing the lid, he put the container inside a slightly larger cardboard box, sealed it, and addressed it to the Moscow station chief care of the security officer.

"Deliver this to Agent McCall's boyfriend. I'm certain he will convey the sad news of that pig Polyakov's demise. Perhaps next time she'll think twice about recruiting our people. *Suka!*" Golikov cursed.

• • •

Telephone rings cut through a brief silence as a herd of suit-clad diplomats shuffled through the consulate section. It was lunch time at the

American Embassy in Moscow. The station security officer, Grayson "Six" Chance, glanced at his watch as his stomach rumbled. His gut told him he'd miss lunch again, and the phone rang just in time to confirm Grayson's suspicions.

"Siiiiix," the duty officer said, the tone in his voice teasing. Grayson's nickname was the source of several running jokes. His IQ. The number of times it took him to pass his last lifestyle polygraph exam. The number of women he bedded the night before. But his skin was thick and his temperament easy. "We've got an ID on the hand. You might want to get up here," the officer continued.

The light at the end of the tunnel dimmed. He'd planned to serve out the final two days of his sentence hunkering down in a corner and working in solitude until time to hop his flight to Dulles Airport. Golikov's thugs had decimated his hopes.

"Give me two minutes." Six typed the last two sentences of his final after action report. When the meeting ended, he'd let the administrative officer clean it up. After grabbing a pen and notebook, he made his way to the stairwell, preferred to take the steps up to the secure area.

His anxiety swelled with each step. He needed to tie up the last of his administrative loose ends in order to return stateside. But, in this moment, his thoughts centered on J.J. McCall. Why hadn't he realized sooner? She meant more to him than he knew.

No woman had ever made him feel that way, simultaneous apprehension and lust. He'd built barriers to maintain his cover and conceal his heart. But J.J. cut through it all, straight to his core, his truth. She'd slipped beneath his cloak and dagger to see him for whom he really was. And she loved him in spite of it. The debacle, his sloppy exit from her life, had left a wide gulf between them. But nothing worth having was easy, and Six was up for the challenge of getting her back.

He'd become a man on a mission. He'd served his country as a clandestine case officer, then a security officer in his latter tours. Now he was just one flight away from her. For the first time in over a decade, he looked forward to returning to Langley.

Four flights of steps and a few paces through the main corridor, the one connecting the State Department's political and economic sections to the "Company's" section, and he had arrived at his destination. He badged into the secure space and headed for the conference room. Upon entering, his eyes locked on two reports sitting on the table in front of the seat left open for him. He turned to the duty officer, whose face wrenched in knowing discomfort. Six knew from his expression the stakes were higher than anticipated. Even the new boss had stopped by to check on the progress of the investigation.

"Six, come in and have a seat," said Mark Levin, the new CIA Station Chief. He'd arrived three months prior and had been in crisis mode from day one.

Six gripped the chair back, pulled it from beneath the table. He positioned himself beside the station chief. The sound of shuffling papers disrupted the silence. On edge, he waited for one of them to break the bad news.

"The legat had NCIC run the prints for us," Mark said to Six, referring to the embassy's FBI legal attaché. "The hand belonged to Mikhail Polyakov. We'd been handling him on behalf of the Bureau since he left Washington and returned to Moscow Center last year. He was valuable, gave us information that's still saving our asses on a number of critical operations. This is a significant loss."

"Indeed," Six said. He hesitated a moment before asking, "Who was the FBI case agent?"

Mark dropped his chin to his chest. "I'll give you two guesses."

"J. and J."

Mark nodded.

"Do we have any idea who gave him up?"

"Same bastard who gave up her last source, I imagine," the duty officer said to Six. "It's clear at least one agency in the Community has a mole problem. We think he's in the Bureau and the Bureau thinks he's in the CIA."

"What else is new?" Six replied, shaking his head at the silent war. It had endured between the FBI and CIA for more than six decades and intensified with each passing day. "Any possibility this is ICE Phantom?" Six asked, referring to a top secret multi-agency operation to find a rumored mole in the Intelligence Community.

Mark's eyebrows rose. "That operation's dead—the Russians succeeded in making us chase our tails. Ten years, millions of dollars in wasted resources. Langley hasn't expended this much effort on a mole hunt since Angleton," he said. Angleton ran the CIA's decade-long Cold War mole hunt that destroyed the careers of dozens of case officers and never yielded an insider spy.

The duty officer chimed in, "There's no proof that ICE Phantom even exists."

"Except two dead sources," Six replied.

"*FBI* sources," Mark injected.

"Yeah, *one* of which we ran on their behalf until his hand arrived in the mail yesterday," Six countered. "ICE Phantom or not, we better figure out who the hell is responsible before Golikov sends another— and the next one could belong to the source we *can't afford* to lose."

Mark nodded again. Six had made his point. The most high-placed recruitment they'd ever had within the SVR ranks was in danger. At least until the FBI apprehended ICE Phantom. Losing him would cripple their operations, not only in Moscow, but around the world.

"Agreed. Time to get Langley involved. And someone will need to report this to J.J.," Mark said as he turned to his colleague. "Six?"

He agreed to deliver the dreaded news. *Damn!* Six thought to himself. J.J. would conceal her devastation well, but he knew another depression loomed. Losing her second source in as many years, her unbearable guilt for leaving another family without a father, might propel her over the edge this time. He'd warned J.J. a thousand times that her job wasn't to care. Her job was to recruit and exploit. J.J. cared too much. Loyalty and emotion drove her business—a fatal flaw for an FBI agent. Her steadfast concern both annoyed and endeared her to him. J.J. would succumb to the sadness; she always did. But consolation was just days away. He'd resume his rightful place in her life, help her pick up the pieces—and

then make J.J. his wife.

CHAPTER 1

Saturday Morning...

The lashing FBI Special Agent J.J. McCall planned to deliver to her traitorous boss must not be tempered by common sense or conscience, and her mind churned over that thought as she arrived on the edge of the bourgeois Northern Virginia suburb. She couldn't wait for her visit with Jack to end. For J.J., time crept by, and the entire morning dragged. *Why me?* she asked herself again and again like a tired, broken record. Her burgeoning anxiety was irritating at best, so she leaned on Belvedere despite her promise to Tony. Only a small sip, though. Just enough to soothe the nerves and loosen the tongue.

Except for the barbed wire and armed correctional officers, the state jail looked more like luxury condos than a place to imprison hardened criminals. She took a deep breath, flashed her credentials and ambled inside the detention facility, dreading the moment she'd be forced to see his face, hear his voice. Her heart thanked Tony, the best co-case agent she could ask for. He was already inside waiting on her to arrive, refused to let her go it alone.

A sheriff led her through a series of security doors to the interrogation room where Jack awaited her arrival. The door buzzed, and the lock popped before she walked inside. Her teeth ground as she headed toward her seat, the one farthest from him and closest to the exit.

Jack sat solemn, pensive, shackled at the wrist. He rapped his hands on the table and waited for J.J. to sit down and speak. Seemed relieved, a feeling that no doubt dissipated when he realized the sentiment was in no way mutual.

"Jack," she spat, unsmiling and cold. She fought the urge to tell him how well he looked in orange. She couldn't force even a microscopic modicum of sympathy, not after he'd destroyed so many lives and treated her like shit for so many years.

"Didn't think you'd show up," he replied, in no position to spout his usual venomous remarks.

She pursed her lips and folded her arms across her chest, gave him "The Hand" with her hardened stare. "If Cartwright hadn't asked me to come, trust me I wouldn't have bothered. Now, can we please dispense with the idle pleasantries? Tell me whatever it is that you need to say so I can get the hell out of here. Confinement depresses me."

Jack's shame-filled gaze fell onto the table. He nodded and laced his fingers together. "The thing is..."

Then nothing. For seconds that seemed like hours, nothing.

Her patience had dwindled to non-existence, especially given that he'd done nothing but show her his ass over the years. She couldn't wait to show him hers.

Karma's a bitch.

J.J. had already decided to swiftly vacate the premises if she experienced even the slightest hint of an itch, any minor discomfort. He could spout his lies to someone stupid enough to believe him, find someone else with whom to share his sob story. She had a source to save and neither the time nor patience for his antics.

"You had every reason not to come here today. And now you have every reason to leave, but I'm asking you to please hear me out." He rubbed his hands together in a rapid, nervous motion. "Nothing is what it seems."

What's this? she thought. Jack's shoulders slumped and red veins peppered his eyes. He appeared sleepless and pathetic—not a good look.

"I know I've been a prick."

"Uhhh. . . correction," she interrupted, wagging her index finger. "A racist prick." Her hand began to tremble so she clasped both together under the table. She attributed the shaking to her welling anger toward Jack.

He nodded and hung his head in shame. "All right. I'll accept that. I'm a lot of things, not all of them good. But God as my witness I'm not a spy."

Please, Lord, bring on the itch.

Anything.

She hoped, wished, and prayed. Just one little sign that he was lying. She'd dash out of the interrogation room so fast there'd be nothing left but skid marks and vapors.

She waited and waited. And waited and waited.

Nothing.

Son of a bitch!

He lifted his head and locked his eyes squarely onto hers, didn't falter, didn't back down, didn't cower in the face of her evident doubt. "Somebody framed me, J.J. and I think it may be someone close to us."

She shot him a skeptical glare and turned her head toward Tony, certain he was standing behind the one-way glass listening to every word. He'd *never* believe Sabinski. J.J.'s only consolation was that Tony would stand behind her decision, whatever that may be. That was the nature of their relationship, something she could always depend on. "What about the poly? You failed miserably. Twice I might add."

"I don't know what to say. They hooked me up and my heart wouldn't stop racing. Never happened to me before. I have no idea what could've caused me to experience such a reaction."

J.J. wanted so desperately to tell him that being a mean bastard who pops Snickers bars like popcorn might have something to do with his condition, but she resisted the temptation. After all, her snide remarks would serve no useful purpose and certainly wouldn't repair the damage he'd done to her career or her sources.

"Did you take any drugs, alcohol, or anything that might've caused a negative physiological reaction?" she asked.

"No, nothing that I didn't report."

Still no reaction, she thought. *Damn!* He'd probably never been this honest in his life and, just as J.J.'s luck would have it, he batted a thousand at that moment.

"What about the money? I'm told your prints were all over the bag."

He exhaled, cupped his reddened face in his hands. "I don't know what to tell you except that I buy trash bags for the house. Maybe the person who framed me got a hold of one I touched and used it to hide the money. Trust me, if I had all that cash, I wouldn't be living in that piece of shit house or driving my piece of shit Hyundai, that's for certain."

Even if he was lying to himself, he certainly believed he was telling the truth. Still no reaction, much to J.J.'s dismay.

"After everything you've said to me, put me through, do you really expect me to trust a word you say? To help *you*?"

Without hesitation, he nodded.

"Guard!" J.J. called out. "Could we get this man an ice pack, please?"

"Ice pack?" Jack asked.

"Yes," she snapped. "Because you've bumped your head if you think for one moment I'm going to risk what's left of my shitty little career— no small thanks to *you*—to help save yours!"

Jack wrung his hands together, desperation seeped through his pores.

"The FBI has a mole. And this one is even more dangerous than Hanssen."

"Yes, *you* are."

"It's not me!"

She cut him a wicked sideways glance. "We've been trying to tell you about this problem for years. And you didn't want to listen, at least not until the chicken came home to roost. Now it's roosting like a mother-fucker, huh?"

"J.J., he's compromising every sensitive HUMINT operation we're running. At this rate, all FBI assets will dry up. We'll never get another well-placed recruitment. Human intelligence in the FBI, as we know it, will cease to exist. This is serious. It's no game. And it's because of our history that you're the only one I can trust…if you agree to help me."

Everything in J.J. wanted to smirk, but deep down she knew Jack had finally come to his good senses. He'd spoken a lot of hard truth. Nobody would trust working with FBI counterintelligence. The Bureau's foreign partners would no longer share intelligence. The CIA was just looking for a reason to cut the Bureau off from their most sensitive human intelligence. The FBI would be isolated and unable to effectively conduct any kind of intelligence operation. And at the end of the day, the country would suffer. Even though J.J. knew her days at the Bureau were numbered and she fought every urge to give a damn, the truth could not be denied.

"Mhm-hmm. I see. So why'd you ask me to come here? What do you expect me to do? Run some rogue investigation to help free you from the bondage of your own willful ignorance?"

"If you're half the agent I think you are...then, yes. I do."

A slight sensation emerged behind her eyes, causing her to blink. Of course, that would be the one answer he'd lie about. Made perfect sense, though. Why would he believe she'd trust him under these or any other circumstances?

"Flattery doesn't suit you, Jack."

Without another word spoken, she stood and raised her arm to signal the guard to open the door. She wanted his jaw to hit the floor; she wanted him to feel a fraction of the hopelessness and frustration she'd felt over the years.

When she turned to make her grand exit, Jack said, "Walk away if you want, but take this with you. If he set me up, do you think he'll have any problem doing the same to you?"

J.J. froze where she stood. Jack's remark, however desperate, got her attention. She returned to her seat so she could ask a few more questions. After all, he must've had some inkling or suspicion that drove him to believe the mole was in the FBI as opposed to the CIA or some other agency. "So, if you had to guess—"

"The bigot list," he said. "It's someone from the bigot list."

Director Russell Freeman controlled a "bigot list" that contained the names of personnel with access to "the vault," an ultra-secure Headquarters facility. Agents planned and executed the nation's most complex and damaging espionage cases from this space. Only employees with "need-to-know" could enter. Inside, secure file safes locked in four secure breakout rooms held key intelligence from the most valuable counterintelligence sources. One compromise, one dead source, one slip of the tongue to a dimwitted congressman with no sense of national security, and hell would be paid—and the bigot list ensured the FBI knew exactly where to start the search.

An innocent man, prick as he was, had been unjustly arrested, and there was little she could do to spring him. Certainly couldn't stroll over to the U.S. District Attorney's Office and say, "Drop the charges. He's not lying. How do I know? Well, my generational curse gave me the power to detect lies, and he didn't make me itch. No, really."

That idea was a non-starter. Taking on this mission meant conducting an unsanctioned mole hunt for the man who made her work life a living hell. She shuddered when she thought about the vile comments he'd made about her and the McCall family name just days ago, and now he expected this? She'd be required to gamble with what was left of her career. Going rogue to help him? Not a chance she was willing to take.

CHAPTER 2

Two days before…

Thursday Morning at FBI Headquarters, Washington, D.C.

J.J. searched for serenity in bottom of a Belvedere bottle. The wait for his sugar-coated lies had dragged on for too long; she'd lost patience. After glancing around the small reception area to ensure no one was watching, she removed from her purse a silver flask and smiled. It was filled to the brim with relief. One small gulp and the soothing burn slipped down her throat, calming her prickly nerves. Inside she felt on the brink of dissolution. The 10 am swallow was just a necessary evil. It would get her through the meeting, until time for her next dose of repose.

Another dead source. She couldn't stomach the thought of his demise. Two had been more than her fair share. The unceasing cycle of loss had worn her resolve thin. She'd refused to let another family suffer that pain if she could in any way prevent it. J.J. wanted to tell the FBI where to stick her badge and gun, but she had promises to keep. Promises to Viktor. Promises to herself. No matter what Cartwright said, she'd see her case through until the end. And the end was as near as nightfall because the op was simple and would go off without a hitch.

J.J. stiffened her back and squared her shoulders as the elixir took effect. Her posture mirrored that of the powerful yet graceful eagle perched atop her FBI badge. She'd eyed it, waiting for the carefully choreographed denial and deception ritual to begin.

Blur the truth. Fool the enemy. Protect the state—or the Bureau as it were.

From Naomi Jones McCall to Johnnie Mae Gibson to J.J. McCall, the long-practiced routine hadn't changed much. Forty years and still the same old shit. For almost a decade, she'd operated under the blind faith of equal opportunity for all, but J.J. finally lost her last modicum of hope that positive change was inevitable.

"Agent McCall," Assistant Director of Counterintelligence James Cartwright called from the door of his vast office. Only Director Freeman's office was larger. A wave of apprehension gripped J.J. as she smoothed her hair down to the shoulder and stood to face him. She'd been twiddling her thumbs for twenty minutes, waiting for him to deliver the promotion board results.

Cartwright's jaw tightened and his face contorted before he said "Please come in and have a seat."

"Yes, sir." Her tall slender frame towered over his as she offered a respectful nod and strode inside. She flipped her navy blue suit jacket backward before parking herself in the burgundy leather executive chair facing his desk.

Cartwright pressed his lips together and grimaced, expelling a long breath as he closed the door behind her. Once seated, he clasped his fingers together and tightened his lips. "You're looking a little tired. When's the last time you took some time off?"

J.J. didn't understand why people had taken so much effort to tell her she looked like crap in recent weeks. A few sleepless nights had begun to take their toll. All she needed was a good night's rest and she'd be better than her usual "okay." But her appearance was not what she had been called in to discuss. He knew it. And she knew it. "Come on, Mr. Cartwright," she smirked. "You didn't call me in here to talk about planning my Disney vacation. I'm fine."

"Listen, I've had a long discussion with Jack and the members of the board today. Even though you're long overdue for a supervisor slot, they...*I* can't recommend you during this cycle. However, you should know that your co-case agent, Antonio Donato, is still in the running."

She leaned forward in her seat, her expression incredulous. She'd spent the last twenty-four hours mentally preparing for the inevitable, but an unexpected burst of rage rushed through her at the sound of his hollow words. "Tony? You mean the junior case agent that I've been training for the past year? The one who's been shadowing *me* on *my* cases?"

Three class-action suits over the last 15 years. Tens of millions in discrimination settlements. Zero lessons learned. The FBI hadn't changed one iota. The speech should've been old hat. After all, she'd heard the same one, almost verbatim, three times before. Somehow, the sting cut just as deep as the first.

"I see." She shifted in her seat and braced herself. The tired and overdone "we need you on the street" portion of his speech was next.

"This decision in no way reflects on your performance. If I may speak frankly, you're one of the best counterintelligence recruiters the Bureau's ever had—no one disputes that."

"With all due respect, sir, no one could. I think my record speaks for itself."

He nodded and shifted his gaze toward the window. Then he turned toward her and dropped his head into the palms of his hands in. His frustration was apparent. "Summa cum Laude at Howard University. Top of your class at Quantico. Your mother would be proud of the woman, of the agent, you've become. But please understand, my hands are tied right now," he implored. "With this mole situation, the Bureau...hell, the country can't afford to lose you—or your sources. We need you on the street."

"Ugh!" she grunted as her leg jutted out. He'd lied and the itch felt more like a stab…in the back.

"You okay?" he asked.

"Yeah, it's nothing, the thing, you know," she said, shifting in her seat, trying to brace for another untruth. "Anyway, you and I both know, if this was about the streets, I'd be working out of Washington Field, not Headquarters. I was really hoping for something a little more original this year."

"So, Mr. Cartwright—"

"Please, Jim."

"So, Mr. Cartwright, you're implying that if I performed my job poorly, I'd be eligible for promotion?" J.J. eyed him with a skeptical gaze.

He leaned back in his seat, heaved a long sigh, and shook his head. "Really? That's how you're going to carry this? You know that's not what I'm saying."

"Then I'm confused," she said snidely. Her eyebrows scrunched in feigned bewilderment.

"Honest to God, my hands are tied. I just *can't* help you right now," he pleaded, almost as frustrated as she. He clearly wanted to assist but couldn't. "You wouldn't believe the stress I'm under. I'm on my last leg here, J.J. I could crash and burn at any minute."

She braced for the sensation, but none came.

"You're right, sir. I wouldn't believe it." She looked at her watch and then at Jim. "I really hate to cut this short, but I'm running late. Donato and I are supervising an op today. Are we finished here?"

Cartwright's face burned red with what appeared to be frustration as he nodded. "But before you go, hear me out. We've known each other for years. Don't think I don't understand what you're going through. Jack is…well…*Jack*. I'll make good on my promise to help you if it's the last thing I do, but I'm certain you're onto something major, maybe the biggest case of your career. You've got to promise me you'll hang in there a little longer."

She pursed her lips. He wouldn't allow her to quit, and she didn't understand why. She had a job to do, one he apparently needed her to finish. "You know me. I won't leave until my job is done. But, frankly, you'll never understand my predicament," she said, standing to leave. "The core of your humanity will never endure this kind of challenge. We, as minority FBI agents spend every damn day defending rights that we are *still fighting* to fully enjoy right here at the F-B-One. Don't you see? When all goes according to plan today, we will get the answers we need. And when this case is over, so is my career."

He grunted as J.J. huffed and turned to leave.

"They won't let you resign, J.J."

His words stopped her cold. She turned back toward him. His face had turned pale. "Excuse me? *Let* me resign?"

"They need Viktor Plotnikov and he won't work with anyone but you."

"I beg your pardon, but I don't need the Bureau's permission to quit."

"But you'll need your reputation. The FBI's reach is far and wide in the investigative community. You know what they'll do. And let's face facts, you don't work well with rules. You've given them plenty of ammunition to leverage," he said, his face now unnaturally colored as if he'd decided to hold his breath until she relented.

She whipped her head toward the door and willed her feet to follow.

"Ahhhhgggggghhhh!" Mr. Cartwright yelled out.

Her head snapped back toward him. His entire body shook; his face turned a deep red and finally blue. He collapsed against the back of the chair then his body slid onto the floor.

"Mr. Cartwright!"

She dashed to his seat, watching his body thrash like a caught fish. White foam formed on the edges of his lips, and the veins in his crimson-colored neck bulged above his collar.

J.J. kicked his chair toward the wall, dragged his desk across the floor. Another inch closer and he'd have a concussion. She forced her hands under his back and flipped him onto his side. If he was going to choke, it'd be by her hand and hers alone.

"Mrs. Slater! Call the nurse!" J.J. yelled to Mr. Cartwright's secretary praying she'd returned. "It's Mr. Cartwright! He's having a seizure!"

She heard a faint reply. Fortunately, FBI Headquarters had a small medical facility for such emergencies.

J.J.'s heart thumped through her chest as she watched his hopeless flail subside. She knelt down beside him and put his head on her lap, felt as if a million minutes had passed. The faint sound of harried footsteps padded closer.

"It's gonna be okay, Mr. Cartwright. Help is on the way." She wiped the sweat from his brow. Her hands trembled more than usual, but she attributed that to the moment's intensity not the more likely cause. "And the next time I don't believe you, Jim, you can just swear on the Bible. This was overkill."

A weak grin struggled to part his lips.

Time had changed nothing in the FBI. And J.J. had a double dose of the Bureau's glass-ceiling blues. She was a minority to the second power—black and a woman. Every single day she'd begin at square one, proving herself the next day as if she'd done nothing the day before. Work twice as hard, be twice as good, to earn half the respect. The stodgy old white males who ruled Russian counterintelligence in the FBI? They didn't give a damn about equality. And the youthful ones were too naive to perceive the lack of it.

Her stellar record was mandatory.

Mistakes a liability.

In a long, slow, faith-shaking siege, she buckled under the weight everyone's expectations, as well as her own misguided belief that she must achieve perfection at all personal costs. She could not fail her sources. She could not fail her co-case agent. She could not fail her mother's legacy. She could not fail the hundreds of agents who might someday like to walk on the ground she'd broken. And on the many days, like this one, when she felt like utter shit, she could not afford to feel anything other than "okay."

J.J. and Tony would soon nail the bastard. The next in an infamous line of treacherous snakes—Aldrich Ames, Earl Pitts, Robert Hanssen, and the new son of a bitch—ICE Phantom. Three years' worth of investigation rode on Karat making the drop. If he delivered as promised, J.J. would draft her last and final resignation letter—and this one she fully intended deliver. She'd free herself from the stifling space beneath the glass ceiling and lift off to soar on untested wings to a destination unknown.

CHAPTER 3

Her thoughts churned, nerves constricted. The Cartwright episode shook her.

Everything's under control. Everything's under control, she told herself.

She didn't *need* a drink that second. She just *wanted* it. As far as she was concerned, until she needed it, she had no drinking problem. She dug in her pant pocket and pulled out the half-eaten pack.

Doublemint gum.

That would do the trick.

Tony didn't buy her logic, but she did. He was a fine Jersey Italian and his accent was as strong as his proclivity for beautiful women. J.J. was no exception. His striking deep-set dark baby browns and toned rippled physique did little to help J.J. maintain her professionalism. And with a nose like a bloodhound, Tony wouldn't miss a beat.

She promised him she'd slow down too many times before. This was no time to blow the appearance of propriety. She quickened her pace to the office, each step heavy and purposeful. Then she drew in a few calming breaths before placing her hand on the doorknob. Once the door opened, she'd step back into the fray. With the promotion board's decision, she'd approach the day's mission with a new goal.

The Espionage Unit was half empty as most agents were out running down leads. But her co-case agent Tony Donato was standing there waiting for her, holding a steaming cup of java in his hand. He beamed a bright smile, clearly deluding himself that life was fair.

It wasn't.

When she didn't reciprocate, Tony slipped into the empty chair beside her desk. She eyed him briefly and then avoided his gaze. She hated the look of pity, didn't need it either.

"So, uhhh, how'd it go?" Tony asked, his expression warm, attentive. The wicked slant in her eyes and pasted on grin betrayed the put-on bounce in her voice. "It seems congratulations are in order, for both of us. You're still in the running for the supervisor slot."

He didn't flinch, avoided eye contact.

She turned to him and didn't budge until he faced her. "You knew?"

"Well...I'd heard something from one of my boys while you were gone."

"What? What did you hear?"

"Uhhhhh…"

"Come on, Tony."

"Well, uh, two things really. First, the board, they know you've got heart and you're loyal, which makes you a great recruiter. But they...they think you're soft. In a life and death situation, they wonder if you're strong enough to pull the trigger. They want a supervisor who can make the tough choices, who will pull the trigger."

She sat blank-faced.

"I don't think they mean it literally but..."

"I know exactly what they mean." She rolled her eyes.

Any excuse would do. Pull the trigger. Make the tough choices. All buzzwords for we'd prefer to have a white male in the position instead of J.J. But she refused to play the race card. Filing a complaint would only sully her stellar reputation in the too small and tight-knit federal law enforcement community. Those perceived as stirring up trouble were ostracized. She'd need her contacts when she started her own firm.

"Will you accept the supervisor slot if they offer?" she whispered.

"Me? No fuckin' way. I'd rather take one in the head than be a supervisor, especially in this place. Too many freakin' headaches."

"Well, as soon as this operation is over today, I'm done. Finito. Finished."

He caught his breath. Surprise didn't quite convey his reaction as far as J.J. could see. Perhaps it was disappointment. Or fear. Yes, J.J. had been frustrated for some time; he probably assumed she'd take the hit on the chin. She always did. Resigning obviously wasn't the trigger he wanted her to pull. "J.J., I'm not gonna let you quit. I know you're pissed right now, but if you quit that jerk-off Sabinski wins. Cartwright's gotta make good on his word."

"Tony, you know as well as I that I'm playing this *tired* game with two sets of rules, neither of which weigh in my favor. Whadaya gonna do?" She playfully mimicked his Jersey accent. No emotional eruptions as usual, just dispassionate, flat, didn't give a damn. She had one foot out the door, and her sense of duty couldn't hold her hostage much longer. Not if she was determined to go.

He studied her face and leaned in, warmth emanating from his body. "Are you...okay, J.J.?"

She locked her eyes on his. "I'm . . . okay."

He sniffed. "You didn't take any—"

"I'm fine!" she snapped, her first impulse. Then her gaze softened. It always did when she looked at him. "I'm sorry, really, but we've got more important things to discuss. Karat is afraid Golikov's people might be on to him, we need Jake on this op today. I presume he's in the conference room?"

Jake McGee was one of the best Gs in the Special Support Group— the FBI's eyes and ears. They kept a close eye on the Bureaus spies, terrorists, and high-value targets, lurking from the shadows. But when the Bureau wanted the target to know they were there, they knew.

"Yeah, but…"

"Uh-uh," she interrupted as she stood to leave, "*Buts* are for guns and strip clubs. Before we go, you said there was something else."

He leaned in closer. "Sabinski's ordered a random file inspection specifically targeting *our* cases in the vault."

"Figures," J.J. said. "He's dirty. I can feel it."

"Yeah, well, we've gotta double check our 'duplicate' file for Karat and the other cases. Or you and me might not be so employed come tomorrow."

"Damn!" J.J. said, frustrated but unsurprised by Jack's action. After all, she and Tony had long suspected he might have turned. "All right. Jake can handle the op on his own. We'll get him on the road and head into the vault. By the time we're done squaring the files, the op will be over and we can clear the drop. If Jack gets his hands on the real file, Plotnikov is as good as dead."

"Exactly," Tony said as they started out the door.

A few minutes later Tony and J.J. arrived at the breakout room inside the Strategic Information and Operations Command center—SIOC. J.J. had no idea why Cartwright reserved it. They usually planned ops in the vault. Then, it struck her, what he said during their meeting. He said she was on to the biggest case of her career and urged her to stay. Then he set up this space. *He must know more than he's letting on.*

When J.J. and Tony entered the breakout room, they startled Jake, who quickly shut the lid on his laptop. Nervous, he ran his hands through his dark, Ryan Seacrest-inspired locks.

"Flipping through pictures of your girl again, huh?" Tony said to Jake, who answered with a sheepish grin and turned toward J.J.

She took a seat at the head of the table and flipped through a case file, searching for the name of her NSA contact in case Plotnikov came through with the encryption codes and frequencies.

"You all right, J.J.?" Jake asked. "Looks like you're having a rough day."

She cut her eyes at him then grinned. "On the contrary. My day is getting better by the minute."

"So what's the deal with this op again?" Jake asked.

J.J. glanced at Tony and answered. "Plotnikov is a clean diplomat with access to information on Russia's stance on the missile shield. The J2 at the Pentagon would like to get that information, but Plotnikov has suggested on numerous occasions that he's afraid he's under suspicion, scared of Golikov's people." She lied well. Their cover story was elaborate but necessary for her source's protection.

"With good reason." Jake nodded. "Okay, I'm with you."

"So, we set up a meeting with an Army Intel cutout today to help us assess him. We need your team to make sure that neither Golikov's people nor Russian counterintelligence trails him. Otherwise, we might not get another chance at him anytime soon."

"Roger that."

Only a handful of people knew about Plotnikov, that he and Karat were one in the same. To the Gs and other agents in the vault, he was no different than any other diplomat in an embassy. Outwardly, he received no exceptional treatment. Only two people understood his value. Only two people knew Karat might solve the one mystery that the Intelligence Community couldn't solve in ten years' worth of investigations.

Tony flipped through a notebook of handwritten notes. "Where are the contact instructions? I swear I had my hand on 'em yesterday."

"I don't know. Maybe you left them in the vault," J.J. said. She hoped the mole wasn't responsible for the disappearance. The entire op could be blown before it got started.

J.J. glanced down. Her watch read 1 pm. Time was running out. "Shouldn't you be on the road already?" she asked Jake. "You've been slipping on your job lately, chief. Keep playing around, and I'll make that sparkly new Charger disappear like a hooker in a vice raid."

Jake cringed. J.J. was notoriously passive aggressive. Her jokes were usually veiled threats that she almost always made good on. It'd be all fun and games at the start, right up until a Barbie Dream car occupied his parking space.

Tony shot J.J. a wicked eye. "Yo, J.J., why you gotta be a ball buster, eh?" He turned to Jake. "Don't pay her no mind, ya hear me? She's just bustin' your chops. I got your back."

She folded her arms across her chest. "Oh, I see. Two guys against one girl? That's okay, I can take both o' yous. Square up, let's go." She erected herself into a boxing stance. The swift motion coupled with the Belvedere's effects threw her off balance. She wobbled and dropped her hands.

Tony stood in front of J.J. and eyed her from toes to ta-tas, towering over her hourglass five-ten frame by an intimidating six inches. She shriveled into a shy teen. "You might be many things, but you ain't a *girl*," Tony oozed. The subtext knocked J.J. unsteady again. His frequent overt flirts disarmed her, raided her heart. One by one he pilfered the chunks of wall she'd built to keep love safely at bay.

"You're a sexual harassment suit waiting to happen. You know that, right? I can handle it though. Besides, mama needs new shoes," J.J. said, rubbing her thumb against her fingertips to signal the money Tony would need to pay out. Then she laughed through her blush, hating the power he had to shift her emotions at will, his ability to render unsuccessful her every attempt to slough off his jibes. She glanced down at her watch again and then sneered at Jake. "As for you, *think pink.*"

"Yeah, yeah. I'm quaking in my Timberlands. Whatever you get, just make sure it's convertible," Jake scoffed putting on a little bravado for

Tony. Then he double-timed it to the unit entrance, concealing his newfound urgency.

Jake grabbed the wrinkled Burger King bag containing the now cold Whopper from office secretary's desk. He'd scarf it down as he paced to his Bureau-assigned beauty.

J.J.'s trust in Jake never wavered, but everyone knew his technique was slipping, including Jake. She didn't hesitate to chew him out for it either. Coasting on those cowboyish, hot rod ways, the source of her admiration for him, was no longer an option. J.J. realized that tracking suspects all day with seven years at Princeton, two degrees, and the downgrade from his broken dream to become an FBI agent hadn't inspired him to greatness. Even still, his "G" status seemed to give him sufficient (if not equal) satisfaction, half the paperwork, and a set of credentials nearly identical to those issued to FBI agents. He'd developed a gift for anticipating his targets' next move, but now his success seemed more luck than skill. His teammates, J.J., everyone joked that he was "whipped," distracted by his new girlfriend. J.J. believed he just quit caring. She had no idea why. She just wanted to the old Jake back.

Jake's team was always the first called, the most eager to serve. True professionals, all of them. Never overstepped the bounds between meddling and mission, and were all crazy enough to hell ride with the Russian during their rip-roaring, piss-your-pants surveillance detection runs. They lingered in the shadows when the Russians wanted them in the open and knew precisely when to back off because aborted operations did little to help the FBI identify dirty Russian intelligence officers.

And they knew it, they meaning Jake and the rest of the motley crew.

The Gs were the FBI's "gift with" purchase. Buy a diplomatic visa, get a G-team. On the street. In the woods. Under footbridges. Their eyes were watching. And the fate of J.J.'s sources depended on it. Her future depended on it. The future of the FBI's counterintelligence program depended on it.

• • •

Upper Northwest, the location of the Russian Embassy, was thirty minutes from FBI Headquarters in traffic. Jake turned down his window and allowed the cool September air to wash away the ill-effects of his ritual adrenaline rush, then mashed his gas pedal to the floor.

His Charger cut through the wind as he hot-dogged it to Tunlaw Road, double-fisting his wheel like a gray-haired grandmother. He steered tightly and carefully, though; another accident would set him back even further.

His chronic distractions might cost him more than a few traffic tickets if he didn't pull it together. Two electric poles and a marked Secret Service police car sideswiped in the heat of surveillance, the list of damaged vehicles had expanded as fast as his personnel file.

Jake glanced at his watch and exhaled. He'd arrived before schedule. He scanned the area to ensure he couldn't be seen, and then shook his head in dismay. Why in hell would the State Department give the Russians land on the highest peak in the Nation's Capital? The location was a signal collector's dream. They could tap into communications from every U.S. government agency east of the Mississippi.

Jake slipped on his sunglasses and then flipped the switch on his secure radio. Everyone would be expecting an update by now.

"Breaker breaker one-nine. This is J. Swiff behind the wheel of steel. I'm in position. Let's keep it short, guys. Our friends are listening," Jake reminded the crew. Russian Impulse officers monitored the area for FBI radio traffic. The Gs' radio signals were encrypted so the Russians couldn't hear conversations. But increased signal activity put them on alert.

His stomach growled as he rifled through the remnants of his Burger King bag with his free hand. "Waiting for Plotnikov to exit the building. Jiggy, what's your twenty?"

"Copy that Swiff. I'm at the corner of Wisconsin and O Streets. Cham and Money T are a few blocks south of you at Calvert. Jazz and the rest are running a picket near the choke point. Over," Jiggy responded.

"Roger that, everybody! Sounds good." J.J. said on her long range radio. "Tony and I are headed into the vault and won't have any reception for a few minutes. But this is just a simple routine coverage. Stay loose and keep an eye out for Golikov's people. Piece of cake. We'll see you back here in a couple of hours."

Jake swallowed hard, bit a hunk out of his burger. Anticipating the trouble ahead, he braced himself for a long afternoon. "When all hell breaks loose," he mumbled to himself, "only the devil survives."

Moments later, Plotnikov, dressed in a black suit cloaked beneath a cliché trench coat, stepped outside the embassy doors as scheduled.

Jake exhaled. The op should go down as planned. What could go wrong? A second later he was sorry he asked.

His heart thumped, he grabbed the radio. *Fuck!* "Houston, we have a problem."

• • •

Maps of the Washington, D.C. area poked with colored thumbtacks adorned the walls in J.J.'s and Tony's tight compartment inside the vault. At a small round table, they scanned through each file, frantically flipping pages to ensure Jack would find no information that could damage their cases. And there were only three files for Russian intelligence officers operating in Washington that they needed to be concerned about, the most important of which belonged to Karat.

Documents relating to Aleksey Dmitriyev, a counterintelligence officer linked to Karat since the day he arrived, must also be scrubbed. If any FD-302s mentioning him and Karat (as Plotnikov) didn't reflect the information from the fake file, the jig was up. The file of Aleksandr

Mikhaylov was last. The lookouts had spotted him in the company of both Dmitriyev and Plotnikov on multiple occasions. J.J. had been tailing him since he'd stepped on U.S. soil. She didn't know if any pertinent information existed, but she'd scrub the file just in case.

Call it a hunch. Perhaps an intuition. But Mikhaylov made her skin crawl. He ran the most insidious and evasive cadre of Russian spies—illegals. They assumed the identities of American citizens to gain access to classified information. Almost impossible to catch because the Bureau had little success in identifying them until the 2010 New York bust.

"Tony, I haven't seen the most recent volume of Karat's file. You don't have it do you?" J.J. asked.

"No," he said as he checked through his stack. "It's not in my stuff. Maybe we left back in the breakout room."

"Hmmm. Maybe. I'm gonna check as soon as we get out of here."

They studied each case file, lookout log, surveillance report, and photo and decided to tuck the real files inside the jacket folders of long dead sources. As J.J. placed her hand on Plotnikov's photo and prepared to stash it away, she recollected the moment she dug the hole into her present predicament, her promises to Viktor. Promises she wished she hadn't made. Promises she wished didn't have to keep.

CHAPTER 4

Two Years Ago…

Before Polyakov's hand arrived at Moscow station, there was ICE Phantom's second victim and J.J.'s second source—Kostya Belikov. He disappeared, vanished like billowing smoke in the night air. J.J. slept for what felt to her like five minutes a day in the following months. She was consumed to the point of obsession, determined to identify a replacement asset. She needed someone who could not only provide information on Belikov's fate, but help her identify the FBI scourge who had all but delivered the fatal bullet to his head. When she wasn't thinking and planning, she drank. Not guzzles, but little sips, every couple of hours, every day.

Her barely conscious hours were spent at Dulles airport monitoring Russian diplomatic arrivals and departures, hoping to spot a new mark.

And there he appeared.

A diminutive schlep of a man in a slightly oversized navy-blue business suit. His shiny dome and silver-framed spectacles, unimposing and unremarkable, clashed with the more dapper attire of the counterintelligence officer accompanying him—Aleksey Dmitriyev, a Second Secretary and fairly high ranking for an intelligence officer..

Weeks later, J.J. cornered Plotnikov in an empty men's bathroom at an outlet mall during an embassy-sponsored shopping excursion. He'd just shoplifted over a thousand dollars' worth of goods–grand larceny and a lot of trouble if she chose to threaten him. But that's not how J.J. operated.

She quickly crafted an out of order sign out of a paper towel and chewing gum and waited for him. Listened. Smelled. Gagged. Her stomach convulsed. The odor permeating the room would make a Marine cry foul. When he emerged from the stall, her tall frame blocked the exit.

He froze.

"Who are you? What are you doing in here?" He appeared startled at first, but a moment later the tension in his shoulders released. Now his expression alarmed her.

J.J. paused before speaking. His colleagues might be searching for him. She had to be careful. Looking downward with her hand covering the visible side of her face, she poked her head outside.

No passersby. All clear.

She closed the door and moved toward the nearest stall. In it, she could conceal her presence if someone walked in.

"I'm Special Agent J.J. McCall with the FBI. Please. Feel free to go ahead and wash your hands."

Plotnikov eased over to the sink, pressed his hand against the soap dispenser. He sucked in a deep frustrated breath as he thrust his hands under the stream of water. "Yes. Agent McCall," he said. "You are quite legendary in the Embassy—or perhaps a better term would be infamous? What pray tell brings you to the men's room on this glorious afternoon?"

His comment told her the one thing she hadn't been sure of until he spoke—he was an intelligence officer. A clean administrative officer would have no concerns about the FBI.

"Well, if you've heard the legend of me," she fought the urge to roll her eyes, " then I think we both know why I'm here."

He silently walked over to the hand dryer, rubbed his hands beneath, and looked down at his expensive watch. "I'm a diplomat and have no interest in speaking with the FBI. Leave immediately or I'll file a complaint with the State Department."

Her skin prickled, and she flinched.

"Listen, you don't have to lie to me. I'm not your security officer. Consider me more like family. I'm not going to talk about your recent acquisitions from Lord & Taylor and Macy's—nice Movado, by the way.

"Instead, I think it would be more productive to our relationship if you'd permit me to share some information with you…about your father," she offered, opting to take a more sensitive approach. He mattered, and J.J. wanted him to trust her. Sources who believed they mattered divulged the most secrets.

"Don't you dare speak of my father! Don't you speak his name!" he said, his expression gruff.

She froze. The sound of footsteps neared. She watched the door and waited, prepared to conceal herself in a stall. Within seconds, they passed.

"Sergey Plotnikov, right?" she asked, eager to glimpse his reaction. If he was angry, well...anger was a good sign. "I know what the KGB did to him. And I know what he did." She said, poking the bear to get a reaction.

He breathed heavily and growled, "He was innocent!" His stark expression hardened, knowing and cold. The scars from his memories were still fresh and soul-deep. At that moment, she believed he'd secretly willed her to show up. Somewhere. Anywhere. She would be the vessel he used to exact his revenge.

"They used him as a pawn, as if they really needed another excuse to justify the Cold War," she said. "He never worked for us. We targeted him, but he feared for his family's safety so he refused to cooperate," she said, referring to U.S. intelligence services, the CIA in particular. "Can we talk?"

"But I—I have to . . . we're returning to the embassy in a short time. I must leave."

J.J.'s eyebrow rose. A plan. She needed a plan. She expected to cast the bait. She didn't expect the big fish to bite on the first try.

• • •

To his embarrassment, J.J. staged a fake arrest and in conjunction with the mall police. J.J. arrived in the small holding area and found Viktor seated and sipping on a Coke. Now, he and she could have a tête-à-tête before Vorobyev, the embassy security officer, suspected Viktor had uttered so much as a cordial hello to an FBI special agent.

To J.J.'s surprise, they fell into easy conversation. The SVR gave Plotnikov shit work. Stuck him in a low-level position, assumed he'd never do any harm. But Viktor was sharp. Smarter than they gave him credit for. And he had loyal friends in the right places. The more they conversed, the more the deep-seated pain from his past bubbled to the surface. Plotnikov's eyes flooded and he crumbled with emotion.

"My Papa," he said, his voice trembling, "was a former KGB Colonel who'd been falsely accused of working with the CIA and committing treason in the 1970s. Golikov's father orchestrated his execution, tortured him, shot him in the back of the head with a high-caliber pistol. The penetration so powerful it blew off his face, so I'm told."

J.J. gasped as she choked down her own tears. With her own mother's death still looming heavily on in the fabric of her life, she could relate to the pain spilling from his eyes.

"Dear Papa. We never got a chance to say goodbye or visit his burial place. Golikov's father and his thugs threw my father into an unmarked grave, face down, so his soul would go straight to hell. Our family was shunned, stripped of everything we owned, isolated from everyone we loved, betrayed by everyone we trusted. From a very young age, I vowed to one day make the KGB pay, to avenge our destitution."

His eyes tightened with contempt. He was a Predator drone, pre-programmed to strike in perfect time.

"Twenty years later, the report was released. An American mole, one of the senior FBI or CIA officers controlled by our service, passed information that would set me on course to exact my revenge. Although one source was executed as a result of the intelligence, my father was exonerated, cleared of all charges."

"So you decided to work for the Russian intelligence?"

"Yes, it was still the KGB at the time, in 1993, just before the break-up of the Soviet Union. They recruited me and a colleague from the Foreign Language Institute, gave me a dead-end government job with a promise of foreign travel to assuage my wounds. It was the KGB way. Keep your enemies even closer than your friends."

Nothing he confessed sparked a backlash from her gift. His hunger to avenge his father's death seeped through his pores, loomed heavily on the conviction in his expression and the acid in his voice.

Confident of his intent, J.J. set up a communications plan and gave him the code name KARAT because encryption codes were as good as gold. They would make periodic phone calls for updates and mark signals for emergencies. She also provided him with a throw-away cell phone to be used in only the most catastrophic situations. He concealed it inside the crumpled piece of paper stuffed in his new tennis shoes.

"I understand how important family is to you, Viktor," she remembered saying to him as their first meeting drew to an end. "I'll do everything in my power to protect you and your family. You will not meet your father's fate, not on my watch. That's a promise."

Who had recruited whom?

Plotnikov served as a code clerk, one of two to three embassy personnel responsible for transmitting and receiving every classified and unclassified communication to and from Moscow Center, Russian intelligence headquarters. He owned the proverbial keys to the kingdom—encryption keys as it were. If he passed those codes to U.S.

Intelligence, the FBI could decrypt intercepted Russian classified communications.

In his first dead drops, KARAT had only given the Bureau a few gold nuggets. To seal up the leak and identify the mole, the FBI needed Fort Knox, the identities of American government and military employees cooperating with Russian intelligence service. If he passed the codes used to transmit counterintelligence message traffic, they'd find ICE Phantom. She had no doubt. So J.J. pressed for the intel. And pressed hard.

KARAT hemmed and hawed, suggested he'd see what he could do. Weeks later, during a pre-scheduled phone call, he came through, or so he intimated. Finally, he told J.J. he had compiled the information she needed. He'd schedule the drop as soon as he could do so without alerting internal security.

She'd compromised herself and her career, overstayed her long-vanished welcome in the FBI in order to protect KARAT and his family. If anyone—Jack or, God forbid, the Director—ever found out the depth of her deception, she wouldn't have to worry about quitting. She'd be fired on the spot.

It all seemed so easy at the time. Like every other agency in the Intelligence Community that was aware of the breaches, she believed the mole to be CIA, not FBI. She'd made a promise she thought she could keep.

Her ability to fulfill her promise had been hampered by one thing.

One person.

And the time had finally come to find out who the hell he was.

CHAPTER 5

Thursday Afternoon…

""Uhhh, heads up everybody. Plotnikov has departed the main building," Jake said. "But he's not alone—and his hands are full."

"I don't even understand why J.J.'s so pressed to watch this guy. He's a nobody," Jiggy complained, speaking freely because J.J. and Tony were in the vault. "I could be at home catching up on the *Young and the Restless*."

Jake let out a strained chuckled and hopelessly watched his mark. The counterintelligence operational line chief for Washington's Russian intelligence residency escorted Plotnikov from the residential wing to his diplomatic vehicle and jumped into the driver's seat. "Well, J.J. doesn't have to worry about Golikov's people or counterintelligence *following* him. Aleksey Dmitriyev is his fucking chauffeur."

"What the hell?" Jiggy said. "Plotnikov can't meet our guy with a counterintelligence guy in the car. I mean, aren't these the guys who tortured and shot spies working for the FBI?"

"Correct," Jake said. "And it looks like they're carrying luggage."

Dmitriyev had two jobs in the residency: one—recruit American intelligence personnel willing to collect classified American intelligence and sell it to the Russians; and two—prevent Russian embassy personnel from cooperating with American intelligence. With Dmitriyev at his side, Plotnikov could do nothing except buckle his seatbelt and enjoy the ride.

When the words "leaving with luggage" finally processed through the team's minds, murmurings bubbled across the airwaves.

"Wait a minute," Jiggy said, interrupting the chatter. "You said luggage. As in suitcases?"

"No. As in suitcases," Jake replied. "Something wrong with your English today?"

"Could be comms equipment." Jiggy said, apparently trying to avoid any thought of the worst-case scenario.

"I doubt it," Jake said. "Shit! J.J. and Tony are in the vault and I don't have the number to the bat phone. Should I stay with them or abort?" Jake hoped Jiggy would suggest aborting the op. What purpose would going through the motions serve?

"We should be asking you—Obi Wan," Jiggy replied.

"I'm thinking no way he's gonna make the meet with a security officer in the car."

"That may be true, but I say we stick to Plotnikov like honey to a bee's ass no matter what," Jiggy said. "I refuse to be the one to tell J.J. we dropped coverage and don't know what happened to the mark."

"Good point," Jake said.

The gates opened. Jake peered into his targets' car through his Steiner binoculars. Embroiled in a heated discussion, Dmitriyev didn't bother scanning for surveillance which meant he didn't give a damn about the G presence or he knew he could evade them.

Jake made a mental note and prepared for the ride as he watched them pull through the exit gate. "Okay, team, they're out. I've got the eye."

Time to rock, Jake thought.

Dmitriyev's vehicle approached a stop sign at the corner of Tunlaw and Calvert Road, a few blocks from the embassy grounds. Jake pulled in behind them, using the three civilian cars he'd allowed to pull in front of him as cover.

"Traffic's heavy," Jake advised his team. "We shouldn't be crappin' our clothes during hairpin turns today. I'm heading east on Calvert. You in position, Jiggy? If I should lose him, you gotta pick him up."

The team decided to use leapfrog surveillance, switching the eye among multiple cars posted in positions ahead of the lead eye—in this case Jake. The Russians would never see the same face, the same car. But Dmitriyev, a seasoned counterintelligence officer, would expect the Gs to be there whether he spotted the team or not.

"Copy that, Jake. I'm locked and loaded. Ready to roll," Jiggy responded.

Minutes into the surveillance, Plotnikov's arm pointed out the window toward a Starbucks on Wisconsin Avenue. He motioned Dmitriyev to pull over to the right. Once at the curb, Dmitriyev stopped and got out. When Jake radioed the status, the silence suggested the move had left everyone scratching their heads.

"Since when do counterintelligence guys hop out for coffee? Something's not right," Jake said. "Get a shadow on him, so we can find out what the hell is going on in there. He knows we're watching. Any other units nearby?"

"This may be a stretch, but any of y'all ever think he might be going in for a Caramel Macchiato?" Jiggy joked. "I'd pimp my sister for one right now. I'm just sayin'."

They had no time for jokes, but everybody laughed.

"Jumping out! I've got this one," Cham's voice called out. She always took control when the boys lost focus.

Jake watched in his side-view mirror as she exited her vehicle and approached the store entrance.

By the time she reached the door, Dmitriyev had returned to the entrance with two steaming coffee cups in hand. He bowed his head at Jake before getting into the car, a provocation if he'd ever seen one.

Jake slammed his hand against his thigh, infuriated by Dmitriyev's blatant smugness. With that, Jake authorized himself to cover more aggressively. He'd hug their bumper no matter what J.J. said.

Dmitriyev waited for a break in traffic and eased out, then exploded down Wisconsin Avenue. The Daytona 500 had slower starts. Jake reacted too late.

He'd been duped.

Dmitriyev made the stop as a ploy to draw out surveillance, and it worked.

Zigzagging in an out of traffic, Dmitriyev weaved through the streets like a fucking nutcase. Jake's Charger engine roared, tires hugging the road as if on train rails. He tried to stay on Dmitriyev without breaking cover or killing an innocent bystander, but the pockets of stopped traffic and wayward pedestrians proved too much to avoid. As they approached the intersection at Wisconsin and R Streets, he saw her. A grandmother with a rolling walker and two kids at her side stepped into the crosswalk against the light.

"Noooo, get out the way!" he yelled, leaning forward on his steering wheel.

They moved onto the road. Only twenty feet ahead. Jake was going too fast.

Too fast.

SCREECH!

He slammed his brakes, fishtailed to a stop, and banged his hand against the steering wheel. Dmitriyev disappeared and left nothing in his wake except smoke and exhaust fumes.

Jake snatched his radio from the passenger seat. "I've lost him. I've lost him! He's on fire. Headed down Wisconsin. Here we go people! Jiggy he's less than two minutes away. Don't lose him!"

"Dude, already? He beat you in the paint!"

Jiggy idled at the intersection of Wisconsin and O Street, a one-way street a few blocks down from where Dmitriyev smoked Jake. Jiggy's itchy foot hovered over the gas pedal, waiting to slam and roll the minute his target appeared. No sooner than Jiggy spotted him, Dmitriyev careened over the horizon and hooked a right, barely avoiding a head-on collision with Jiggy's vehicle.

"Shiiiiiit!" Jiggy yelled. "He turned! He turned!"

Dmitriyev's car tilted as it spun onto the street. His hair-trigger move put the fear of God in Jiggy.

"Idiot! You almost side-swiped my door!" he yelled. Dmitriyev was long gone. "Damn! Too much traffic coming."

He jerked his head left and right, looking for an out. Nothing opened up. Couldn't make a U-turn fast enough. Change of plans. Jiggy decided to hook a right on Wisconsin Avenue. He'd catch him a block down, off P Street.

"Jiggy you got him? You got him? What's goin' on?" Jake yelled. He'd begun to sweat from his armpits, nervous.

Jiggy fumbled for his radio. *Damn, he was supposed to go straight!* he thought. He had selected the position on the one-way street explicitly so Dmitriyev couldn't turn into him from Wisconsin Avenue. And that bastard did it anyway.

It's almost as if he knew where I'd be sitting, he thought.

"Damn! He's in the wind! Gone." Jiggy said, after wrapping his sweaty palms around his radio. "I think he's headed south toward M Street. I'm gonna try to get turned around and catch up with him! Cham? Money T? Anybody else got eyes on?"

"Negative," Cham replied. "We're stuck at S Street. Dmitriyev ran the light and MPD rolled up behind us. If we pursued, we'd have gotten pulled over and lost him anyway. But I've got a hunch about where he may be headed. Money T and I are going south."

Once traffic cleared, Jiggy circled back on the next block, accidentally blowing a stop sign. Dmitriyev's car was nowhere in sight…but another was. Not two seconds later—*Whoop! Whoop!* The melodic stylings of the D.C. police sirens.

Son of a bitch!

Jiggy grabbed his radio. "Jake, what's your twenty? I've got a big negatory on his location."

Jake blew out a long hard breath. "I'm heading back to headquarters."

"Don't know what to tell you dude. I've got no idea in which direction he's driving, and MPD just pulled me over. Dmitriyev drives like freakin' Dale Earnhardt on crack and *I* get popped."

CHAPTER 6

The STE, a secure phone J.J. often referred to as the 'Bat Phone', rang inside the vault. She and Tony had nearly finished fixing and photocopying the files, so they could prepare to head to Rock Creek Park to clear the drop. The end to this "mole business," as Mr. Cartwright called it, was near.

"McCall," J.J. answered.

"I'm back. And I'm afraid I don't have good news." Jake's voice sounded like burnt coffee and cigarette smoke. "Meet you at your desk."

Her stomach plummeted to the floor. Something had gone wrong, and she instinctively knew. Best-laid plans always went awry.

J.J. glanced at Tony with an oh-shit face. They both raised their eyebrows, silently left the vault, and entered the fray.

Back in the office, spastic phones rang and gun-toting, business casual-clad FBI agents milled about the office trying to look important and busy. She approached Jake whose face bore the weight of failure and a sheepish grin.

"Whatcha got for me?" J.J. asked.

"We lost him." His voice was flat. Day old pancake flat.

J.J. suppressed the emotional surge and maintained her cool. She couldn't afford to rattle Jake or arouse suspicions about Plotnikov's true importance. She'd already ripped him a new one several days prior. His skills had degraded and he knew it. The Russians had all but requested him to provide surveillance coverage.

"I don't understand," she began, "this was supposed to be a routine op. What the hell happened?"

"Dmitriyev," Jake said. "He got in the car with Plotnikov. Drove him."

"Dmitriyev?" It struck her that Dmitriyev had met Plotnikov at the airport when he arrived.

"We stayed on them but about two miles into the surveillance, but they juked us...well, me." He went on to explain the painful details.

"Son of a bitch!" Tony grumbled before J.J. could nudge him. "So we don't know if he, uhhh, met the cut out?"

Jake shook his head.

Cool had officially left the building. A slight sense of panic crept in. The pit in J.J.'s stomach evolved into a galactic wedge.

"To be honest, J.J., I don't think staying with them mattered much since Dmitriyev was escorting him. That meeting wasn't gonna happen." Jake threw up his hands. "Besides, looked like he was carrying baggage. With intelligence officers, you can never be sure about the contents, but..."

"Plotnikov's got over a year left on his tour," J.J. reasoned out loud to restore the slight sense of hope Jake had robbed. "Had to be Dmitriyev's comms equipment or something."

Visions of a bullet piercing Plotnikov's skull whirred through her mind. She could barely stifle her rage, frustrated and fearful for yet another source's life. How could she resign now? She promised he wouldn't suffer the same fate as his father. She had a sinking feeling it might be too late for him. Too late again.

She wanted a drink, needed one.

The irony. For the first time in months, she didn't want to quit. Yet once Sabinski found out *another* source might've disappeared, he'd probably fire her anyway. She pursed her lips and hung her hand high on her hip, the way a mother does before scolding her child. Then she shrugged. The time for lectures had passed.

"Well, that does it, huh?" Tony said, heaving a long sigh.

"Sabinski's gonna chew me a second one," J.J. added.

Jake's glance grazed the floor as he headed toward the door. "We'll get him next time. Let's just be glad the information wasn't critical."

She turned to Tony. "The hits keep on coming," J.J. mumbled. "You would've loved my resignation speech to Sabinski. A ten minute dissertation loaded with suggestions on new locations to stick my badge and gun. Looks like my escape's on hold."

Tony exhaled, appearing more relieved than empathetic. "What do we do now?"

"One thing's for certain: I'm not going anywhere until I find out what happened to my source. And if that mole had anything to do with Dmitriyev's little ride along today, he better pray to God that I don't find him before Washington Field does."

Jake shuffled toward the door, his chin hanging below his balls.

"Hey!" J.J. shouted to Jake. He hesitated before turning toward her. "Do me a favor. Have the lookouts contact me the minute Plotnikov and Dmitriyev return to the embassy."

Jake nodded and disappeared into the hall. J.J. turned to Tony and lowered her voice, as if keeping the monumental screw-up secret was even a remote possibility. "Every day I'm more certain that Jack is the mole. Only five of us are aware of Plotnikov. The Gs don't have enough details about what's going on to even attempt to compromise him."

"I agree. I just wish we had the evidence to pinch that son of a bitch. If only Viktor had made that drop, we could've proved it." Tony consoled her, gently rubbing her back. "Listen, I realize it's a long shot, but I say we check to see if he left the signal anyway."

She gave him the side-eye.

"Yeah, yeah, he probably didn't," Tony continued. "But it can't hurt to look, can it?"

J.J. weighed her options and Tony's suggestion was about as good as it would get. "All right. You've got a deal. Let me write up this Pulitzer Prize winning report about today's adventures and turn it into Jack. Then we'll get the hell out of here."

"There's something else you oughtta know," Tony whispered, pulling J.J. inside his cubicle. "One of my boys in the Inspector General's office stopped me in the hall. He got word that Cartwright is launching a new internal investigation to find the ICE Phantom, whoever he is. And they're starting with everyone on the bigot list with access to the vault."

"Well, it's about time! I wondered how many cases we'd have to lose before someone got a clue that we've got a problem. I mean I'm lying like a cheap toupee to protect our last source. How bad do the breaches have to get?"

"I heard they suspect he's a CIA case officer, but they're gonna put all of us on the box if one more FBI asset gets recalled to Moscow."

"Put us on the box?!" J.J. yelped. She remembered where they were standing and lowered her voice to a whisper. "You're kidding, right? This is a problem. A *major major* problem."

Tony leered at J.J., confused. "A problem...*for us?*" he asked. "I don't understand."

"Tony, we're both cursed to the grave with Catholic guilt. And the only accurate information we've written in our Karat reports to Sabinski are the *dates...sometimes.* Do you think we have a snowball's chance in hell of passing a polygraph? And if we tell the truth about our double reporting methods and Sabinski finds out..."

"Ahhh!"

"Exactly! And I don't even want to think about what'll happen if we *fail,*" she said.

"We'd become the prime suspects for ratting out our own sources and get locked up."

She shook her head. "That's just for starters. Sources have been murdered because of this mole. Whoever gets arrested for *these* compromises isn't just going to jail...or Supermax. We're talking death penalty charges."

Tony expelled a long heavy breath and glanced at J.J. Her shoulders curled forward and she swallowed hard.

"This is no time to breathe," she said. "Say your Hail Marys and hope like hell Viktor left the drop so we can stop Jack before he drops the hammer on us."

For some time, both she and Tony had been of the belief that Jack was the ICE Phantom. He'd been accessing files with no need-to-know, a narcissistic personality with an equally grandiose sense of self-importance, all smothered in a Grand Canyon-sized grudge. In his estimation, Bureau executives lacked sufficient intelligence to give him the senior executive position he believed he so richly deserved. His contempt for the Bureau was barely surface-deep.

Compromise. Ego. He displayed the classic motivations to commit espionage and seemed the most logical to turn. But they had little more to go on than a hunch.

J.J.'s thoughts returned to Plotnikov as she contemplated on her conversation with Tony. Her stomach turned and fear flooded every crevice and pore. If Viktor didn't make the drop, where was he? Where did Dmitriyev take him? She didn't know if he'd return to the embassy—or in how many pieces. She was helpless and could do nothing except glance at her cell phone every thirty seconds, waiting on the lookouts to call. As much as J.J. despised the mere thought, she needed to inform Jack…as if he didn't already know what happened.

Traitorous son of a bitch.

She relished in one small hope, the day she'd collect enough evidence to arrest him.

J.J. paused to mentally rehearse her speech when she saw them, smarmy agent Chris Johnson and his co-case agent Lana Michaels. She was a brunette, blue-eyed bombshell who exuded sex and sin. With his Tom Cruise looks and an added six inches in height, they were a match made in a Tommy Hilfiger underwear advertisement. One behind the other, they paced toward her, prepared to insert themselves into Tony's and J.J.'s conversation.

J.J. huffed.

The mid-winter arctic was warmer than the relationship between J.J. and Lana. There was zero love lost between them. Zilch. Sentiments abundantly clear from the scorched glares they exchanged every time they were forced into each other's presence.

As for Lana and Sabinski, well, they shared a mutual respect for one another. She kissed his ass, and he returned the favor. She'd been at the Bureau nearly seven useless years and hadn't recruited a single source—yet Sabinski never missed an opportunity to give her a leg up, so to speak. All of Lana's cases had been reassigned, clipped from the hard-working agents who'd developed them. All under the guise of requiring Lana's Russian language skills, a ridiculous notion given Russians serving under diplomatic cover must be proficient in English to be selected for U.S. tours.

Sabinski had once threatened to transfer Karat to Lana, but Plotnikov would hear nothing of the sort. He adamantly refused, arguing he didn't require a translator. Then he threatened to cease cooperation with the FBI if J.J. didn't remain his handler. His refusal may have saved his life. Few agents would have lied to protect him the way J.J. had.

"What are you two doing here?" Tony asked. He and J.J. were both surprised to see them in the office. They were scheduled to provide assistance on a joint task force with Coast Guard Intelligence all day. A crap assignment Sabinski had doled out in order to feign fairness. "Thought you were on surveillance today."

"Yeah, we were on the water this morning," Chris responded. His awkward glance toward Lana spoke volumes. "But, uhhh, Lana here dropped her weapon in the river."

"Again?" J.J. and Tony remarked simultaneously. This was the third weapon in three years. Every competent agent in the vicinity rolled their eyes. For a brunette, Lana had blond tendencies.

"It was raining. My hand slipped," she said, in a lame effort to defend herself, wearing her usual too-tight skirt and boobs seeping out of her too-tight silk blouse. Every day in the office with Lana was akin to a night at the Kitty Kat Club. She'd been ogled and gossiped about since she first sashayed through the entrance, and she couldn't care less. To her, sex equaled power, and she brandished her feminine wiles more often than her 9-mm.

"Oh yeah. Sabinski's looking for you," Lana snapped, a slight hint of arrogance evident. Lana's self-righteous sneers usually meant trouble. J.J. had landed in the hot seat once again. No surprise given her crap-filled afternoon.

Lana smirked and sauntered off. J.J. rolled her eyes and prepared for his wrath. She grunted and sucked her teeth.

"McCall! Get in here. Right now!" the portly one bellowed from his nearby sty.

Tony pointed the finger-gun at his head and pretended to pull the trigger against his temple. He offered it to J.J.

"Please, don't tempt me."

J.J. trudged toward Jack's office, just a few feet away. She rapped her knuckles against the frame. Jack peered up from a file sitting on his wooden desk, suitably dark enough to hide coffee and Kit Kat stains. He pulled off his glasses and grunted, "Yeah, close the door behind you and have a seat."

She sat in one of the two guest chairs across from him and peered at the ordered obsessive-compulsive chaos on his desk. Each item in its place. Not neat, just in its place. She scanned the office as he finished flipping through a case file, then glimpsed Plotnikov's photo just before he closed the jacket. A look of disgust seized her face.

Jack slammed the folder shut.

When the hell did he get Plotnikov's file? She'd just noticed it missing and his signature wasn't on the log. Tony had mentioned the comms plan was missing too. The reason was now quite evident. Thankfully, he had a copy of doctored file. No information inside would get Viktor killed.

She struggled to hold his glance.

Jack's eyes narrowed. "You got an update on Karat?"

She ran her fingers through the strands of hair dangling over her shoulder, grasped the back of her neck and let out a long frustrated breath.

"I know what you're gonna say, but understand that the Gs had him…at least until the target made a cover stop and shook them. But KARAT couldn't make the meet today anyway. He had an escort."

"An escort? Who?" Jack asked as if he already had been told the answer.

"Dmitriyev." She waited for a change in his facial expression, a sign of shock or surprise. The sign never appeared. "Tony and I will be leaving to check the signal shortly. Just in case."

He grabbed an individually wrapped Twizzlers from the family-sized container on his desk, noisily crackling the paper. After he chomped a licorice stick, the arrogant glutton folded his arms across his rotund belly and cocked his head to the side.

"Don't even bother!" he snapped as he bent forward and wagged the uneaten portion in her face. "Cham and Money T picked up Plotnikov and Dmitriyev near Dulles as they entered the airport parking lot. Plotnikov was on the afternoon Aeroflot flight back to Moscow."

"What!" She lurched forward in her seat. *No. No. No!* The screams echoed in her head. Her eyes flooded with contempt. How could Jack sit before her so nonchalant and unaffected knowing Plotnikov had disappeared and he was responsible?

The sound of a gunshot ripped through her mind, sending a chill through her entire core. She envisioned Plotnikov collapsing on the floor and squeezed her eyes shut, trying to force the thought from her mind. J.J. vowed to prove Jack's guilt. He'd get locked up before he struck again.

"Yeah. Another one bites the dust." His glib tone was almost too much for J.J. to withstand. Her eyes darted across the surface of his desk, scanning for potential murder weapons. A paperweight. A lamp. A

Twizzler. "He's probably dead by now with his hand in a parcel headed to Moscow station thanks to you."

His words dripped with snide condescension. Given the day she'd had, J.J. would've have liked nothing better than to stuff the Twizzler down his throat until he shit red licorice sticks. An incredulous look consumed her expression. "If I didn't know any better, Jack, I'd be inclined to think you were making an accusation."

"Well, somebody better get me some fucking answers. This is the fourth source recalled in almost seven years. Three out of four of them belong to you. I wonder why *you*, of all the agents assigned to work counterintelligence, are so . . . *unlucky*."

Because I work for a traitor! she thought. J.J. stared in stunned silence. Couldn't believe what the asshole had suggested. He had some gumption, taking so lightly the deaths of men who risked more to protect the United States than he ever would.

"Could it be because I'm the only one who's recruited anyone in four of the last seven years?"

J.J. struggled to stay composed, but she had no choice except to hold her tongue. She'd need to keep her job for a little while longer. Locating her source and nailing Jack's ass to the wall were more important than acting on professional grudges.

"I should've put Lana on this one. She's a fuckin' pro. You on the other hand..."

She clasped the armrests to push herself up from the chair. The decorum-deficient piece of her mind burned across her tongue and nipped at her lips as she inhaled a calming breath.

"Let's not go there. You and I both know I'm the best recruiter you've got. Lana hasn't recruited a single source in nearly seven years and has more guns floating in the river than the Gambino Family. Blond hair, blue eyes, and big boobs do not a professional make. Now if you'll excuse me..."

Jack leaned forward in his seat and sneered. "Neither do shit brown daughters of domestic terrorists . . . or your little guinea wise guy partner," Jack said of J.J. and Tony. His father had been a capo in the Bonanno family before getting arrested on racketeering charges seven years before.

J.J. froze and glared at Sabinski, then shifted her body at an angle as if to avoid the sun's glare. She tightly pinched her lips together, until she could feel teeth marks in her flesh. Every ounce of common sense in her body screamed, begged her to lay the badge and gun on his desk and tell him where to shove them. Her tongue was locked, loaded, and ready to fire. But she'd put her yearning to verbally thrash Jack aside. An insubordination complaint would pit his word against hers. And the words of a woman, especially a black woman, meant a little bit of nothing in this man's FBI.

Too crackbrained to know when to quit while he was behind, Sabinski continued his rant. "As your E.E.O. rep, I'd advise you to report me. But I don't feel like entertaining any reports against me," he chuckled, his teeth as yellow as a tub of I Can't Believe This is Butter.

She failed to see the humor.

How she longed for it, the day when she could slap the handcuffs on him and drag him to jail by the lone strand of hair left on his watermelon-sized nugget.

She bolted up from her seat and started toward the door. Attempted to leave before choice four- and five-letter words spewed past her lips. Why give him the satisfaction of knowing he could make her completely lose her composure. She did, however, leave him with one final thought.

"If you ever spit those hateful comments or utter a single syllable about my father again, I promise you an E.E.O. complaint will look like the Tea Cup ride at Disneyland compared to the nightmare I'll bring to your doorstep!"

She strutted to his desk, her breath heavy and fingers trembling with fury as she reached toward him. Jack's eyes bulged and his countenance lit with panic. There was no question. He wanted to scream at her, but the sound locked in his throat.

J.J. proceeded to knock over every OCD-arranged knick-knack she could reach. She then dry washed her hands and threw them up in victory. With his bottom jaw scraping the floor, she turned to leave.

Jack sat back hard against his seat. This was a different J.J. and she could see he was caught off guard. She'd never jumped down his throat heels first; rather she'd normally grin and bear his verbal vitriol. He paused, unsure of how heavily to tread. "I won't tolerate your insubordination! Touch my desk or speak to me that way again, and I'll you have fired."

He had no idea how much she wanted to dare him. No sooner than the words passed his lips, a slight sensation emerged in her earlobe.

Bluffing, as usual.

Emboldened, J.J. shot a glare over her shoulder. "You promise?"

CHAPTER 8

J.J. burned with angry fire. As she raced from Jack's office, her feet pounded hard against the floor. She charged toward the vault entrance, frustrated. Pissed off. Thirsty. She hadn't planned to walk into the vault except for the fact that she could take a swig without everyone staring down her throat. J.J. had been teetering on a thin line for years and Jack had managed to push her over. Now she didn't want a drink, she needed it.

"What's going on, J.J.?" Tony asked, concerned. He hurried his pace to catch up with her. Once he was out of earshot of their nosy colleagues, she stopped and turned to him.

"Refresh my memory. What's the penalty for first-degree murder?"

J.J. badged into the vault, placing her index finger into the new biometric scanners, the most hi-tech security used in the Bureau outside of the labs at Quantico. She waved her badge in front of the infrared reader until the lock clicked and then entered; Tony followed close on her heels.

"What happened? What did he say?"

She collapsed into a chair and buried her face in her hands, tried to shake off the disastrous meeting. Then she pulled her spare flask from a desk drawer and opened it in front of Tony. He bit his lip; his neck stiffened.

"J.J."

She took a short gulp and twisted the cap shut. She never took more than a sip or two at a time. A slow drizzle. "Trust me, when I tell you what happened you're going to want some too." She handed the flask to him. "What do you want first, the *bad* news or the *worse* news?"

"Gimme the worst first," he said, sitting at attention and wagging his hand to refuse her offer.

"It's Plotnikov...he was recalled to Moscow." She returned the flask to the drawer. "He's gone, probably dead by now if Golikov's people had anything to do with it."

"You're yankin' my chain. I don't even believe this shit!"

"Believe it." J.J. peered at him and then tilted her head toward the ceiling. "I just got word from Archie Bunker. He tried to pin the blame on me, said he should've assigned the case to Lana. No, no, please contain your astonishment."

"Lana? Get the fuck outta here! She couldn't recruit a Mouseketeer into the Mickey Mouse club."

He took a seat beside J.J. and rubbed his hand against her back. Their eyes met for a moment, but she never held his glance for longer than a few seconds at a time. His glare pierced her, exposed her vulnerabilities in a way she'd prefer not to reveal to him...or any man for that matter.

"Listen don't let him get to you. He probably forgot to take his crazy pills today."

J.J. shrugged. "Well, looks like we're all getting hooked up to the box unless we can find this damn mole. I'd half hoped the package from Karat might give us a clue as to his identity. But, right now, we got nothing'."

"I know. Let's just hope we're the last on the list to take the polygraph. It'll buy us some time to figure out what happened to Karat and find the rat. And I gotta tell ya, I feel sorry for him when I do," Tony threatened.

"Maybe we can send him to Supermax to keep Hanssen company. He probably needs a new boyfriend right about now."

Tony smiled, happy to see her spirits lifted once again. "Thatta girl … anyway, let's grab something to eat and we'll go check the signal," he said.

"You eat. I'll drink."

The fates bestowed upon her the boss from hell and the co-case agent from heaven and leaving one meant leaving both behind. If Sabinski had a fraction of Tony's good nature, she might not be so willing to turn in her badge. "Sounds good but I gotta make a quick phone call first. You think Kevin Douglass from the Organized Crime-Drug Section still has the pink convertible Mini Coop they seized from the Bonanno raid—" She winced, cut herself off a moment too late.

Whatever discomfort Tony had, he shrugged it off. "Probably. I don't think it's been auctioned yet. Why you wanna know?"

"Remember my promise to Jake?"

Tony nodded and chuckled. "Remind me to light a candle for your soul at mass this Sunday. Yeah, make the call. I wish I could see his face."

"Hey, he asked for a convertible. A convertible it is."

• • •

Thursday Evening…

At the Hawk-n-Dove, J.J.'s favorite watering hole, Tony gulped the last of his lager as she drank him in. He was easy on her eyes as Sunday morning and hard on her feminine sensibilities. Tony's glance lingered in her direction more times than she cared to admit, but she kept her mind locked on the task at hand. Usually. Besides, they were both relationship-challenged workaholics. Neither one had a personal history conducive to…humans. Hard to believe it'd only been a year. They meshed well inside the office and out.

J.J. felt Tony's eyes on her. He sat unnaturally still twirling his fingers as she shamelessly inhaled the last of her burger and fries. She loved that about him, the fact that he didn't judge when she scarfed her food down.

But she didn't like his expression, the one that said a lecture was imminent.

"We should talk about the white elephant in the room," he said.

"I prefer blue gorillas," J.J. joked in an effort to lighten his tone.

"Blue gorilla, white elephant. I don't care. I'm just gonna say it," Tony began, his voice laden with apprehension. "I'm a little worried about you. I mean, you say you've got everything under control but this shit has a way of sneaking up on ya. I gotta make sure you're all right. You're the one who has my back. Maybe you should think about gettin' some help."

Tony. He'd never been this direct, nor the look of worry so pronounced, evident. She felt in control. Mostly. The timing, the problems, everything else was out of balance. As soon as her troubles ended she'd recover, get back to her old self.

"First of all, I'm okay. When have you ever seen me sloppy drunk or out of control? Never. So, I take a sip here and there to knock off the nerves. It's no big deal," she said, delivering her rehashed speech. "Besides, if I went to get the help that I obviously *don't need*, I'd have to report it to security. And you think I can't get a promotion now? That's all the excuse Sabinski would ever need to put me on airport surveillance for the rest of my career."

"But—"

"But nothing Tony. I'm going through a lot right now. She died 25 years ago next Friday. Did you know that?"

He shook his head.

"And then Polyakov's hand, Plotnikov's departure, and only God in heaven knows where he is, if he's still alive. So cut me some slack. I'd be more surprised if I *weren't* drinking." She twirled her thumbs to relieve her own tension. Finally, Tony's shoulders relaxed. "Now, can we just toss back a couple of beers? If it bothers you that much, I'll lay off the booze. Just a beer every now and then. Is that satisfactory?"

He nodded, seeming unsure of whether to believe her or whether she even believed herself. But he nodded.

"You know, if I was one of your boys, you'd offer to buy me a beer and just say I was blowing off steam."

"But you're not just 'one of the boys' to me, J.J. That's why I give a damn. *Hai capito?*"

She nodded and smiled in the uncomfortable silence. He cared for her, and she knew it. She just didn't have time to care as much for herself. They both took long sips to finish their first beers and sat the glasses at the end of the table, seconds were on the way. She was much more relaxed until she stoked Tony's ire. The details of her conversation with Sabinski didn't go down as smoothly as the beer.

"I don't understand why you don't report that scumbag. I mean, there's gotta be something we can do."

"Please, Tony. You've been at the Bureau almost as long as I have. *You know* what happens to supervisors accused of racism, sexism, or any other kind of 'ism'."

Tony picked up his glass to take another sip of his beer. "Yeah, they get promoted."

"Bingo. Then spend the rest of their careers making your life a miserable hell from a high-ranking position. And with even greater authority to fire your ass. No thanks. And I don't need anymore drama than I'm already mired in."

"Well, just wait and see what Cartwright's gonna do. He's the AD for crying out loud. If anyone can make the situation right, he can."

"As soon as we nail this bastard and take care of Plotnikov—" she began, avoiding his piercing stare. She couldn't face him when speaking of leaving. He too often made her want to stay.

He leaned forward and smiled, his deep gaze forcing her to look at him. He effortlessly disarmed her, shifted J.J.'s thoughts from her misery to his eyes, just as she knew he would.

"What?" she said, feeling naked in a room full of strangers.

He chuckled. "Nothing. Just wanted to make you forget what you were about to say."

Her lips curled upward as she bowed her head in concession. "Mission accomplished."

• • •

The burnt orange and amber-colored leaves drifted in the fall breeze as Tony pulled up to the street corner. They'd arrived at the mailbox designated for the dead drop. Idyllic brick cape cods lined the streets in the residential area surrounding the signal location. They made it convenient to the embassy for a reason. Karat could reach it by just taking a leisurely 20-minute stroll.

Peering out of the passenger window, J.J. was thankful the last ray of sun had yet to fade. She could check the box without drawing undue attention with a flashlight. She snatched her glasses off in frustration and sat back hard against her seat.

"Nothing. Damn!" she said, disappointed. Against her better judgment, she'd already begun to kid herself, thought Tony's bright idea might yield a sliver of hope.

"What were your instructions?" Tony asked.

"A vertical chalk mark on the south side of the box. This is the south side. No mark."

Tony leaned forward and examined the area as if he'd see something with his "man" vision that she couldn't.

J.J. rolled her eyes, shot him a glare. "Really?" she asked, her voice slathered in sarcasm. "Nothing's there."

He shrugged. "Dmitriyev was with him so…whadaya gonna do?" Glancing to his right, Tony's eyes locked on something in the distance. "You want ice cream?" Tony asked. "There's a shop just up the block."

"If this is some feeble attempt to help me eat my troubles away, well…you should've thought of it sooner."

As he spun the steering wheel to the right, J.J. pressed her forehead against the window. The ice cream shop was just a few hundred feet away. In an act of sheer desperation, she eyed the box from her peripheral vision.

She gasped. "Wait a minute. Stop, Tony. Stop!"

"What is it?" he yelled.

"Back up to the box! I think I saw something."

"Jesus! You scared the crap out of me," he said.

She grabbed his arm, pulled him toward her.

"Look! Right there!"

Tony's gaze shifted in circles. Then his chin collapsed into his lap. "How the hell did he pull that off?"

They'd spotted the faint but visible mark. Plotnikov had placed it on the wrong side of the mailbox. J.J. blinked a few times, believing her imagination had run wild.

How in hell could Plotnikov mark the signal with Dmitriyev in the car? Her mind churned. Maybe he slipped out in the middle of the night and made the drop? Hmmm. No, the lookouts would've seen him leaving and noted the incidents on the log. A piece of this puzzle was missing—something important. And she had no clue what it was.

But the package was there. Encryption codes. ICE Phantom's identity. The unknowing, the stress was unbearable.

"We've got to check the dead drop location now. We'll get ice cream after. The park's about to close."

Tony shook his head. "What happened to your priorities?"

CHAPTER 9

Thursday Evening…

Russell Freeman, the first African-American FBI director, took the weight of a nation on his shoulders. A little more than a year before, he vowed to leave no stone unturned. The source of the compromises in his department would be identified, and he promised to protect those brave individuals who'd risked their lives to help the FBI accomplish its mission. In the second of his ten-year term, he'd still failed to deliver. Two men had been murdered for political defiance, one man had gone missing, and Freeman still had no idea who the culprit was. Aside from vague references to some ICE Phantom, blaming rogue CIA officers for intelligence failures had been the Bureau way for years, evidenced by the initial botched handling of Robert Hanssen's investigation. The core of his gut told something he'd denied for too long—the problem was close to home, much closer than he cared to admit.

Freeman sat behind the stately executive desk in his expansive office. It was decorated with the obligatory accouterment. An FBI seal was mounted on the wall behind him. An array of state and government flags flanked him on either side, all neatly arranged to complement the head-man-in-charge air. He scanned through his daily emails and replied to the most important message, a note from the Director of National Intelligence. He'd requested an urgent meeting with Director Freeman the following week because of the brewing storm, a storm purportedly created by the ICE Phantom or someone like him.

The DNI had recently become aware of potential compromises in his own organization, so he asked Director Freeman to assign agents to support initial inquiries. With tensions mounting between Russia and the United States over the U.S. missile shield, and the economic downturn, too many vulnerable government employees had begun to fold under the pressure, sought opportunities to sell secrets for a quick buck to the highest bidder.

He glanced down at his watch in time for his five o'clock appointment. He normally didn't take meetings at the end of the day, especially before a celebration his wife had planned for his 58th birthday. But he made an exception. No sooner than he turned to face the entrance, Jack Sabinski and Jim Cartwright entered his office, greeting him with nods and hellos.

"Jack, Jim, it's good to see you both. Please, shut the door and have a seat," he said, his expression growing as grim as his tone. "Wish we could be meeting under better circumstances."

Sabinski and Cartwright each sat in the two chairs directly opposite Freeman's desk. Both appeared nervous, uneasy.

"We do as well, sir," Sabinski interjected as he placed the file on his lap.

Freeman clasped his fingers together. "In our last session, I requested that you both intensify your efforts to identify the source of these compromises. This ICE Phantom. Are *we* the problem? Is CIA the problem? Another agency? I've got a meeting with the DNI next week, and I need some answers. What's the status of your preliminary inquiry?"

Cartwright exchanged awkward glances with Sabinski before he conceded the floor.

Jack sat erect and tugged his suit jacket forward. His excessive, rotund waistline could not be concealed and did not go unnoticed by

Freeman or Cartwright. Agents did, after all, have standing fitness requirements. "Sir, we're certain there's a mole, but we're much less confident about whether the problem lies in the FBI or CIA...or even NSA. Almost every civilian agency in the intelligence community has lost valuable Top Secret intel and HUMINT sources. But based on an NSA assessment, our comms networks appear to be secure. This is a HUMINT problem."

Freeman rubbed his throbbing temple. "Listen, I don't want another Hanssen situation, not on my watch. The FBI can't afford another embarrassment. The nation can't afford to lose such valuable sources and intelligence. This is no time to play point the finger."

"We understand this, sir."

"If either of you has an ounce of suspicion that we've got a problem, then I will do everything in my power to find this son of a bitch and prosecute him to the fullest extent of the law," he barked, agitated and nearly losing his composure. He sat back hard in his seat; his tone grew calm and more measured. "So, the question I'm posing to both of you is this: what are we doing? I'm not in the habit of launching accusatory stones from glass houses and I won't start now."

Cartwright leaned forward, elbows to thigh. Freeman could see the stress from his job had aged him in the four short years he'd been the AD. When he accepted his position, his hair was coal black, now almost every strand had been subsumed by gray. Bags of stress buckled beneath his eyes. Too many anxious days and sleepless nights.

"Russell, we're doing everything possible to secure our remaining sources. As of today, we've revoked vault access to everyone on the bigot list. Each and every agent and analyst will be required to undergo a polygraph examination to regain their entry privileges."

Jack pulled out a sheet of paper from the file folder marked "SECRET" in red at the top and bottom and passed it to Freeman . It was titled "REVOKE ACCESS" and contained a list of names, including

J.J. McCall, Antonio Donato, Lana Michaels, Sunnie Richardson, Christopher Johnson, Jacob "Jake" McGee, and a few other unit colleagues.

Freeman grabbed the paper and scanned it carefully from beginning to end. "Jack, this list should include *everyone* with vault access, including you."

"Oh uh...an unintentional oversight, sir. Actually, my polygraph exam is scheduled for first thing tomorrow. As the supervisor, I thought it was important that I regained access immediately so I can properly supervise my unit," he said, puffing out his flabby chest.

Cartwright nodded in agreement. "Good thinking. We need you back on this case as soon as possible. If anyone fails, call me first and I'll arrange to have their personnel files sent directly to Washington Field. I want full investigations opened immediately. No preliminary inquiries."

"Yes, sir," Jack replied.

"Sounds good, gentleman," Freeman said to them. "Now, if you'll excuse me, I've got to get back to work. Who would've thought terrorists would demand as much attention as Russian spies," Freeman said. He stood and placed his hands on the desk to brace himself as he leaned forward. "And don't forget the lessons learned from our last major internal investigation. We're all human. We all have vulnerabilities. Exploited by the wrong person at the right time, any one of us could turn."

Sabinski and Cartwright stood almost in unison and headed toward the door. Freeman followed closely behind and shook their hands before they exited. "Okay, our mission is clear, and time is of the essence."

CHAPTER 10

The sun hung low in the horizon when Tony and J.J. wheeled into Rock Creek Park. The drop only steps away, the end to years of compromised cases and dead sources were finally coming to a close. And in the location where it all began for them mere months before. It was perfect for her, D.C.'s largest recreational area. The park contained many nooks and hidden places to suit her operational needs. Off-the-beaten path walking trails, rocks, and footbridges, it was replete with ideal locations. Dead drops could be easily concealed and signals marked without being disturbed for days, even months.

They pulled into a cul-de-sac, a semi-circle shaped parking lot right off Beech Drive, a main thoroughfare. Very little traffic passed through the spot in the late evenings because no lighting had been installed on the walking trails. J.J. reached in Tony's back seat to find the operational backpack they stored in his car for those occasions they needed to retrieve drops at night. Inside was a flashlight, rubber gloves, and evidence kits. The rubber gloves ensured they wouldn't contaminate any potential evidence with their own prints. Crime lab techs lifted prints on everything. The skull caps and black nylon windbreakers were reversible, gray and black, in case they needed to alter their appearances while on foot. But this night the lot was desolate, no one but them, the bats, the trees, and the chilling breeze. Concealing their identities was the least of their concerns.

"Listen, Tony, we need to step up the pace. Park Police will be making their rounds to lockup soon. I don't want to have to explain that we're FBI agents here to pick up the Top Secret documents that our Russian spy left for us in a dead tree stump." She stuffed the gloves in her pocket. "They get just south of pissed when the FBI doesn't advise them about ops on their turf."

"True. True," he said as he removed his seatbelt.

"The last thing we need is for some keystone cop to call Sabinski and rant about our failure to follow protocol."

"You got that right," he said, twisting his head toward the back seat. "The flashlight's still in there, right?"

"Uhhh, I think so."

When she turned to dig in the bag, a blinding light obstructed her vision. Headlights. The car turned into the lot and eased closer toward their car. She blinked rapidly, suddenly felt as if she needed to use the bathroom. She could see nothing.

And time was working against them.

J.J. and Tony couldn't afford to lose a single day. She couldn't tell whether the car had takedown lights. The sky was blue-black.

"Please tell me that's not Park Police," J.J. said. "You know they'll order us out."

Tony craned his neck, but couldn't discern. "Damn it's dark out here. I can't tell yet."

The car pulled into a parking space a few feet away. The engine stopped.

"No, can't be Park Police. They'd have rolled up behind the car to keep us from backing out," Tony said. "Probably some kids up to no good."

"*Whew!* Okay, let's roll."

J.J. opened her door, planted her foot onto the moist asphalt. A choir of crickets sounded as a light breeze swept across her face. Then a second set of headlights appeared. The take-down lights were visible this time. She glimpsed the faint shadow of an arm maneuvering a floodlight hanging on the driver-side mirror.

J.J. poked her head back in the car and lowered her voice. "Shit! This *is* Park Police! What are we gonna do?" She pulled her foot back inside and closed the door.

"Where's your gun?" Tony asked, his breathing markedly faster.

"In the holster on my back," she answered. She hoped his solution involved something other than flashing their credentials.

"Good. Mine too," Tony said. "Now just play along."

Before J.J. could inhale and process what he'd said, he grabbed her shoulder, yanked her to his chest, and kissed her deeply as if they'd just said "I do." J.J.'s eyes opened wide when they should've closed, and drifted closed when she should've been pulling away. He cupped her cheeks; the heat from his hands warmed her. Her fingers roamed, found their way into his hair, onto his shoulders, and down to the small of his back. *My God—his lips,* she thought. She'd never felt such softness, such tenderness. Slowly he eased his mouth open, and hers followed. Their tongues intertwined in a beautiful dance. J.J. felt drugged with the purest form of Ecstasy. She lost track of time, of space. She'd been transported to a dream.

Bam! Bam! Bam!

And awakened by reality.

The officer banged on the window. His light shone directly in their faces. Then on the floor and in the back seat.

Tony turned down the window and placed his hands on the steering wheel so the officer could see them.

"Didn't you read the sign when you drove in? The park is closed after dark. You'll need to leave immediately so I can lock up."

J.J. didn't hear a word the officer said. *Is he even speaking English?* she wondered. Neither her body nor her mind had returned from wherever

Tony had beamed her a few seconds before. The other car pulled off, distracting them all for a moment. The officer turned his attention back to them.

"Oh, sorry, sir," Tony said. "But my wife, she dropped her wallet when we took a walk here earlier. It's our anniversary and this is where we first met. Guess we, uhhh...got a little carried away. You know how it is."

Did he just say wife?

J.J. tucked her left hand under her thigh so the cop couldn't see her ringless finger. Tony words had whizzed her back to reality, caught her off guard. So did the itching sensation that ensued a few minutes later. Her leg jerked noticeably before she could compose herself.

"You all right, Miss?"

"Yes, it's a condition. Forgot my medication."

"So you dropped your wallet, huh?"

J.J. nodded sheepishly and balled her fist. She wanted to jab Tony in the arm.

"Women! Whadaya gonna do, right?" Tony added.

They shared a man laugh at her expense. J.J. frowned at Tony, cocked her head to one side and shook it. He'd pay for that remark later.

"I dunno," the cop said, debating whether to let them go.

"Pleeeeaaase, officer?" J.J. begged. "If somebody steals it, I'll have to replace my driver's license, social security card, everything. And hubby here will never let me live it down."

He paused. "All right. All right. I can't even count how many times I've had to call out a search party to find my wife's purses and crap. Sheesh!" the officer said. "You've got five minutes and then I've got to lock up. I'll make another stop and come back. You got a flashlight?"

"Uhhh...yes, sir. Right here." She reached her arm behind the seat into the duffle bag and pulled it into his view. "See? We're good to go."

"Okay. I'll be back in a few. Good luck finding your wallet."

Tony stepped out of the car, waved at the officer. When he pulled the cruiser onto the parkway, J.J. and Tony jumped out.

"That there was some fancy footwork, partner," she said, sucking her teeth and speaking with a cheesy Yankee Texan accent. J.J. shifted her gaze to her watch, and then grabbed an evidence bag from the duffle. Time was ticking and they hadn't reached the drop location.

As they padded down bike trail, a sliver of a moonbeam and a flashlight illuminated their path. Tony led the way, his pace swift and urgent, his body shielding her from whatever lay ahead. The sound of falling leaves set her nerves on edge.

Within minutes, they arrived at the footbridge, roughly forty meters in. She shone the light on the adjacent grassy area as Tony eased down the rocky slope, then tossed him the flashlight so he could see where Plotnikov had stuffed the bag.

Alone in the blue blackness, J.J. flinched, placed her hand on her holster every time noises sounded in the trees. Birds, bats, whatever. Sunday dinner was but a shot away.

Wordlessly, Tony searched the crevice between the wooden planks and the slope.

"You see anything? The package may be small if he's passing codes." She looked at her watch again. "We've only got a couple minutes left."

"No. Nothing. You sure this is the right location?"

"Uh yeah. Picked it myself."

"Still don't see...oh, here it is! Lemme see if I can grab it. He wedged it in here pretty good."

Wedged? J.J. thought. *How could a small package be wedged?*

After a few grunts, he emerged. He followed the light up the jagged rocks embedded in the hill, climbed to the trail. The large, dark green trash bag sealed with duct tape along the seams was classic Russian tradecraft.

"*This* is the package?" J.J. questioned. The discovery wasn't quite what she expected. "Rather large to contain codes, wouldn't you say?"

"Yeah. Sure is," Tony replied. "Feels like a stack of documents."

They both shrugged off their concerns for the moment, grateful Karat made the drop at all. His recall to Moscow was unexpected and probably as shocking to him as to them. His cooperation may have prompted his own murder and that thought quelled their excitement.

J.J. shook her head, held the evidence bag open so Tony could drop the weighty package inside. Karat must've cleaned house knowing the opportunity might be his last. Seems he wanted to stick it to the SVR before he met his fate, and now J.J. would bring his desires through to fruition.

"He did it. He fuckin' pulled it off." Tony grabbed the evidence bag from J.J. and paced toward the parking lot.

Her initial elation subsided and sadness set in. "Yeah, but at what cost?" J.J. followed closely on his heels. "You think they're gonna kill him...like the others?"

"Probably. But risk is the nature of this business. Everybody knows that. He understood the stakes. We paid him to take those chances. And he gave his family a better life. If this information is solid, whether he's dead or alive, we'll work with the CIA to get the money where it belongs. We've kept our end of the deal."

"No, you and I kept *our* end of the deal. But the FBI didn't. Some self-serving bastard didn't keep his end of the deal," she spat as her anger welled inside. "He didn't honor the oath, and Karat might pay for his treachery with his life."

"Listen, I realize you're frustrated and angry. Hell, I am too," Tony said. "The best thing we can do for Viktor is to make sure that he doesn't die in vain. We're going to take this information and use it to find the rat scum sucker, whoever he is. But right now we gotta get to the car before that cop gets back. If he catches us with this big ass trash bag, we're toast."

In no time, they arrived at the car. J.J. tossed the drop contents into the back seat, the Park Police officer drove up and turned down his window.

"You guys find what you were looking for?"

"Yeah, we got it," Tony smiled. "Thanks, officer. We'll be on our way now."

"Have a good evening," he said, before turning to J.J. "And *you*…take better care of your belongings."

She smirked at the scolding.

Tony and J.J. slipped into their seats, and the engine revved. Rock Creek Parkway would put them at headquarters in twenty minutes.

"Looks like we're gonna have another late night. Let's take this stuff to the office and review it," Tony said.

J.J. shot Tony a glare suggesting he'd put his brain in the bag with the drop materials. "Are you kidding me? Not after the day I've had. Not even at gunpoint. Let's just head to my place to review the package and we'll take it to the vault in the morning."

"And violate Bureau security regulations?"

J.J. shot him the side-eye. "Gimme a break. Before you started working with me, you didn't even know the Bureau *had* regulations."

He laughed. "Yeah, and I only learned the regs because you're always in trouble for breaking them. Someday, I'll teach you how not to get caught."

"Tonight let's just focus on finding the evidence to arrest Jack," J.J. said. "And tomorrow, all of our troubles will be over. Right?"

J.J. turned on the radio. The slow romance-filled melodies of Quiet Storm show filled the silence. She and Tony rode mostly in silence toward her "uptown" condo in D.C.'s Woodley Park area, anticipating the moment she'd open the package and find it…

The smoking gun.

It had to be inside. Had to be. The one piece of evidence that would help her lock up Sabinski up for the rest of his life. Her mind churned, longing for the moment she could confront him.

Distracted by a familiar song, she broke out in song. Her father said she had the voice of a nightingale. And a love song transported her mind back to the intimate moment she and Tony had earlier shared. The kiss felt too real. Tony had awakened a sleeping beast, and she needed to knock it back to sleep fast. She'd pulled out her mental shovel and prepared to bury the memory of what happened in the deep recesses of her mind at the precise moment Tony's brain succumbed to his ego.

"Look J.J., if you wanted to invite me over to your place, you only had to ask. You didn't have to pretend you didn't want to go to headquarters. I realize I can sometimes have that effect on women. *If* you know what I'm saying."

She shook her head and blinked rapidly. His sweet moments were touching, but, oh, that Italian machismo. "Earth calling Tony! Welcome back to reality," she said. "If *you* wanted to *kiss me*, you didn't have to put on that performance with the Park Police. You only had to ask. I realize I can have that effect on men. *If* you know what I'm saying."

He winced, laughing uncomfortably as they approached the stoplight. Tony locked his eyes on J.J.'s and a sexy grin sliced between his lips. She leaned into him and smiled, her face a reflection of his. Softly, she traced her index finger along his jawline, down his neck, to his bicep. "Well, since we're here together, in this car, on this glorious moonlit night . . . and we're on the way to *my place*. I've got an important question I'd like to ask you."

He cleared his throat and then shot her a gloating I-know-you-want-me glance. "Yeah?"

"Why don't we pull over," she paused, "at that McDonald's up the street. I still want ice cream."

He shook his head. "That was cold."

"No, the ice cream's cold," she said. "That was just funny."

Despite their deep-seated desires to explore the "something" between them, whatever it was, they never crossed the line. They treaded along the edges with tight-rope walker precision but never crossed it because both had insurmountable familial obstacles to overcome.

Tony was supposed to fall in love with and marry a good Sicilian woman, one who would stay home, cook, and birth male heirs.

As for J.J.?

Well, her father, a former Black Panther, would go ballistic, melt out of his skin if his only daughter waltzed through the door with Tony on her arm. She and her father had grown close, almost inseparable since the crippling loss of her mother. Each week she ate Sunday brunches with her brother and father; they helped keep the family together. She visited without fail despite Max's criticism of her career choice and the constant chidings she took for not finding herself a good black man, as if they grew on the "Brother Tree" and all she needed to do was pluck one from its ripe fruit and marry him.

If only finding a good man of any color was that easy.

Love had mostly evaded her for thirty-two years. Mostly. She'd almost been taken once, but her gift saved her in the nick of time. With Tony, there was a major difference between her past and present, one thing she couldn't deny: Tony was the only man in three decades of life who never made her itch. With the exception of the wife comment in the park, her discomfort in his presence emanated from only one source—her heart.

Chapter 11

Thursday Night…

The unit was desolate and dark. The only the exception was the light from a desk lamp in Sabinski's office. He'd stayed late to type up a few reports, thumb through some closed cases, several involving Russian sources that had mysteriously disappeared in mid-2005. He wanted to find out why. Could ICE Phantom go back that far? He considered the possibility when Lana tapped on his door.

She stuck her head inside, scanned to ensure the coast was clear. "Hey, Jack. I was trying to put my files away but couldn't get into the vault."

Jack ran his hand along the back of his neck and then waved her inside. "Come in. Close it."

Sabinski's eyes clung to Lana's every move. Her sexy grin sucked the air from the room and rendered him stuporous. His eyes locked on her hands as she unfastened her suit jacket. Each button she opened revealed a sheer white blouse agape to the waistband of her mini skirt. Her nipples were taut and visible through the sheer fabric. He licked his lips hungrily as she sauntered toward him and bent over his desk just enough. A hint of cleavage was all he needed to see to make him wild. Then Lana eased into the lone chair in front of his desk.

Sabinski spun his seat sideways. "Come on now, Lana. You know that's not your seat."

She glided to him, as a stripper to her pole, claimed a seat on Jack's lap, and pressed her lips to his.

As the passionate kiss lingered and Jack's member swelled, neither noticed Chris. He'd forgotten his wallet inside his desk and swung by on the chance that Jack was working late. And working late Jack was.

Chris heard voices and peered through the venetian blinds. There she was. He wondered why she hadn't answered any one of his dozen phone calls or two dozen texts. Visibly flushed, his jaw tightened and stomach burned; the tips of his fingers rolled into his palms. He wanted nothing more than to storm inside and bash Jack's head in. Lana belonged to him and him alone. But she'd be livid if he didn't stick to her plan. That's why he created one of his own, a plan to rid himself of Jack and ensure Lana could live without the fat bastard's interference.

Chris turned away, stormed to his desk. He wouldn't be played for a fool this time. His hands juddered as he grabbed his iPod and earphones from beneath the clutter in his desk drawer. Hurriedly, he plugged the buds into his ears. The device took a moment to tune in. His buddy in the headquarters' Special Projects Unit, the "Q" of the FBI, modified the iPod so that it no longer played music. Rather, it functioned as a receiver for the wireless transmitter Chris had planted beneath Jack's desk. He huddled into the corner of his cubicle, concealed in the darkness, and tuned into Jack's and Lana's conversation.

Just as the signal came through, Jack cried out a loud moan.

"Ahhhhh…you're amazing," Jack said. His zipper sounded. "You sure know how to make an old man feel young again."

"Please. I don't see any old men in here," she hummed.

"What are you doing here, Lana?" he asked.

She relieved her knees and returned to his lap.

"A girl like you could have anyone you want," Jack said. "Why me?"

"Why not you? Seems you and I differ in our perceptions," she said flirtatiously, peppering his fat head with kisses.

Chris struggled to restrain his gag reflex. Hearing them coo at each other like a pair of fucking teenagers made him sick. The things he'd done for the love of that woman, but she'd warned him from the beginning that her career was her first priority—and she would go to any lengths (or stoop to any depths) to fulfill her mission. But he hadn't banked on her tryst with Sabinski becoming part of the package deal. Disgusted, he couldn't stand to listen to another gut-wrenching word. He slammed the iPod in his desk drawer and slipped out of the office unnoticed.

"Now back to our discussion," Lana reminded Jack, easing into a business-like tone. "You were telling me about the vault."

"Oh, yeah. I met with Freeman and the AD about this compromise business. They've revoked access to everyone on the bigot list. We'll all have to take polygraphs. No access until we pass."

"*Everyone's* got to take it? Even *you*?" she asked.

"Everyone. I just finished drafting the list and you and I are the first two. I want to make sure we don't miss a second of precious time finding this fucking mole."

She swallowed hard, noticeably more uncomfortable than moments before.

"What is it?" Jack asked, concerned.

"Now that you mention this mole, I've been hesitating to speak with you...about Chris. It's probably not my place to say anything but, uhhh...he's been acting strangely as of late. Well, more strange than usual. I think he's in trouble, and I'm not certain I can help him."

Jack sat forward in his seat. "What kind of trouble?"

"I don't know. He's secretive. He's been spending insane amounts of money, buying very pricey gifts, too expensive for an agent's salary. There are also the crazy mood swings....and the flash drive. I've seen him with it in the office."

"Is that right?" he asked. "Well, I'll definitely follow-up on the flash drive issue. They're not authorized in the SCIF. As for the money, well, anybody could see he's got it bad for you."

She shook her head. "Well, he's certainly not in love with me. Obsessed maybe. I was really hoping you could just...I don't know...have a talk with him."

He nodded. "I'll speak with him tomorrow afternoon and see where his head's at."

"Appreciate that Jack." She stood in front of him, sighing in relief. "So, what about J.J. and Tony?"

"What about 'em?" Jack snapped.

"Another one of the agents mentioned they're targeting a diplomat providing intelligence on European missile defense negotiations. They might need access sooner than we do."

"Her case is shit. Karat's not giving up anything of value, so I made certain they're the last two on the list. They aren't scheduled to take the exam until Friday. I'll assign you to work her cases until she gets access if she ever gets access again. Wouldn't surprise me if the bitch is guilty."

"Wouldn't surprise me either. Which begs the question, why is she still working here? I've been telling you to get rid of her for years." Lana cut him a sideways glance. "Don't tell me you've bought this competent act of hers. She's not good. She's lucky."

"Lana, give me a break, will you? I've denied every promotion she's ever been up for. I've made her working environment as hostile as I can without getting myself fired. I don't get it, either," Jack replied. "Something tells me she won't leave until she finds what she's looking for."

"Looking for? What do you mean by that?"

"J.J.'s father was a Black Panther, one of those hoodlums who killed cops for sport. I've overheard her talking to Donato about COINTELPRO a few times. She's probably biding her time until she can access the restricted files," Jack said, referring to the FBI's 1960's covert program. J. Edgar Hoover created it to neutralize the Black Panthers and other black civil rights and dissident organizations. "And don't even let me get started on Donato. His father's a former Capo in the Bonanno crime family. He's serving seven years on racketeering charges. Trust me when I tell ya, the rotten fruit don't fall far from the tree."

"So you're suggesting the crimes of the parents apply to the children? If so, my father doesn't have a clean past either. I mean, he didn't before he died. So, what does your little theory make me?"

"Beautiful." The glint in Jack's eye suggested he'd finished with his conversation. He wanted to talk about a more appealing subject. "Now, are you coming to my place tonight so we can finish what we started? I don't know about you but I need an *entree* with my appetizer."

"Let me wrap up my report. I'll see you later. Maybe I'll even pour your favorite *cocktail*," she answered.

Chris, without realizing it, had held his breath as he waited for her. Concealed in the FBI garage's darkness, he stood statue-still and fixed his eyes on the exit door. *What's taking her so long?* he wondered as he stewed in his own disgust. He watched until she appeared in the doorway. His gaze stalked her until she entered her vehicle, the convertible Benz he bought with the spoils of his dirty work. He clenched his eyes tight, trying to shake the image of Lana and Jack from his mind.

Never again, he thought. *Never again.*

He had one trump left. One trump that could make the Jack problem disappear for good. And the time had come to play it.

CHAPTER 12

What the hell was I smoking? J.J. thought, wondering what possessed her to invite Tony to her cozy slice of sanctity. It was a foreclosure she got for a steal. Inside the elevator, she hit number ten on the panel and watched the numbers light up as she tried to dim her anxiety. The maid service had been rescheduled for the following day, so she hadn't had a chance to do the ritual maid pre-arrival clean up.

Now she was afraid of what he would think of her.

When they finally entered her condo, a slow smile brightened his face. His lips parted slightly as his gaze roamed J.J.'s sparsely decorated apartment, from the sectional sofa and naked dining room table, to the Crate & Barrel wall shelf supporting her 51-inch flatscreen and Bose stereo system (she loved her toys). He halted abruptly before passing the photos of J.J. with her father and brother. Another photo of J.J. with her mother, aunt, and grandmother as a child.

Then her heart stopped. Tony's expression told her he'd spotted the one she never meant for him to see.

"Nice place. Decorate much?" he said as he made a bee-line toward the shelf.

She tried to intercept him, but her reflexes were slow. She couldn't position herself ahead of him.

"Well, well, well, what have we here?" He snickered at the photo of J.J. wrapped in the arms of her last relationship faux pas. He grabbed the frame and held it up facing her. "Who the hell is this *douche bag?*"

Douche bag? He can tell from the picture?

J.J. would never give Tony the satisfaction of knowing, but he'd hit that nail on the head. At the age of thirty-two, she'd never suffered a *severely* broken heart thanks to her gift. It protected her from dating liars for longer than an outing or two. Except for this one.

Grayson Chance was known as "Six" to his friends and the many victims of his smash-and-dash. Six could light a fire with the heat from the sexual vibe he radiated. Tall and chiseled, his body was carved from a mass of perfection. His face was sweet as sugar cane; he was Easter Bunny brown…and equally hollow. He could donate a sliver of his ego to every living person on the planet and still have enough left over to rate pompous asshole.

He'd been recruited by the CIA in college and became a counterintelligence case officer when he graduated from The Farm, the CIA's training academy. For the last ten years, he'd been both a case officer and security officer, mostly serving in overseas embassies and consulates. His job was to catch CIA case officers cooperating with foreign intelligence services such as the Russians, thus a joint investigation at the Agency a few years ago brought J.J. and Six together.

They shared a torrid on-again-off-again affair. She was drawn to his mystery, his charm, his sense of humor. Nobody had ever made her laugh more…except Tony perhaps. They shared moments when their souls connected on heights she'd never before allowed herself to reach. And the sex! He did sensuous things to her body that made her shiver at the mere thought. One or two of his moves might be illegal in every state except California and Kentucky. The problem with their relationship? He couldn't stop living his legend, always undercover. The real Grayson rarely stood up and the legend always lied, so she always itched. Couldn't stand to be around him except when their time together didn't involve speaking, which was often, but not often enough. His career and lifestyle forced them onto separate paths. Her path led to sanity, his path led to the land of ill repute. Six's career consumed him. Somewhere along the line, he lost himself...and so he lost J.J. The break-up was difficult, at least for J.J. Six, on the other hand, possessed an ice-cold resilience when it came to failed relationships. But, all in all, J.J.'s decision to let go was probably the best for both of them. Probably.

She still battled moments of doubt, the instances of which had nearly disappeared unnoticed until…

"His name is Six. And why's he got to be a douche bag?" She snatched the frame from his hand and replaced it on the shelf. For some time now, she'd been planning to take the damn thing down. But with Tony Snoopers in the house, she'd have to wait until he departed for the evening. She refused to give him a second's pleasure of thinking that his sneers had any effect on her decision to remove it.

"What kind of name is Six, anyway? His folks hadda give him a name he could spell?" Tony drew the number six in the air with his index finger.

"Ha, ha, ha! You're so funny. No. He graduated Summa Cum Laude from Princeton. I assure you he has no problems with his spelling," she said, avoiding an explanation she didn't want to provide.

"So what's with the 'Six' already?"

"If you must know, Six is a nickname he received because he can bounce a quarter on his six-pack," she joked, patting her stomach.

Tony rolled his eyes and pretended to vomit. "Oh. I thought it might be his rating in the sack."

"No. If that's what it stood for, they'd call him *Ten*." A pregnant pause followed shortly behind her quip, a testament to the jab's effectiveness. J.J. kicked off her shoes and squiggled her feet into the plush carpet. "What's it to you anyway?"

"Hey, it's your business. I was just askin'." He carried the trash bag toward the dining room table, ran his finger across the surface, collecting dust along the way. Then he shot her a "bad housekeeper" look, as if she didn't already know.

"So, how long you been *dating* this. . . *Six*?" he asked, his tone amusingly bitter.

"I'm not, not anymore."

"Is 'at right? So what's his picture still doing on your shelf then?"

"Haven't had a *chance* to take it down yet." She avoided his gaze and headed toward the bedroom. "Now, if you're done with your inquisition, I'm gonna change."

J.J. closed her bedroom door and flopped back-first on the bed. Her hands smothered her face as she cringed. She knew bringing him to her place would be a mistake, one she realized too late.

She brooded over Six's picture every day in the first few months following the break-up. Finally, she'd forgotten it was there, that is, until Tony dredged it up. He'd opened an old wound, picked the scab. How long before it healed again? She rolled over, pulled a flask from her nightstand drawer. Two gulps. Just a little something to take off the edge. That's all. She glanced at her watch. *Scandal,* her usual evening indulgence, would have to wait. They'd have a long night ahead of them.

She grabbed a can of lemon-fresh furniture spray and returned to the living room. When she approached the table, J.J. could see Tony's eyes meander down her body, starting from her face and caressing each bend and curve until he glimpsed the pink foot coverings resting on the plush beige carpet. He stifled a chuckle and backed up his chair so she could spray and wipe the table down. "About time you cleaned this place."

"I'm an FBI agent, not Martha Stewart."

She shot a puff of lemon-scented spray wax in his direction. He coughed dramatically and fanned his face.

"Now, can I get you a beer before I sit down?"

"Sure," he responded.

Tony was thirsty, but maybe not so much for the beer. Out of the corner of her eye, she could see him. He drank her in with his eyes as she opened the refrigerator door. After a lingering stare, he diverted his attention to the work at hand. He laid the evidence bag on the table and pulled rubber gloves from his pocket.

She arrived a few moments later. The two long-necked bottles of Yuengling had begun to perspire. She opened the first with her teeth, stunning Tony into silence. He gawked at J.J. as if he'd just witnessed her swinging from a chandelier in a porn flick.

"What? You gotta be The Hulk to open a beer bottle? Get over it." She placed the bottle in his hand.

He bowed his head in gratitude and tapped the mouth of his bottle against hers. "Salut!"

"Salut!" She smiled weakly. Her knees buckled.

Mmmm, she mumbled. The touch of Sicily in his voice danced in her ear, sent chills through her body. Her emotions welled within. Suddenly, she was the one who needed to shake him off.

She placed the mouth of the bottle to her lips and drew the cold lager inside, allowing the cool fluid to wash across her tongue. She wished his lips had met hers instead and longed to repeat that moment in the park, but she was more than a little relieved they'd resisted the temptation. "What are we toasting to?" she asked.

"Hmmm. Why don't we make it to...a productive night."

• • •

Thursday night…

Russell Freeman devoured the dinner cooked by his divine wife, Rayna. She tried to force him to take the night off. No work, no phone calls. But all to no avail. His mind was on the job. He stared at the remnants of his T-bone until his vision blurred.

"Honeeeeey, it's time to blow out your candle and make a wish," Rayna sang. Her glowing latte-colored skin almost negated the need for candlelight. Russell had been too distant, too consumed with his mystery case to notice. "Honey? ... Honey? Rayna calling Russ. Is anyone home?"

He snapped out of his daze and forced a smile. He'd been outed in the worst way. "Oh, I'm sorry, baby. My mind was somewhere else."

She shook her head. Her brilliant smile disappeared behind a look of indifference. "As usual. Now, blow out your candle before I use it to set you on fire."

He gazed at her, his every expression pleading for her forgiveness. But her unforgiving expression replied, "Go to hell!" Russell let out an uneasy chuckle, smoothed her cheek with his fingertips. "Okay. Okay. Here we go." He closed his eyes just long enough to make a wish. Then puckered his lips and blew.

She picked up the cutter from the linen table cloth and sliced hard into the mango cake, his favorite. The little things mattered most, and she showed him every day. Oh, he knew she loved him deeply. She was, after all, his high school sweetheart. But after four years of college, three years of law school, fifteen years serving as an FBI agent, twelve years as a federal prosecutor, and seven years as a judge, her patience had worn toilet-paper thin. She'd made no secret of the fact that she longed for the day when he'd belong to her, and only her, once again. Most days, she lived with a ghost, a man home with her in spirit but his mind and body were someplace else.

She slipped a piece of cake on his plate. "It's about work, right?" she said, filling the empty seat beside him.

"Yeah...you know how it is," he said, feeling the warmth of her hand rub along his thigh, her signature move. Most days, it would be sufficient to motivate him into the boudoir. At that moment, however, it felt more irritating than stimulating.

"Care to talk about what's going on?"

Her question was met with silence. Perhaps sensing his reticence, she pulled back.

He exhaled in frustration. Certainly, he wanted to share the details of his day with her but he couldn't. Most husbands had license to disclose the nine-to-five drudge. Russell's job was nine-to-infinity, and the specifics were mostly classified national security information.

"I—" he started, preparing to offer yet another excuse for his silence. But she interrupted. He needn't bother.

"Never mind! I know, I know. If you tell me, you'll have to kill me." She shrugged and snapped. "That line's getting old, Russ. Old and tired like me. Or hadn't you noticed?"

"Baby…," He tried to put his arms around her shoulder, but she jerked away and slipped out of the chair.

"I'm exhausted. It's been a long day," she said, heading toward the staircase.

"I'm following right behind you."

She stopped in her tracks and turned to him, her body stiff, the lilt in her voice smothered in venom. "Do me a favor, Russ. Don't!"

Sadly, Freeman felt more relief than guilt. Off the hook for the night, he let out a frustrated sigh and dropped his face into the palm of his hands. If he didn't find out who'd been compromising these cases sooner than later, his marriage might meet the same sticky end as the Bureau's sources.

• • •

Early Friday Morning…

More than two hours later, Tony and J.J. had sifted through everything Karat passed, the massive pile of documents he had smuggled out of the residency before the SVR recalled him to Moscow. He didn't provide the codes as they had expected, as they had hoped.

No, the material he passed was infinitely more important, of greater valuable than anything they could've imagined.

Pages and pages of Xeroxed files, operational files, no doubt slated for encrypted transmission or for transport by diplomatic pouch to Moscow Center.

U.S. military intelligence information reports, CIA communication cables. Pages and pages pilfered from FBI case files and surveillance reports. NSA signals intelligence reports. Defense Intelligence attaché reports. Human intelligence source reports on Russian intelligence officers operating in the United States and abroad. An intelligence disaster as bad as Hanssen and Ames combined.

The sound of J.J.'s heartbeat thumped in her ears, her body tensed. She could feel her veins constrict the flow of blood through her entire panic-stricken body. The compromise wasn't as bad as they initially thought.

No, it was worse.

Much worse.

Her level of distress compounded a hundred fold each and every time she turned a new page. All the major agencies in the community had been burned. No, burned didn't adequately describe the massive security failure that had left the Bureau and the intelligence community with their balls flapping in the wind. They'd been charred to the core, gutted like a school of mahi-mahi at a midnight Luau. With this information in the hands of the Russians, the community would need to shut down half the nation's intelligence operations targeting Russians around the world. Not tomorrow—yesterday. And the CIA would have to exfiltrate at least three assets operating in Moscow or they were dead, Golikov cautionary tales.

"FBI, CIA, NSA, DIA. This traitor's giving up the baby and bathwater," she said. But one question nagged at her. "How could a code clerk get his hands on this? I mean, look, Tony. These are photocopies of original documents. He wouldn't have had access. Encryption codes and cables, yes. Original documents? No."

Tony shrugged. "I'm at a loss. I'm just glad we've got 'em so we can find this nut job." He wiped his perspiring brow with the back of his hand. "Looks like Plotnikov photocopied every document the rat passed. Case files, surveillance and lookout logs, message traffic, everything. And we're even more screwed because most of this information is available to the entire community through the joint communication system, except some NSA SIGINT collection and the military special ops reports."

"Yeah. Every agency, military and civilian, has access. Anyone with a log-on and password could pull this information from the network. Even with cyber forensics, it would be nearly impossible to pinpoint the source."

"Yeah, you're—" Tony started. He flipped through the stack of papers carefully before sinking into his chair in disbelief and resignation. "No...not the surveillance reports and lookout logs. That information is only available at FBI Headquarters and the field offices. We don't share these reports on the Joint network."

"Shit! I'll be..."

"Damn!" Tony yelled in frustration. Tony turned to J.J., his face solemn. "You know what this means, don't you?"

"Yeah. No one else could access the surveillance and lookout logs. I can't speak for the other intel, but whoever took *these* documents has got to be an FBI agent. And judging from these cases," she heaved a weighty sigh, "he's someone with access to the vault. Someone who probably smirks in our faces every damn day knowing that we're working our asses off so that they can cash in our cases in for a few thousand dollars and a Jaguar."

"A few thousand? No, J.J. This information is potentially worth millions of dollars, you hear me? Millions."

What they had once only suspected, Plotnikov's drop had removed all doubt. The FBI was at least one source of the problem—not the CIA, not the NSA, not DIA, but the FBI. And they still didn't have enough evidence to convict anyone, including Jack.

J.J.'s anxiety was compounded by Tony's earlier revelation. If his contact from the Director's office got his information straight, the next few days might spell the end of at least two careers. They would be subjected to polygraph examinations that both were doomed to fail.

They were working against time, and every second that passed brought them one step closer to becoming the primary suspects, locked up, and facing death penalty charges.

Tony eyed a typewritten sheet of paper and scratched the faint stubble on his chin. "Now, this one's interesting. It's a photocopy of a typewritten note. Looks like it's from the source. Check it out."

He handed the paper to J.J. and she began to read it aloud.

The house we built was strong, but I'm beginning to detect a few cracks in the foundation. They must be sealed before the entire structure collapses. My best to Mikhaylov. Juliet Charles. (Solnyshko).

"Solnyshko? What the hell does that mean?" she asked.

"I don't know," he said, smirking. "But Lana's a Russian speaker. Why don't we take this to her in the morning and ask? I'm sure she'd be happy to help."

J.J.'s expression hardened. "Yeah, right. Over my cold, dead, maggot-eaten body. I think Sunnie's a Russian speaker. I'll ask her." Sunnie was one of only two black intelligence analysts within the headquarter-based counterintelligence organization. Recruited from Howard University, J.J.'s alma mater, she was the go-to-girl for all analysis. She'd made an art of creating actionable intelligence, something they could use to build cases, make arrests. She idolized Condoleezza Rice, the only other African-American she knew (living or dead) who also spoke fluent Russian.

J.J. leaned back in her chair, trying to calm her thoughts. "God my head is spinning. I don't think I can process anything else tonight."

Tony examined the note again, and then looked at J.J. in frustration. "I hate these cryptic fucking notes. Why can't people just say, 'My name is Joe Smith. I work for the FBI and I'm a traitor."

"A little thing called the Supermax . . . and lethal injection."

She yawned long and deep, exhausted from the days misadventures. Tony succumbed a few seconds later.

"It's nearly 4 am. Let's get some sleep and take the package to the vault late tomorrow afternoon. Then we'll report it," J.J. suggested.

"That's easier said than done," Tony said. "If we're right and the mole has access to the vault, who can we trust?"

Chapter 13

Friday Morning…

Jack, blank-faced and disoriented, sat wired to the computerized polygraph instrument, his pulse beating at an unusually high rate. He attempted to clear his mind, stare at the white space on the wall in front of him as his examiner had instructed, but his thoughts refused to be stilled.

Memories raced, replaying visions of the less-than-honorable moments of his life, as a film loop turning over and over again. Such as the time he stole a candy bar from the local corner store when he was ten and Mr. Sharma chased him for two blocks. And the times, three times to be exact, that he cheated on his case studies during his sixteen weeks of new agents' training in Quantico. And the dozens of times he'd concocted reasons to reassign J.J.'s cases with no warning or justification in order to boost the subpar career of the woman he loved. And why could he not shake the memory of the moment he removed Plotnikov's file from the cabinet safe without signing the log? Or the countless nights he engaged in classified pillow talk with Lana, divulging details of sensitive investigations of which she had no need to know?

The closet-sized room's stark walls closed in around him. The perspiration sensors on his digits pinched his fingertips as he gripped the edge of the armrest. He tapped the heel of his shoe against the floor tile in rapid motion. The sound resonated like the timer of his life ticking down to nothing. Why had his last polygraph been so much easier, so much less painful? His heart didn't ram through his chest the last time, not this fast. Not this hard. Sweat didn't rain through his pores as if he'd just run the Marine Corps marathon.

There was only one difference between this day and the morning of his last exam. A night with her.

Lana.

He tried to free his mind of the negative thoughts pushing their way through. She adored him as much as he loved her. Perhaps he'd gotten too excited during their tryst. After all, he could hardly control himself in her presence. One glance at her supple breasts sent his nature in the fully loaded and upright position. She'd always been more woman than he could handle. But, even at his age, he'd welcomed the challenge, the intensity of his desire for her. He sought to quench his thirst every chance he got, a thirst that could never be satiated. He couldn't let her go.

The irony of Jack's predicament struck him. He was only two years away from his 57th birthday. Two years away from collecting his hard-earned retirement and pension. Two more years and he wouldn't be subjected to these silly examinations ever again. But two minutes from this moment, his career might be over.

• • •

In an adjoining room of equal size and blandness, they stood in front of the polygraph laptop, the primary and observing testers, Mike Sullivan and Don Anderson. They were perplexed. The test results from the four-hour long examination had stunned them into silence, and both of their faces bore strained expressions.

"Check out his heart rate. The readings run clear off the charts. His perspiration level is higher than I've seen on any human being. And look at these readings here. He had an especially marked reaction on questions related to his honesty and whether he's working on behalf of a foreign government."

"Damn. I don't think I've ever seen anything like this. All of his ranges are above normal, even his control questions. But you're right, the two you noted are especially high. Did he have any kind of medication this morning? Or take any kind of drugs whatsoever?" Mike tried to give his old colleague every benefit of the doubt. He and Jack worked together back in the day. He'd polygraphed a few of Jack's sources.

"I reviewed the questionnaire and asked him outright. He said he didn't ingest any kind of drugs or vitamins today. Claims all he's had is his usual breakfast and coffee," Don said.

Mike swept the palm of his hand over his face and grabbed his chin. "I've known him for twelve years. Sabinski's a career agent and only two years from his retirement. We'd better make damn sure we get this one right. Let's look over the results one more time."

They both examined the charts with microscopic intensity and then turned to face one another.

"Hate to say it, but looks like we've found the mole," Don said as he stood to exit the room. Mike followed. "Let's go talk to him."

Jack's fake smile appeared when Don and Mike entered the room, put-on like the mouth of a Mr. Potato Head. Mike disconnected the blood pressure monitor and offered Jack a box of tissues to wipe his sweat.

"So, we all done? Feels like I'm in the ICU at Washington Hospital Center with all these wires coming out of me." Jack grabbed a couple from the box and dabbed his brow. "I'd like to get out of here and go grab something to eat. We've been in here a long time."

Don and Mike stood stoic and expressionless for a moment. Then each took a seat in his respective chair. "Jack, I'm not sure how to tell you this," Don began, "but there's really no other way. You failed the examination. I mean, you 'do to not pass go, do not collect two hundred dollars' failed."

"Me?" he said, each breath labored, his voice strained. "That's impossible!" he cried out. He knew. Before they entered the room, he knew. His bold-faced lies were equally ineffective on his conscience. Don had only confirmed his own suspicions.

"Do you have any *issues* you'd like to discuss? What's on your mind?"

Jack's stomach sank; he shifted nervously in his chair and lowered his gaze. He'd begun living his worst nightmare. Without question, there was a problem with his polygraph results. Hell, he could feel the surge of anxiety as he began taking the test.

Even so, Jack's expression was incredulous. "Do I have any issues I need to talk about? What the hell could I possibly have to say? Mike's here. He and I have known each other for years. Ask him! He knows I'm not capable of committing treason against my country."

"Yes, Jack," Don said, "he told me you've known each other for years, but we've got a job to do. Whatever he or I might *believe* is irrelevant in this matter, you're having some statistically significant reactions when you answer questions relating to whether or not you're working on behalf of a foreign government."

"Impossible."

"Afraid not. Listen, you've worked counterintelligence for thirty-three years. If you were standing here and I was sitting in that seat, what would you think?"

"I demand a retest!" he barked.

Don let out a long, labored breath. "We can't test you again today. We've been at this for too long. You need to get some rest, meet with security, and we can try again in a few days."

Jack's eyes widened; his bravado disintegrated as his voice shriveled. "A few days? No! You have to retest me, tonight," Jack pleaded. "Mike, please don't let me walk outta here with that monkey on my back.

How am I gonna face my unit, my colleagues, with this kind of suspicion? This is my career we're talking about. I'm not leaving until you test me again."

Don stared into Jack's eyes, studied his expression. "All right. All right. We'll go over the questions again and conduct a retest. Just give me a few minutes to set up the equipment."

Mike led Don out the door and waited just outside.

"I'll go ahead and retest him," Don whispered. "You call Cartwright and tell him we've got a problem. A big one."

Chapter 14

Friday Afternoon…

Chris forked his salad and glared at her, wondering how he arrived at this place in his life where he simultaneously dwelled at the gates of heaven and in the depths of hell. In his wildest imaginings, he hadn't planned for his path to take such a dark turn.

Every day, he droned through the motions, accomplished the minimally acceptable for ten passionless hours a day. Until, that is, he met his lovely Koshechka. In and out of bed, she loved him with fervor and an abandon he'd never before known. He'd fallen under her spell and willingly succumbed. She dominated his thoughts, controlled his mind, and he indulged her every whim. Chris fulfilled her every demand and then asked what more he could do, anything to ensure he held onto the love he'd longed for since the day he could conceive that love existed.

She listened. She supported. She was the first woman truly interested in him as a person, not "the Agent." He shared his desires, thoughts, feelings, and she soaked it in, like an emotional sponge. She empathized with his every concern, understood him in depths no one had ever explored. When he told her he'd grown bored of his mind-numbing theft cases, it was she who suggested he make a career change, pursue something more exciting, like terrorism or counterintelligence.

"Yes, counterintelligence," she said. "You are perfectly suited."

And when she purred in his ear a few nights later, he took it as a sign, a sign that the Russian program might be the right fit. His darling Koshechka was pleased, and he so loved pleasing her.

Once assigned to the Russian Espionage Unit, he clashed with Lana, who was nothing like his Koshechka, except for the sex exuded in their appearances. Lana's tightly wound brunette bun and conservative spectacles contradicted her short skirts and revealing silk blouses. Everything above her neck said business. Everything below, anything but.

He questioned how he could feel like two different people in their presences. One changed him into the man he'd always dreamed he'd become, and the other had devolved him into a man he despised.

In the back of his mind, he realized she'd have to play the same game with other men of his ilk. His only consolation was the promise of a long life together after the game ended.

And end it soon would.

After the long morning he'd had with Lana, his heart smiled with Koshechka. She made angels spread wings, and the sun rise and set around her. He loved the way her silky blond locks flowed across her shoulders and into the curve of her back, like a soft, shimmering blanket. Really, he loved all of her hair colors, like the pink she wore when they played maid and master, and the red she wore when they played actress and director, and even the brown she wore when they played agent and spy. But her naturally blond hair was his favorite.

"I called you last night after I left work. You didn't answer," Chris said with his chest thrust out and a vein protruding through his forehead. He held his glare steady until she looked up from her salad and caught his expression.

"No," she replied, barely blinking. "I didn't."

He laid down his fork and clasped his fingers together. This was no time for mind games. What he wanted, no what he *needed*, was to be reassured. If nothing between them had changed, he wished to hear the words from her lips.

"Don't look at me that way. You know I would never do anything to hurt you if I didn't have to," she said. "Jealousy does not become you, my dearest. We should live the rest of our lives stuck in our dead-end jobs because of your insecurities?" She made no effort to conceal the fact that his impatience wore thin on her nerves.

"No," he replied. "But you don't have to enjoy it."

"You think I enjoy this?" she exclaimed, insulted by the accusation and annoyed by his insecurity. "I hate it. I hate every second. But if this plan is going to work then I have to put aside inconsequential concerns and do what I have to do. Otherwise, my cover will be blown and I'll go to jail. Is that what you want?"

He studied her expression. He just needed one sign, any sign, that she might be lying, but he couldn't detect any. Maybe he was going crazy, wouldn't be the first time. "I'm just glad it's almost over."

"Over? What do you mean when you say 'over'?" she asked.

"Nothing. Nothing at all." Chris's voice trailed off as he stared out into the abyss at the many tourists passing along Pennsylvania Avenue. He eyed the fountains encircling the Navy Memorial, his gaze drawn to the American flags billowing in the wind. He wondered how he could dare set his unworthy feet in such an honorable place. How could he? Especially when he'd betrayed everything it stood for. "Since meeting you, I've become someone I don't even recognize anymore. And when I call and you don't answer... I—I just had to see you, I guess." He reached across the table and ran his finger along the silhouette of her cheekbone. "I need to know that you and I are okay."

She grabbed his hand, laid a soft peck into his palm, and placed it against her cheek. "Don't you realize how much I love you? I'd do anything for you, Chris. Anything for our future. Can't you see that?"

"Sometimes I think I've seen too much," he said, his voice flat as he recalled her office visits with Jack. "I'm sure I have."

"Haven't we all?" She smiled and reached across the table to stroke his cheek then looked down at her watch. "We really must return to work, but first let's discuss a little business. Who's next? J.J. must've identified her next target by now. Have you heard anything?"

Chris shrugged. "I don't know anything you don't already know, except Jack pulled the plug on her next promotion."

A satisfied smile seized her expression. Then she noticed Chris appeared disturbed, distracted. "What's wrong, my love?"

"Guess I'm still anxious about taking this polygraph on Thursday. No way in hell I'll pass." Chris glanced at his watch then sunk deep into his own thoughts.

"You afraid?" she asked.

He didn't hear her. He couldn't. For the first time, fear distracted him more than her charms. "Sabinski still hadn't returned to the office when I left." The vacant, far off expression vanished a moment later. "His poly is probably going as well as mine will."

"Don't be ridiculous."

He shrugged.

"Look at me," she waited for him to turn to her. "You can do it. You have to."

He turned away, dragged his gaze across the room and locked in on an older gentleman with a square jaw and weathered skin. He reminded Chris so much of his grandfather. A sudden wave of guilt tugged at his conscience. *What would Granddad say if he knew?* Chris thought. "I don't know if I can do this anymore. Maybe I should—"

"No!" she cut him off abruptly. "You must put an end to this weak thinking. I-I couldn't let you do it."

"Maybe *you* don't have a choice anymore," he warned.

She couldn't sway him, so she sunk into her own thoughts for a few moments before saying, "I can help you if you let me. There's a better way."

Emotionally defeated, he shook his head. "A better way? Better than what? More…of this?" he asked, doubt still clouding his expression.

"We can teach you simple techniques so that you can beat the exam. Or at least get an inconclusive finding. We've done it before, we can do it again."

"In three days?"

"Two," she replied.

"I see." His eyebrow rose. He appeared more skeptical than assured.

"Dearest, I love you, and I want to spend the rest of my life with you. Trust me, okay. Just trust me. If you go down, I go down. You don't want that for me, do you? Or for…*our baby*?"

He appeared dazed and his voice rose an octave. "Baby? You mean you're…"

She nodded yes, her cheeks flush with happy tears. "That's why I asked you here today."

Chris forced a half smile; part elated and part doubting the baby was even his.

• • •

Early Friday Afternoon…

Hopper Mack noticed the neighbors peering out their windows, watching seven black, unmarked sedans screech around the corner a short distance from Jack's house. Moments later, the passengers padded across the driveway, a dozen Agents wearing navy blue raid jackets with "FBI" emblazoned in golden letters. Plastic gloves and evidence kits filled their hands.

The front door was locked so they broke out a window panel and entered Sabinski's house on orders from Cartwright. "If an ant shit in Sabinski's house, you better find it!" Thanks to Freeman, who, on

Cartwright's request, called in a favor with a judge, they received an expedited warrant. The agents scattered throughout the house, carefully examined every crack and crevice for evidence, anything indicating Jack cooperated with the Russians. The allegations were incontrovertible. The assumptions of guilt evident. But their mere presence at his home, not even two hours after he'd miserably failed his poly, was a clear indictment.

A new agent on the evidence team, Hopper trekked down a darkened staircase to the basement, the air musky and humid. He reached up for a pull cord hanging at the base of the stairs and yanked. Shook his head when the lights revealed the disheveled chaos brewing in the bowels of his house. Jack, an extreme packrat, had saved dusty boxes overflowing with old magazines, including an extensive collection of *Playboy*. Judging from the sheer volume, he'd probably been stockpiling them since his teenage jerk-off days. Just beyond one stack of boxes he noticed a light in a back room. He waded through the mounds of junk until he arrived at the security door. The padlock was open, hadn't been returned to the secure position. He pushed the door forward to find a neatly organized office area.

Metal shelves loaded with old paint cans lined the walls, the labels had been alphabetized and were perfectly aligned. The paneled floor felt spongy beneath his feet. But the space was too tidy, not a thing out of place, not a speck of dust. With the OCD-like organization, the room was a stark contrast to the rest of his home. The agent grew suspicious. What was so special about this room? Especially when the rest of the basement was a pit? He walked over to the large wooden desk, opened the drawer with his gloved hand, and grabbed an assortment of items as his mind flashed back to his counterintelligence instructor at the Quantico.

Bingo!

He pulled his radio from the pristine leather holder on his belt and yelled, "Get down here in the basement. I've got something."

CHAPTER 15

Late Friday Afternoon…

The sun hung high in the afternoon sky by the time J.J. dragged herself out of bed. She trudged to the bathroom for a hot shower. Needed to restore life into her tired, haggard body. She and Tony wouldn't arrive at the office until late in the afternoon since they'd pulled a late-nighter. As the lead agent on the case, J.J. kept all of Karat's information with her overnight. Not that she didn't trust Tony implicitly. She figured she should be the one to take the fall if Jack caught them. After all, it was her idea to take the package home in the first place. Her stake in keeping them safe was considerably higher, too. Her source's fate, and indeed her own, depended on her ability to make smart moves over the next few days. She must get the information to the vault and exploit it for any and every clue that might lead her to ICE Phantom.

On the face of it, all the information appeared rock solid, the best intelligence from any source they'd ever recruited in the past. Still they needed to follow certain procedures if for no other reason than to protect themselves from insider spies and double agents. She only hoped they could keep Chris and case-stealing Lana at bay and stop the intelligence hemorrhage before too late. Tony's early morning suggestion to report Plotnikov's drop to Cartwright was as good a choice as any. She trusted Jim, not implicitly but more so than any other person of authority.

Torn about the day's wardrobe, J.J. finally opted for a navy blue pantsuit with a white button-down blouse over the Dockers then she headed to the office. Stress fueled her appetite, and she was starved, craving her favorite coffee. But she couldn't stop, not until she arrived at headquarters and locked up the drop materials. The sewage from the cafeteria pawned off as coffee would have to do. As she sucked in a cleansing breath to calm her thoughts, her phone rang.

"McCall," she answered.

"McCall. Ha!" Jake said. "You mean McCrazy, don't you?! Where the hell is my Charger?"

"Great balls of fiyah! Why, whatever do you mean, Sir?" she snorted, her voice steeped in deep Southern syrup and an octave higher than normal. "I *de*-clare, I have no *i*-dea what you are referring to, Mr. McGee."

"I'm referring to the pink convertible clown car sitting in my parking space this morning!"

"You asked for it, you got it." J.J. said, trying to contain the laugh but exploded before she could lock it down. Jake's demeanor sounded somewhere between mildly amused and annoyed as hell.

"Yeah, yeah . . . yuk it up," Jake said. "Just remember, he who laughs last, laughs best."

"Why Mr. McGee? If I didn't know betta, I'd *swear* you were *threatenin'* me."

"No ma'am," Jake said, putting on an accent of his own. "I'm a gentleman. We don't make threats...we make *promises*."

"All right, all right, already!" she conceded. "I'll call the police and tell them to pull your car around. But let this be a lesson to you, Jake. I *always* keep my promises."

"Yeah, yeah," Jake said. "Will that be all?"

"Don't be mad. It's like you always say," J.J. said, snickering in Jake's annoyance, "when all hell breaks loose, only the devil survives. I'm the devil today."

"Don't sweat it, J.J.," Jake said. "My turn is coming…"

Moments later she pulled into the FBI Headquarters garage. Her stomach growled in a sound audible to outsiders. As soon as she locked the drop materials securely in her cabinet safe, she'd run upstairs. Food was a necessity before the research commenced.

At the elevators, she ran into Tony and exchanged greetings. He looked rather fetching in his Dockers and denim blue-colored button down. He juggled a cardboard drink carrier containing two Starbucks coffees; the hazelnut aroma seized her senses. The Dunkin Donuts bag was no doubt filled with their favorite blueberry muffins. He had anticipated the suffering they'd endure after their long night.

J.J. held the door open for Tony and a choir of hushed whispers met them when they entered. The room was eerily quiet with the exception of a few agents huddled around their colleague's cubicles. She glanced back at Tony and his eyebrow raised. No one noticed that they had walked in, each was so engrossed in their conversation. But J.J. sensed the anxiety, and their colleagues' faces were each painted with distress. A wave of uncertainty flitted through her mind.

 The weight of the briefcase in her hand jolted J.J., reminded her that she had a mission to accomplish. Refocused, she charged straight for the vault and swiped her badge.

A red light.

Her brow furrowed. She tried again.

"What the hell is going on? I can't get in!" J.J. placed her finger in the biometric reader and scanned her badge several times. The light blinked red again—no entry.

Hmmm, she thought. *Maybe the lock's malfunctioning.*

Then her second thought: Maybe Sabinksi had found out she and Tony had misrepresented information on their administrative reports for months. Maybe he'd revoked their access. Suddenly, her face warmed as if she burned with fever.

"Here, let me try." Tony sat down the coffee and bag on the floor beside his feet and scanned his badge. Same result.

"Something's wrong. Very wrong," J.J. said.

• • •

Admiring his new discoveries, the new agent listened as the patter of feet tapped across the upstairs floors. The team was headed toward the basement entrance.

"Copy that. We're on the way!" a colleague called out over the radio.

Hopper smiled smugly. He couldn't wait to get back to the squad. A rookie, they called him. *Junior.* They'd have to respect him now. This was the ideal way to kick off his counterintelligence career. He set the box of black trash bags, a carton of Crayola chalk, two rolls of white duct tape, and several case files classified "Top Secret—Human Intelligence" on top of the desk, then searched the area for more evidence.

Even as a new agent fresh out of Quantico, he had been trained to recognize traditional spy tradecraft. Chalk and duct tape were often used to mark signals. Trash bags concealed classified documents so they wouldn't be destroyed if left outside in the elements. Rudimentary but effective—and classic Russian tradecraft. The file had probably been intended for the next dead drop. Fortunately for the Bureau, Sabinski's previous drop would be his last.

When he rose from the desk chair to place the items in the evidence bag, one of the floor panels gave way beneath his feet. *Floor panels on a basement floor?* he said to himself. Most people install Berber carpet, pile, or even ceramic over the concrete. Curious. He lifted a loose plank and then blinked rapidly. Thousands in unmarked hundred-dollar bills lay beneath his feet. He pulled a stack from the floor and flipped through each, carefully eying the serial numbers. All sequential.

Son of a bitch!

"Well, I'll be damned, Junior! Look at what you dug up!" his senior colleague said as he peered through the door. "We've got ourselves a spy!"

• • •

The Espionage Unit agents were solemn and quiet, some visibly angry. A misty-eyed Lana emerged from her cubicle and approached them. J.J. couldn't stand the sound of her voice—she or her partner-in-crime for that matter. They always made her eyelids tingle.

"Lana, what's going on? We, uhhh, needed to get a file from the vault and neither one of our badges works."

"Oh my God, so nobody's spoken to you."

"Spoken to us about what?" Tony said.

Lana tugged on Tony's arm and pulled him aside; J.J. closed in the circle.

"It's Jack. He's been arrested for committing espionage."

"What!" Tony and J.J. yelled in unison.

"When...when did this happen?" J.J. asked, overcome with shock. She'd witnessed Jack choke down a lot of food in her time, but never his just desserts. Finally, they'd been served on a hot platter. Her joy swelled. Had she sufficient floor space, she'd have turned a cartwheel and a backflip or two.

"Only moments ago. Apparently he failed his polygraph exam so badly Cartwright got an emergency search warrant. They found the evidence at his house in less than an hour. A hundred thousand dollars in cash beneath a floor panel in the basement. Some Top Secret documents, trash bags, chalk...you know the drill."

I knew it! I knew it! J.J. thought. She'd suspected him all along. It made perfect sense. All those days he'd accused *her* of compromising her own sources and he'd been the one selling out the Bureau to the Russians the whole time. While her stomach soured at the thought of the information that he potentially had passed to his handler, at least the mystery had been solved.

Tony and J.J. eyed each other knowingly.

"Yeah," she continued. "The AD and Freeman revoked everybody's vault access and ordered that we all take polys. Jack failed."

"No one's informed us yet," J.J. said. One of Tony's buddies had passed some RUMINT, rumor-based intelligence, but they hadn't officially been notified.

"Yeah, well apparently everything happened pretty quickly. They'd planned to notify us today, and I believe they're still going through with them."

"So, how do *you* know?" J.J. asked.

Lana's mouth fell open, she touched her throat. "Uhhh...Someone told Chris."

"Shit!" J.J. yelped as she pressed her fingers against her eye. Lana had lied, and the itching intensified. She couldn't take it, would've clawed her own eyes out with her fingernails if she could. J.J. bent and placed the briefcase on the floor, tried to blink through the tears streaming from her eyes.

"J.J., what happened?" Lana asked.

"You okay?" Tony asked as she stooped over to get a look at her eyes. She couldn't blink them open, so she held them closed until the sensation passed.

"I'm...I'm okay, now. Just an allergic reaction to this new eyeliner I tried out this morning."

"You don't wear eyeliner," Tony piped in.

J.J.'s snarl pierced him; he snapped his mouth shut.

Tony looked at J.J. suspiciously, his expression skeptical, unbelieving. A few seconds later, Chris walked up behind Lana.

"Guess you guys heard about Jack, huh? Good riddance, if you ask me. Fat bastard. I hope he gets the death penalty. I'd love to see him roast."

CHAPTER 16

Early Friday Evening…

Although their loathing for Jack was quite mutual, J.J. didn't understand Chris's reaction. Why had he expressed so much hatred for Jack? After all, he was teamed up with Jack's golden girl. Everything Jack did to benefit Lana, inevitably benefited Chris. He should've been near tears as was Lana.

Lana's reaction, her fear, was understandable. She didn't want the Bureau to hire a new supervisor whom she couldn't control with her breasts, who wouldn't excuse her ineptness. And if justice existed anywhere in the world, the AD would replace Jack with a *woman, a* straight woman who wouldn't give a damn about the height of her skirt, the depth of her splits, or the volume of silicone in her cleavage.

Lana's head snapped around toward Chris and she glared at him, a fire brewing on her tongue. But instead of exploding, she yielded. "I'm off to take my poly now. See you guys later."

Chris watched her hips sway as she walked way. "Good luck with that." He turned to Tony and J.J. "They booked him in Alexandria, and I hear he's not talking."

"Not talking? There's something new and different," Tony quipped. "Well, I'm sure they'll get some agents from Washington Field out there to grill him before long."

Chris shifted his glance to J.J. "Oh, by the way, Cartwright wants to see you in his office immediately. He told me to let you know as soon as you arrived. Said you should just go on upstairs."

"Me and *Tony?* Or just *me?*"

"He didn't mention Tony. Just you."

"About what?"

Chris shrugged. "I have no idea; he didn't say. Why don't you get up there and find out?" he asked as he walked away.

J.J. faced Tony, her distress visible. *Why in hell would he want to speak to me without Tony there?* she asked herself. She didn't understand.

"Guard this with your life," she said, sitting the briefcase next to Tony's feet. "I'm going to head upstairs and see what he wants."

He leaned in and whispered, "You gonna tell him about the drop?"

J.J. bit her bottom lip, unsure of her response. "I honestly don't know right now." J.J. scanned the area to ensure no one was listening. "I mean, I realize we'd planned to tell him. But if Lana passes her polygraph today then he's going to order us to turn all of the information over to *her.* Let's just wait and find out what he has to say."

• • •

J.J. tugged on her suit jacket to smooth out the wrinkles as she approached Cartwright's open office door. When she peered through the threshold, he was standing next to a cabinet safe, flipping through some files. Jim glanced up just as she opened her mouth to speak.

"Ah, Agent McCall. Come in. Have a seat." He moved back toward his desk and slipped into his chair. A sullen expression blanketed his usual jovial appearance. He seemed pensive, more intense.

She took a seat in the guest chair, nervous and somewhat anxious. She had no idea why he'd asked to meet with her. Maybe he'd heard Jack had harassed her in the past.

"So I guess you're wondering why I called you here this morning," he asked.

"Uhhh…yes, sir. The question had crossed my mind."

"I'm assuming you've heard about Jack's arrest," he asked matter-of-factly. The supervisor of her unit had been arrested for espionage. Of course, she'd heard. She struggled to contain her elation.

"Yes, sir. Agent Michaels told me the bad news just a few minutes ago. She didn't give me any details, though."

"His polygrapher called me yesterday during his exam to express some serious concerns. He failed his poly and failed it miserably. I asked Director Freeman to request an emergency search warrant and sent an evidence team out to his house. Minutes into the search, we found a hundred grand in cash, trash bags, chalk, duct tape and several case files, including one for Karat."

Minutes into the search? J.J. found that odd. As an FBI counterintelligence agent, especially one who had helped draft the Hanssen damage assessment, seems he could've done a better job of concealing the dirt under the carpet so-to-speak. But she shrugged it off and inhaled deeply. Her only comfort was that Sabinski didn't have the real case file. He'd taken the one with the doctored reporting inside. A surge of anger burst through her as she thought about his accusations, his indictment on her father's and Tony's father's pasts. Nothing but the pot calling the kettle black.

Still she had to perform for effect.

"My God." J.J. pressed her hand against the chest. "But I've had my suspicions. I saw him reading the file yesterday and he hadn't logged it out."

"Is that right?" Cartwright responded.

"Yes, sir. He called me in to tell me Karat had been recalled to Moscow."

A thousand pounds of uncomfortable silence hovered between them before Cartwright spoke again.

"I'm afraid Jack refuses to talk. After we booked him, he evoked his Fifth Amendment rights and clammed up. He's hardly said two words together since. Except...he's, uhhh, he's asked to speak to you. And you *alone*."

J.J. drew her head back stiffly then cocked it to the side. She wouldn't have been more surprised if Cartwright stripped naked, sprouted wings, and flew out the window. Why in hell would Jack want to speak to her? She'd be the first person to pull the switch if he got the chair.

"Me? W-why me?"

"That's what Director Freeman and I would like to know," Cartwright responded.

Confused, J.J. shook her head. Her instincts refused his request long before she could speak the words. "You don't understand. Jack and I have a very contentious relationship, to say the least. Now, I hadn't previously come forward with complaints. We both know that's a useless exercise in this place. But, please understand, we have nothing to say to one another. And trust me, anything he might say to me wouldn't be worth listening to."

Cartwright sat forward in his chair. "J.J., you and I both know headquarters isn't that big, and I've known Jack since the Academy. Trust me, I'm well aware of that river of bad blood between you two."

"Well, *that's* the biggest understatement since the discovery of fire."

He half chuckled. "Jack's reputation precedes him, but I need you to talk to him. The Bureau needs you to speak with him. We've got to find out as much as possible about his cooperation. We can't begin our damage assessments without his statements. And our secure intelligence collection channels are still vulnerable. Most importantly, we must adjust our HUMINT operations—both in the Bureau and throughout the Community—so we don't lose any more sources. This is a mission imperative."

J.J. began to waver against her own will. She looked down at her lap to gather the strength to fortify her resolve, but to no avail. If nothing else, she owed it to her dead sources and their families to listen to what Jack had to say. She didn't need to say much in return. And the visit would offer her a prime opportunity to do something she'd wanted to do for years, gloat and relish in his misery. As she contemplated her concession, the thought of Jack bound in handcuffs brought her a fountain of joy. She needed no more convincing.

"I'm asking you to do this as a favor to me. Hear him out, report back to me, and you're done. You never need to see or speak to him again as far as I'm concerned."

She hesitated, for the sake of show, and then blew out a long breath. "Okay, okay. I'll meet him. But if he so much as blinks the wrong way, with all due respect to you, Mr. Cartwright, he's going to be *begging* for the death penalty."

CHAPTER 17

Saturday Morning – Back at the Alexandria Jail

More than a decade earlier, during the Hanssen damage assessment, a sketchy Russian source suggested a second mole was burrowed deep within the Intelligence Community. The heads of all Intelligence Community agencies initiated Operation ICE Phantom—Intelligence Community Phantom—to find the turncoat allegedly more dangerous, more insidious than Hanssen and Ames combined.

A stagnant search had since yielded nothing, nothing except a dead-end ghost chase. As of late, the only mark of his existence was J.J.'s dead sources. They'd been dropping off too quickly, suggesting the mole was afraid, desperate. These facts were all but completely ignored by senior leadership who opted to claim ignorance, a game J.J. and Tony could ill afford to play.

One source vanished from the face of the earth and the other was brutally murdered. Only one remained thanks to the son-of-a-bitch selling secrets like popcorn at National's stadium. And the new target would no doubt be Viktor Plotnikov, codenamed Karat.

J.J. broke every rule and regulation to protect him: falsified FD-302s, the Bureau's official interview reports; intentionally wrote a false assessment identifying him as a low-level diplomat to conceal that they knew his true identity; and Robert Ludlum couldn't produce better fiction than that found in his "duplicate" case file. She even designed his codename as an operational security measure. The misspelling would differentiate those who'd seen his file from those who'd merely heard about him. She refused to lose another source to the ICE Phantom or Golikov's thugs.

Jack drowned in denial, and J.J. and Tony had long suspected his reasons were rooted in more than professional self-preservation. ICE Phantom had struck during his duty, his watch. The blame was squarely at Jack's doorstep. Rather than confront the problem, Jack thought it better for his career to simply ignore the problem. Rumors of moles deterred other agencies from sharing intelligence with the Bureau and frightened sources that feared arrest, imprisonment, death, or some combination of the three. Not to mention, they wreaked havoc on an already tenuous relationship between the FBI and CIA.

Now, sitting in jail, the problem had returned to bite Jack squarely in the ass.

"The bigot list? Who do—"

"Chris," Jack said with hardly a moment's pause. Didn't even allow her to finish the question.

"*Chris?* Wait, Lana's *Chris?*"

"Yeah, I think he's in love with Lana," Jack said. The red in his face intensified. He squeezed his hands and cracked his knuckles repeatedly, the sound of which made J.J. cringe. "No. That's not true. He's very much in love with Lana, almost to the point of obsession."

J.J. shifted in her seat, constantly examining her feelings. "And? What's that got to do with *you?*"

He looked at J.J. stone-faced. She waited for an answer when the gravity of his statement pulled her smack into the reality of his insinuation. "Wait. *You*…and *Lana?*" The words propelled from her mouth like vomit.

J.J. dropped her head in shock and disbelief. What could Lana possibly want with Jack?

"What can I say? She came onto me."

"Uhhh...rewind," J.J. said, twirling her finger counter-clockwise. "*She . . . came onto you?*"

"Yes."

Still no reaction.

Wow.

After some thought, his story made sense, even with the Lana detail. Everyone knew she'd cozied up to him to advance her career. J.J. didn't know how cozy until that moment. If Chris had truly been obsessed with Lana and became aware of her relationship with Sabinski, what better way to get rid of his competition than...set him up for espionage?

No, didn't make sense. Obsessed people stalked their victims, let the air out of their tires, poured sugar in their gas tanks, and pushed the objects of their desire down flights of stairs in fits of jealous rage; they didn't frame them for espionage. Just didn't quite add up. Not that she should care. He wasn't her problem.

"Well, that explains everything, doesn't it? Who knew she was so . . . *multitalented,*" she snipped, suppressing the urge to slip in another dig. "So, let me ask you this. If you thought enough of Lana to reassign my cases to her, then why didn't you ask *her* to come help you?"

"I called for the person I believe I can trust."

"So, are you saying you *don't* feel you can trust Lana?"

Silence.

He didn't respond, just stared into the distance.

J.J. stood to leave again.

"She's through with me. You know it, and I know it. I'm in jail and can no longer help her career. I've never deluded myself about our relationship," Jack said. He lowered his head, pressed his hands against his temples. "Besides, other than you and Tony, I'm beginning to wonder who in headquarters can be trusted. Think about it J.J., I take a polygraph one minute and the next I'm in jail? That's not Bureau procedure, and you know it. Why was there such a rush to search my house? No one had enough pull with the judge to get an expedited warrant except Free-man…or—"

"Cartwright," she said.

He'd made a valid point. Something definitely didn't add up. But *Cartwright* ordered the search. The same Cartwright who pressed J.J. to stay and dig deeper. If involved in setting up Jack, why would he ask J.J. to pursue the mole when he himself might be the one she'd end up arresting? That didn't make sense either.

"Will you help me J.J.?"

The door buzzed, and she wrapped her fingers around the handle. "I don't know, Jack. We shit-brown daughters of domestic terrorists and sons of Guinea wise guys will need some time to consider your request. In the meantime, make sure you sleep with your back to the wall."

The venom spewing from her mouth brought J.J. as much discomfort as it probably had Sabinski. Perhaps the Belvedere had loosened her tongue too much.

A vision of her mother's countenance flashed in her mind. Her mother's disappointed voice spoke to her heart. "J.J., I raised you better than that!"

She turned back to him to apologize but couldn't choke the words out. Perhaps a full apology was a step too far. After a second's hesitation, her voice softened. "They got you in solitary?"

He nodded. "They don't mix cops in with the population," he said. "J.J…the prosecution's asking for the death penalty."

Why did I even have to ask? she questioned. That's the part she hated about being a woman. Compassion beyond reason.

Based on J.J.'s reaction to Jack's story, the Bureau had arrested the wrong suspect, and Jack had just enough honor to ensure he'd never cop a plea for this charge and leave the real mole on the streets.

Her only questions were whether the investigation had been ordered to frame Jack.

And if so who was *really* behind it.

J.J. forced herself not to look back again. She couldn't. The sincerity in his desperation had somehow managed to permeate the wall she'd built to protect herself from his verbal floggings. The armored door slammed closed behind her, and the resulting breeze made the skin on the back of her neck prickle.

J.J. took a few steps into the hall when Tony greeted her. He ran his fingers through the silken twists in his curly black hair, distracting her for a brief moment.

"I take it you heard everything," she said.

"Yeah, I listened to the whole sob story. The snake," Tony responded. "I gotta tell you, I'm glad the ass wipe got pinched. I'd love to see him go down for this, especially after what he said to you. And it'd sure solve our problems."

All J.J. could do was stare, and then she rolled her eyes up to the ceiling. If she allowed Jack take the rap for the compromises, she and Tony wouldn't need to worry about taking the polygraph examinations or losing their jobs. And she'd never have to deal with Jack's ass again.

On the other hand, the Bureau would still have a mole to contend with. Their sources would still be in danger of compromise and death. And the son of a bitch traitor would continue to walk free.

"What's with the face? You don't actually believe this guy, do you? I mean, c'mon, suggesting that Cartwright had something to do with setting him up? He's reaching, don't you think?"

"Please, I haven't heard a taller tale since O.J. pled not guilty. But as far-fetched as his story may sound, I know he'd rather be roasted alive on a spit than ask *me,* of all people, for help."

"Well, if you think I'm lifting a fucking finger to help that jerk-off, you can fughettaboudit. Ain't happenin'. After what he said to you? He's getting exactly what he deserves as far as I'm concerned. Let him fry."

"But Ton—"

"I don't want to hear it. You help him; you're on your own."

What else did she expect? He didn't know what motivated J.J.'s change of perspective. And she couldn't explain her reasoning, not without sounding like a lunatic. She was singing a new song and he'd gotten stuck on the old one.

"You're really not gonna help?" she asked as she started toward the exit.

"You heard me!" he snapped, refusing to budge an inch.

Stubborn fucking Italian! she thought to herself.

She couldn't believe he was so determined to remain defiant.

"Fine," she growled, matching his coarse tone. "The Bureau pays me to catch spies, so unlike you I'm just going to do my job. On my own!"

Tony huffed as they both plodded to their cars quietly seething.

J.J. had never seen this side of him before and didn't care to see it again. Ever. In the time they'd worked together, he'd never held his ground so firmly. Now she was truly screwed. Not only did she need to find the mole and clear the name of the boss she despised, she'd have to do it alone.

CHAPTER 18

Late Sunday Morning…

J.J. strategized her next move on the way to her standing Sunday brunch reservation at the McCall house. Tony's ultimatum hadn't helped her present dilemma, but could she really blame him? For months, they'd both believed with every fiber of their beings that Jack was the mole—and they were both wrong. Thanks to her so-called gift, she was the only person in the FBI who knew the truth. Shit pissed her off. Not only because she didn't want to help the racist bastard, but whatever investigation she conducted to find the real mole would benefit Jack. As much as she wished she could take Tony's attitude and let him fry, one simple fact remained—the mole was still free. And as long as he remained free, no operation or source was safe from his reach. She'd been forced by circumstance to do a job she never thought she'd have to do—clear Jack's name. To make matters worse, she still had few clues to go on. They had sufficient information to confirm the presence of a mole, but too little to identify him.

Work called, but she'd first need to endure her father's weekly diatribe on the ills of singledom. *Ugh.*

The scent of fried eggs and bacon wafted into J.J.'s nose as she entered her father's 1960s, all-brick duplex off Irving Street, where front porches still had swings and neighbors were still nosy. Photos of a young Max McCall posing with Huey Newton, Bobby Seal, and other Black

Panthers hung throughout the house. Her mother was undercover at the time, managed to stay out of most photos.

Special Agent Naomi Jones McCall was among the first black women recruited by the FBI near the end of J. Edgar Hoover's tenure. He established a Top Secret program to recruit educated black agents that not even Hoover himself would publicly acknowledge. She received orders from the COINTELPRO director, who ran a covert program to "disrupt and neutralize" subversive "Communist" organizations and political dissidents such as the NAACP and the Black Panther Party. Naomi targeted the latter. The Bureau sent her undercover to infiltrate and quell illegal arms activity that might undermine U.S. national security. Her operations were only documented in Hoover's secret files, most of which were destroyed by his long-time secretary shortly after his death.

A star agent, Naomi's gift helped her to identify and arrest corrupt Panther Party officials involved in harboring illegal firearms—of which they were few and far between. Certainly fewer than she'd expected given the propaganda she'd been indoctrinated with only days after raising her right hand at the academy graduation.

Eventually, she met and fell in love with the disarmingly handsome Max McCall—the one man who never made her itch. Her mother's gift revealed an inner goodness Max's gruff, disillusioned exterior concealed. And his greatest crime against society was establishing school breakfast program at the local elementary school. Max told J.J. that after he proposed marriage, her mother had planned to quit the FBI "soon." But "soon" never came. She had sensitive sources to protect and no colleagues she regarded well enough to trust, not with their lives.

Before she could resign, she was critically wounded in the line of duty during some mysterious operation, the details of which had never been fully disclosed, at least not to J.J. For years she inquired about what happened but no one provided answers, not even her father. As she grew older, in the recesses of her mind, she'd planned to someday get the answers straight from the FBI.

She stopped off at the powder room to wash her hands before entering the kitchen. When she stepped into the doorway, Max turned to her, his smile warm with affection.

"Ahhhh, there she is! My daughter the pig!" He held his arms out to welcome her despite his too frequent digs about her employer. Max McCall, now in his mid-60s, donned distinctive salt and pepper hair, and his usual Sunday attire, a black Reverend Run Adidas sweat suit.

She walked over and embraced him before grabbing the coffee pot. "That's *federal* pig to you, Dad, which would make your son a city pig."

He shook his head. "Mhm, mhm, mhm. I'm sure I raised y'all better. But to each his own, I suppose."

"You reared us just fine," J.J. said taking her seat at the table. "You call us pigs and *we still* come to Sunday breakfast every week. That's got to say something about us, doesn't it?"

"Yeah. It says neither one of you likes to cook." He laughed. "Did your brother call this morning? Probably gonna be late as usual."

"No, I hadn't heard from him, but you know the police chief has them working a bunch of overtime in the All Hands on Deck program. No telling when he'll get here. And I'm too hungry to wait. Sorry, bro!"

"If that boy ever showed up for brunch on time, I might die and have a heart attack."

"Well, don't tell Malcolm. The way you two are constantly at each other's throats, he'd probably start coming on time out of spite. And I personally kind of like having you around."

Max reached into the cabinet above the stove and grabbed a couple of the "good plates" his wife spent three hours selecting at Woodward and Lothrop in the months before she passed away so many years ago. He'd bought them for their twelfth anniversary present. After her eleven years of guilt-tripping him about their Justice of the Peace wedding and non-existent reception, he finally conceded even though his money was still a little funny. She couldn't be with them in body, but he made sure she enjoyed Sunday brunch with them in spirit.

He lifted the cast iron skillet from the burner, slid some eggs onto their plates, and his daughter all but collapsed into her seat, looking weary and sleepless. His expression shifted from one of joy to concern.

"Looks like you've got bags under your eyes," he said as he laid the plates on the table. He pinched her arm. "You've lost some weight too. I keep telling you, J.J., if you die working yourself into the ground it'll be in vain 'cause all they gonna do is hire a white woman to replace you. What they got you workin' on, anyway?"

Bags? Lost weight? J.J. wondered why her father exaggerated so much. She'd checked herself in the mirror before leaving the house and she looked "okay," just as she felt. She shrugged off his comments as the bantering of a concerned father and poured coffee into the supersized mugs resting on the kitchen table. "I could tell you, but—"

"You'd have to kill me. Yeah, yeah, yeah...I know."

"Come on, Dad. You know the drill. Can't talk shop, so there's no sense in you worrying yourself to death about my work. I'm Max McCall's girl. I can handle it."

He nodded in agreement. "Okay then, how's your love life? You datin' yet?"

She stuffed an overflowing fork full of eggs in her mouth and mumbled, "I'm not allowed to talk with my mouth full."

He rapped his fingertips against the mahogany table. "That's okay. I've got all day."

She chewed up the food and swallowed with a hard gulp. "Jeez. I think I'd rather talk about work."

"Ohhh, noooo, young lady, we're talking about this right now."

Ever since her thirty-second birthday two months prior, Max had made it his goal to ensure *her* lady eggs were harvested to produce a grandchild. "Dad, you'll let this go if you want to live long enough to see your grandson graduate from the FBI academy," she said, chuckling. "Stressing over my nonexistent love life will surely kill you."

Dad shuddered and gave me the side-eye glance. "At the rate you're going, you'll be eligible for the *Guinness Book of World Records* by the time you give me a grandson."

J.J. smirked and leaned back. "Careful, Dad. Your 1950s are showing. Besides, Malcolm doesn't have any kids; he's not married. Why don't you hassle him for some grandbabies?"

He shot her an incredulous glare.

"What?" she said. "All those women he's got chasing him, you could have your own rug rat assortment from multiple babies' mamas."

"Don't even get me started on your brother. If I say go right, he goes left. If I asked him for some grandbabies, he'd probably bring me a pet fish. Hate to break it to you but your brother's an idiot, God love him. Can't blame a woman for not marrying his crazy behind. You on the other hand…"

She turned to him; her expression serious. "Well, I kind of met someone, if you must know. He's smart, he's an agent, and, uhhhh… he's just a little white. . .*ish*?" she said, lowering her volume to a level perceptible only to a few breeds of dog and some small rodents.

"What you say? 'Cause *I know* you didn't say what I thought you said!"

CHAPTER 19

Even though she had no plans whatsoever to pursue a relationship with Tony, part of what held her back was a paralyzing fear of her father's reaction. To say he wasn't a fan of non-black people was the understatement of the century.

He became a small successful businessman strictly serving the black community to avoid working with them, talking to them, or dealing with them in any way shape or form. His body was in the now, but the 1950s and 1960s would forever color his perceptions of the world, relationships, and view of a woman's place in the family. She thought she'd pitch him the idea of a multiracial relationship to gauge how receptive he might be to the idea. If he didn't melt like the Wicked Witch of the West in a thunderstorm, then maybe....

J.J. tried to feign some semblance of courage. *He's sitting here crying about grandbabies. Why does the daddy's color matter? All sperm swims in the same direction, doesn't it?* she thought to herself.

"I said . . . he's white . . .*ish.*"

"Ohhhh, *lawwwwd*!" he cried out, getting a little preacher in the pulpit dramatic. "My child's been brainwashed by 'the man'! What the hell is white-*ish*? Either he's white or not. Ain't no 'ish!' Bad enough you workin' for those racist Gestapos that ki—."

"What dad? What were you gonna say?" she asked. Sounded as if he was about to say "killed." Did he know more about her mother's death than he admitted? J.J. didn't know but trying to get it out of him, once he became aware of his slip, would be like trying to squeeze water from a rock. She'd broach the subject another day.

He shook his head. "Don't try to change the subject. You bet' not bring no white boys up in the house. All these good black men out here—girrrrrrl, you gon' get my pressure up."

"He's Italian."

"Shoot, Italians ain't no better. They'd just as soon as call you 'the magic word' as some bible thumping rednecks from the Mississippi sticks. Didn't you see *The Sopranos*...or *The Godfather?*" he asked. She hadn't realized how skewed his perception of reality had been for so many years. Or perhaps it was her perception that was skewed for the worse. "I'll never forget that line talkin' about give the drugs to the black folks and spicks. 'They're animals anyway, let them lose their souls,'" he said, imitating the accent. "That's what Italians think of us! You remember those words when you're flirting with Giuseppe!"

"That's ridiculous. Zaluchi said *the line* because it was *in the script*. What if Tony said he knew what all black people were like from watching *Good Times* and *The Wire?*"

"Well, that Puzo cat wrote *the line* because that's what they believe."

They both sat silently for a moment. J.J. thought about what he said, and one thing she realized with her and Tony, their union would be a two-way street as far as family goes. His mother probably wouldn't be anymore excited to welcome J.J. into the Donato family than her father would be to welcome him. She tried to wash the thought out of her head.

"Don't get your boxers in a wad. I'm messing with you, Dad. I'm not setting my sights on anyone, white, black, or otherwise. Besides a man can only serve two purposes in my life right now anyway."

He paused for her answer.

She let him stew in anticipation for a few seconds.

"Take out the trash and keep my truck clean. Now, let's finish eating before the food gets cold."

Silence had won again and it was good.

Max fixed a delicious meal. All those years of cooking for his children had improved his skills considerably since Naomi died. J.J. couldn't jab her fork into her eggs fast enough when her cell phone rang. Normally, she'd ignore it, knowing her father would be displeased if she answered for work purposes while she was sitting at the table. But something inside tingled telling her she probably shouldn't let this call go to voicemail. She fished her phone from her purse, looked at the caller ID, and answered.

"Well, well, well, abandoning us this morning?"

"Hey, Sis," Malcolm said. "How's breakfast? Had your serving of *nag* yet?"

"Yes, a heaping pile of it and no one to share it with," she said. "You still working?"

"Of course. What else is new?" he said. "Listen, I got stuck at work today because I made an arrest in the middle of the night. When I checked for his identification, I found your business card hidden in his wallet."

"My business card?"

"Yeah, thought you might want to get down here and talk to this one."

"Who is it?" she asked, sitting at the edge of her seat. The curiosity nearly killed her.

"Some diplomat from the Russian Embassy," he said. J.J. could hear paper shuffling in the background. "Anyway, how about those Red-skins?"

"Malcolm!"

"I think RG III will make a fine addition to the team."

She clenched her teeth. "Keep it up and I'm gonna tell your girlfriend you still sleep with a woobie."

"You always were the ruthless one," he said. "Okay, it's Aleksey *Dmitriyev*, a Second Secretary."

"Dmitriyev?" she said in delight…and then the confusion sunk in. "How in hell did Dmitriyev get my business card? I've never met him." She tipped her head back and turned her face to the sky. All the while trying to temper her emotions.

Malcolm wasn't aware that J.J. recruited spooks because she'd dipped, dodged, and evaded that bullet for years.

Max looked at J.J. curiously as she hung on her brother's every word. Her mind spun at the possibilities of getting a counterintelligence officer to cooperate.

"Hmph. That's interesting indeed." Her mind churned.

How could he get my card? How could he get my card?

Then she realized it. He took Karat to the airport. He must know about Plotnikov's cooperation.

"Ohhhh God!" J.J. whispered as grief overcame her. "He's dead. He's dead."

"What's wrong, Sis?" Malcolm asked. "Who's dead?"

"N-nothing!" she said, avoiding the urge to curse to the high heavens. She forced the emotion down and pulled herself together. "I, uhhh, Dad's here. Can't really get into it. But why'd he get arrested?"

"We caught him soliciting a prostitute. Leona."

"Leona? You mean the transvestite on 14th Street?"

"That would be the one."

She chuckled and tilted her head to the side. "Wow. I suppose smarter men have been duped by her…his…her beauty, right?"

"Indeed. We caught a city official soliciting her a few weeks ago."

"No effin' way. Which one?" she asked. Thirty-two years had passed and she still had never uttered a single curse word in front of her father.

"You know the drill, Sis," he replied. "I could tell you but I'd have to—"

"Yeah, yeah, yeah. Preaching to the choir. So, has he claimed immunity? Have you called the State Department yet?"

"No. And no. He was too drunk to claim anything except intoxication. He's sleeping it off."

"Don't call them. Don't do anything with him until I get there, do you understand me? This could be the break I've been waiting for."

She hung up the cell phone and threw it back into her purse, which she slung over her shoulder, scrambling to get out of her seat.

"Who's dead?" Max asked.

"Can't talk about it, Dad. I've got to get down to 4-D."

"So you're just gonna run out in the middle of breakfast?" her father said, his disapproving gaze burning a hole through her.

"Can't be helped," she said, her every move urgent and swift. "I'm gonna slap my breakfast on toast and eat it on the way. Duty calls."

Dmitriyev had sent Plotnikov to his death. J.J. was certain of it. But the only way to get the information she needed from him was to help him. It wouldn't be easy to secure his cooperation. Hands down, Russian counterintelligence officers were toughest to recruit. They'd been schooled in the FBI's dirty tricks. The puppet show held no secrets or surprises; they knew which strings would be pulled. And more than anything else they understood the dire consequences spies suffered for cooperating with agencies like the FBI, especially in the age of Golikov. But he was the last person seen with her source before he got recalled to Moscow. As hopeless as the situation seemed, they had to talk.

She needed Tony's support on this one—she couldn't play good cop, bad cop without a bad cop.

Can I do anything to change his mind?

She decided to make Tony an offer he couldn't refuse.

CHAPTER 20

Sunday Afternoon…

With his father locked up, Tony made a point to spend as many weekends with his mother Mona as possible. Once a major babe, often compared to Sophia Lauren, she'd aged much less gracefully under the weight of her husband's criminal transgressions. Seemed he'd gotten stuck in a revolving prison door, and each time he went up, his absence picked away pieces of her soul, burrowed crevices of worry along her eyes and forehead. She'd almost grown numb to the pain and had even begun to allow her leg to drift into Senior's side of the bed. The lone glimmer of light in her life, Tony, the one child who hadn't gotten caught up in "the life," brought as much joy to her heart as his three siblings gave her angst. She cooked for him every chance she got, and Tony never missed a meal.

"Yo Ton'! Is 'at you?" Uncle Paulie called from the living room after Tony finished greeting his mother. Uncle Paulie was his mother's brother and owned a pizzeria in Baltimore's Little Italy. He was a grey-haired, beer-gutted grouser who worshiped the Budweiser gods and thought black socks with brown slippers was a fashion statement. He'd never gotten caught up in the life despite Senior's offers to help him find employment in one of his racketeering operations back in the day.

"Yeah!" Tony answered, walking to greet him. "Heeeey! Uncle Paulie. Good to see ya!" He kissed him on both cheeks careful not to disturb his beer.

"C'mere have a seat. How's life? Job treatin' you okay?"

"Yeah. Yeah. Everything's good," Tony said, nodding his head.

Uncle Paulie sat up in his seat and turned down the TV volume. "Your mother keeps naggin' me to talk to you about settlin' down. You seein' anybody yet? I know you had it pretty rough after Olivia."

Olivia De Luca was to Tony what Six was to J.J. He had suffered from superhero syndrome all of his life. He had a "thing" for projects, and what a project Olivia had been. A single mother (of a cute, precocious kid) with a drug habit she concealed for months. She wanted "the family" life, the clothes, cars, furs, and jewelry, and Tony's interests were too far on the right side of the law, thus ending their brief, passion-filled relationship.

He shook his head. "Nah. Well . . . there is this one lady. Her name is J.J. McCall."

"McCall? That ain't Italian."

"No...she's not Italian. She's black."

Uncle Paulie whipped his head toward Tony. "She's a black?"

"No, she's not *a* black. She's black."

"There's a difference?"

"We're not dating yet. I just think she's interestin'. That's all."

"Yet? She ain't one o' them welfare broads with six kids and seven babies' daddies, is she?"

Tony snapped his head toward his uncle in stunned disbelief. "Hell no! She's an agent. A damn good one, too."

"An agent, huh?" Paulie said. He leaned forward and his hand flailed to the rhythm of his speech. "Listen. It's all right to get yourself a piece every now and again, but you don't bring 'em home. And you don't marry 'em eitha!"

"I don't see what the freakin' problem is. We're living in a new day, Unc."

"Hey, this might be a new day, but Italians are old school. Years ago I hadda thing with a fine mulignan. *Che bella donna!* Satin skin. And the body?" He shook his head and bit his bottom lip. "The things she did for me would bring a grown man to his knees. And she was a good person, kindhearted. But I hadda walk away, couldn't work. Then I met your aunt Gloria and look at us now."

Tony cut him a sideways glance. "She chased you outta the house with a butcher knife last week. You slept on Ma's couch for three days."

Paulie sneered. Tony hit a sensitive nerve. "That's beside the point. Don't think I don't unda'stand your plight. Take my advice and don't go down that road. Besides, what's it gonna do to your mother? Isn't she going through enough right now with your father and all?"

When Mona finally joined Paulie and Tony after making a pot of spaghetti sauce big enough to feed the Italian armed forces, Tony's phone rang. She threw her hands in the air, knowing he'd again be called to work before he could eat.

"Did I catch you at a bad time," J.J. said, excited and breathless.

"Nah, I'm with my Uncle Paulie at my mother's place. She's cookin' dinner for lata," Tony replied.

"Well. I need you Tony. There's been a break in the case and I can't handle this alone," she said.

"A break? What happened?"

"Dmitriyev was arrested early this morning…and my business card was in his wallet. You know what that means."

"Wait a minute. Your card was in his wallet. But—oh no."

"My sentiments exactly. We need to persuade him to cooperate with us so we can find out what happened."

"We?"

"You've got to help me, Tony. I'm asking…no begging you. And I promise, if we discover *one more* piece of information that implicates Jack, I'll let him eat his just desserts."

Tony pondered the deal for a moment, blowing his nails and whistling to himself as he lingered in a long, painful pause. He combed his fingers through his hair and shook his head.

"Well?" Sounded as if she was holding her breath in anticipation.

The corners of his mouth lifted. He could never say no for long. "All right, J.J. You've got a deal. *One* piece of evidence, I don't care what it is, and we end this and let Sabinski fry."

"Agreed," J.J. said, sounding relieved. She blared her horn causing Tony to pull the phone away from his ear. "Get the hell out of the way! I swear. Freakin' Sunday drivers."

"Easy there, Danica Patrick," he said. "I'll see you in a few."

"Great. Meet me at 4-D and hurry. We don't have much time," J.J. urged.

Adrenaline pulsed through Tony's veins. Even better than receiving information on Plotnikov's whereabouts would be to recruit Dmitriyev. J.J. and Tony knew Aleksey had one weakness—he loved America. At least that's the information they received from a clean diplomat they'd been running for years. It was a vulnerability they could exploit. He'd served in London for six years, postured himself for a U.S. tour. By all accounts, he was a rising star. They wouldn't have another opportunity like this one. Then a smile emerged on Tony's face as he replayed J.J.'s words in his mind. *I need you.*

Tony sucked in a breath, intoxicated by the spaghetti's aroma. He'd miss eating this meal fit for a king, or a prince as it were. But wouldn't miss Mona's musings on the ills of bachelorhood.

"I gotta go, Ma. Work calls," Tony said. He stood into a deep stretch, oblivious to his exhaustion at the week's events. He'd have time to crash after the case ended. Until then, no rest for the weary. For now, coffee would have to suffice.

"Not again! Every time you visit me, it's work, work, work. Dolce far niente."

"What's 'at?" Tony asked. He understood little Italian and spoke less. She could tell him in the time it'd have taken for him to translate.

She threw her hand up in frustration and opened the kitchen cabinet door. Plastic food containers tumbled to the floor as she pulled several to pack Tony's Italian delights.

"I swear if I didn't push you out for 36 hours I'd wonder if you were really mine. It means you need to stop workin' so hard, that's what it means!" Her hands actively flailed, speaking volumes above her voice.

Mona reached into a second cabinet beneath the sink and pulled out a shopping bag, the Big Brown one with the sturdy handles. She sat it on the countertop and loaded the buffet inside. Tony's eyes followed her as she fluttered around the room. Funny, he hadn't eaten and yet he was full...*of guilt*.

"Hey. I gotta work so I can afford your grandchildren."

"Grandchildren? Ha! You gotta roll the cannoli every now and again to make a baby! All you do is work! Work, work, work!"

Tony cringed and laughed aloud. The gibes she let pass her lips.

At once, she froze and cut through him with her gaze. "Hmph. But since you brought up the topic of grandchildren, when are you gonna find a good Italian girl and settle down? That Rosa was nice. What happened with her?"

Hesitant to answer, Tony dug his hands into his blue jeans pockets. He rocked back forth toe to heel, searching for the right words to explain to the woman who set them up that Rosa was a whack job.

Mona met Rosa at Saturday evening mass. By Sunday breakfast, she was the first Mrs. Antonio Donato, at least in Mona's and Rosa's minds. She lit candles and said two hail Marys. Little did she know Rosa was this side of crazy—controlling, obsessive. His intentions were to obtain a restraining order, not marry her. "Rosa and me, we didn't work out so good. We go out on one date and already she's namin' our kids. I wanna find someone for myself who makes me happy…and who isn't a few pepperonis short of a pizza pie. Did you hear that, Ma? Me. I."

She paced toward him, stopped, and hung one hand on her hip as she motioned dramatically with the other. "How many times I gotta tell ya, huh? Marriage has nothing to do with happiness."

"Look at you and Pop . . . well, *before* he got pinched." Tony started motioning his hands to mirror his mother's. It was contagious.

"Exactly! Look around you. Think back to when you were a kid in Jersey. You call that perfection?" She took a seat next to him, grabbed his hand. Her eternally wrinkled brow and weathered skin bore the weight of a worried mother. "You kids, you want everything to be perfect. The body, the hair, the pretty face, love, romance, please! Chi troppo vuole, nulla stringe!"

"What's 'at mean?"

"He who wants too much doesn't catch anything. Stop being so freakin' picky. Find a warm place to hide your sausage. Make sure she can cook and keep house. Then make it work. Simple! You young people these days, you make life too hard. Life's not that hard."

She patted his back and resumed her task. "So what you're saying is, I should just settle."

"Yes," she deadpanned. "Settle shmettle. No woman is perfect. Neither is love. And here's another newsflash, my dear Antonio. Neither. Are. *You*!" She pinched his nose.

Tony chuckled and shook his head. His mother had done her worst and he'd survived. Time to go. But not before checking up on the old man. Tony might be dead to Senior, but a father was a father. "Before I go, you uhhh...you heard from Pop?"

CHAPTER 21

Ten years had passed and they hadn't spoken a single word to one another. Not hello. Merry Christmas, Happy Birthday. Or kiss my ass. When Tony graduated college and chose the FBI over the family business, his father, a "made" man, broke ties immediately. His son's choice was an act of treason against the life. His sisters, Carla and Adrianna, married wise guys. His younger brother, Dante, became heir to the family business and the number-one draft pick.

He was groomed to be a soldier before Tony took the Bureau job. But in rejecting the family way, Tony ended Dante's career before it began. Got feds in your family? Can't be a wise guy. Dante was forced to go legit and he held a monster grudge against Tony. Wouldn't even acknowledge his presence on the street, despite the fact that Tony didn't work in Jersey and skillfully avoided Bureau attempts to recruit him into the Organized Crime section. Tony gave up nada. He didn't know anybody. Never saw anybody. Never heard anything. That's the way it had been. That's the way it would always be. He never took the vow of silence, but he honored it.

Tony had sacrificed a lot to live life on his own terms and follow his own path. The same stubborn determination he'd inherited from his father, was the same quality that ripped his family apart. His education, the one he received before he shunned the life would serve him well in his new occupation. Operational security techniques. Recruiting soldiers from other families to stay informed about the enemy. Avoiding face-to-face meets. Detecting surveillance. Tony entered the Bureau with better practical training than Quantico could ever provide.

Mona let out a long sigh and turned her face to the heavens. "Yeah, he's good. Well, as good as you can be in the pen. Your uncle Paulie went to see him last week, took him some groceries. Your father's still stubborn as a mule though, make no mistake about that."

"Did he ask about me?"

She looked away from him, avoided his gaze. Her melancholy expression betrayed the answer before she could speak. "Your father loves you, you know. His life isn't your life. You did the right thing. Don't doubt yourself for a minute. Your family will always be your family whether you agree with each other or not. Always remember, you can't choose family, so you can't lose family. Besides, I couldn't bear to see you in—"

She broke down. Not full-on waterworks, just a few streaks; this was significant for Mona. Tony walked over to her and let his arms console her. "It's okay, Ma. It's okay."

She recovered quickly, her sleeve soaking up her tears. Then she pinched and, palm open, double patted his cheeks. "You go on to work and make sure you eat, you hear me? Your mama's gonna be fine. I'm always fine, aren't I?"

Tony grabbed his bag and headed for 4th District.

He hated to leave Mona in her sullen state, but it was time to shift gears. Dmitriyev could be a major score, and his performance would have to be convincing. Their routine was trite but effective. As long as J.J. was on her A-game she'd seal the deal. Dmitriyev would be singing canary-style before nightfall.

• • •

Tony arrived at 4-D thirty minutes later. J.J.'s brother met him at the door as expected. He smiled as Tony approached. Tony wondered whether J.J. had mentioned him outside the context of work. Malcolm was a tall guy, like his sister, and equally likable. His down-to-earth attitude was genuine, and he lacked the "fuck you" attitude cops often had toward FBI agents. His sister had no doubt made him Fed-friendly. Tony admired their closeness, even envied them at times, the way she spoke of him with such adoration. Could never be him and Dante, not as long as he served the nation. The possibility had all but vanished once Tony took his oath of office. No matter what, he'd still show up for any one of his siblings. If they ever needed him, he'd be there. Whenever. Wherever. Without hesitation.

Tony's glance darted around the precinct. Only a skeletal staff remained on Sunday duty. They took a stairwell to the basement lockdown. Dmitriyev's holding cell was located a few feet down a narrow hall on the left. The interrogation room, separated by two sets of alarmed steel doors and metal detectors, was on the right. Malcolm waved to the duty officer who buzzed them inside.

Tony followed Malcolm through another short hall and stopped when Malcolm peered inside a small window inside a door on the right. "He's in here. We have someone monitoring you behind the one-way glass so just motion us when you're ready to leave." Malcolm turned to walk away. "His twenty-four hours is almost up. We'll have to call State or send him to Central Cell Block soon."

Tony took a deep breath, tapped into his inner asshole, and stepped inside. He understood his mission: Make Dmitriyev feel more miserable than he already looked.

And he looked like twice-hit road kill.

"Well, well, well, so we finally meet in person, Mr. Dmitriyev," Tony said with a smug smile pasted on his face. He pulled his credentials from his back pocket and gave them a customary flip. "Special Agent Donato at your service. Been following your career for a while now."

Dmitriyev nodded his head to acknowledge Tony's presence. Then Tony handed Dmitriyev one of his business cards.

"You recognize this, don't you?"

Dmitriyev pursed his lips and stiffened his frame.

"You sure?" Tony asked, fully expecting silence he met. Tony was just the warm-up act. "Man, you don't look so good. Rough night, eh?" Tony rested himself in the empty chair directly across from him. "I've never seen a green Russian before. Can I get you something? Coffee? A little hair of the dog, maybe?"

Still nothing. Tony couldn't blame the guy. After all, a rock and a hard place would've been heaven for Dmitriyev, especially given the humiliation facing him if he returned to the embassy without the veil of Bureau secrecy protecting him. Tony cringed on Dmitriyev's behalf. Unless Aleksey spilled his guts about what happened to Plotnikov and cut a deal, his life would stink like twice-dead road kill too.

Dmitriyev sat stone-faced and shackled with his fingers locked together on the wooden table. The sweat beads surfacing on his forehead appeared to be hangover symptoms rather than a sign of nervousness. From what Tony had read, Dmitriyev's long-time friend and colleague Stanislav Vorobyev, a First Secretary and the senior-most counterintelligence officer in the residency would choke Dmitriyev if he found out about this fiasco. He'd have no choice except to send him home. Stan-the-Man, as J.J. affectionately referred to him, was a declared member of Russian intelligence and his affiliation was known inside and outside embassy circles which meant he could never engage in operational activity—clandestine or otherwise. He was mostly an internal administrator who supervised the operations of other intelligence officers, such as Dmitriyev.

According to Russian reporting from another Embassy contact, Stan had privately warned Dmitriyev about some unspecified sketchy behavior but J.J. and Tony had no idea he had an appetite for prostitutes, especially black ones. Apparently, he didn't listen. As a result, he was destined to find himself on an express flight back to Russia. Not to mention the fallout from his wife's reaction.

Dmitriyev's stakes were high and most intelligence officers deplored the idea of being forced into some mind-numbing desk job in the Center.

Tony continued, "Listen Aleksey. We both know you don't want to go back to Moscow, especially not under these precarious circumstances. I mean, soliciting a prostitute? A black, transgender prostitute at that? Well, I can only imagine how that's gonna go over at the embassy. And assaulting a police officer? It'd suck for you if that story somehow found its way to *The Washington Post*," he said, tapping his index finger against his chin. "Which section do ya think that would make? Entertainment maybe? And Stan...he probably won't look favorably on your extracurriculars, neither will the State Department. You might get PNG'd."

Being declared persona non grata in the United States was tantamount to a death penalty for intelligence officers—a career death penalty. It virtually assured an intelligence officer would never work in a Western country again.

"If I have to call Stan, we both know where you'll end up," Tony said. "I'm not going to sit here and insult your intelligence because we're both counterintelligence; we know how the game is played. I guess the only question you need to answer is...what do you want to do? You can work with the Bureau or declare immunity and, well, you know the rest. Just understand if you want to stay in the U.S. of A, and finish out your tour, all roads lead through me. So, ball's in your court."

"What do you want?" Aleksey asked flatly.

"You're counterintelligence. If you can't figure that out then this meeting's over and my friend at the *Post* will enjoy an informative…" Tony looked down at his watch and glared at Dmitriyev, "brunch."

They stared each other down and a muted tension seized the room. Each refused to give an inch. Dmitriyev had been threatened, blackmailed, disrespected, and insulted.

Mission accomplished, Tony thought. *It's J.J.'s turn.*

CHAPTER 22

Late Sunday Afternoon…

J.J. stood in line at the Starbucks, biting down on her lip as her pulsed blitzed. *Will he confess to sending Plotnikov to his death? And how in hell will I cover his ass if he cooperates?* Without a strategy, a pitch would be useless. She wouldn't be able to offer him the thing he needed most—the ability to return to the Embassy without the threat of a recall to Moscow. The pressure was on. Dmitriyev would be a major score if she got him. No harm, no foul if she didn't. After all, no one at Headquarters knew about the opportunity except her and Tony.

Of all the intelligence officers at the embassy, he had the fewest vulnerabilities to exploit, up until his arrest. He'd kept his nose clean, stayed out of trouble, didn't stand out for any negative reason. Other than his apparent taste for black prostitutes, his only vice seemed to be a three-cup a day Venti cafe habit. Prostitute trouble and a recall to Moscow could not guarantee his cooperation. He might opt to take the hit on the chin, suffer the humiliation, and accept a desk job at the Center. But the occasion felt too ripe with opportunity not to give a pitch a shot.

"Venti dark roast, extra hot, please," J.J. said to the barista. "Oh, and can I have two small cups with that?"

"Sure, ma'am. Coming right up."

Piping hot coffee. A necessity. The only things Russians liked cold were beer and Borscht. Cold coffee wouldn't tempt this spy, particularly one trained not to accept food or drink from the likes of the FBI or CIA. Russian intelligence officers still suffered from Cold War paranoia. They wouldn't eat or drink anything for fear they might be drugged with mind-altering narcotics, truth serum...or French vodka. A refusal of such offerings was akin flipping an agent the bird as if to say, "Fuck you, and your weak American coffee."

She bought it anyway. If he drank it, she'd know, the way you know about a good cognac, whether Dmitriyev would trust her enough to cooperate. Without a single word spoken, he'd offer his services to the FBI.

J.J. grabbed a few sugar packets, jammed them into her pocket, and high-tailed it over to 4-D. By the time she arrived, Tony would be finished. Then J.J. would step in and make magic happen.

As soon as she slipped inside her car, it hit her. An idea. A way to cover Dmitriyev's ass, an offer he couldn't refuse. She phoned one of her reliable U.S. Park Police contacts. Rice McPherson, an auto technician, was the color of a Chai latte and his hair rice white. She had to cash in on yet another favor. Thankfully he accepted payments in Redskins' club seats. She only hoped he'd be able to come through with such short notice. It'd be worth the trouble if Dmitriyev gave her pitch even half of a second thought.

"Mr. Rice, it's Agent McCall."

"Well, young lady! Haven't heard from you in a month of Sundays. What can I do for you?" he asked.

"I've got a big big favor to ask. I need to get a car towed from MPD to the Russian Embassy. And before it reaches the gate, it *must* be mechanically challenged. Can you get over to 4-D within the hour?"

"4-D? A little bit out of your jurisdiction, don't you think?" he asked. "What kind of seats are we talking about?"

"Front row. Club section. Platinum parking."

"Well, why didn't you say so before? Anything for my favorite FBI Agent. I'm on the way!"

• • •

Tony sauntered out of the interrogation room, appearing full of himself, overstuffed with sanctimony. J.J. felt assured all had gone as orchestrated. She peered inside the interrogation room. Aleksey was inches from death—or at least very much *wished* he was. He'd devolved from hung over to dangling on the edge of life by a half a shoestring. "I presume that look on your face means you got him warmed up for me?"

"Yep. Standard procedure."

"Listen, before I go inside I need you to do me a favor."

"What's 'at?" Tony asked.

"Tell Malcolm to get a hold of Dmitriyev's cell phone. We need to drain the battery. If we're lucky it'll be an iPhone, and it won't take too long."

Tony's eyebrows scrunched together leaving deep creases in his forehead. "Okay," he said, noticeably confused. "If you say so."

"Trust me."

J.J. strolled in the interrogation room, smiling her usual smile. Dmitriyev eyed the steam rising from the lid of the Venti Starbucks cup. She placed the cup holder on the table, alongside the two extra cups the barista kindly supplied. J.J. eyed him as she turned the cup's opening toward Dmitriyev, allowing him to inspect inside. Then she sat the two cups on the table and poured coffee into both. After resorting to an infantile game of *Eenie Meenie Miney Moe* to select her cup, she took a short sip of the steaming java, just to reassure him his drink was safe. On edge, she watched for any gesture, motion, or sign that the cup would meet his lips. There was none. Of course, he'd make the visit harder than it had to be. It was the Russian way.

She pushed the second cup toward him, careful to maintain a respectful distance. "Thought you could use this. I brought you some cream and sugar, but based on your newly discovered preferences, I thought you'd prefer it *black*." A slight smile lifted the corners of her lips.

His face scrunched, perhaps her joke was ill-timed, too soon. He responded with defiant silence.

"Okay. Don't say I didn't ask."

J.J. waited, stared at his face. It was six shades of green, propped up by a shaky hand on the table's edge, his body slightly bowled over. She tilted her head in empathy. "Umph. Perhaps you'd prefer a cyanide capsule."

He managed a slight grin, but his silence remained unbroken. A window of opportunity? Now it was time to convince him that she was there for him, on his side. And what better foe to unite against than Tony.

"So. I heard Agent Donato gave you a hard time," she said, her voice thick with Guido. "Sorry about that. Fucking Italians. Whadaya gonna do?"

Aleksey chuckled again but still refused the coffee. J.J. was on notice. She hadn't charmed him quite yet. Although she wasn't ready to start the routine, his insolence forced her hand. She pulled her credentials from her jacket pocket and flipped them open.

"Do you know who I am?"

He nodded. "No introduction necessary. I know you who you are. And I know what you've been doing."

J.J. grew uneasy. She drew back and tugged at her shirt sleeve when her thoughts turned to Plotnikov. Dmitriyev was counterintelligence. Had he turned over her source to Golikov? Even more troublesome was the fact that his statement failed to make her skin prickle. He knew something she wasn't aware of. At the same time, she knew Malcolm found her card was in his wallet; he was still unaware of that little fact.

She gazed at him curiously. "Is that so? May I ask how you *think* you know me?"

"You may ask," he responded calmly, too cool for someone in his predicament. His was not the behavior of a man facing a humiliating recall to Moscow and an inevitable grilling by Golikov's people. No, he was crazy or fearless. J.J. suspected the latter. She only needed to figure out from where he'd derived his courage.

They sat in silence, stared at one another, the way you look at a lottery ticket before the numbers are called, each hoping the other would pay off. The difference was she was on her own turf. She hadn't disappeared from her residency the day before. And she wouldn't have to face the security officer...and potentially Golikov. J.J. had the upper hand no matter what game he played. Still, the stalemate could go on all day. J.J. decided to feign impatience in order to force his hand, throw him off his game.

She sat forward and folded her arms on the table. The time had come to cut out the small talk and get down to brass tacks. "Listen, my time is valuable, and I've got more important work to do. I'm here to offer you some assistance with your, shall we say . . . *predicament?*"

"Oh, so this is what you Americans call it? Assistance? In Russia, we call it blackmail."

"I beg to differ. In Russia, you call it standard business practice."

"Is there a point to this, Agent McCall?" he said, his voice short, terse.

She chuckled and wagged her finger. "I know what you must think. But unlike some in my profession, I don't believe in blackmailing those whom I hope to someday call friend. Somehow seems counterproductive to developing a trusting relationship," she said, intently watching his expression. "So we're clear, I'm offering my assistance whether or not you choose to cooperate with me."

J.J.'s remark stunned Dmitriyev. His face contorted briefly, but he regained his composure almost as fast.

"Sounds like *bad business* to me. What's in it for you?"

"If you choose not to speak with me? Nothing. It's never bad business to treat people with decency and respect," she said. "Now, according to my watch, you should've returned to the embassy...ohhhhh, about *fifteen hours* ago. I'm sure Stan and Golikov's people will be anxious to speak with you when you return. On the other hand, I've got all day. It's your ball to play, Mr. Dmitriyev."

He leaned back and folded his arms across his chest, studied her expression, and waited for a flinch. In fact, she yawned. Little did he know, *flinch* was not in J.J.'s vocabulary.

Her expression didn't crack. She maintained her stance a few seconds longer and then prepared to concede for the moment. If he wanted to cooperate with her later, he had her business card.

"Okay. Well. While Agent Donato was speaking with you, I arranged for a U.S. Park Police tow truck to take your now malfunctioning vehicle back to your embassy, and we've drained your cell phone battery. Now, you have an excuse for not returning or checking in."

Dmitriyev sat forward in his seat, appearing intrigued and mildly impressed...or amused. She couldn't quite discern which.

J.J. continued. "Just tell your security officer you were doing whatever Russian officers do in the middle of the woods—checking a signal or something—and you had car trouble, after your cell phone died of course. They'll see the Park Police, and my buddy Rice will make it all legit."

She twice patted her hand on the table and stood to leave. "Well, since it appears we're finished here, I'll be in on my way. I'd wish you good luck on the rest of your tour, but that would be bad for Bureau business. So, I'll just bid you adieu."

She looked into the one-way glass and signaled Malcolm to open the door. When she placed her hand on the doorknob, Dmitriyev called out, "Agent McCall."

J.J. turned toward him and huffed impatiently. "Yes, sir?"

Dmitriyev smiled and grabbed the coffee cup. Before she could inhale her next breath, he took a sip from the cup she'd poured earlier, and returned it to the table.

She shot him a sidelong glance, her lips parted slightly. Was he toying with her or signaling his readiness to cooperate? She remained silent, waiting on him to say more. When her diminished patience was met with silence, she again turned to leave. His voice rumbled. "By the way, did you enjoy your reading the night before last?"

"My reading?" she asked, realizing seconds later he was referring to the day she and Tony retrieved Karat's drop.

Before she could temper her reaction, she turned to him, her eyes and mouth opened wide and she hissed, *"You,"*

"We have a saying in my country," Dmitriyev said. "The enemy of my enemy is my friend. Hello, friend."

CHAPTER 23

For the second time in almost as many years, J.J. had slipped and fallen into a Russian intelligence treasure trove. It made perfect sense. The embassy would never suspect a code clerk of working with American intelligence. As the counterintelligence operational line chief, Dmitriyev had some, if not limited, access to American sources. Plotnikov wasn't passing the documents, *Dmitriyev* was. Plotnikov was merely a cut-out.

But still, the pairing was highly unusual. There was more to their story than the surface revealed. The truth was hers to find.

Her only plan for the day had been to pitch him. All of a sudden, she was conducting an initial debrief. No time to get him to a safe house. She'd need to elicit as much information from him as possible—in less than an hour—so he could return and avoid more suspicion regarding his whereabouts.

J.J. excused herself from the interrogation room before the debriefing began.

Strategy. What's my strategy?

As a counterintelligence officer, his bona fides were solid, and he had a year left on his visa, a visa that could be extended if the FBI could help him appear productive. His cooperation would deal a significant blow to his service's operations in Washington D.C., New York, and perhaps even San Francisco. But she must find out the source of his motivation, and eliciting personal information from counterintelligence officers was akin to milking a cow for peanut butter.

Tony would know what to do. He greeted her in the hall with Malcolm just a few steps behind.

"Hey Bro, I need a favor. Find me a digital recorder. You guys must have one around here somewhere," she requested.

"Hmmm...yeah, I think so. I'll check with one of the duty officers," he said, trotting down the hall. She and Tony watched him until he was out of earshot.

"Well, this is an amazing turn of events, wouldn't you say?" J.J. said.

"I know, right? Certainly explains how Karat got the intel and made the drop before he left."

"He had help from the line chief."

"Yeah," she said, heading for the door, waiting for Tony to follow behind. "You don't want to sit in on the debriefing? I mean, even though your heart's not in this one, this is *our* case."

"No, no. You got this. Besides, I don't want to spook him. He's got to be pretty concerned about his security," Tony said. "I'm just gonna run out and get more coffee and cigarettes. They help loosen the tongue."

She flashed a comforted smile. "You're the best. By the way, I need a disposable bat phone from the backpack. Just in case."

"You got it," he said. "And if I could offer one piece of advice, don't over-think this one, J.J. He wouldn't be here if he weren't ready to talk. Just let him talk."

Malcolm switched J.J. and Dmitriyev from the interrogation area to a small, more comfortable conference space with a circular table, a few chairs, and a view. Dmitriyev's eyes brightened when he saw the gifts J.J. bore. Now, a dense smoke filtered the sunrays that shone through the window. Welling with anticipation, she sat down and rested a digital recorder in the center of the table as he chain-smoked cigarettes. She could feel the cancer building on her lungs. The smokeless ashtray she had purchased years ago for such purposes had been rendered all but completely useless. No more time to get ready. It was time to get done. She had dispensed with the pleasantries and eased him into the conversation about Karat.

"So, my brother Malcolm tells me you've been formally introduced to Leona."

He smirked, inhaled a long drag from his cigarette, the smoke swirling about his lips and the wisps vanishing into air.

"You mean *Leon*? It was like scene from *Crying Game*," he joked, exaggerating his raspy Russian accent. "There's not enough vodka in Russia to force the memory of that godforsaken moment from my mind."

J.J. laughed, surprised at Dmitriyev's sense of humor. She glanced at her watch. Time was passing by too quickly and the longer they talked, the more she feared for his security.

"So back to Plotnikov. Earlier you mentioned you and he are very close."

"Our fathers served in the KGB together. First Department, First Chief Directorate. They were both stationed in London until an MI-6 officer defected and falsely claimed Sergey, Viktor's father, was passing information to them. After a show trial, he was tortured and killed. Then my own father came under heavy scrutiny. Our lives were never again the same."

"Ahhhh, so this is the reason you both decided work with the Bureau. But how did you both come to work for Russian intelligence, especially after what happened to your parents?" She knew the answer of course, but she wanted to ensure their stories matched up.

"In another ironic turn of events, our fathers were exonerated by one of the two big U.S. spies. I can't be certain which, but the information was credible. Both had collaborated with the MI-6 defector and confirmed that our fathers had not been recruited by the American or British security services," he said. "The KGB would never admit such a mistake. Ever. But when we applied to the Foreign Language Institute we were accepted immediately. Exemplary students, we were recruited by the KGB just before the break-up and offered premier assignments."

"I see. Is Viktor okay? I mean, they didn't—"

"I don't know," he said with a shrug. "Haven't heard from him since he left. According to the rumors, Golikov thought the FBI was black-mailing him over the shoplifting and feared he was prepared to pass codes."

J.J. shuddered inside but tried to maintain her cool exterior.

"He's been detained. And if we don't clear his name, and I mean soon, Golikov will murder him with or without sufficient evidence," Dmitriyev urged, his forehead creased with worry. "He's my brother and the only family I have left. He said he could count on you, said that you keep your promises. And I know that if you were the mole, he would already be dead."

"I made promises, yes, but he's in Moscow now and I have no power outside of the United States. None. And requesting the Agency to exfiltrate him means a shit load of bureaucratic red tape that will expose him to even more insider threats...and I suspect it will take a lot of time that we don't have."

"Is there no one at the Agency you can trust?"

J.J. immediately thought of Six, but he answered to the powers that be and there was no telling who was dirty.

"I don't—" She hesitated and shook her head no.

"Then you have to find a way to help him from here. You must." Dmitriyev peered out the window into the distance, then turned to J.J. as he tapped his cigarette in the ashtray. "I do not mean to rush you but we really must hurry. I've got to get back."

She glanced down at her watch again. The window of opportunity had drawn to a close. "My hands are tied, but I'll see what I can do. Just a few more questions and we'll get you out of here," she said, running her finger across her notes, checking for critical gaps. "What do you know about a '*Juliet Charles*'? The individual from the letter you provided in the drop."

"He's a well-placed asset. Based on the information he's provided, I believe he's FBI. I've been told he's made drops two to three times a year over the past four or five years, but I'm not aware of his true identity. We only communicate through dead drops and signals. No phone calls, no electronic communication, no personal meetings whatsoever. Classic tradecraft. It is my understanding he slipped a note in Aleksandr Mikhaylov's car some years ago when the window was cracked."

She hesitated. "Wait. We thought Mikhaylov was Line N, an illegals support officer, not counterintelligence."

"Seems you know our *rezidentura* quite well," Dmitriyev said, somewhat taken aback. "Yes, Mikhaylov does support illegals and deep cover operations, but if your mole were seeking to volunteer, he'd only need to see a diplomatic license plate on the vehicle. Doesn't matter whether he knew Mikhaylov was an illegals support officer."

She nodded in agreement. "One thing I notice. You keep saying '*he*'. . . but Juliet Charles is a woman's name."

"Ahhhhh. Very good observation. When I cleared the drops, I noticed a man's shoe prints in the mud. I've no doubt it's a man."

"So you're his handler?"

"Yes, *one* of them. Since there are no personal meetings, he has several."

Dmitriyev handled ICE Phantom himself. Good to know, but the SVR had mastered the art of compartmenting information and assets so that any counterintelligence officer could service the source but only a handful—maybe fewer—might be privy to the source's true identity.

Even worse, as a counterintelligence special agent, the mole would be skilled in burying his tracks.

"So, does anyone else in the residency have access to his true identity or files?"

"Well, normally such information is maintained at headquarters, but I believe Stanislav Vorobyev, the security officer, maintains a special file which contains his identity. It's in a safe that only the security officer can access."

J.J.'s stomach hardened. She propped her elbow on the table and let her head fall into her hand. "Damn! He's scheduled to depart on Friday," she said, throwing her hands in the air, defeated. A breakthrough was imminent. She could taste it. But recruiting Vorobyev? Impossible. She certainly couldn't do it in such a short period of time if she could at all. And she had nothing on which to pin her hopes, nothing except the possibility that the mole would pass a document that would reveal his identity...someday. But they'd have to wait months, perhaps even years for that to happen. Unless by some miracle from heaven they could recruit the next security officer.

"Do you know who his replacement will be? We haven't received notification from the State Department about any new arrivals."

"In this case you would not," he said, "because Vorobyev's next re-placement is already in the embassy."

"In the embassy?"

"Yes," he answered.

"Well...who is it?"

A smile parted his lips. "Me."

J.J. heard him but couldn't quite bring herself believe what he'd said. *Me?* she thought. What did he mean by *me?* His words zapped through her spine and hit the Hallelujah nerve. She glanced down at her notes, then snapped her head back toward him.

"I'm sorry. I must've been imagining things. Did you say that *you are* Vorobyev's replacement?"

He nodded.

"You mean on Friday— *this coming Friday—you* might be in a position to identify the mole?"

"It's very possible. Trust me, no one wants the mole caught more than I do. As long as he's out there neither Viktor nor I are safe. But you must do everything you can to keep him from finding out that I'm cooperating with the FBI. And I've got to find a way to keep Golikov's people in check," he said, his expression strained. "Of course, I'm sure you understand that even though Russia has initiated a moratorium on the death penalty, the Russian mafia, thieves-in-law from the Solntsevskaya organized crime group, are serving as guns for hire for their friends at the Center. Golikov will kill me if I'm caught."

"Golikov and his henchman are no strangers to me," J.J. said, thinking of Polyakov's hand.

"They're here in Washington under the guise of conducting inspections. His people have been assigned to all Western embassies including here in the United States," he said. "I trust you because the man I called brother trusted you. However, until I find out the mole's identity, *you* cannot trust *anyone.*"

Shit. Every step forward ended in one step back. The answer was close, but not quite close enough. "I will do everything in my power to protect you," she said, remembering her promises are what held her prisoner in her current predicament. She reached into her purse and pulled out a cell phone specially fitted with a transmitter to provide him with a means of emergency communication. She also handed him a sheet of paper with dead drop instructions.

"Mark a signal if you need to contact me. Only use the throwaway phone in life-threatening situations. Now, we'll get you back to the embassy."

Keeping Dmitriyev alive wouldn't be easy, not with Golikov's goons looming and ICE Phantom still deeply concealed.

CHAPTER 24

Monday Morning…

Newton's cradle kinetic balls clicked in a soothing rhythm as Director Freeman waited in his office for Cartwright to arrive with an update on the status of the remaining personnel polygraphs and Jack's arrest. Freeman's stomach twisted and turned when he received the news, another fucking FBI agent arrested for committing espionage, and he still hadn't reconciled himself with Jack's guilt as so many others had, despite the evidence. His instinct told him to keep looking, and his instincts had never steered him wrong before. Jack was an asshole but Freeman never figured him for a spy. Hell, he wouldn't have pegged Hanssen either truth be told. CIA case officers were trained to lie and break the laws in foreign countries of interest. They always tread a thin, murky line between mission and miscreant. He'd rarely been surprised when the CIA case officers turned, especially those from Russia House. But for FBI agents, the lines were clear. They were trained to uphold laws not break them.

He'd already been called to the Hill to testify in front of the Senate Select Committee on Intelligence. They wanted answers, answers Freeman couldn't provide because Sabinski refused to cooperate. Maybe Cartwright had made some headway.

"Has Jack started talking yet? I'd hoped he'd open up after a few days in solitary confinement."

"Unfortunately, not," Cartwright said, intense and focused. He crossed his legs and laid a notebook across his lap. "The only thing he's told us is that he's innocent and he wanted to speak to Agent McCall—and Agent McCall alone. She met with him a couple of days ago, but she hasn't briefed me on her discussion yet, which suggests to me she probably didn't find out any more information than we already knew."

"Hmmm, I see. The minute we're done here, I want you to get her in your office. Everyone's riding my ass about this case, asking questions I can't answer. Don't drop the ball on this, Jim. I can't stall for much longer."

Cartwright nodded yes and made a notation on his notepad.

"Anyone else had poly issues?" Freeman asked.

"No, sir. So far, everyone else has passed. Agent Michaels and Sunnie Richardson, our analyst, took theirs yesterday. Neither one had any issues to my knowledge, but I'll double check to make certain."

"Who's left?"

"Three agents—Johnson, McCall, and Donato. Johnson's poly is scheduled for Thursday. Donato and McCall for Friday morning. The examiner had scheduling issues due to this recent hiring surge and couldn't fit them earlier."

Freeman noted the dates on his calendar and then spoke without looking up. "What about yours?"

"Sir?" His head flinched back, he reached for the base of his neck.

"Jim, you're on the bigot list. I realize the test is a pain in the ass inconvenience—and a mere formality, but I'm not ready to put all my eggs in the Jack basket yet. I want to keep searching so you'll just have to take this one on the chin for the team. Are we understood?"

"Yes, sir. Understood," Cartwright said flatly and then stood to leave. "I'll schedule mine in the morning. They should be able to get me in next week."

"Don't bother. I've already got you on the schedule for 10 a.m. tomorrow," Freeman said. "You call me immediately after you speak with Agent McCall. And remember the door is open if you have any issues you need to discuss. Now if that's all…"

Cartwright nodded in agreement and hurried nervously out of the office.

In a moment less than an instant, Cartwright's face turned pale. His chest rose and fell dramatically. Fleeing down the main corridor, his expression grew panic-stricken.

Cartwright's secretary, Sue Slater, was on her way to the cafeteria to grab some breakfast when she noticed his urgency and stopped him mid-stride. "Are you okay, Mr. Cartwright?"

He tried to force the words and respond, but nothing came. He charged ahead, his breath labored and his forehead dripping with perspiration. He flung open the door to a stairwell. It led to the main entrance. Soon the hurried clack of his shoe heels against the steps echoed louder and louder, down ten flights of stairs, until he reached the exit.

Air.

He needed air.

• • •

J.J. had dragged herself out of bed and schlepped into the office, her stress level off the charts. The ICE Phantom skulked around headquarters like a sly serpent stalking its next prey. Her worse nightmare had been realized—Golikov had detained Karat. But she'd recruited the most important Russian source to cooperate with the Bureau since…well…since her last source.

Each limb attached to her body felt as if it weighed a hundred pounds. Every movement an endless slog. The unyielding turmoil had taken a physical toll, even though her mind felt sharp and geared for action. She'd half considered setting up an intravenous Starbucks drip in the office so she could survive the rest of the day. Instead, she stopped at the second-rate coffee shop across the street to grab coffee before heading into the office.

When J.J. finally reached the Hoover building's Pennsylvania Avenue entrance, Cartwright swung the door open. It nearly smacked her in the face. He stepped outside and sucked in a breath of cool exhaust-filled fall morning air before he even noticed J.J. Although he tried to collect himself, he appeared disturbed, flustered.

"Mr. Cartwright. You look ill. Is everything all right?"

"I'm fine. It's the air in that place. Sometimes you have to get out," Cartwright replied, wiping his brow with the back of his hand.

J.J., unconvinced, felt a tingle on the back of her neck. She reached her free hand back to soothe it. He was lying...but about what she had no idea. He didn't feel fine. He didn't look fine. She only questioned why. Maybe he was again caving under the pressure. After all, she'd personally witnessed him meltdown before.

"Fancy meeting you here," he said. "I was just telling Director Freeman that I planned to call and find out how your meeting with Jack went. We can't thank you enough for attempting to speak with him."

"No problem." She took a deep breath to brace herself in case he told a lie that brought on a more intense reaction. "Glad I could be of service."

"So what did he have to say? Probably not much right?" Cartwright asked, his voice reflecting more hope than certainty.

"No, sir. As a matter of fact, he had plenty to say," she said, watching for any change in his expression. "He claims he's been framed and that someone in the Bureau is responsible."

He tilted his head to the side. For a moment, he appeared shaken but he recovered quickly. "Yeah. The problem is no one could fail the polygraph exam twice on Jack's behalf, except Jack. He was the only one hooked up to the box. He must take you for a fool to believe you'd fall for that."

"Yeah, I'm always amazed at what people take me for." Careful to keep her expression neutral, she said, "If you want to hear something crazier, he seems to think he can identify the person responsible. What do you think about that?"

"Did he name him?"

"*Him?* No," she said, finding it curious Cartwright specified a male. Maybe the suggestion was just a function of the English language. Perhaps there was more to it. "But if his allegations are true, we'll get him eventually. What's done in the dark will always find its way to the light."

"I agree. I agree. At least we know where his head's at, right?" Cartwright shifted his gaze to the sea of brake lights flashing in rush hour traffic. He looked toward the ground, deflated. "Uhhh, did he have anything else to add?"

"Yeah. Just one other thing. He questioned the speed at which the investigation was conducted before he got arrested. But I'm sure you believed he'd be a flight risk, especially with all the cash."

"Of course. That's exactly what I thought. And I acted within the bounds of the law."

An itch spiked through the center of her spine.

"Damnit!" she yelled.

Her knees buckled and she grabbed Cartwright's arm to keep her balance.

"You okay?" He placed his hand against her back to ensure she was steady.

The sensation passed a moment later. She composed herself and continued. "I'm okay...just fine. The last few days have been exhausting. I think I probably should've grabbed some breakfast with my coffee—woozy."

He nodded. "Well, if that's all you have for me, I really must be going now. I'll be sure to pass the information on to Director Freeman."

He started to walk away but stopped. He spun around to face J.J., his expression sullen.

"You know, as FBI Agents, the weight of our country's security rests on our shoulders. Unfortunately, not all of us bear the full weight of that responsibility gracefully."

"Yes," she said, her mind focused on ICE Phantom. "And apparently some of us can't bear it at all."

Both turned to walk their separate ways. A few steps into his journey Cartwright called out, "J.J.! Wait a minute." He moved closer. His eyes were glossy, dampened with the remnants of almost stifled tears. "Meet me in my office first thing tomorrow morning. I have some important information you need."

"About what?"

"You ever play chess, Agent McCall?"

She tilted her head to the side. "Sure, a few times in college. Why do you ask?"

"Well, sometimes when playing chess, one has to sacrifice the pawn to get the king."

J.J. paused for thought. "So, uhhh, am I supposed to be the king or pawn in the scenario?"

"Neither. Right now, you're the most important piece on the board—the queen. I'll see you in the morning."

CHAPTER 25

D istracted by Cartwright's elusiveness, J.J. literally ran into Tony at the office door. They exchanged morning greetings and turned to go to their cubicles when who should appear but Chris and Lana. If the two had some romantic bond that made Chris maniacally insane at the thought of Lana's extracurricular activities with Jack, she couldn't discern. Lately, Chris appeared a little colder, emotionless. Maybe he had finally come to his senses. Maybe the voodoo that she do so well no longer wooed him into stupidity.

"Hey. You two have been quiet lately," Chris said, stopping them as he stepped away from Lana's cubicle. "Either you're keeping a low profile to stay out of trouble or you're up to no good. Which is it?"

"Neither," Tony responded, agitated. Chris was probing for information. From the look on his face, J.J. could anticipate the smell of bullshit about to seep from his greeting. "We've been investigating. You know, the work the government pays us to do on behalf of the American people. The work you'd be engaged in if you weren't so busy playing footsie."

Both of J.J.'s eyebrows popped up.

Chris's expression hardened, his voice rose. "You're one to talk." He motioned his head toward J.J.

"We could take this outside if you want to discuss it further," Tony said. He went express Jersey on Chris, with his chest puffed and back rigid. Chris had crossed the line. And J.J. was caught in the middle of Testosterone City.

"All right, boys. All right. That'll be quite enough, thank you," J.J. said. "Knock it off or I'll send both of you to the principal's office."

Why Chris had suggested Tony and J.J. were intimately involved, she didn't know. Didn't really bother J.J. but Tony was more than mildly perturbed. As she watched them argue back and forth, J.J. noticed Chris had something of a slick nature, his every gesture, every word reeked of used car salesman. If indeed he was ICE Phantom, he'd still need motivation and nothing logical came to mind. He'd come from a fairly well-to-do family, graduated from Stanford, never smoked or drank—no drugs. Major health nut. A bit narcissistic but not overly so, not for a third-generation legacy FBI agent. J.J. was a second-generation legacy, so she couldn't hold that against him. Besides, a certain level of cockiness was expected and, to some extent, required to be effective at this job.

His only weakness (as far as she could tell) was his addiction to blond, blue-eyed, big busted women. But most men on the planet could confess that sin. He had a reputation for wining them and dining them all the way to his bed. He spread his affections as far and as wide as their slim, toned legs. Then he dropped them cold. His curiosity was only piqued by the aloof, the uninterested. Lana didn't fit the bill on any count. The rumor mill suggested she'd been had by one and all—from Gs to G-men anyone with credentials would do. For Chris, using her body and winning her heart were separate challenges, the latter might intrigue him beyond reason. Lana's tryst with Jack could drive him to jealousy and send him over sanity's edge.

Time and time again the love of a woman had proved more than sufficient motivation to spy for the Russians, especially if Chris believed purchasing her affection would net him the ultimate prize.

The moment, ripe with opportunity, offered J.J. the chance to probe Chris, to elicit information and confirm her suspicions.

"Yeah, everything's been nuts around here since Jack's arrest. Can't believe he asked to meet with *me*...of all people."

"Yeah. Strange indeed."

"I'm rather surprised he hasn't asked Lana to visit yet. They seemed so close," she said. "Why do you suppose that is?"

Chris shrugged, played nonchalant. "I don't know. I've actually been wondering the same thing," Chris responded. No reaction? He was telling the truth. Perhaps he knew less about the details of Jack's and Lana's relationship than she suspected.

"Interesting," she said. "He made some crazy accusations. Suggested a mole in the FBI might be attempting to frame him."

"Is that right? Did he offer any names?" Chris asked, swallowing hard. His interest was obviously piqued.

"Yeah...as a matter of fact he did," she responded, maintaining her poker face. "*Yours.*"

Chris ran his hands through his hair. "Me?"

She paused and watched as his breathing became labored. She'd learned all she needed to know.

"No, I'm just kidding," she chuckled. Her laugh fake, insincere. "Your secret's still safe...for now."

He held his hand against his chest. "Man, you had me going for a second. Thought I was going to have to empty out my Swiss bank accounts and move to Russia," he joked in return.

Her eyebrow rose. *No responses to* his attempt at humor at all, not even the slightest hint of an itch.

"Careful what you say to me, Chris," J.J. deadpanned. "I'm an FBI agent."

A jovial expression seized her face. He had no idea how dead serious she really was.

J.J turned to glance at the wall clock and noticed Lana. She lingered like month-old fish odor at a nearby cubicle. When J.J. turned as if planning to leave, Lana gave up the pretense of being busy and injected herself into the discussion. Just as J.J figured she would.

"So, what did he have to say for himself?" Lana chimed in.

"Just wanted to apologize for the, uhhh, contentious relationship he and I have had over the years. Trying to atone for his past sins, I guess," J.J. lied. "Must be trying to get in good with The Man Upstairs before he fries."

Chris nodded. "I suspect he'd have to offer more apologies than he could possibly make in *this* lifetime to stay out of hell," he said.

A slow smile crept upon J.J.'s lips. "Yes, there's a special place in hell for traitors...*like him*." She hoped they both would take the comment to heart. She shifted her glare to Lana. "I like to think hell's fire burns a little hotter for those who betray their country."

Lana returned J.J.'s glare, unyielding, defiant. "I'm a patriot. I *would never* betray my country."

J.J. dismissed Lana's remark as fake and disingenuous as her breasts and braced herself for the physiological fall-out. But none came.

Perhaps Lana had some semblance of honor, even if she was inept and had only succeeded in stealing other agents' cases.

Chris flashed a sheepish expression. "So, do you think he did it?"

"I have no doubt he's guilty," J.J. lied. "And none of his half-assed apologies would ever alter my opinion of him."

If Chris was indeed ICE Phantom, all evidence and suspicion must still point to Jack. Then Chris would continue to operate business as usual and catching him in the act would only be a matter of time.

An uncomfortable silence hovered between them. J.J. changed the subject.

"So, did you guys take your polys yet?"

Lana nodded. "Yes, I passed with flying colors. I'm back in the vault."

"Motherflubber!" she yelled as her knees buckled.

Her skin crawled at the sound of Lana's voice, but she wouldn't be standing in the office if she hadn't actually passed. Why did her remark about passing with flying colors ring untrue? Her mind plunged into another round of uncertainty. The situation served as a prime example of the reason J.J.'s "gift" was often more curse than blessing. To know someone had been untruthful was far less useful than knowing the reason why.

Lana turned to J.J. and sympathetically patted her shoulder. "Your…*issue?*"

J.J. nodded and tapped her forehead with the back of her hand.

"Well, you'll have time to get some rest. In Jack's absence, Mr. Cartwright instructed me to take over all of your cases until you pass your polygraph. So, I'll need access to your cabinet safe," she said, waiting to sink her claws into J.J.'s cases.

J.J. struggled to stifle the flippant bitch inside crying to get out. "Fine," J.J. snapped. "Have at them."

Plotnikov's real case file still rested safely in the vault, housed inside a folder belonging to a deceased source. And Plotnikov was in Moscow. There'd be no reason for the mole or Lana to pursue more information about him. She looked to the ceiling and thanked God Dmitriyev's information rested safely with her because she and Tony had been locked out of the vault before filing his case. Her two most important sources were safe, at least from Lana's ineptness. And if Chris were indeed the mole, keeping their identities from him would no doubt mean the difference between life and death. He must never know about them. And he never would.

J.J. eyed Chris and he returned her glance. "So when's your poly, Chris?" she asked.

"I got an email this morning. You, Tony, and I are the last three. I get the pleasure of the first appointment Thursday morning. Both of you are scheduled for Friday. Although when I arrived this morning, I heard

Freeman ordered Cartwright to take one, and he's not at all happy about it."

"This morning?" J.J. asked, remembering her run-in with Cartwright outside the front entrance. He seemed off-balance, even panicked. She might've caught him right after Freeman broke the news.

She and Tony exchanged glances. "Yeah. Apparently he thought he was exempt, but Freeman thought otherwise. One thing you can say about Freeman is he's fair."

Or covering his ass. If J.J. were the director, she wouldn't want to be called to the Hill to explain how senior executives *don't usually* spy so Cartwright wasn't expected to take the examination. Freeman hadn't been fair, he'd been smart.

"Well, Tony and I have some issues we'd like to discuss in private, so we're gonna grab an empty office. Who's the acting supervisor?"

"Me," Lana said. "But you're free to use Jack's office if you want. I'm not sitting in there...at least not yet."

Tony mocked her, turning his head and silently mouthing the words, "At least not yet."

J.J. shrugged half-heartedly then checked her jacket for lint, hoping Lana would evaporate into another dimension.

"Hey, J.J. Before you guys meet can I speak with you for second?" Lana lowered her voice. "Alone?"

"Sure," J.J. answered, humoring her for humor's sake. "Let's step in-to the hall." Lana followed her out the office door.

Lana hesitated for a few seconds. She stammered and stuttered be-fore collecting herself. "Listen, I know you don't think much of me," Lana said. She paused as if waiting for J.J. to disagree.

J.J. pursed her lips and nodded. "Go on."

"Even though Jack would never admit it, I think we all know the ICE Phantom exists," Lana said. "And whatever you may think of me or how

I do my job, I have as much interest in finding the asshole as anyone. So, just hear me out."

How could J.J. resist hearing more with a start like that? "Agreed. Continue."

"The night before Jack was arrested, I expressed some...some *concerns* I had about Chris's behavior. With his attitude today, I'm even more worried."

"About what?" J.J. waited for any reaction.

"That he might've played a part in what happened to Jack."

Hmmm...no reaction, J.J. thought to herself. However, her only surprise was in the apparent ease in which Lana thrust her partner, and presumably her lover, squarely under the bus.

"He's been acting strange, more obsessive than usual. Buying expensive jewelry that I'm not sure he can afford. He has volatile mood swings. And I believe I saw him with a flash drive; they're forbidden in the SCIFed area. I just think you should be aware."

"Me? I'm just a recruiter. You should report it to security so they can make the proper inquiries," J.J. responded, choking out the words. Given their history, it pained J.J. to help. But for all J.J. knew, Lana's concern was genuine. "Now I need to get back inside so I can meet with Tony."

"Sure, sure," Lana said. "See ya later."

Lana flashed a thinly veiled smirk as she walked away. J.J. wondered for a brief moment if strangling Lana with her own brunette tresses would still constitute murder.

• • •

Moments later in Jack's office, Tony kicked his feet up on the desk, clasped his hands behind his head like a boss. "How do I look?" He shooed J.J. with his hand. "I take my coffee black, please."

"Well, if you wanted something hot and black all you had to do was say so—here I am!"

He shook his head and revealed his sexy grin. He had quite a few smiles—his joking smile. His cocky smile. His cat that caught the canary smile. But the sexy smile was J.J.'s favorite.

"*Whatever*," J.J. continued. "While I must say the look of success agrees with you, you do realize Jack probably farts in that chair."

Tony vaulted up from the seat as if someone had lit a fire under his ass. He pushed the chair aside and scanned the office for another one. "Leave it to you to steal my little bit of thunder."

"Ass thunder is what I saved you from," she said chuckling before her mood soured. "While I appreciate the diversion, we've got to figure out a way to find this mole and save our source. I'm gonna hit the ladies' and I'll be right back."

Chris. Mr. Cartwright. J.J. churned over the information overload falling into her lap. She had reason to suspect both, but insufficient evidence to implicate either. She paced down the long corridor replaying Lana's and her conversation in her mind. Why was she so quick to hurl Chris under the bus with hardly a second thought? If J.J. suspected Tony had been involved in illegal activity she would've investigated him herself and made damn sure she had a leg to stand on before uttering her suspicion to a single soul. J.J. suspected Lana probably knew more than she admitted. About what? That was the fifty-million-dollar question.

CHAPTER 26

If one wanted the dirt on a senior FBI executive, there was only one source—the secretary. They were all-knowing, like the maids in stars' homes. Both Freeman's and Cartwright's secretaries entered the bathroom ahead of J.J. and she planned to strike up a casual conversation.

By the time she stepped into the ladies' room, her targets were already deep in discussion from their stalls. But the chatter stopped when she swung the door opened. So, she pushed the door open once more as if she'd walked out, and then tiptoed past them into the last stall on the end. Sitting on the toilet, she pressed her feet against the door and waited for them to continue their conversation freely.

"So what are we doing for lunch today?" said Mrs. Whitehouse, Freeman's secretary. Her voice was distinctively Southern and her dress Southern conservative. Every day a tight hair bun, knee-length skirt suits, and mother's pearls. And she could talk a boundless hole in any head. "If it was up to me, I swear before Jesus I'd have a liquid lunch. I could use a couple of shots after the morning I've had."

"Honey, you're not alone," said Sue Slater, who worked for Cartwright. She was the opposite of Ms. Whitehouse in all ways except Southern charm. "If I had my way I'd keep a bottle in my desk with all the mood swings I have to deal with on a daily basis. I swear that man must be bipolar."

"Get outta here. Mr. Cartwright seems like such a nice guy and a considerate boss. I mean he did give you a gift certificate to the Outback last Christmas. All Mr. Freeman gave me was a word of thanks for all my hard work during the year. Cheap bastard."

The stall doors swung open and shoe heels tapped toward the sink area. They raised their voices above the sound of streaming water.

"I'd gladly take a word of thanks if it meant I didn't have to work with Dr. Jekyll. His mood goes up and down like the friggin' Dow Jones average. One minute he's as happy and jovial as he can be. The next minute he's one Prozac short of the wacky ward."

"Shut your mouth!"

"I swear. And did you hear about his psychotic meltdown yesterday? He freaked out something terrible when Freeman told him he had to take a polygraph exam," Sue said. "We have to take one every five years for our reinvestigations, so I didn't know what the stink was all about. Just unnecessary."

"Unnecessary is right," Delores said. "Why would he have a problem? He couldn't be any more squeaky-clean if he tried."

"Squeaky-clean? Please. That man has more skeletons in his closet than Arlington cemetery." Sue lowered her voice to a whisper. "Rumor was a few years back he had a little sexual rendezvous with an employee in the garage."

"And? If we fired every man in this building who's had an affair, we'd be left with the chaplain and five high school interns."

"Ain't that the truth!" Sue said. "Normally I would agree with you one-hundred percent. But it's my understanding that this employee was *a man*. Yes you heard me correctly—a man!"

Delores gasped. "Stop lyin'!"

J.J. turned her head toward the ceiling, clenched her eyes shut, and shook her head, all the while keeping her gasps inaudible.

"I wish I was, trust me. That's more information than I'd like to know about anyone, especially my boss," Sue said. "Apparently, the person who witnessed the incident didn't offer any proof so Cartwright got off...no pun intended. They gave him a slap on the wrist and promoted him."

"That's the Bureau way," Delores said as they cackled like a couple of hens.

"But he's got a wife and two kids."

"Please! What does that mean these days except that he married some poor gullible woman and screwed her long enough to procreate a couple of times? Haven't you heard of the '*down low*?'"

"No," Delores said. "But I know *low down* when I hear it, and you can't get any lower than that. What a terrible thing to do to his family!"

"He literally hadn't been the same person since the incident happened. All the drama must be taking its toll. But he's certainly lying in the bed he made for himself. He's got no one else to blame," Sue said. "But you better believe this...I'm gonna blame you if I starve to death, that's for sure. Let's get out of here and drink some lunch."

J.J. washed her hands and high-tailed it through the vacant corridor. Cartwright had been involved in a homosexual extramarital affair. He certainly had omitted that tidbit of information on his SF-86, the form required to apply for security clearances. Tony's shock at the news would no doubt mirror her own. More importantly, the secretarial chatter put Cartwright right back at the top of the list.

J.J. paced back to the office. All the pieces of the puzzle fit, but maybe too well. Regardless, the potty gossip more than justified a deeper look. She ripped through the office entrance and brushed past Chris before dashing into Jack's office and closing the door hard behind her.

His curiosity piqued, Chris detoured from his planned trip to the cafeteria and circled back to his desk to retrieve his iPod receiver from its hiding place in his drawer. After slipping the headphones into his ears, he bobbed his head as if listening to music until J.J.'s and Tony's conversation faded in.

"I think we need to move him up on our suspect list. Like yesterday."

"That musta been some trip to the bathroom," Tony said. "What's goin' on?"

"Well, it appears as if our golden boy, Mr. Cartwright, is more like tarnished brass. I overheard that someone caught him having a 'sexual liaison' in the garage a few years back."

"He sure as hell wouldn't be the first," Tony responded nonchalantly.

"He isn't?" J.J. said, squinting daggers from her eyes. "Have you?"

"I plead the fifth," Tony smirked. "Anyway, this is about Cartwright not me. Get back to what you were sayin'."

J.J. eyed him suspiciously. Her mind now more focused on what he'd been doing in the garage and less on the case. "Mhm-hmm. But don't think this subject is over. We'll hit that one again later. Anyway...the rub is his partner was a man."

"Get the fuck outta here. No way," Tony said.

"Yeah way. And I have to meet with him tomorrow. He says he has some information about the mole he wants to impart. Can you imagine that conversation? Awkward!" J.J. said. "And before you ask, no. He didn't give me even a slight hint about what he has to say. Very mysterious. Misty-eyed. If I didn't know better, I'd think he planned to turn himself in."

"Wait wait wait. My head's gonna fuckin' explode," Tony said, hands flailing. "He's a family guy. Two beautiful kids and a wife. No way he was gettin' *Brokeback Mountain* in the garage with some guy. Just didn't happen. Who'd you hear this from?"

"His secretary."

Tony paused. "Hmph! You know what they say about secretaries..."

"You're starting to sound like me," J.J. remarked. "With him so scared to take the polygraph and this secret he's been keeping—something's definitely rotten in Denmark. Even still, being gay isn't a reason people turn, at least not nowadays. Back in the 40s and 50s maybe."

"Yeah," Tony said. "But he wouldn't want this information to get back to his old lady—or his kids, God forbid."

"Mmm. Good point. Perfect opportunity for blackmail. You think Chris is the one putting the screws to him?"

"No offense, but he's too much of a pussy to blackmail anybody."

"Well, if it's not him...then that would mean our guy is innocent. Or..."

Tony hesitated. "Or—"

"Don't say it!"

CHAPTER 27

J .J. hadn't given the network idea more than a passing thought before she spoke to Tony, a spy ring seemed like a very distinct possibility. Now, it was at the forefront of her mind. A network of moles that may or may not know they were working toward the same cause. Wouldn't be the first time. Multiple spies could be providing information to the Russians, perhaps operating from small cells unaware of the others' existence. With Russians so fanatical about compartmenting their cases, even the best agent or analyst would need a Moscow Center view of their operations to connect the dots between sources and determine how much they truly intertwined.

"I'll check the emergency signal to see if our friend at the embassy has any news. Hard to believe he's only got three days left. Then we'll have all the information we need to nail this treasonous bastard. He won't know what hit him."

• • •

Chris gasped. He snatched the buds from his ears and slammed his iPod into the desk drawer.

Another unfortunate turn of events.

No greater misfortune could befall him than J.J. recruiting another source he and Lana didn't know about. A source with access to the files of valuable Russian assets. A mole in the Russian Embassy. Only counterintelligence officers could access those files.

• • •

Monday Evening…

Later that evening, lit scented candles and boxes of hot lo mien helped J.J. and Tony wind down from a long day and gear up for another late night. J.J.'s condo would serve as a makeshift vault but at the moment it was their retreat. Each time the world quieted and they were alone, with no one or nothing to face except each other, the affection and yearning they fought to suppress bubbled to the surface. With every word spoken and unspoken, with every accidental brush of their hands, courteous gesture, or lingering gaze, they tap danced around the white elephant in the room, the issue simmering beneath their already tenuous exteriors.

"You done with that?" Tony asked, reaching his hand out for her empty plate. "I'll take care of the dishes."

J.J. understood Tony's unspoken language. As macho as he could be, he wanted to enjoy the pleasure of showing he cared and she allowed it, smiling and handing him the plate. She admired the sexiness of his form as he strode into the kitchen, each step accented with a magnetic swagger she could barely resist. He rinsed off the dishes in the sink. "Thank you, Agent Donato. You want dessert?"

He pressed his hands against a hand towel and stood in the doorway. "Mmmm," he said in a low throaty rumble. "Whatcha servin'?"

"Cheesecake." She shook her head playfully as she squeezed through the doorway. She brushed against him and every nerve tingled as her back grazed his chest. His body warmed hers for that brief moment.

She'd never wanted anyone as much as she wanted Tony, but they both had so much to lose—including each other. Risking their friendship to satisfy physical yearnings might deliver ecstasy for a night. But the morning would bring a reality neither was prepared to face.

He eased behind her, looking into the refrigerator over her should, his pelvic area lightly pressed against her backside, his excitement undeniable. "Chocolate?"

She snapped upright and turned to face him, her body wanting, her heart falling. Breathless, she said, "Cherry."

He smiled and moved closer, his body invading the empty space between them until none remained. He gazed so deeply into her eyes she could feel the warmth of his soul greeting hers.

With the chill from the refrigerator cooling only her back, she ran her fingertips along his chest until she reached his face. As she laid her palm against his cheek, her eyes drifted shut. With his lips barely a breath away...

They both jerked their heads toward the dining room. J.J.'s cell phone blared in a loud annoying tone.

J.J. snapped out of her trance and tried to force work back to the forefront of her mind.

"I, uhhh...I better get that," she said.

Tony was so hot, and she was willing. But everything happened for a reason. Perhaps they were destined to be apart.

She lifted the phone and checked the caller ID.

Six.

"Figures," she mumbled beneath her breath. It was his Northern Virginia number. *He's back in town.* Memories began to flood her mind, but she pushed them back and refocused her attention on the matters at hand.

Tony looked at her curiously. "Who was 'at?"

"Trust me, you don't even want to know. We should probably get started."

• • •

Overwhelmed with the influx of information they'd been deluged with, the case needed a gut check. They reviewed everything to ensure they weren't spinning their wheels, pinpointed the top suspects so they'd know where to focus their energies.

Positioned at the table, Tony and J.J. glanced at each other and smiled. The air was still thick with possibility, but the moment had been lost. Tony taped to the wall sheets of paper containing the names of everyone on the bigot list.

"Okay. Let's take it from the top. We'll start by assuming neither one of us sold out. So pull down our names right now," J.J. said, grinning. "Unless of course you've got something to tell me, in which case I'll be more than happy to read you your rights and place you under arrest."

J.J. knew the sexy lilt in her tone straddled the line, so she'd have no one but herself to blame if Tony's teasing demolished it.

"Is 'at right? You gonna handcuff me?" he said, batting his eyes playfully. "If so, I gotta tell ya... I prefer the fluffy pink ones...with the little red hearts."

"All right now. Let me find out you've got some freaky sneaky going on!" J.J. said, laughing. Tony in pink fluffy handcuffs? She didn't think so...on second thought. "Listen, I think you better exercise your right to be silent or I'm going to have to charge you with one count of shameless flirting and one count of sharing too much information. Now let's get to work."

"You're the boss," Tony said as he stripped his and J.J.'s name from the wall. "Okay. Now we're left with Jim, Lana, Chris, Director Freeman, Jake, and Sunnie the clerk?"

"Analysts. Don't ever say clerk! You know they hate that," J.J said. "Anyway, I'm going out on a limb and say we can eliminate Freeman. He hadn't yet been briefed on two of the HUMINT operations at the time they were blown, so he couldn't compromise cases he didn't know about."

"Good point," Tony said, pulling Freeman's name from the wall and turning his attention to Jake. "Jake has access to the vault but doesn't have the combos to the cabinet safes, and he's never inside the vault unless he's escorted. No way he could get into the files without one of us noticing."

"True, unless someone else in the vault gave him access. Any chance of that?" J.J. asked. She had no idea whether or not he'd developed relationships with anyone else. Sure, he'd eyed Lana once or twice, but every man in the Bureau had eyed Lana *at least* once or twice.

"Nah. Highly unlikely," Tony responded, removing his name next.

She nodded. "Alright. Jake's off the list," J.J. said. "What do you think about Chris Johnson? This is Jack's prime suspect. And with good reason if the information about his obsessive relationship with Lana is true. And Lana has all but co-signed."

"Yeah, based on what Jack said, he's certainly got the motive to set up Jack. Seems a little extreme though...and where would he get the money? I mean who can afford to let a hundred grand sit in evidence? *Unless* that represents the proverbial drop in the bucket," Tony said. "If you think about it, he's also got the initials. Juliet Charles—J.C., C.J."

"Hmmm. Well, Chris does give me the creeps sometimes. That's for sure. And did you notice his reaction when he found out about Jack's arrest?" J.J. asked. "He stays on the list. He's scheduled to take his poly the day before us. We'll wait and see if he passes and proceed from there."

Tony chuckled and moved Chris's name up to the top of the wall.

"What about Jim Cartwright? Another J.C. –Juliet Charles. I know. I know. They wouldn't be that obvious," Tony said. "Besides, he seemed like a pretty solid guy…until today." Beginning his career in white collar crime, Tony had known Cartwright only a short time but he'd trusted J.J.'s instincts.

"Every mole seems like a pretty solid guy at some point. It's how they get hired," J.J. said. "But he didn't want his family to find out about his leanings. That alone made him vulnerable to recruitment."

"Yeah, and since Cartwright spearheaded the entire investigation, if that's what you want to call it, he should definitely stay on the list," he said. "Moving on. What about your favorite person—Lana?"

"Oh, you mean, Miss Every-case-she-touches-turns-to-shit? I don't trust her as far as I can throw her," J.J. said. "Wait let me take that back because I could probably toss her a few hundred feet on a good day."

"You probably could, but aside from excessive blondness, what's her real crime? Granted, I've never seen an agent lose so many service weapons," he said.

J.J. couldn't have agreed more and standing in Lana's presence physically set J.J.'s nerves on edge.

"Trust me, if she had a penis and big feet she'd be at the top of my list, but Dmitriyev specifically noted male footprints."

"Okay. Lana's off the list. What about Sunnie…the *analyst*?"

"I heard she took her polygraph exam today and passed with flying colors, so we can pull her off the list. This means she's got vault access, so she can help us out. Bat those beautiful brown Italian eyes at her and she'll do anything for you, Ton-nyyyyy," J.J. said mimicking the sing-song sound present in Sunnie's voice whenever she spoke his name.

"Gimme a break, she's the same age as my little sister. I don't think so," Tony said. "Anyway, we're looking at Chris Johnson, Jim Cartwright, and we may as well keep Jack on the radar. So, what's next on the game plan?"

They both knew the drill. Espionage cases were textbook. Follow the trail of the agent experiencing professional, personal, and financial lows, and you'd find the rat. Time to dig a little deeper. And only one place in the Bureau held the information they needed.

"Well, I think you need to ask our favorite analyst to get her hands on their personnel files so we can look at their financial statements. That's gonna be pretty tough for Cartwright because he's an assistant director, but she knows people who know people."

"We also need to keep an eye out for polygraph results." Tony's face lit up. "My boy Mike Sullivan is a senior polygrapher. We were in the same class at the academy. I'll reach out to him and let him know what's going on," Tony said.

Tony always "hadda" guy or "knewa" guy.

"I wonder if Cartwright has taken his polygraph. You heard anything?" Tony asked.

"I don't know, but that's a damn good question. Contact Mike as soon as you can. If we can eliminate him from the list, we'll know exactly who the ICE Phantom is."

CHAPTER 28

Early Tuesday Morning…

"It's Jim." Cartwright woke up and immediately left a voicemail for J.J. She couldn't miss this meeting. It wasn't quite 5 am. He knew she wouldn't answer but hopefully she'd detect the urgency. Their meeting was critical to the advancement of her career—and the *end* of his. "Don't forget about the plan this morning. It's critical."

Sleepless, Jim Cartwright lay in bed thinking about how much he adored his little girls, watching the sunlight drift through the picture window. They'd been the light of his life since the day, no, the moment he first laid eyes on them. Twins. Seven fertility treatments and fifty thousand dollars to become the father he'd always dreamed he'd be. But as his misfortune would dictate, his children would be delivered in the midst of his financial ruin. When Gloria told him the news, he'd just returned from his attorney's office where he prepared to file for bankruptcy, even though doing so could have cost him his security clearances and thus his job. He understood the consequences of taking such an extreme financial action. After all, he'd once taught the very same security classes that now haunted him.

Report changes in your financial situation.

Report all contacts with foreign nationals.

Secrets and lies. Lies and secrets. What a tangled web we weave, he thought to himself. He'd done neither and now he'd be forced to pay the piper a few short hours later when it was his turn to take his polygraph examination. He thought he'd have a little more time to strategize and ensure his family would be okay if for some reason he never returned home. Amazing how one call from the FBI Director could help clear the polygraph schedule the next day. For Freeman, ordering the examinations was simply a matter of course.

For Cartwright, however, it'd probably mean the end of the life he'd worked so hard and sacrificed so much to build.

He reached onto the nightstand and grabbed his cell phone. Dreading the call, he took a few deep breaths before slowly punching her numbers into the phone. He was tempted to hang up; she answered before he could press the button.

"Yes," Alex said, her voice cold and dry. The call was contrary to his communications plan, and he knew she'd be irritated. But since it would be his last, he didn't really give a damn about protocol. "I thought I told you never to call me at this number. It can be traced."

Her Russian accent was unusually perceptible, perhaps because she sounded angry.

"It's an emergency. I had no other choice."

"An emergency," she snapped. "What is it?"

"I have to take a polygraph at ten this morning, and I think we both know this will not go well," he said. "And frankly, I—I can't do this anymore."

"I understand," she responded, "but what will your family do for money?"

"They'll have my pension. And I was hoping in exchange for some information about the mole investigation, you might be willing to provide me with one last payment, so I can leave them with some financial security."

She paused.

He fully expected her to say no as compassion wasn't in her vocabulary.

She grumbled. "Okay...meet me at the usual spot. Nine o'clock."

Cartwright sat on the edge of the bed and pushed his feet into his brown leather Father's Day slippers. He placed his arms into his like-colored Christmas robe and made his way to his favorite place in the house.

"Girls! It's time to wake uuuuuup," he sang as he entered the twins' bedroom. Every morning, he was the one who got the kids off to school because Gloria worked the midnight shift at the hospital.

He waited for them to respond, knowing they wouldn't (as part of the routine), so he knocked on the door and cast his eyes on his pretending-to-be-asleep princesses. "Good morning sleepy heads!" he said as he eased over to their bunk beds. The sound of his steps getting closer and closer made the oldest (by one minute) giggle with her head beneath the blanket.

"Annnniiiie," he sang, "Time to wake uuuuuup."

She giggled again as he pulled the blanket back and blew a zerbert into her cheek, causing her to roar with laughter. "Morning, Daddy!"

"My turn. My turn," Abby said, laying on her side with her cheek poked out from beneath the bottom bunk. "I'm ready."

"You're supposed to be sleeping!" Annie admonished and then pouted. "You're ruining the whole thing,"

"I beg to differ," Jim said to Annie. "A zerbert is the best part of the day, even if you know it's coming. Now you two get up and get dressed. Daddy's got a long day ahead of him."

"You gonna lock up some bad guys, Daddy? Like the last time we saw you on TV?" Annie asked, referring to the FBI's press conference following the FBI New York office's arrests. Cartwright served as a spokesperson for the case involving Russian spies operating under commercial cover.

"Yes, baby. Daddy's gonna take care of one *big bad guy* today, and get him off the streets," he said, turning away quickly so they couldn't see his sullen expression.

His chin fell to his chest. This time *he* was the bad guy he'd send to jail.

He rushed the girls through their morning routines in order to steal a few moments to collect his thoughts before he did what his conscience demanded. He'd known for many months he couldn't keep up with the pretense in his life anymore. Sooner or later truth would find its way out. He'd only hoped he would be in a position to do some damage control for his family's sake. Now, *he* was controlled by the damage—and the consequences would be severe. But when he looked at his hazel-eyed angels, those two precious souls, in his mind his actions, no matter how deplorable on the surface, were equally the greatest gifts and the greatest curses of his life.

He stepped into his walk-in closet to select his suit for the day. He first picked up a light gray suit with a pinkish shirt, but he knew there'd be a lot of sweating involved. Next he looked at the black suit but it felt too morbid. Finally, he settled on the navy blue suit. It was his kids' favorite. Enough said.

He poked his head out of his bedroom door. "Girls? You getting dressed?"

"Yeeeees!" they yelled in unison.

"Okay, well, you've only got ten minutes before we have to leave so hurry up!"

The choir sang, "Okay, Daddy!"

He took a brief shower and dressed as quickly as possible. His appointment started at ten a.m. and it was already past eight. Where had the time flown? His mind had sunk deep in thought swirling with fear. He took the envelope he'd prepared and wrote on the front of it. "For J.J. McCall only."

In the sole quiet moments of the morning, the drunken moment that would forever change his life flooded his mind.

CHAPTER **29**

It was December 2005, years before Freeman had been appointed Director and subsequently banned all alcohol-related events at FBI facilities across the country. Although seemingly drastic, Freeman's extreme policy followed an agent's fatal hit-and-run accident which killed a civilian after a holiday party. The Organized Crime and Drug Section hosted what would be the last and final of the headquarters' Christmas shindigs. Drunken executives and agents, who wouldn't as soon spit on you if you were on fire when they were sober, sloshed around hugging a little too long, kissing a little too often, and touching a little too much.

One conversation about everything and nothing led to one surreptitious touch. One touch led to many lingering stares. The lingering stares resulted in a leisurely stroll to the FBI garage where they'd planned to release the drunken passion simmering within.

Jim's mind had become foggy and unfocused. He couldn't have been thinking . . . *straight*. Because if he had been thinking straight, he would've remembered his wife and his children that night, and he'd never have let Rex stand so close to him. He'd never have allowed Rex's lips to press against his. He'd never have found himself stripping his shirt off in the backseat of a fogged up Bureau-issued vehicle. And when their carnal cravings had nearly reached their drunken peaks, and they reached to unbuckle their respective belts, he'd never have glanced through the window to see those piercing blue eyes glaring back at him with contempt and disgust.

And he would never have accepted the $200,000 in payments that freed him from creditors, but held him hostage to his extortionists and his own lies and deceit.

Nothing of the sort would ever have happened if he had been thinking . . . *straight*.

"Daddy! We're ready!" his girls cried out to him, a welcome interruption to his ugly thoughts.

He wiped the warm tears from his cheeks. "I'll be down in just a minute!"

He'd finished collecting all the important documents and the last of the proceeds from his illicit activities, which his wife would need in his absence. Between the cash and his pension, they wouldn't have to worry about money for some time. He placed everything Gloria and J.J. needed in her lingerie drawer where she'd be sure to find them that evening. He checked in the mirror and gave himself a last once-over, straightened his tie, and made his way down the stairs and out of the house.

As they backed out of the driveway he'd resurfaced on a rare free Saturday, he took one long look, not at his house, but at the home he'd made for his wife and children.

He smiled.

"What's so funny, Daddy?" Abby asked.

"Daddy's not laughing," Jim said. "I was just thinking you girls make me so happy."

"Turn on the cd, pleeeeeease?" Annie asked.

"Sure, sweetie," he replied.

He pressed power button and the sounds of *Barney and Friends* filled the car.

Fitting, he thought. *It's time to face the music.*

• • •

Jim checked his watch, his stomach twisting into tightly wound knots. It was 9 am. The irony of it all. He'd worked his entire career to be the good guy, to build the reputation of an agent who was impervious to corruption, to serve as a patriot. After his inevitable failed polygraph and subsequent confession, he'd be hauled off to jail like a common criminal.

What his wife would say? What would his girls think of him?

Would they remember with pride the father who tucked them into bed every night and read them bedtime stories? The father who made them Mickey Mouse-shaped pancakes and brushed their hair into crooked ponytails? Or would they remember with disgrace the father who sold out his country, who had affairs with men, and who they'd be forced to visit behind barbed-wire fences for the rest of his natural born days? And how could he, the father who loved them so, live with the thought that each morning when they arose and each night before they fell asleep, they'd know their father couldn't kiss them goodnight or wake with them in the morning because he was locked up in some eight-by-eight cell for twenty-three hours a day? He cried the kind of heaving sob your soul releases when filled with the deepest sorrow and regret.

Jim pulled into the scenic overlook on George Washington Parkway and stared at the rainbow of fall leaves across the river in the Georgetown area as *Ava Maria* blared from his radio. A few moments later, Alex arrived, parked her car beside his, and slipped into his passenger seat. He shifted in his seat to face her. She appeared angry and agitated and immediately began scanning his vehicle.

"What are you looking for?" Cartwright asked Alex.

She opened his center console with her gloved hand. "I just want to make sure you don't have any recording devices."

"I know you're pissed, but I had no idea Freeman would make me take the poly," he said, shifting his head with her every move.

"My concern is not that you must take the polygraph. My concern is what you plan to say during the pretest examination. For me, the stakes are too high for weakness. I have everything to lose, including my life," she said, reaching her hand into the glove compartment. She pulled out his weapon and aimed it at his head.

"I swear," he pleaded, trembling as his face drowned in fear-borne tears. "I will not reveal your identity."

She reached into her coat pocket and retrieved a small unlined notepad. The first sheet contained a pre-written note.

"I know you won't!" she said. "Now, shut up and copy this!"

Jim trembled and shook his head feverishly, so afraid he could almost smell death permeate the car. "No, I won't."

"Copy the fucking note!" she screamed maniacally, breaking her usual cool demeanor.

Cartwright's hand trembled and tears washed down his face as he retrieved a pen from his suit pocket and began to write.

"Put it up there," she said, motioning her head toward the dashboard.

Jim slipped the note on top and shook his head as tears swept across his cheeks in waves of sorrow. She grabbed the notepad and shoved it inside her pocket.

"My girls!" he said. "Please, don't do this."

She pressed the barrel of his Bureau-issued Glock firmly against his temple. Shivering, he clamped his eyes shut until his girls' smiles appeared.

Cold and empty, devoid of humanity, she pulled the trigger.

Blood and brain fragments splattered on the window. Some on her own person. Unfazed she wiped her fingerprints from the gun and placed the gun in his hand before allowing it to fall to the floor. Cartwright's body slumped against the door, life abandoning his body on a brief, shallow breath.

"Rest in peace, *golubaya bl'yad!*" she hissed, spitting the words *gay whore* in Russian as she exited the car.

Fall had become Jim Cartwright's favorite time of the year. He fell in love in the fall. He married in the fall. His children were born in the fall. And, in disgrace and despair, he died in the fall.

205

CHAPTER 30

Later Tuesday…

Chris busied himself around the office through the early afternoon, passing the time, collecting his thoughts. His mind whirred with fear after eavesdropping on J.J. and Tony. If they had indeed recruited a Russian counterintelligence officer at the Embassy, Chris's days were numbered, life as he knew it was over. Unless he could somehow rid himself of the source first.

The office walls bore down on him. His mind clouded, and he couldn't think straight. He decided to get some air to soothe his angst. He pulled open the door to leave and literally bumped into Lana on the way out.

Her hand covered her mouth as she repeatedly sniffed. Streaks of black mascara tracked down her cheeks. She dabbed a tissue under her eyes as Chris placed his hand on her shoulder and eased her backward into a corner so they could speak in private.

"What's wrong with you, Lana? What happened?"

Distraught, she could barely compose herself to speak. Instead of words, she released sobs. "You...you didn't hear what happened?"

Chris let out a long breath. His patience had vanished before she spoke. He didn't care what happened. Nothing could be more important than the mole in the Russian Embassy. "I've got a bunch of shit on my mind right now, Lana. Hear what?"

"It's Cartwright. He's dead!"

Chris froze in shock as his knees gave way. Struggling to catch his breath, he nearly stumbled toward the floor. He pressed his hand against the wall, trying to prevent his free fall, but he was six years too late. His descent had begun long ago, when he met *her*. He started to ask why but he knew the reason for Cartwright's death before Lana uttered a syllable.

"He killed himself. Virginia State Police found him….at an overlook . . . off the GW parkway," she managed to say between heaves.

He fought to fill his lungs but the guilt strangled him. Darkness and evil gripped his heart. Had anything he'd done or any of his sorry reasons been worth ending a good man's life? He grasped for the strength to not just to look at Lana, but to see her…for the first time.

"Shot himself in the he—" she cut herself off. "Are you okay, Chris?"

"But...but h-h-he's got two kids! I...I can't...breathe," he stammered, each word labored. He pressed his back flush against the wall as he slid to the floor.

Lana knelt down beside him, wrapped him in her arms.

"What have I done? What have I done?" he cried in a whisper.

"Chris, listen to me, now. Listen to me!" she urged, clenching her teeth together, angry at his weak display. "You've got to pull yourself together. How can you blame yourself?"

He peered at her, glared with contempt, pulled his body back as if disgusted by the threat of her touch. "How can you, of all people, say that to me?" He propped his elbows on his thigh and dropped his face into the palms of his hands.

"I can say it because it's the truth," she replied, her voice suddenly cooler, more callous. "Now be a *man*!" she scorned through gritted teeth.

Lana shifted her emotions like flipping a switch, too busy playing hardened agent to express any genuine emotion. He marveled at her disaffection. Relations between them had chilled. With every day that passed he wondered if he really knew her at all. He longed to be in the arms of his Koshechka, only she could make his hurt go away.

"No one could have predicted Cartwright would go this far. Not you. Not me. Not anyone. Rumors have been flying around the Bureau for years. You know that better than I do. He should've been forthright."

Chris drew in a shallow breath, his head fell back against the wall. "Hmph," he said. "Maybe that's the real lesson here—honesty."

"Look, I won't let you fall apart over this," she snapped. "We all liked Cartwright, but *you're* an agent, *you're* still here, and *you* still have a job to do."

He raised his head, ran his fingers through his hair, grabbed the back of his neck, and arched his back before working his way to his feet.

"You okay, now?" Lana said, patting his back. "Please, don't do this to yourself."

His stood and traced the grout lines in the floor tile with the tip of his shoe. "I'm done talking about this," he continued. "You've advised me of the situation. It's over," he said. "Now, I need to get out of here for a few minutes and clear my head."

"Look, I'm here for you. Really. Anything I can help with?" she asked.

"You haven't done enough?"

What he needed she could clearly no longer give. Perhaps she could shed light on upcoming embassy events instead.

"On second thought, maybe you can," he said. "Listen, I need to know. Have you received any reports indicating something unusual's going on at the Russian embassy in the next few days? More specifically in the next three days?"

She combed her fingers through her hair, tapping her heel at a rapid pace. Finally, she shook her head. "Nothing springs to mind why?"

"Damn! I was hop—"

"Oh! Wait a minute," she interrupted, "Vorobyev! The security officer is scheduled to depart on Friday," she said. "I haven't seen a visa notice for his replacement though. Still keeping an eye out for it."

"Vorobyev?" he said, the sound of his heart pounding a panicked rhythm. "Shit!"

Chris threw his head back and expelled a frustrated breath. Of course. It must be Vorobyev. He'd have access to the asset files and would probably know the mole's identity.

His body core burned like fire, sweat beads forced from his pores. Scared, confused, he didn't know his next move. He'd grown so tired. Cartwright was dead, and Chris had blood on his hands, as if he'd pulled the trigger himself. And the light at the end of the tunnel was attached to the barbed-wire fence that secured Supermax.

Spending the rest of his life in prison was a chilling prospect but paled in comparison to his present misery. The boat, the cars, the houses, probably worth a few million. But none worth the price of honor or peace of mind. He'd become a prisoner of his own lust. And with one path leading to execution, only one escape remained.

Vorobyev.

Chris couldn't allow him to pass the mole's identity to J.J. and Tony. His life would be over and his dearest Koshechka would be embroiled in the biggest counterintelligence scandal in the history of the United States.

"And?" Lana asked, still baffled by his concerned expression.

"He's the highest ranking counterintelligence officer in the residency...and he's leaving in *three* days!"

Lana shrugged. "I'm turning grey here."

He lowered his head and whispered. "I think there is a very real possibility J.J. and Tony recruited Vorobyev."

"What...what makes you say this? Vorobyev is declared—he can't engage in operational activity."

"I, uhhh, *overheard* them talking in Jack's office earlier today. J.J. mentioned that on Friday she'd have all the information she needed to nail the mole—ICE Phantom. She specifically said 'her friend' only had three days left."

She shook her head, her expression more urgent, tense. "No. This can't be right. If J.J. recruited him, we'd have a record of it. I've reviewed all the active case files."

"I know what I heard. Too bad your precious Jack is locked up and can't get you access," Chris growled. "I'm sure you'd love to get your hands on that one."

She spat in his direction and then spun around sharply to walk away. He grabbed Lana's shoulder to stop her, faced her, and then placed a gentle finger beneath her chin.

"I'm sorry. I didn't mean what I said. I'm just…the pressure's getting to me. And I'm taking my frustration out on you," he said. "I need to get out of here."

"Where are you going?"

He shrugged. There were few places he and his pregnant Koshechka could hide from the FBI. *The escape plan*, he thought. *Now is the time.* They had passports, a flat awaiting them, and a hero's welcome. Just one more financial boost, courtesy of Vorobyev, would give them the cash they needed to ensure their security for years to come.

CHAPTER 31

Tuesday Night…

Chris visited his Koshechka's house, a small cape cod in the Van Ness area of Washington, D.C. She turned the fixer-upper into an updated masterpiece; it was modest enough to suit her cover. And for Chris, it was home, the place where he could wrap Koshechka in his arms and confide to her his deepest fears. She soothed his mind; her soft body warmed and blanketed him in security. Her touch triggered a passion he never wanted to end.

"Listen, my dear," he said basking in their post-coital glow. "In light of this Cartwright's death…and not to mention the Vorobyev information—"

"Stop!" she interrupted. "Are you *positive?* He's very well respected. I've known him for years. He and my father worked together in Washington."

"And?"

"And we must verify what you believe you overheard before we act. I forbid you to report this without my approval. And furthermore, I'll see to it that you receive no payment."

"*Forbid?* Don't you understand?" He propped up his left elbow and rested his head in his hand. "We have no time to verify. We work in intel. There are no absolutes. We base our decisions on the best information available at the moment. This is what we've got."

"We're talking about a man's life here. Not to mention the fact that I have no diplomatic immunity. I'm a citizen now. Don't *you* understand? I'm subject to Title 18, with no diplomatic immunity, just like you!" she said.

"A man's life? What about Cartwright?"

In silence, he stared at her in the eerie calm.

Her tone still urgent, she continued, "If you're wrong, they'll intensify the search for the mole. Relations between Russian and the West are deteriorating because of that fucking missile shield. If the security officer is arrested for cooperating with the FBI and the resident lodges a complaint with the State Department, this could have international implications."

Chris remained defiant, refused to concede. "If Vorobyev passes that information to J.J. *You and I may both die.* I can't take any chances. We have an emergency plan to defect so let's execute it."

"Only as a last resort."

"Can't you see, my love? *This is* the last resort." He lowered his voice to a heavy whisper. "Do you want to give birth to our baby in prison *before you die?* Is that how this ends?"

"No," she said. "But—"

"But what? This is game over. If we don't give up Vorobyev, he'll give up you and me," Chris implored. "Even if we sacrifice Vorobyev, we'll be on an even shorter list of mole suspects, especially with Jack in jail and Cartwright dead. We must defect."

"There's got to be another way. I'll think of something."

"Are you kidding me? Why is this still under discussion?" he pleaded. "Now, either you're with me or you're against me. *I've made* my move."

He bolted out of bed, feeling through the darkness for the lamp. She gripped his arm firmly, yanked him toward her. Although small in stature, she was government trained in hand-to-hand combat. She could take

Chris on her worst day. And unlike him, she had the balls to follow through on any threat.

She lowered her voice, her tone angry and stern. "Cross me and you'll be making the mistake of your life. Allow me to come up with another solution," Koshechka urged, desperate to change his mind. She pulled the covers back to expose her negligee and distract him, but Chris would not be deterred.

His glare sliced through her as he snatched his arm from her grip. His lips flattened as he snarled, "I'm afraid it's already too late for that!"

Chris dressed himself as she handed him his clothes to hasten his exit. He charged through the living room, his feet padding hard against the pristine wood floors. A moment later the door slammed, rattling the windows. For the first time he exerted his will, strengthened his backbone. The deed was done, and there was nothing to left to do except wait.

• • •

Koshechka grunted in anger as she lifted her cell phone from the mahogany antique dresser, the one for which she haggled during an antiquing jaunt in Williamsburg, Virginia. Raking her fingers through her hair, she scanned the room, caught her glance in the mirror, and immediately looked away. She'd underestimated her control over Chris, a critical mistake. Now, Chris had backed her into a corner and her mission was incomplete.

She dialed the phone to call him. She hadn't planned to fall in love but...his smile. He flashed it during a training class. She couldn't resist it, nor his chiseled frame and cocky charm. She was drawn to confident men. And unlike Chris and Jack, he possessed an inner strength neither of them could fathom.

He answered after the first ring.

"I should've known he couldn't be trusted but I thought I could contain him. He's such a fuck up!" she said. "All these years. All this work."

"Calm down, baby. Calm down. What's going on?" his sweet voice trilled in her ear.

"There's no time to explain right now. But what's that thing you always say? When all hell breaks loose, only the devil survives?"

He smiled. "Yeah. Made that up myself."

"Well, we need to make arrangements to defect—this week—or we won't survive."

• • •

Early Wednesday Night…

Freeman lay in bed, sleep-deprived, restless. Cartwright's death stirred up a tornado of conflicting emotion. Anger. Confusion. Resentment. Sadness. They'd been friends for years, since Freeman's prosecutor days. They were golf buddies. He'd attended Jim's daughters' christening, and now he was gone, a single gunshot to the head. Rita had pressed him to go to bed and attempt to sleep, but not even three Hennessey cocktails could settle him down. He crept downstairs to his office, thought he'd catch up on some reports in his favorite recliner and leave his Rayna undisturbed. Nothing like a stack of National Security Letters to knock him out for the count. As sleep skulked in an hour later, soft footsteps padded on the staircase and an angel's voice sounded from the study's threshold.

"Baby," Rita said, "I know you're sick about Jim, but you really need to come to bed. Let's go. It's almost two in the morning, and you've got to wake up for work in a couple of hours."

He smiled, laid his eyeglasses on the side table, and turned out the lamp. "I just was on my way upstairs when I heard you tiptoeing in here."

"Good," she said. "Had to make sure you weren't down here making 1-900 calls again."

Russell laughed. He hadn't had many occasions to do that in recent days. The stress was stifling, but Rayna was his balance personified. Thankfully, for his sake, she'd forgiven him for the birthday debacle.

"How about I give you a little back rub to help you relax?"

He smiled. Tonight he was in the mood to accept and reciprocate; he needed the comfort of her touch. "All right, now. That's what I'm talking about," he said, following her to the staircase.

The second he placed his foot on the first riser, the secure phone rang, the one the Bureau had installed in his home for emergencies. *This damn well better be important*, he thought, anxious to receive what his wife had waiting for him.

He let out a hard frustrated sigh. "Let me get this and I'll be up shortly. Must be urgent for them to call me at this time of night."

"You want me to wait for you?"

"No, no," he said with a wink. "I'll see you upstairs in a few minutes."

He paced to his desk and placed his hand on the receiver. It stopped ringing. Just as he turned to leave, it rang again.

"Freeman."

"Uhhh...yes, sir. This is John," said John Nixon, the Acting Deputy Assistant Director for Counterintelligence until Cartwright's replacement could be identified. "Sorry to call you so early but we've had a few developments, and I thought you should be aware of the situation before you arrived at headquarters in the morning."

"Uhh...no problem. I couldn't sleep anyway," Freeman said. "What's going on?"

"Well, sir, we received a call from the chief of Russia House at the CIA," John said, referring to the CIA's center for Russian operations. "He's received very reliable information indicating Stanislav Vorobyev, the security officer at the Russian Embassy, has been detained and interrogated for cooperating with the FBI. As you know, targeting a declared officer violates long-standing diplomatic protocols. Now, the SVR Resident, through the Russian Ambassador, is planning to lodge a protest with the State Department first thing tomorrow."

"What?!" Freeman said, folded over, barely still on his feet. He gripped his forehead. "Vorobyev is not working with us, and my agents would never target a declared officer."

"Well, the Russians seem to think they have it on pretty good authority that he's indeed cooperating with the FBI."

"Lord, have mercy," Freeman said.

"There's more, sir."

"More?"

"Unfortunately, yes," John said. "According to Russia House, Moscow's planning to expel the CIA security officer from Moscow station in retaliation."

"You're shitting me!" said Freeman. "Always tit-for-tat with these guys."

"And the Chief of Station."

"What!"

"And every operations officer they can identify, which according to the list is all of them except three NOC officers operating under commercial cover," John said. "This will decimate the station and it will take the Agency years to refill those slots."

"Jesus H. Christ."

"They'll all be expelled, possibly PNG'd, and forced to leave their posts within days unless, by some miracle, we can somehow prove the accusations are false."

He collapsed into his chair. The ramifications would be disastrous. An expulsion only meant they'd have to leave the country. Officers declared persona non grata had to leave and could never return. Ever. It was a career-ending diplomatic sanction that would no doubt further endanger the already tenuous cooperation between the FBI and CIA.

"What the hell is this, the Cold War?" Freeman said. "Did Scottie beam me back into the 1970s without my knowledge? The CIA has got to be livid."

"I believe that should win the prize for understatement of the decade, sir," John said. "And they want Agent McCall's head roasted on a spike and her operations shut down. Unless we do some real damage control and find out who's at the root of all these compromises, we are going to be the scorn of the intelligence community . . . more so than we already are."

Freeman exhaled. "I refuse to throw my agent under the bus and they don't tell me how to run my agency. Agent McCall is doing her job. I won't suspend her unless she's broken the law," he said. "With that in mind, we're not going to take this on the chin."

"What do you need, sir?"

"Pull together a list of all Russian intelligence officers operating in the United States, *including* their NOCs. Let the State Department know we are prepared to reciprocate, officer for officer, if a single CIA employee is expelled," Freeman ordered. "If it takes us years to recoup, it'll take them decades. That should shut down this noise until we can figure out a long-term solution."

"Yes, sir."

"We'll discuss this further in the morning. Bright and early. Will that be all for now?"

"Isn't that enough?"

What a fucking nightmare! Freeman thought to himself. He hung up the phone and stood to head upstairs to his bedroom. His chest tightened and his left arm went numb, just for a moment. The feeling subsided with a few deep breaths. His job had already taken an emotional toll on him and his marriage. Now it was gunning for his body.

Whatever the blood-pumping organ inside his chest had planned, it would have to wait. He simply did not have time for the heart attack and nervous breakdown he so richly deserved. No, there were far more important things on his agenda.

And at the top of the list, he had a mole to catch.

CHAPTER 32

Wednesday Morning…

"**M**ake them stop, Aleksey!" Vorobyev cried out, his body writhed in pain. "I know you're watching. I am innocent! For God's sake, make them stop!"

The linoleum tiles cooled Stanislav Vorobyev's face, still stinging from the jarring strike that sent him crashing to the floor. The gash in his forehead, left by the ringed hand of Golikov's goon, dripped the blood that trickled into and burned his eye. His vision blurred, and he could no longer distinguish facial features, only darkened shadows. Each attempt to push himself upright was met with a brutal shoe tip in his gut. The force of a heel in the core of his spine numbed his limbs. He was innocent of the trumped up charges, but reasoning with the insane proved a futile exercise. He had served his country with honor and so steeled his determination to rise from this undeserved hell.

"You pig!" Igor, Golikov's junior officer, spat. "We have very reliable information from our source that you are spying for the Americans and passing critical information to the FBI. Tell us who you're meeting with and what you've told them."

Vorobyev pushed the palm of his hand against the floor, struggled to get his bearings. "I . . . am a man, not a dog, nor a pig! I will say nothing more until you allow me to sit up and speak to you like a man."

Vasiliy, a large man with an enforcer build and mentality, stepped out of the room and returned a moment later. He and Igor wordlessly glanced at each other before grabbing Vorobyev by his arms and pulling him up. With his eyelids pressed together tightly, he braced himself. It was coming. The fist would collide with his abdomen.

And then...the unexpected.

A chair pressed against the back of his legs. They sat him down.

"Talk," Vasiliy barked.

He folded his hands together, as if preparing to pray. "For the last time, I have told you I am not working for the Americans," Vorobyev snarled. "*I am not* working for the FBI. *I don't know* who your so-called reliable source is, but if this is the intelligence they have passed to you, then you better re-evaluate the validity of all his information."

The back of Vasiliy's powerful hand collided with Vorobyev's jaw. He fell to the floor in a painful thud, blood spurted from his mouth. Silence filled the room as Vorobyev anticipated the next swing. He couldn't see, but he knew who dealt the blow. Every sound and smell was magnified. Vasiliy reeked of cigarette smoke and Igor of cabbage and coffee. Suddenly, the clack of the shoe heels shuffled toward the door. It opened and closed. The two goons had exited the room, leaving Vorobyev sprawled in the floor.

He was alone. Heard nothing except the sound of his heartbeat...and betrayal.

Vorobyev propped up his upper body with his forearm, turned toward the one-way glass, and cried out, "Aleksey! I know you're there! How could you let them do this? You know the truth. End this madness . . . or be a man and kill me yourself!"

His cries were met with silence as his body wrenched and curled into a fetal mass.

• • •

Dmitriyev could barely stomach the mushrooming guilt. His mind took him to a cruel place when he imagined what his and Plotnikov's fathers must have endured at the hands of their own interrogators. How they must've begged and pleaded for their own lives, with each appeal landing on deaf ears. He could almost hear Uncle Sergey declare his innocence until his very last breath echoing and alarming until the bullet shattered the back of his skull.

The imaginings haunted Dmitriyev, obliterated his self-denial. Retribution for a family wronged was no longer sufficient. The means no longer justified the end, not in the wake of his own treachery.

Before watching Vorobyev's thrashing, Dmitriyev had never questioned whether cooperating with the FBI had been the right thing to do, for him, for his family, for his country. His thirst for revenge seemed just, especially for a country that thrived on the backs of its citizens and governed with intimidation and a dogged lust for economic and military supremacy. Even in the new democracy there'd been little freedom. Voting rights were laughable. What democracy could exist in this Russia where the communist KGB and the new political elite were one and the same? The old guard had gone "legit" during the break-up of the Soviet Union, but nothing had changed except the color of the uniforms, the names on the buildings, and the effort expended to cover-up the human rights realities. Democracy stood among the biggest frauds Russian politicians had perpetrated against its citizens in the 21st Century.

Dissidents had been committed to Russian mental institutions and drugged into comas for the audacity of independent thought. Such "traitors" understood better than most citizenry that corruption and deceit had become so deeply woven into the fabric of Russian society, its people could no longer distinguish might from right.

Dmitriyev realized he loved Russia, not for what it had been, rather for what it could be—but only if....

Still the unintended effect of his revenge glared down on him like the eye of God. Innocent men would be tortured, their families made to suffer for crimes they had not committed. He was no better than the state he scorned.

Standing at the fork in the road, Dmitriyev could choose one of two paths. On one side, he could turn himself in and confess. On the other side, self-preservation. Dmitriyev's path was clear and ungenerous. He could barely muster the courage to watch, let alone make the confession necessary to end Vorobyev's suffering and initiate his own. And his fate was tied to his brother's. If he attempted to interfere in the interrogation, the suspicion surrounding himself and Viktor would most certainly intensify. Even if he could subject himself to such scrutiny, he refused to implicate his brother. No, he needed a way to help Vorobyev without implicating himself. Agent McCall must agree to help him clear Vorobyev's name. If not, he would cease cooperation immediately and provide no further information, including the name of the traitor they so desperately desired. He had no choice.

Shoulders slumped, Dmitriyev stood stoically as he watched Vorobyev endure strike after endless strike, each meant to weaken his resolve and loosen his tongue. Only he knew Vorobyev had nothing to confess. He thought, for one brief moment, that Vorobyev appeared ready to concede in order to end his own suffering, but his comrade Stan was proud, a family man, and even if a confession meant the end of his own suffering, it would certainly spell the beginning of worse for his loved ones. So Vorobyev refused, willingly accepting each blow, indignant and defiant as an innocent man should be.

Vasiliy and Igor had meted out their worst and Vorobyev survived bruised but not broken. They left the interrogation room to speak with Dmitriyev.

"He refuses to talk," Igor said, sweat pouring from the bulge protruding from his neck. "What should we do?"

"Perhaps it is time to consider that he has nothing to say. Or, if he does, he will never speak it to us." Dmitriyev turned toward the interrogators. "Get him cleaned up and offer him something to eat. Sweep his room for any kind of communications equipment, then we'll hold him in his residence until it is time for him to depart on Friday."

"Ah, good idea," Vasiliy said.

"I'm certain we'll get nothing from him tonight and he must be strong enough to stand trial," Dmitriyev said.

"Trial? Ha!" Vasiliy interjected. "He should be so lucky. Golikov has been informed and will certainly be awaiting his return on Friday. He and that pig Plotnikov will die together."

Dmitriyev shuttered at the chill in the Vasiliy's voice. He needed an excuse to leave so he could mark an emergency signal and request Agent McCall's assistance. He'd been diligent about establishing his daily habits and routines. No one would be suspicious when he left for Starbucks.

"Listen, while you both inspect his room and help him get cleaned up, I'm going to pick up my coffee and smokes. Looks like we are in for a long day and, possibly, an even longer night. I'll be back shortly and then we can draft our reports to Moscow."

Igor and Vasiliy both chuckled, and then Vasiliy said, "Whatever would you do without your daily coffee fix, Comrade Dmitriyev? We'll see you when you return."

• • •

Vorobyev jumped abruptly, his nerves stood on edge as the distant footsteps closed in on him. Igor and Vasiliy re-entered the room and a slight breeze wafted across Vorobyev's bloody face.

"You're finished for the day," Vasiliy snapped. "We're taking you to get cleaned up and eat. You'll need your strength for what awaits you when you return Moscow," he said with an evil grin as he turned to face Igor. "He's got bony wrists. Mashkov will have fun with this one!"

Vorobyev yelled at Vasiliy. "I am innocent! You convict your people without evidence, sentence them to death without trial! Take the words of some ridiculous treacherous American over a loyal government servant without a second thought." Vorobyev lowered his voice and growled. "And you call *me* a traitor."

The two men wordlessly stared at Vorobyev, stunned by his defiance. He'd never revealed such strength in their previous dealings. They mumbled to one another as they carried him, one under each arm, to his residence.

Back inside his apartment, Vorobyev showered as he waited for Golikov's goons to finish conducting their searches. The warm water washed over his head and face, soothing his wounds and renewing his strength.

Vasiliy cracked opened the bathroom door. "We're finished in here. There is food on the table. Don't try anything stupid, okay? Security will be standing outside the door at all times."

He poked his head out from behind the shower curtain, bowed his head in acknowledgment, then listened for his the front door to shut. Vorobyev hurried to finish bathing for he had much to do. He wrapped a towel around his waist and wandered up the hall still dripping wet. His left eye had swollen shut, but he could partly see out of the right. He used his hands to feel what he wasn't visible in the periphery.

Vorobyev had much to do. Since they would never allow him to make any phone calls, he decided letters would suffice. Letters to his wife and children, to say goodbye and let them know how much he dearly loved them. They must know, with every fiber of their beings, that the man to whom they'd entrusted their lives, the man whom they'd kissed good morning every day and goodnight every evening, would never betray them or his country. Even though he wondered whether the letters would ever be delivered, he felt comforted in the belief that his old friend Aleksey Dmitriyev would ensure they were provided to his family. Dmitriyev was no doubt subsumed in guilt over the day's events, events Vorobyev knew Aleksey was powerless to prevent.

He slipped into the kitchen area and ran his hand along the cabinet until the handle felt cold on his fingers. He pulled it and brushed his palm along the top shelf, pushing aside several cereal boxes. It was still there. A large ceramic canister. He removed the lid, dug beneath a layer of cotton balls until the metal from the small .22 caliber Smith & Wesson cooled his fingertips.

He'd kept the gun for protection as he had heard that parts of the city were dangerous and refused to be the victim of some random street crime. Little did he know, the biggest crimes against him would be committed by his own people. He exhaled, relieved they did not find it during their search. For what he bought for his protection would now become his savior.

He tucked it back inside and returned the canister to its place. It was time to complete his unfinished business and end this travesty.

Vorobyev swore Golikov would never torture him for another man's crime if indeed one had been committed at all. He vowed to die in his own time, on his own terms, by his own hand.

Stanislav Vorobyev had lived in honor.

He refused to die in disgrace.

CHAPTER 33

Wednesday Morning…

J.J. was anxious, on edge. Only two days left before the polygraph exam, and an arrest was no more imminent than when they started. The ICE Phantom still lurked about, and J.J. had no idea whether the traitor knew she'd turned up the heat on the hunt. How the following days would unfold, she didn't know. The evidence wasn't coming together quickly enough.

Stay calm, she thought. *Avert disasters.*

If she could keep Dmitriyev's identity concealed for two more days, meet with Cartwright to get what she suspected would be his confession, then Dmitriyev would have no need to leave an emergency signal and the nightmare would end.

She pulled next to the mailbox where Dmitriyev was directed to leave a chalk mark, sucked in a deep breath, and held it until she glanced at the spot.

Nothing. She exhaled and shrugged.

She had instructed him to mark the signal in catastrophic situations only. The likelihood of such an event occurring in such a short time period of time was highly unlikely—possible but unlikely. But her instincts, they told her, *Turn the corner. Check the other side. Just in case.* Plotnikov was prone to marking the wrong side. Perhaps Dmitriyev would do the same.

She pulled around and carefully examined the other side. "Damn, damn, damn!" she said out loud, relieved at first that she found it...and then not. The mark portended bad news, and she didn't want to face it. But she needed to hear it. She did a double take to be certain. "What the hell could have possibly gone wrong now?"

Strike number one. It was a blow but not deadly. J.J. still had the meeting with Cartwright. If he turned himself in, all other problems would be moot.

J.J. blew out a long, hard breath and braced herself for Dmitriyev's news. No sooner than she pressed the accelerator and reached the next stop light. Her phone rang.

"What's up, Donato? I'm in a hurry."

"We get anything?" Tony asked.

"Yeah. He left an emergency signal."

"Already?" Tony said. "Shit, that ain't good."

"I know, and if I don't get to the other side of town in twenty minutes, I'm gonna miss the first call. Who had the bright idea to select a phone booth in West-freakin'-Cucamonga anyway?"

"I'm afraid you'll have to take the blame for that, Ms. McCall."

"Damn! Hate it when that happens. Anyway, what's up?" she asked. "I'm sure you didn't call to chit chat."

"You're right, I didn't. I've uhhhh...," he began, "I've actually got some bad news."

"What?!" she replied almost expecting Tony to say Dmitriyev was on his way to Dulles airport like all the others.

"Relax, it's not Dmitriyev, but it still ain't good," Tony said. "Rumor has it, Jim Cartwright off'ed himself early this morning."

J.J. gasped, abruptly pulled over, and put on her flashers. When the news settled in, her chest rose and fell in desperate sweeps as she struggled to catch her breath. *Cartwright is dead? We were supposed to meet this morning...and now he's dead?* She didn't believe Tony at first.

"What exactly happened?!" Her mind swirled in confusion. She couldn't speak to Dmitriyev in this mental state. She needed to shake off her humanity and allow Agent McCall to take over. But the news cut deep. She fought to stifle the tears pushing their way to the surface, dabbed the corner of her eyes to dry the few that broke through. His wife, his beautiful girls, he loved them so. Then without warning, her mind flashed back to their conversation, the one they'd had the day she'd planned to quit.

"Park police found him in an overlook off the G.W. Parkway with a bullet in his head."

"My God, did he leave a note?"

"Yeah, apparently he left some cryptic note about betrayal in his car, along with a goodbye to his wife and kids in his own handwriting."

"You're kidding me!" J.J. said. "Why would he do that?"

"Why indeed," Tony said. "Looks like our list just got a little bit shorter, huh?"

"I'd say so," she said, holding her forehead. "Listen, let me make this phone call and we'll talk when I get back to the office. Every time I think things can't get worse, they do."

Cartwright killed himself? Why? Was jail worse than the suffering he'd put his family through in death? J.J. wondered. The despair he must've been drowning in. Nothing else would separate him from his girls. She couldn't imagine sinking so low. *Strike fucking number two.*

Her consternation over Jim's death would need to wait. She made tracks across town. Dmitriyev would be calling any moment.

In the advent of cell phones, few actual phone booths remained in the city. Those on which one could receive phone calls were even further and fewer between. After a week of searching, J.J. found two obscure locations. She'd instructed Dmitriyev to mark the signal by 8 am and call the first number at 11 am sharp, the same day. If she missed the call, he would try the second number 30 minutes later. If she answered neither, he was to return to the embassy and try again in two days. But two days would be too late for J.J. and Tony.

She pulled into the small convenience store right off Pennsylvania Avenue in the Southeast. The telephone booth on the outside corner of the store's exterior was only a few feet away. Her mind still distracted by Cartwright's death, she didn't notice the handset was missing...along with the rest of the phone. Panicked, she rushed inside.

"Can I help you?" asked a slight Asian man protected behind bullet-proof glass.

"Yeah," she said breathlessly. "What happened to the friggin' phone. It was here two weeks ago."

"They take day before yesterday. Nobody use anymore. They use *cell phone.*"

"Shit!"

"Sorry..." he said, delivering his apology with all the sympathy of a roll of paper towels.

J.J. grunted and made her way back to her car. She jammed her key into the ignition, missing several times before it slipped inside. *The time. I've got to watch the time.* She glanced at her wrist. Rush hour still hadn't ended. She might not make the next call. The next stop was twenty-five minutes away and she had only twenty minutes before Dmitriyev made his last and final call for the day—and maybe ever.

Horns blaring, swerving in and out of traffic, J.J. aggressively maneuvered her way through the crowded lanes. Her destination was finally in sight. Eddie's Carryout. It was just across the Maryland-D.C. line. She sped into the almost empty lot, nearly losing her balance as she stumbled out of the car and scrambled to the phone booth. It rang. She was still steps away. She extended her arm and grabbed the handset.

"Hello . . . hello!" She waited for a sound, any sound. Nothing. Only the crackle of static.

"Hello?" she repeated. Nothing still.

Just as J.J. reached to return the handset, a voice broke through.

"Hello?" the man's voice said.

"I'm here," she replied. Then she remembered the parole, the script she crafted for operational security to ensure each the other was not an impostor.

"Good afternoon," Dmitriyev said, his voice strained, unsure. "Did you watch the Redskins beat the Cowboys?"

"Yes," she responded as written. "The game brought me much pleasure."

They both exhaled in relief.

"Agent McCall. It is good to hear your voice. I'm very glad you received my message."

"You too," she said, equally reassured but still tense. His life must be in danger. "Are you okay?"

"For the moment. But we have a problem. A significant setback," Dmitriyev said, his voice heavy, thick with angst. "Vorobyev has been detained for committing treason."

"Vorobyev? Why?"

"Your mole, he passed information in an emergency drop last night which implicated Vorobyev…instead of me. Golikov plans to kill Vorobyev when he returns to Moscow this Friday, along with Viktor. It's all my fault." His voice trailed off. Knowing his past, she could sense the guilt. It was almost palpable.

Son of a bitch! She screamed in her head. Just as she suspected, the mole was indeed getting desperate, and his mistake was too close for comfort. Of all the intelligence officers in the residency, he nailed the guy only one position away from her source.

But why implicate a declared officer who'd never cooperated with the FBI?

J.J. struggled to figure out why he fingered Dmitriyev. If she could, it might lead her to his identity. J.J. shuddered at the thought of the repercussions, the chaos, both inside the FBI and the Agency. Moscow Station must be reeling.

"Agent McCall. Are you still there?"

"Oh...I'm sorry. Yes. Just trying to figure out why the mole would implicate Vorobyev, that's all. He's never worked for us and he's declared. Doesn't make sense. Have Golikov's people gotten to him?" she asked as her mind whirled. If her suspicions were accurate and the mole had access to the vault, he had seen or overheard something.

"Yes, but he's still alive. Barely. The mole offered no proof, no additional information. He just provided a name, said you recruited Vorobyev, and mentioned something about 'three days.' And, of course, Vorobyev denied cooperation, but Golikov's people are trained not to believe the truth. He and Viktor will be killed together when Vorobyev returns to Moscow on Friday. We have to do something before then. We simply must," he implored.

"Hmmm. Three days?" J.J. asked. She half listened to Dmitriyev as she wracked her brain. Who could've been in the position to snitch on Vorobyev? She and Tony hadn't spoken of Dmitriyev around anyone. Except in J.J.'s apartment, her car and . . . Could he have overheard their conversation? But as she recalled she purposely did not mention Dmitriyev's name, even in the privacy of Jack's office. *The privacy of Jack's office...*

"I'll. Be. Damned!" J.J. yelled.

"Excuse me?"

"I'm sorry. I just—I think I know what happened." She slapped her forehead.

"Agent McCall . . ."

"I'm sorry. Got distracted for a moment."

"I hate to complicate this situation further but you are well aware of my past. I could not in good conscience continue to cooperate with you if Vorobyev suffers or is killed because of my crimes. Besides, since

Vorobyev was detained, Golikov's people have taken control of the case. It would be a great risk to attempt to access it."

"So what are you saying?"

"I'm saying I can't assist you. At least not you clear my brother and Vorobyev and Golikov's people stand down."

On her list of shit she didn't want to happen, she never considered losing her key source as an option. One step forward, two steps back.

"Obviously, your position is disappointing, but how could I not understand with everything that happened to you and Plotnikov?" she said. However calculated, her empathy was sincere. The more concern she expressed for his personal safety, the more loyal he'd be over the long-term. But at the moment, her patience had thinned. "I'll figure out a way to make this right."

Strikes fucking number three and *four.*

Again, she nearly asked what more could go wrong. But the universe always answered in exasperatingly troublesome ways. Now she not only needed to identify and arrest the mole, but also clear Plotnikov and Vorobyev. While she admired Dmitriyev's concern for his comrade, he had seriously monkey-wrenched an already impossible situation.

"Can you share any information that might help *me* help *you and them?* I gotta tell you, we're running on empty and we can't do this without your help. We just can't," she said, exaggerating to milk from him as much information possible.

"Well, I glimpsed two things in his file before I handed them over this morning. One, the mole supposed to be making another drop Thursday morning. He requested a payment immediately. Normally, we'd verify the information before requesting authorization for such action, but because his intelligence has been so invaluable, the Center agreed to pay him half."

"What's half?"

"Based on the information he usually provides, my guess is the payment will probably be somewhere in the neighborhood of $100,000. But it could be more, could be less."

More than my salary, she thought. *Perhaps I should consider a change of professions.*

"Where's the drop location?"

"Rock Creek Park. They took the file before I had time to view the exact drop time and location. But one of Golikov's people will be retrieving the package to avoid any future compromises."

"Sheesh, do you know how big that park is? We'll need every G east of the Mississippi to cover down on the location if we want to catch him," she said. Then another idea struck her. One that might get them they help they needed. "If you overhear any information on the location at all, I need to you to text me from the throw away cell I gave you, and it's critical that you throw it away."

"Okay, I will try my best." He paused for a moment. "Listen, I must hurry back to the embassy but there is one more piece of information that might interest you."

CHAPTER 34

Wednesday Afternoon…

J.J. waited anxiously for Dmitriyev to deliver the additional piece of information she hoped would help her break the case once and for all.

"The mole, he's part of a joint operation that counterintelligence has been working with illegals support for at least the last six or seven years…maybe longer."

"Counterintelligence working jointly with illegals support?" she said. It was an FBI agent's nightmare. Tactically, they were the hardest targets to work against—one cunning and the other elusive, a tough combination. "Wait a minute. That's why Aleksandr Mikhaylov is one of the handlers." She stated her suspicions as fact to see whether Dmitriyev would confirm or deny. She'd believed he was dirty from the moment he came into the country and his ability to shake the Gs and operate almost entirely in the black confirmed her suspicions.

"Ahhhh, I'm impressed," he said. "Yes, he is the primary handler and has been since day one. Apparently, the asset dropped a note in Mikhaylov's car window to establish the first contact years ago. We've been working them jointly because the illegals support operational line is short on officers and Mikhaylov is nearing the end of his second and possibly last tour."

"That's odd," she said. "The mole is FBI so he should've been passed off to your counterintelligence department…*to you.*"

"Correct," he said. "These circumstances are very unusual indeed. The Center always has its reasons. I'm still unaware of what they are."

When their call ended, J.J. questioned whether the mole had a specific reason for approaching Mikhaylov or happened across his open car window by coincidence. It seemed highly unlikely that the incident was mere happenstance, as might be the case with someone who doesn't know Russian intelligence—but not with an experienced FBI agent. No, the mole *selected* Mikhaylov—the illegals support officer—for a reason.

Illegals, Russian intelligence officers under the deepest covers, came to the United States from friendly, benign foreign countries, such as Canada. They then sought U.S. citizenship and sensitive government positions, usually communicated with US-based Russian intelligence officers or the Center through the most covert means—dead drops, coded and encrypted communications transmissions. She questioned what would prompt the mole to place a letter in Mikhaylov's car. Some kind of personal relationship? The notion, while far-fetched, was certainly worth considering.

Dmitriyev's call had sparked more questions than it answered. But two things were certain: First—she and Tony needed to devise a plan to save Karat and Vorobyev's hides if they wanted maintain access to Dmitriyev. Second—they needed to consider the possibility that the mole could be an illegal. And if indeed one of J.J.'s colleagues from the vault was involved, personnel files might contain critical answers. If J.J. and Tony could stop putting out fires long enough to ask Sunnie to review them, the information may tie one of the bigot listed personnel to a friendly foreign country. Then they could arrest the son of a bitch once and for all.

The pressure mounted, and the sky rained confusion, and J.J. began to fold emotionally. Tony couldn't expect her to keep her promise under these circumstances.

She reached under the passenger seat, grabbed her flask, and checked to make sure the coast was clear before taking a long sip of her savior. She sat still and waited for that moment, the moment when it smoothed the edges on her crumpled nerves.

She slipped the container under the seat, pushed the key into the ignition and put the car into gear. *BAM!* She ran into the telephone pole ahead of her.

"Damn!"

She had meant to put the car in reverse, but put it in drive instead. She jolted her forward in her seat, slamming her knee against the lower edge of the dash. Nothing seemed broken except her front fender, no doubt, but her knee ached like hell. The ensuing adrenaline rush made her hand tremble like the oak leaf she spotted drifting in the strong fall wind.

As if her luck couldn't get any worse, a Prince George's County Police officer, on duty and in uniform, stepped out of the carry-out with a bag of Chinese just in time to witness the entire incident. He was headed for her car.

Shit!

• • •

Later at Headquarters

J.J. met Tony to devise a solution to their new problem—Vorobyev—as well as solve the lingering ones. He reserved a conference room in his old White Collar Crime unit on the fifth floor at her request. If her suspicions were correct, the mole had placed a listening device in the office, probably Jack's office. No conversation was safe until they located and removed it.

When she limped into the cramped room, their Xerox copy of Plotnikov's real case files were sprawled across the table as Tony eyed her with concern.

"What the hell happened to you?"

"I, uhhh, put the car in drive when I meant to put it in reverse. P.G. cop saw the whole thing, but I played blond. He didn't cite me."

He jumped out of his seat and swept to J.J.'s side, pulling a chair out so she could sit down. Then he took the adjacent seat and waited for her eyes to meet his, but she avoided his gaze.

"J.J., you weren't drinking, were you? If you get a DUI, they'll snatch your badge, you know that, right?" he urged.

"I was fine, Tony. It was just a stupid mistake, one that I'll never make again. I was distracted and lost focus. Now, can we please get down to business? We don't have time for lectures."

He nodded, eying her skeptically.

Without haste, J.J. brought him up to speed on the day's events. Dmitriyev had given her an earful about Vorobyev and Karat, the mole's next drop, and the potential illegals connection, which stumped them both.

"So, why'd you ask to meet here? I hadda pull a few strings to borrow this space," he said.

"Well, if my suspicions are correct..."

"And they usually are," he interjected.

"The mole planted a bug somewhere in our office, I suspect Jack's office. That's the only place where you and I discussed Dmitriyev without specifically mentioning his name."

"A bug in headquarters?" Tony appeared dumbfounded by the accusation. He leaned forward, waiting for J.J.'s explanation.

"Remember the conversation we had in Jack's office when I told you we'd have the answers to nail the bastard in three days?"

"Yeah."

"Let's assume the mole overheard me, which I believe he did. I never mentioned Dmitriyev by name. I called him 'our friend' and mentioned that, in three days, he would have the information we needed to nail the mole."

"Right. I'm with you."

"Well, if the mole checked to see what was happening in the embassy within the next three days, he would've found out that Vorobyev was departing, then he wrongly assumed that I was referring to Vorobyev—not Dmitriyev."

"Wow," Tony said, his frustration obvious. "We've got to get in there later tonight and locate it. Only someone in the unit would've had access to Jack's office."

"Exactly."

She grabbed an old photocopy Plotnikov's real case files from the table and flipped it open. The page containing the list of operational locations in Rock Creek Park that she'd compiled over the years was located near the back. "So now we gotta figure out a way to clear Vorobyev and Karat, not only to save their lives but to ensure Dmitriyev will maintain contact with us. He's too valuable a source to lose," J.J. said.

"How the hell are we gonna pull that off? Walk up to the embassy and tell Golikov's people they got the wrong guy because the FBI said so? I mean c'mon."

"If only the answer were that simple," J.J. nodded her head. She pushed her fingers through her hair, scratched the scalp as if doing so would stimulate her brain. "I got nothin'. I mean that idea's about as crazy as getting the mole to say, 'My bad! I made a mist—.'"

She cut herself off, her eyes widened.

"What?"

"That's it! That's the solution! Even when you're not brilliant, you're brilliant."

CHAPTER 35

J.J. swept out of her chair and flounced around the room. Deep in thought, she tapped her finger against her lips. *But could this plan really work?* She shook her head no. It was too difficult, too many pieces had to fall in place, especially at a time when every step forward was always followed by two steps backward. Then again, what was the alternative? Let Vorobyev and Plotnikov die? Lose Dmitriyev? Probably wouldn't work, but they had to try.

"What...what is it?"

"The drop. That's the answer, don't you see?" she said. "If the mole tells the Russians that the information implicating Vorobyev was part of a big set-up, an internal FBI investigation to flush out ICE Phantom, they'll believe him, call off Golikov's dogs, and Vorobyev will be cleared."

"Keep going. I like the sound of your idea so far." Tony folded his arms over his chest. "But I'm anticipatin' one tiny little problem? How do you propose we get the mole, whom we haven't actually identified yet, to confess all of this to the Russians…as if he ever would."

"I'm getting to that part," she said impatiently, rushing to make sense of her own thoughts. "We don't. We switch the drop. And, in our package, we include a note from the mole clearing Vorobyev. They're typewritten. We don't have to worry about handwriting."

"You mean the same drop that's happening in the location we don't know and at a time that we also don't know?"

"Okay, Mr. Glass Half Empty."

"J.J., it's freakin' empty. No other way to see it."

"Yes, there is, if we get our shit together and speak to SAC McDonald, pronto!" J.J. said, referring to the Special Agent in Charge of the Washington Field Office. "We'll ask him for as many G teams as he'll authorize to blanket that park."

"Easier said than done."

"Listen, all intelligence services pretty much use the same tradecraft and I've been through every square inch of the park. I've located all the best operational spots. We'll post the Gs in those locations and pray we get the right one. Unless you have another idea?"

He shook his head no. "Not bad, not bad at all, McCall," he said. "But what about Karat? And what are we going to use for passage material? They're going to be expecting some valuable counterintelligence information not the crap we give up in double agent operations."

"True," J.J. said, moving about nervously. She sat down then stood up again and resumed pacing then blew out a long breath and threw up her hands in resignation. "We have no choice. Double agent passage material will have to do. It's crap, but I don't see any other—"

"What?"

"Wait a minute!" Her face beamed. "You ever play chess?"

"Yeah, what the hell's 'at got to do with anything?"

"It's the last thing Cartwright said to me before he died. Sometimes you have to sacrifice the pawn to get the king."

"Sacrifice the pawn?" Tony asked as he watched J.J. whir around the room. "The question is who's the pawn in this scenario?"

"Karat," she said.

"Wait! You're suggesting we give up Karat…to save Karat?"

She nodded.

"Have you been drinking again?" he said. His face reddened. "You've got to be fucking kidding me, J.J. We've been jumping through our asses to save this man's neck for years and now you want to rat him out to the Russians?"

"Yes…*and no*," she said, a smile emerging on her face. "For drop material, we're going to give the Russians his entire Top Secret operational file, from beginning to end."

Tony ran his fingers through his hair. "You mean, you want to give up *this* file?"

"Hell, no," she said, waiting to see light dawn on Marblehead.

"Then I don't under—" His eyes widened.

"By George, I think he's got it! Now, while I start mapping out the strategy, you call Sunnie and tell her to leave the file in your desk. She's got vault access."

• • •

J.J. and Tony worked tirelessly through the evening. Their justification to conduct the op and request the G support had to be rock solid. They'd broken every rule and bypassed every Bureau regulation in the book. The bureaucratic red tape they hurdled was too long to be measured in miles. No time to get the proper authorizations. One boss was dead, another in jail, and one of their colleagues was spying for the Russians. She'd reasoned they had a pretty good case for taking the more circuitous route to solving this case.

A couple of hours later, J.J. and Tony collected their neatly organized material into a file and locked it in her briefcase for safe keeping. MacDonald, the man who held the collective fate of the operation in his hands, stayed in the office late and had been expecting their death by PowerPoint. So they said their Hail Marys and prepared to talk shit like they'd never talked it before—Tony's specialization without question.

As J.J. and Tony headed toward his car, she couldn't shake the eerie feeling she experienced every time she thought about Cartwright's suicide and what it really meant. There was a reason he killed himself. He must've been entangled in activities so insidious that his only way out was death. The prospect of having to disentangle the web of lies and deceit he'd left behind was nothing short of daunting.

"So what do you think about this Cartwright business?" J.J. asked Tony.

He shrugged. "One way to get out of taking a polygraph, I guess."

"Be serious, Tony. Do you think he did it because of his sexual preference or for some other reason?" She hoped Cartwright's death had raised the same questions in his mind that it had in her own.

"Look J.J., you and me, we're old school. Didn't your mother ever tell you not to go asking questions you didn't want to know the answers to?" he asked rhetorically. "I remember one Christmas, my mother gave me this knit sweater with Rudolf the Red-nosed Reindeer on the front."

She stopped in her tracks and glared at him. "Is this going somewhere?"

"Yeah. Be patient," he snapped playfully. "As I was sayin', I hated that ugly ass sweater but I was gonna wear the thing to make her happy. Anyway, there was this one little thread sticking out of the sleeve. I kept pulling and before I knew it, the whole sweater was nothing but a pile o' yarn."

"And your point is?"

"My point is, you and I keep pulling strings."

She laughed and shot him a sideways glance. "Are we still talking about the case?"

His cheeks blushed red. "Of course. What else would I be talking about?" he asked. "That's what this Cartwright business feels like to me. We've pulled the strings and now a bunch of shit is starting to unravel." He turned to J.J. "What if we've uncovered a network? Given the intelligence in Plotnikov's drop, there's at least one more ICE Phantom. And he's not inside the FBI."

"A spy ring," she said. Speaking the words made her cringe.

Finding the mole had been task enough. She shuddered for the Agent who would be assigned to find the others.

"Well, we do have one last iron in the fire that might provide us with some added leverage," J.J. said.

"What's that?"

"Chris is supposed to take his polygraph first thing tomorrow morning, and I'm pretty sure he'll show up to take it."

"No doubt," Tony said. "If the Russians value him as much as they should, they probably trained him to use countermeasures. He probably won't beat it, but he'll be just cocky enough to think he can."

"He'll make the drop early in the morning and we'll get a confession sometime tomorrow. He may be able to tell us more about the ring, but the Russians are among the best at compartmenting their assets, so there are no guarantees."

"Indeed. Now, let's roll over to WFO and kiss MacDonald's ass for twenty minutes so we can get the Gs. This entire op is riding on his thumbs up."

His metaphor, pulling strings, could perfectly describe their case and relationship. They constantly pulled strings. And the more they pulled, the more their attraction for one another was revealed. But neither dared to face the connection between them—nor the rabbit hole they'd been chased into because of the case.

• • •

Later Wednesday Night...

"It's on like popcorn!" J.J. said, bubbling with excitement. After presenting their case to SAC MacDonald, he authorized seven G teams for one day and one day only. Either they'd catch the son of a bitch on Thursday or Operation OVER.

After picking up the package of passage material to fill the drop, they set out to find the bug in Jack's office. As they stepped off the elevator, they faced a new nightmare—one with the power to put the kibosh on their best-laid plans.

"Ahhhh, Ms. McCall and Mr. Donato. I just left your office. I've been looking for you two," Director Freeman said. His scowl could slice through concrete. Neither he nor the members of the director's security detail looked pleased to see them. J.J. braced herself for his wrath, fearing MacDonald had called and ratted them out. And a quick glance at Tony's expression said he was doing the same. He'd come to fire them on the spot, snatch their badges and guns and march them out the front exit. The jig was up.

"Sir?" they said in unison. Tony and J.J. glanced at each other unable to gauge his disposition. J.J. was all but certain her career would end in T-minus thirty seconds. After a few moments of uncomfortable silence, he waved off his security detail and told them he'd meet them at his office later.

"Mhm. Hmm. Yeah...I got a call from MacDonald. He said I might find you two here."

"Sir...uhhh," J.J. hemmed and hawed. "We...uhhh, uhhh. We didn't—"

"Apparently you didn't realize that SAC MacDonald couldn't author-ize such a significant number of surveillance resources without my knowledge...and more importantly, *my approval*," he said, gesturing his hand forward as he started toward their office. They humbly followed in tow. "What I'd like to know is why you didn't come directly to me?"

J.J. looked at Tony and shrugged, gave him a blank stare, and offered nothing in the way of an excuse. After all, Tony was the better improviser of the two. "Well, see. What had happened was . . . Uh, sir, we were trying to keep the information as safe and as compartmented as possible. J.J. identified another problem and we had no idea how extensive the breach might be," Tony said as they arrived at the office door. He unlocked the cipher and badged everyone in. "If you'll give us a few minutes, we can show you exactly what we're talking about. I think you'll understand."

"Yes, have a seat, sir," J.J. said as she flipped on the light, confident Tony's excuse would get them off the hook. No way Freeman could argue with a fear of bugs—the transmitting type.

Jack's office had been left virtually undisturbed since their last meeting. They immediately dove into their sweep, ran their hands along the chairs, window sills, and the file safe, carefully inspecting each item on Jack's desk. Tony crouched down behind the wooden mass and felt underneath. J.J. watched and winced. With Jack, anything could lie beneath.

Toward the back underside, Tony's fingers brushed across two thin plastic-coated wires. Barely an inch away was a second small, flat object. "Bingo! I got it," he yelled. "Son of a bitch!" spilled from his mouth before he remembered Freeman was sitting only a few feet away. "You nailed it, J.J."

He yanked the small device from underneath the desk, held it out for J.J. to inspect. She shook her head and examined the wires. When Tony showed Director Freeman, his body stiffened before he propped his elbows on his knees. Then he tilted back in his seat, his face tired, drawn.

"You mean this bastard placed a bug in headquarters?"

"Yes, sir. That's why we had to be careful," J.J. said. "Karat's been detained, and I'm sure you've heard about what happened to Vorobyev by now. The CIA probably can't wait to get me off the streets."

He nodded. "I'm supposed to deliver your head on a spike by Friday."

She chuckled. "Well, we believe that's how the mole got the information that falsely implicated Vorobyev, a discussion Tony and I had about Dmitriyev."

"Dmitriyev? Why would you be discussing Dmitriyev? He's not working with us."

"Uhhhh...that's inaccurate," Tony interjected. "Not only did J.J. recruit him a few days ago, long story. But he's slated to replace Vorobyev and had intended to identify the ICE Phantom when provided access to Vorobyev's files on Friday."

"The mole's identity? He's handing it over *this* Friday?" Director Freeman said, on the edge of elated relief.

"Well, he'd planned to. But that was before Golikov's people detained Vorobyev," Tony said. "Now he's spooked. Apparently Golikov's people are running security now and Vorobyev got roughed up pretty bad."

Freeman cut his eyes at both. "And of course you couldn't report this due to..."

"The bugs," J.J. said, cutting her eyes at Tony. "We have no idea how extensive the breaches are or where else in the building he may have planted devices. So we had to be careful."

"Shit, this is a sensitive compartmented facility," Freeman said. "You do realize that for the transmitter to work inside a SCIFed area they had to listen from inside the office. No way they could pick up a signal from the street."

"Well, sir. There are twenty-two people working in this office, at least eight of which have access to the vault. We'll find out which one is involved tomorrow, if you allow us to go forward with the op."

He nodded and let out a long sigh. "In the meantime, I'm ordering security to sweep this entire building. They can start tonight before our perceptive employees arrive in the morning and rumors become another distraction."

He stood and patted Tony's shoulder before walking to the door. "Let me get home before my wife threatens to divorce me...for the *second* time this week. You two get some shuteye. You've got important work to do tomorrow and we're all counting you."

"Yes, sir," Tony said. He secured the door behind him.

J.J. and Tony glanced at each other, relieved. Their shoulders sagged and breathing calmed. Although they'd made some significant progress, they were far from in the clear.

"Whew! That was a close one," J.J. said. "You know I got to thinking if the device is here, nine times out of ten, the receiver is here too."

Without hesitation, she walked straight to Chris's desk. Both Lana and Jack had suspected he was dirty. Maybe he'd left the evidence to prove it. She opened he desk drawers, one after the other. Scouring through his office supplies. Looking for anything that appeared unusual or out of place. Any kind of electronic that could be used as a receiver. When she reached the bottom drawer, she saw it. An iPod with a flash drive embedded in the rear casing. She turned it on, but the display didn't operate normally. The backlight glowed on, but no menu appeared. She examined the seams along the edges.

This has been opened.

She held it up in Tony's view. "I'll bet you ten-to-one this is it. Probably uses the flash drive to save the recordings. I'll take this to security and let them scan it."

"Chris. Rat piece of shit."

"Come hell or high water, he'll get his comeuppance before the day's end."

"Indeed."

The look in Tony's eye said he was now in it for the long haul. Sink or sail, they were in the same boat. She loaded the briefcase and scanned the office. One way or another, the office would never be the same. And two days might spell the end of her ten-year career.

"Listen, I was wondering if I could stay at your place tonight...on the couch, of course. We gotta be in the park by 5 am and my place is farther from the city than yours."

She hesitated to answer out of more than her fear of love; she'd made a promise to Tony she hadn't kept. "Hmmm. Is this because you don't want to drive...or because you want to keep an eye on me...or because you want to keep a hand on me?"

"Maybe all of the above," Tony said, a smile seizing his lips. "Okay, just the first two. Whadaya say?"

J.J.'s skepticism and stress level were both on overdrive. Maybe with the security of Tony's presence she could finally get a good night's rest. Her biggest fear was, of course that neither of them would sleep. She and Tony sacking out in her condo was the definition of pulling strings, and Tony was yanking the hell out of them. Perhaps he didn't grasp the full gravity of his suggestion. Maybe he believed they could resist temptation despite their innermost desires. Or maybe he realized the other night could have destroyed their friendship and he decided to reverse course and suppress his feelings. Or...maybe he knew the position he was putting them in and his desire surpassed all reason. This could mean trouble for the both of them. Big trouble.

But, after all, trouble was J.J.'s middle name.

CHAPTER 36

Wednesday Night…

Tony stared helplessly at the shelf containing a mishmash of cable boxes and receivers. He had no idea he'd need an engineering degree to turn on the television.

"How do you turn on the TV.?" he called out.

"You've been here twenty minutes and already you wanna take over the remote controls," she said exiting her bedroom. J.J. had scuttled away to put on her pajamas as soon as they crossed the threshold, nearly overheating at the thought of a man spending an entire night in her home. After all, she was no spring chicken and it had been a while since she'd been locked in with someone for whom she cared so deeply.

"You mean all twenty of them? No, I'm a one-remote kinda guy," he said. "I'd just like to watch the NFL channel. They're replaying Sunday's Jets-Patriots game that I missed thanks to Mr. Dmitriyev."

J.J. walked to the shelf and turned on everything in about ten seconds, shaking her head at his technical ineptitude.

"Men!"

"Can I get a beer?"

"Sure, they're in the refrigerator. I'll have one too while you're at it." She grabbed the briefcase containing the files and plunked them down on the couch. He gave her a look that said "I wish I could kick your ass back to the 1950s."

She snickered and jumped up to grab one from the icebox, returning seconds later. She placed them atop coasters on the coffee table. "Here you go! Do you want me to throw your clothes in the washer? I pulled out some of my brother's old gym stuff and laid them on the bed if you want to change. You guys are about the same size."

"That'll work. Appreciate the offer," he said as he headed for the bedroom. "Now while I'm changing, no peeking!"

"Don't worry, I don't need to...," she said, "...the camera's running."

She grabbed a stack of paperwork from the dining room table and planted herself in a seat at the end of couch furthest from Tony.

He returned just few minutes later, dressed in a pair of Lakers' basketball shorts and a matching sleeveless T-shirt, exposing everything J.J. prayed hid beneath his clothes but that she hadn't seen in the flesh. Now she wanted to devour him in every heavenly way imaginable.

Lord have mercy on me! she thought to herself. *Jesus be the Great Wall of China!*

She pushed the hot, sweaty thoughts of a forbidden night with him from her mind; her skin grew flush. She glanced away, moving her gaze from the T.V., to the floor, to the ticking clock outside the kitchen, anything was better than dealing with the surge of emotions overwhelming her as she looked at him.

"You all right?"

"Uhhhh...yeah. I'm fine." Without realizing it, she fanned herself with a file folder. "Is it warm in here? I think I need to crack open a window." She popped up and slid open the patio door a few inches to the left.

Tony noticed her flustered appearance and chuckled. "Maybe, you better have a sip of your beer. It'll cool you down." He grabbed both bottles and clasped them between his fingers before opening them. Then he held one out for her. The curve in his pecks called to her as he reached out his arm.

She trembled inside. Only a cold shower or a warm bed could offer the kind of cooling she needed. "Salut. Here's to a few sips of beer," she said as their bottle clinked together. "Now. On your next visit, you are no longer a guest. You can get your own beer...and mine too while you're at it." She returned to her seat at the sofa's edge. She wanted him, to feel him inside her, to press her body against his, but life was too complicated and her fears too stifling.

"Next visit, huh?" He looked at her and winked.

"Careful, Tony. You're pulling strings again."

In one swift motion too fast for J.J. to react to or comprehend, Tony emptied his seat and appeared in the one next to her. Unnerved, her mouth fell slightly open. She planned to run, but he grabbed her forearm before she could flinch. "Hear me out," he said tilting his face toward hers. To fight him would be a futile exercise. She knew it. And he knew it. "We've been, you know, pulling strings for a long time now. I don't know about you, but I'm kind of liking what I see. Maybe pulling strings ain't such a bad thing."

"I'm not sure what you're trying to say." She stared at her knees wondering how long it would take her to fall if she tried to stand.

He craned his neck, tried to draw her gaze to his face, but her eyes remained fixed on her knees instead; they were harmless. They could convince her of nothing.

"I'm saying...I'm saying that we have a lot of reasons to fight against this 'thing' between us—our families, society...ourselves. But when I see your smile, I don't see a black woman. I see my life. Everything in here," he pressed his hand to his heart, "tells me to deal with the bullshit and fight for you...for us."

She gasped and placed her hand over her mouth. Finally, he'd spoken the words she'd longed to pass his beautiful Italian lips. She wanted so much to reach out to him, to melt away in his arms. But their lives were too complicated, love too unpredictable, and society too unaccepting.

Perhaps her wounds from the debacle with Six had yet to heal. Maybe she needed to tend to her own unfinished business before starting something new. Or maybe, for a change, she could stop thinking with her head and leap with her heart. She shuffled the files around nervously on her lap, disturbing the pregnant silence as she fished for a response.

"Well?" Tony asked, his eyes still chasing hers.

She sighed and finally looked at him. Eye to eye. Everything in her heart affirmed her desire, but the timing, the timing couldn't be worse. Then again, it couldn't be better either.

The answer came. Her response required courage she didn't possess at the moment, but she hoped to find it sooner than later. "How about we get through this op and we'll talk about it again when we've put this mess behind us tomorrow? Just one more day."

He reluctantly nodded. "Under one condition."

"What's that?"

"Rub my feet. My corns hurt."

She laughed and shook her head. What else could she do with a man who stopped her heart one moment and cracked her up the next...except share her life with him?

"Oh, I'll rub your feet all right." She grabbed a pillow and pounded him over the head. They bowled over in laughter when he finally submitted.

"Actually," she said. "I've got a much better idea."

• • •

"Ooooooooh, J.J. That. Feels. Soooooooooo goooooooood! Don't stop! Don't stop!" Tony moaned, his eyes rolling in the back of his head. She'd expressed his body to sublime ecstasy.

She smiled, enjoying the sight of him. He was her heaven on Earth. "Is it warm?"

"Mhmmm hmmmm. Warm and wet. Just the way I like it."

"I'm gonna stop in a minute," J.J. said. "You gotta get down here and do me next."

He peered through his half-open lids. "Do *you?*"

"Yeah! My feet hurt, too. You can change the water in the Dr. Scholl's foot bath while I take a seat."

"Oh, all right," he said laughing. "It's only fair."

She smiled to herself, knowing he would.

Tony made her choice easy and yet hard at the same time. Did he really understand what they'd be getting into? She understood the issue of race and America in a way he never would, at least until he started dating *her*. Could he handle the rude awakening, the inevitable moment when society reminded him just how white she isn't? Times had changed in some ways to most people. But not enough to all.

Maybe she was jaded by years of watching her parents in the struggle. Loving Six was easy because he was black. Leaving him was easy because he was an asshole. Loving Tony wasn't easy, it was effortless, a natural state of being. Avoiding him because he was "not black" was the most difficult thing she'd ever done.

There were times when J.J. adored Tony's honesty and the fact that he never made her itch. This was not one of those times.

Decisions. Decisions.

As she later slipped into bed and submerged herself beneath her comforter, she tried her best to drown out the latest string of events. Her mind spun, flustered with the onslaught of challenge after challenge. She couldn't sleep. She reached into the nightstand, grabbed a fifth of Belvedere and gulped until her troubles washed away.

• • •

"Rise and shine sleepy head," Tony said as he poked his head through her bedroom door. Four a.m. came four hours too early for Tony, and he knew J.J. was usually a late sleeper. He could hear the wind rustle the windows as he eased through the threshold. "J.J.? You hear me?"

She still didn't respond, probably couldn't hear him above her snores. He eased toward the bed calling her name and she didn't flinch or move. As he reached on her nightstand to turn on the lamp, the moonlight shone on her face. She looked so angelic, so precious. He wanted to plant the sweetest of kisses on her lips but smiled instead. As he pressed his finger against the light switch, words emerged from her steady rumbles.

"I love you, Tony," she murmured, followed by another round of snores.

He froze and drank in every delicious word. Then he shook it off. *She's just dreaming*, he thought. Then again, she was dreaming of him.

Suddenly, her leg jerked and he heard a glass bottle fall hit the floor. She awakened, just as Tony lifted the empty bottle from the floor.

"Why didn't you wake me up?" she said, running her tongue across her teeth, still groggy from the alcohol's effects.

"Believe me, I tried. What the fuck is this? You promised me!"

"I'm sorry, Tony!" she said, scrambling to untangle her feet from the blankets. She rushed to him, arms outstretched. "I'm so so sorry! I-I couldn't sleep. I haven't slept in weeks. Months. Maybe years. I don't know. I thought with you here, I could—But I couldn't—So I—"

"Stop, just stop it, J.J. I don't want to hear it!" Tony snatched his arm from her grip.

She placed her hand on him again but still he rejected her. "I swear to God, Tony! I wouldn't lie to you."

"Yeah, well, apparently, you have no trouble lying to yourself! Don't you understand we'll be failing a polygraph tomorrow and two men will die if this op doesn't go as planned? There's no way I'm gonna let you go on this operation this morning."

She stopped cold, took a step back. "Let me? You can't ground me like I'm some kid. This is *my* operation… for *my* source."

"Oh, your operation, huh? So I've just been following behind you with my head in my ass, is 'at what you're tryin' to say?"

She shook her head no and walked up to him. Within seconds, his hand was in hers and he was slow to pull away. "No, that's not—. Tony I'm sorry," she began, tears streaming down her eyes. "Everything's been spiraling out of control and I don't know how to handle it. I don't know what to do. But God, if I hurt you. If I lost you, I don't...I don't—"

She released him, returned to the bed, and rained blankets of tears into her palms.

In all the time Tony knew her, he'd never seen J.J. cry. As with everything else in her life, she'd excelled so well at concealing her fears and emotions that the depth of her pain stunned him, stopped his breath. He had no idea she hadn't slept. He had no idea her life was so out of control.

Everything had changed. She had exposed her deepest weaknesses and vulnerabilities to him and he saw her with new eyes—the eyes of a man who loved her come what may. His anger subsided, and he now wanted nothing except to stop her from hurting.

He knelt in front of her, wiped the tears from her eyes, and caressed her cheek. "I didn't know J.J., I didn't know. But I'm here and I'm not going anywhere, Hai *capito*?" he said.

She smiled weakly.

"We'll make it okay," he said, the corners of his lips lifting at the corners. "Whadaya say we just get this op over with today and we'll figure out a solution later...together?"

She nodded and released his hands. Then she dragged her pajama sleeve across her eyes as she stepped into the closet and pulled some Dockers and a polo shirt from their hangers.

Watching her step into the bathroom and flip the light on, Tony teased, "Now, can a brotha get some coffee?"

Before she shut the door, she shook her head and chuckled. "Yeah...at Starbucks. It's on the way!"

Inside the bathroom, J.J. dropped her clothes on the floor and gripped her right wrist so tightly the rush of blood made her fingers turn red. She wondered if she could even hold steady her toothbrush; she couldn't will her digits still no matter how hard she tried.

"Not today," she said in a whispered scream. "Not today!"

CHAPTER 37

Early Thursday Morning…

Usually slow to rise, Koshechka slipped out of bed before the street lights shut off. She knew he'd want his coffee early, even though he had been jittery and his nerves dangled on the edge of breakdown ever since he passed the information regarding Vorobyev to the embassy against her advice. His over-eager chicken shit tongue sparked a chaotic chain of events that threw Moscow and Washington into a tailspin. He'd selected the wrong moment to man up. According to a late-night text from her colleague, Freeman had turned up the heat on everyone. From the cafeteria staff to the entrance gate security police, no one had been left untouched. Full-scale internal investigations had been ordered for everyone. Freeman vowed to leave no personnel file unopened until the snitch had been identified and arrested.

Koshechka understood all too well the consequences which is the reason she urged him to keep his mouth shut until after he'd passed the polygraph, but he refused to listen. Now they'd both pay.

She heard him ease up to the kitchen doorway as she started the coffee pot. Her back to him, she assumed he'd silently stalk her in his usual unnerving way.

"You nervous about today?" she asked, spinning around to see his face. She always monitored his responses. His facial expressions always double-crossed him and revealed his true feelings, even when his words said otherwise.

"I don't think this is a good idea. We have travel documents, and we'll have enough money to take care of ourselves for a long time. Why can't we just pick up the cash today and leave? You know, take the money and run."

"I have no immunity. I must be careful...and I also have a child to think about now. This isn't about you and me. We have another life to consider here. I won't be left with nothing, ever again!" she snapped. Her obvious contempt threw Chris off guard. She stammered for a moment and then softened.

"I'm sorry," she said in a sexy moan. The coffee pot sounded and she deeply inhaled the aroma. "You need coffee, darling. Come, let me pour."

He followed her to the counter as she prepared his cup.

Her voice calmed. "I just don't want to leave here to live in some godforsaken country in the middle of nowhere with a new baby, do you?" she battered her eyelashes and rubbed her hand against his chest. "And when the money runs out, what do we do?"

His spine curved. With a grave expression, he gazed down. "You're right my love," he said. "I'm gonna pull myself together."

"I knew you would honey. Never doubted you for a second."

Koshechka had been running from poverty as a loner for most of her life. She had few acquaintances and fewer genuine friends. Her father's work with the KGB First Chief Directorate, which deployed officers to Western countries such as the United States, kept him away from home for most of her childhood. Her mother, who had nary a nurturing bone in her body, succumbed to a bottle-a-day vodka habit, refused to travel with him. Koshechka's days were filled with squandered money and unpaid bills. As she scorned her mother, she placed her father on the highest pedestal, promising to rise to meet him at all costs.

Her will and determination to succeed at almost any cost, coupled with her introverted nature, set her apart from her classmates at the SVR's Red Banner Institute. So, their plans for her changed—slightly. Directorate S, which closely monitored her progress, decided she was well suited for a clandestine position under a special cover legend they'd been developing for ten years—Madeleine Bouchard. She traveled from the Ukraine to Bern, to Vienna, and finally to Canada. In each country, she established a new identity and abandoned her past. In Canada, she received her final documents a Canadian birth certificate and a passport, virtually erasing the life she'd longed to forget.

The father she yearned to know had just begun his first tour at the Russian Embassy in Washington. She wanted so much to see him, to be near him, to hear him call her *Solnyshko* once again. But maintaining her cover meant she could never go anywhere near the embassy. If the FBI lookouts noticed her walking in, she would come under immediate scrutiny. She was forced to rely on impersonal communication to contact him and so dropped a letter into his vehicle during one of his cover stops. His absence would be her only regret, but he'd return home to her soon. And she'd be there, in Moscow, waiting with open arms and an eager heart.

Although she realized Chris's suggestion to bail and leave the country had been more common sense than nonsense, she had hoped closing in the physical distance to her father would help bridge the emotional one. Then J.J. had to go and fuck up the plans, whining about that pig Polyakov. If Jack had done his job and gotten rid of her as she ordered him years before, she'd have been long gone and the ICE Phantom investigation a memory.

Hanssen's arrogance, narcissism, and greed had led him to his demise and Koshechka's unquenched thirst for her father's adoration and her nation's respect had nearly led her to the same dark sticky end.

Almost.

She entered the cramped office in her intentionally modest home. Although the photocopied files she'd collected and stashed away for the past few weeks *might* serve as Chris's last drop, they *certainly* would constitute her final U.S. operation. She hadn't been in the habit of drinking, but a shot of Stoli would give her the patience to get through the morning without making Chris suspicious of her true intentions. She reached behind her favorite book, *The Daughter of the Commandant* by Pushkin, and pulled out the small flask from which she drew two long sips. She reminded herself of her mother, hiding liquor. Her reflection in the framed photo sitting on her bookshelf, the one into which she'd been Photoshopped, gave her pause. The Stoli slipped down her throat with barely a wince and warmed her to the tips of her fingers. She'd have chased it with a cigarette, but Chris must leave first.

After wrapping the packages carefully to seal the exposed edges with the gray duct tape, she carried it to its courier.

"You ready?" she said, watching him descend from the stairs cloaked head-to-toe in black clothing and an unattractive stench of fear.

"Ready as I'll ever be I guess." He grabbed the package from her hand and bent slightly to kiss her blushed cheek goodbye. She offered it to him so he wouldn't smell the scent of alcohol on her breath. And then she wished him luck.

"What are you going to do until I get back home?" he asked.

"Oh, I don't know. Maybe have another shot of vodka and smoke a cigarette," she said.

He paused until she smiled, then he laughed.

"You're joking," he said, chuckling. "But don't quit your day job."

"Too late. Already did." She patted him on the back and followed him to the front porch. "Don't forget what I told you about the test and you'll be fine. I promise." She watched him shuffle to the car and blew him a kiss goodbye as his car disappeared into the distance.

"Finally," she exhaled. "It's time."

CHAPTER 38

Chris white-knuckled the steering wheel as he weaved through traffic. He debated whether he should take I-66 and drive to Washington Field office; there he could turn himself in and confess the whole sordid affair. But could he do so without implicating his Koshechka? After all, she was carrying his child. No child of his would be born behind bars because he ratted out the woman he loved. Who would care for it? Both of his parents were globe-trotting retirees. Saddling them with an infant grandchild, born out of wedlock no less, was hardly an option.

Refusing the test, which would've placed him under immediate suspicion, was also a non-starter. Employing countermeasures was his only option. He'd pass the test and maintain his cover through the painful four hours. Afterward, he'd have the grounds to insist they defect sooner than later.

He pulled into the park and noticed more people than usual were out exercising. But then again, he had little to compare it to as he'd only been in the location one other time. Still, if the drop site had not been so far down the trail, he might have considered aborting the op. Given the distance, he'd be able to tell within seconds whether he was being followed.

He exited the car, and a cool howling gust made him shudder, sent a chill through his core. He grabbed the package from the trunk then paused and listened, wondering if the universe might be whispering to him, maybe the winds of change. He pressed on, hoofed to the drop location. The sound of crisp $100 bills was, at that moment, his only real concern.

• • •

Koshechka grabbed her cell phone and dialed his number. He was her one true love, the lone silver lining in the dark clouds of her chaotic world.

"Darling." Her voice smiled at the sound of his. Her father would be proud of her choice. He was stronger and even more cunning than she. After all, he'd conned more people in less time. Though years younger, he reminded her of what little she knew of her father, and those characteristics are what drew her to him.

"There's my girl," he sang. "What took you so long?"

"Eh! Took forever to get him out of the house." She placed a few family photos into a large moving box. Their flight was scheduled and they had nothing to do except show up at the airport and survive the security checkpoint. Once through, they were home free. She wished she could see the expression on Chris's face. She'd duped him in more ways than one.

"I'm so glad you won't have to deal with that asshole anymore," he said after his hearty chuckle ended. "What time's his polygraph this morning?"

"I think it's at ten," she said.

"You taught him the countermeasures, right? I can't believe he thought he passed those practice exams."

"I can," she said. "Now, we don't have much time. Unlike my colleagues at the embassy, if they catch me, I have no diplomatic immunity and I'll be no better off than Jack."

"I know. This operation should be over by noon. I'll go home, switch cars, and meet you at Dulles," he said. "We'll be in the air before anyone's the wiser."

"Yes, indeed." Koshechka looked out the window at the autumn rainbow along her fence line. She'd miss her house most of all. Her flat on the outskirts of Moscow would be home for some time. She wished she could transport the Cape Cod to her village. "Now I'll meet you outside the security gate at 1:00. That should leave us plenty of time. Maybe we can stop at Harry's to toast our future before we board the plane."

"You'll have sparkling apple cider, remember? We don't want you to hurt the *baby*," he said, enjoying a sinister laugh at Chris's expense. "Silly schmuck."

"Enough of your jokes already. We need to get moving," she said. "I can see the finish line."

"Me, too. Meet you there."

• • •

The sun's rays broke across the horizon, and a strong acrid breeze whipped through the trees. Thanks to Director Freeman's call to the Park Police chief, the patrol officers unlocked the gates a few minutes earlier than usual to give the Gs a head start. Tony and J.J. watched the surveillance personnel move into their positions—some camouflaged and crouched beneath piles of leaves, others dressed in plain clothes, passing themselves off as early morning fitness freaks.

MacDonald authorized enough personnel to post at seven of the eight areas J.J. had identified as the most ideal operational sites. Jiggy's position was close enough to the eighth that he could view the area with high powered binoculars, yet far enough away that he wouldn't be spotted.

J.J. and Tony positioned themselves roughly twenty-five meters down from Jake, where they could monitor cars approaching on the access road. Jake's cam-car, equipped with video, would capture anything they missed.

As J.J. thought about the significant odds against them, a bout of panic overcame her. The locations she selected might not be correct; the timing might be all wrong. For all J.J. knew, the mole may have already suspected the Bureau planned to roll him up and aborted the operation or changed the drop location. Her hand began to tremble once more, heightening her anxiety.

"Any word from Dmitriyev on the cash drop? Even though we'll have Chris covered for the rest of the day, it'd be nice to get positioned ahead of time. That way we can tape it for prosecution."

"This will never make it to court," J.J. said.

"Not once we get this on camera it won't," Tony said.

She glanced down at her cell phone and checked her text messages. She'd set it to vibrate, thought she might've missed the incoming. "No, nothing yet," J.J. responded. "He's supposed to text me the location after Golikov's people leave if he overhears a location."

"He's not going to text you from his personal phone, is he? What if embassy security checks it?" Tony asked.

"No, no. I gave him a throwaway at our first meeting, remember? He sends one text and tosses it. Those were my instructions and for his own safety he better follow them to the letter," she glanced at her watch. "Time to do a mic check."

She picked up the secure radio. "This is Blue Leader one. Is team number one in position?"

"Ten-four good buddy," Jake interrupted, sounding country strong. "Team one is in position."

"Team two?"

"Roger that, Blue Leader one. Team two is in position."

"I'd like to lodge a formal complaint," Jiggy interjected. "Why am I out here in the sticks by myself? It's dark and these squirrels got me shook."

Jake jumped on the bandwagon. "I just hope you picked the right locations, J.J. Otherwise we might all have a long morning."

"You mean, *you* might have a long morn—"

"Looks like we've got an incoming. Stay alert. Stay alert," Jake said.

J.J.'s head pounded harder than her heartbeat. She waited for Jake to deliver the news they'd long waited to hear—the identity of the mole. A few seconds passed before she realized she'd been holding her breath. She released it and inhaled again. She wanted to grab Tony's hand and squeeze it until the blood gathered in his fingertips, but she resisted. *This is it!* she thought to herself. *We're now at the moment we've been waiting for.* She and Tony eyed each other briefly before Jake spoke again.

"All right, Jake, we're cooking with gas," Tony said. "As soon as you can see the license, give me the number so I can call in the plate."

The car crept along. J.J. watched Jake rock back and forth as if he struggled to see the plate. Through the tinted glass, she could see a figure, a male figure as far as she could tell. The man craned his neck, scanning the park, looking for something, maybe suspicious visitors as if he expected to see someone he recognized. After a few seconds that felt more like a few hours, the driver pulled into a parking space and turned off the ignition.

"Jesus, he's finally parked. I can't see inside the car, but—he's getting out. He's getting out. He's walking around to the trunk. Shit! I missed the plate and he's blocking the number! I can't see it."

The man walked with his head down. Dressed in black jeans and a dark hoodie that concealed his face, he opened the trunk and pulled out a trash bag sealed with duct tape and a pair of gloves. He glanced over both shoulders before closing the trunk and heading into the park.

"He took the package out of the trunk and headed into the park. Looks like we've got D.C. plates—David, Tango, 9-9-2-2."

Tony and J.J. looked at each other and she picked up the radio. "Is that a Black Toyota SUV?" she asked.

"Roger that, looks like a Sequoia."

"That's Chris Johnson's truck," she confirmed.

"Well, I'll be a caught dog," Jake said. "That's Agent Johnson all right. All dressed in black and carrying a plastic bag wrapped in duct tape. I've got the dash cam running."

"We nailed him!" Tony said, giving J.J. a high five. "I knew the son of a bitch was dirty. Smile for the camera, douche bag!"

J.J. nodded in agreement.

"We need to pinch this jerk-off, now," Tony said. "Let's roll him up."

"All in due time," she responded. "Even on the outside chance he doesn't show up for his polygraph, he's not making a single move without picking up that money this afternoon."

"No doubt," Tony said.

"We'll let Money T's team cover him for the rest of the day. As soon as he returns to pick up the money we'll get him. And this mess will be all over," she turned to face Tony. "Mike's going to hold him at the exam site until we give him the okay to let Chris go, right?"

"Yep," Tony replied. He'd spoken with Mike early that morning and made all the necessary arrangements. "He's got that part under control. He ain't goin' anywhere without our okay."

She held the radio to her mouth. "All right, Money T, when he leaves here, you've got the eye. He's got to mark the signal to let the Russian's know it's time to pick up the drop and leave the cash," J.J. ordered. "Let him out of your sight and you'll be the next one with the pink Mini Coop, are we understood?"

"Roger that," said Money T. "Trust me. I'll be on his ass like a summer breeze. He might feel me, but he won't see me."

"That's what I want to hear!"

Not five minutes later Chris left the park empty handed. How he could live with himself, J.J. didn't know but she couldn't wait to pop his ass later that day. The arrest would signal an end to the Bureau's woes and her misery.

"Blue Leader, this is Cham." She posed as a power walker on the trail in order to scout out the exact drop location. "Looks like he made the drop about 100 meters in. I couldn't get eyes on the exact location because I had to keep moving."

"Good work, Cham," J.J. said before turning to Tony. "All right! Time to make the switch."

Tony grabbed the radio. "J.J. and I are going in, Jake. I'm taking the radio. I don't care if you see a bird flying crooked, make sure you radio me if anything looks suspicious. Don't let us get caught out there with our balls hangin' out."

"Roger that, blue team," Jake said. "We've got you covered."

J.J. retrieved the package from the back seat. She and Tony moved quickly under cover of the towering trees to find the drop location. Based on the information they'd received from Dmitriyev the site was approximately 100 meters down and to the right of the walking path in a hollowed log. A twisted Coca-Cola can next to an adjacent rock would mark the area. Her gaze darted around as she scanned to find the precise location.

"Hurry up, slow poke," Tony said. "Chris should be marking the signal any minute and I'm sure the Russians won't be too far behind."

No sooner than the words passed Tony's lips, the radio sounded. "Blue Leader, this is Money T. The subject just marked the signal. White duct tape on a light pole in a shopping center parking lot approximately three miles west of the drop location, off of Connecticut Avenue. I'm hanging tight to see when our friends drive—uh!" Money paused.

"What is it? What is it?" Tony asked.

"He must've been running late. A vehicle with Russian diplomatic plates just passed me. Couldn't catch all the numbers but I'll bet they're on the way to the drop location."

"Copy that, Money," Tony said. He picked up the pace, his feet crunching the fallen leaves as he hoofed along the trail. "You just stay on Chris. Make sure he gets to the Bureau offsite for the test!"

"I'm on him."

"Shit! We've got to hurry up," J.J. said breaking into a run. "If Golikov's people are only three miles away, they'll be here any minute."

CHAPTER 39

Jack eyed Lana angrily as she entered the interrogation room at the Alexandria Detention Facility. He had called and asked her to pay him a long overdue visit. To his surprise, she obliged. After everything he'd done to help boost her career, she owed him that much. In jail nearly a week, he'd had a lot of time to reflect. He finally allowed the seeds of distrust and contempt to take hold and grow as he should've many months before.

"In case you hadn't noticed, I'm locked up. Didn't think you were going to show up," Jack said snidely. He feigned hurt at the absence he'd fully expected. Without power and position he was of no use to Lana. He'd merely been a pawn in some career-driven chess match, her fat needy puppet. Jack had always been under the impression she'd just been trying to get ahead—after all, he often received the same in return, but one particular thought disturbed him more than any other.

Lana shook her head, forcing tears from her beady little blues. "I'm sorry for not coming sooner, Jack. I, uhhh, I guess I just couldn't bear to see you here. You doing okay?"

"Three hots and cot, and a lot of reading. Given my situation, I can't complain. It is what it is," he said. "Listen, I know you want to ask. So let me save you the trouble. *No*, I didn't spy for the Russians."

She lifted her eyebrows and smirked. "You sure about that?"

His eyebrows scrunched. "How the hell could you even suggest— You think this is fucking funny? I could get the death penalty for a crime I didn't commit."

"I'm—I'm sorry, Jack," Lana lamented. "Everybody's on edge. This is all so surreal."

He nodded and accepted her apology, with prejudice. She'd always been a heartless bitch. Why he'd expected anything different now was beyond him. She was who she was.

"Listen, has anyone come to talk to you about Cartwright?"

He shook his head. Besides J.J., Jim had been the only person who'd even attempted to contact him in jail. Even left a message saying he had a plan to get Jack out, but Jack refused Jim's calls. It was Jim's fault Jack had been tossed in jail in the first place. Even though he'd always known Jim to be an upstanding person, somewhere along the line his life had veered steeply from the high road. Cartwright had compromised his ideals, lost his integrity. Thus, he was not the same man Jack had met at the academy so many years ago. Jack mourned for the loss of Jim's character almost as much as he regretted the loss of his own.

"No," Jack said, noting her glum expression. "Something wrong?"

"Afraid so." She sighed. "He's, uhhh, he's dead. Shot himself in the head at a scenic overlook off the GW Parkway."

"My God!" Jack yelled. He fell back in his chair and placed his hand over his heart. He knew Jim's life had gone astray but bad enough to kill himself? "Why? Did he say why?"

"He left a note but gave no reason."

"You must be devastated. He pulled quite a few strings to get you hired."

"Yes, I'm quite devastated." Her voice was solemn and flat. "We know all the rumors about him were true. He must've been afraid his family would find out."

Jack hardened his glare on Lana, his face reddened as the edges of his mouth turned down. "Why would he be *afraid?* Despite the rumors, you, Chris, and I were the *only ones* who knew the truth."

She clasped her hands together as her face turned flush red. "I didn't know he told you."

"He and I have been friends since Quantico. He told me about the incident in the garage years ago," Jack said, his mind churning. "Wait a minute. You didn't use that against him, did you? You're not so blinded by ambition that you would blackmail a decent man and a father of two beautiful girls just to further your career, are you?!"

She shook her head feverishly. "Jack, *no!* I would never tell a soul. It's Chris. It had to be Chris. Oh my God—the money, the erratic behavior—it all makes sense now."

"Lana, you have to report this to security at Washington Field, not Headquarters, Washington Field. You can't let him get away with this."

She exhaled and her shoulders relaxed. "Chris will meet his fate soon enough. He's scheduled to take his polygraph this morning. If we're right about him, he'll leave in handcuffs."

Jack eyed her suspiciously. "You seem awfully confident. My question to you is why?"

She glanced down at her watch. "Look at the time. I hate to cut this short, but I need to get out of here. Busy day ahead at the office."

"Mhm Hmm," Jack said. "Lana, what game are you playing?"

"You know me, Jack," she said, smirking as she stood to leave. "I don't play games. I just win."

• • •

J.J. and Tony paced down the walking path, scanning the area carefully every step of the way. About a hundred meters in, the can was blowing across the trail. The marker had moved.

"Do you see it, Tony?" J.J. said. Her head whipped from side to side. Nervous. Panicked. *Where is it? Where is it?*

Tony threw up his hands in resignation. "No, I don't see anything. You think we passed it?"

"No. We couldn't have."

"It's got to be here somewhere because Chris left empty handed. You go back a few yards and I'll go forward a few yards. I'll holler if I see anything and you do the same."

Tony and J.J. scoured the area in close proximity to the walking path, inch by inch. The sun's light helped them see, but it'd also make it easy for the Russians to spot them if they were caught in the area. The last thing they needed was for Golikov's people to abort the op fearing an FBI sting. Their entire plan hinged on the Russians taking the package.

"I got it! I got it!" Tony said.

A smile slipped between her lips as she jetted back to his location. The op was coming to an end, and so far they'd averted the major disasters. But she caught herself. *One step forward, two steps back.*

"Here it is. A hundred twenty yards on the left."

She shook her head in frustration. They'd wasted so much time.

Then Jake radioed in. "Blue Leader one. You've got an incoming. A silver Toyota Camry sedan with Russian diplomatic plates just pulled into the lot. A white male, approximately six feet, two inches, close-shaven head, and a gray jogging suit is heading your way."

"Shit! Shit! Make the switch. Make the switch," J.J. urged.

Tony dug his hand beneath the thin layer of leaves. He pulled out Chris's package, which was wrapped in a manner almost identical to the one they prepared. He replaced it with the fake package, kicked a few leaves over it with his foot, then shoved the real intelligence into his jacket and zipped it up. J.J. took the radio and slipped it into her pocket.

"I don't see him yet. Let's go!" Her every sense was heightened, every sound magnified, every movement perceptible. "I hear something. I hear something. Walk faster."

As they powered along the trail, the package slipped from beneath Tony's Jacket. He pushed it against his ribcage, held his hand firmly against it. He couldn't let it fall out, not now. They continued down the path until they rounded a turn which took them out of their follower's line of sight.

J.J. held her breath as she slowed down. She pulled the radio from her jacket pocket. "Any sign of him yet? We made the switch."

Jake didn't respond.

"Jake? Jake? Do you read me? Any sign of him yet?"

Nothing but static. Jake had gone silent.

But she heard something else in the distance. Footsteps.

"You hear that?" Tony whispered.

J.J. nodded.

Her heart pounded. Maybe the Russian was lurking around the drop site instead of returning to his vehicle. The footsteps coming from behind quickened, drew closer. Suddenly she heard a noise. Someone padded toward them, faster and faster. If the Russians were onto them, they were shit soup. She softened her steps, as if making less noise could conceal their presence. If they could just make it to the fork in the trail, they could head back toward the parking lot and get a window of time in the clear.

"You hear that?" she whispered. "Keep walking. Pick up the pace."

She turned the volume down to a whisper and shoved the radio back into her pocket. They pushed forward. The faster they walked, the louder the footsteps sounded. Suddenly, the steps quickened until J.J. heard them on her heels. She unzipped her jacket and reached for the holster on her back. Tony followed suit. She whipped her head around and...

"Jake!" she screamed. "Jesus, Mary, and Joseph you scared the shit out of me!"

"You better say a Hail Mary when you get home because you almost took one in the chest," Tony said. The package was on the ground under

Tony's foot. He dropped it lightning fast and placed his hand firmly on the holster in the small of his back. "Why didn't you answer, J.J.?"

"Sorry about that. My radio battery died," he said. "I ran to catch you but didn't want to make a big scene. I've been out there watching him and he's still there. Maybe he caught a glimpse of you leaving the area near the drop site and decided to wait."

Precisely J.J.'s thoughts. Her mouth dropped open. "What are we gonna do now?" J.J. asked Tony. If the Russians suspected for a second the packages had been switched, the entire op was all for naught and Karat and Vorobyev were dead men walking. "You can't walk out of here looking six months pregnant with that thing."

Tony shook his head and shrugged. Both he and J.J. struggled to find a solution and leaving the package in the park to retrieve later was not an option.

"Why don't I take it and hold it for you," Jake said. "As soon as you leave, he'll probably follow you out. Then I can bring the package back to headquarters."

J.J. felt a slight sensation behind her ear. She reached her arm out then hesitated. Jake had never given her reason to mistrust him before. And he certainly wasn't the ICE Phantom. With no regular access to files, he couldn't steal and sell them. Still, her "gift" had never failed her before. Not once. She felt uneasy and pulled the package to her gut. "No offense Jake, but I'm not letting this package out of my sight."

Tony shrugged. "J.J., don't be ridiculous. We've got to wait on the text message, right? Jake can take the package and meet us. We'll let the teams take a lunch break and head back to headquarters to talk to Sunnie."

Tony grabbed the package from J.J.'s hand and held out to Jake. Although she had nothing to go on but a slight sensation, J.J. snatched it back.

"Nope. That's okay. We'll deal with it."

Jake scoffed. "It's me, Jake. Not some spy. Don't worry."

"Shit shit!" she yelped. It was the crotch itch…again. And this time it felt more like a stab than the usual crawling sensation. Her knees buckled. "Sorry, it's the, uhhh, it's the *thing*. You know…"

They both shrugged it off.

Jake had lied big time.

About what, J.J. didn't know, but every fiber of her being warned her, *Don't put the package in Jake's hand!* She had no time to assess him. She glared at Jake, her head cocked to the side. All she could do was stand frozen, weighing her options while Tony glared at her as if she'd lost the little bit of mind she had left.

"We can handle it," J.J. insisted.

Tony's jaw tightened and he stared her down. "Really? Why are you being such a hard ass?" Tony asked, confused as hell, determined to have his way. "What's a matta with you? Give him the package already."

He didn't understand the problem and she couldn't explain, not then, not there. When J.J. didn't budge, Tony snatched the package from her hand and returned it to Jake, who backed out of J.J.'s reach as he shifted his gaze nervously between the two.

"Take it and go," Tony ordered, strong-arming J.J. to keep her from reaching Jake. "See you back at headquarters in a few. And charge up that radio, so we can get a hold of you when the next phase of this op goes down. Ya hear me?"

"Loud and clear," Jake said with a canary-ate-cat smile emerging upon his lips. He trekked down the trail at a rapid pace.

"What was that all about? It's Jake for Christ's sake!" Tony said, admonishing J.J. for her behavior. Maybe she'd gotten it wrong for the first time in her life. But her heart sank as she feared the worst. The package contained TOP SECRET information. *Will he take it back to headquarters? Or disappear?* She didn't know. But based on the physiological reaction, she suspected the latter. Within the hour, she'd know.

"I can't explain."

"You can't or you won't."

"I just had a bad feeling. Call it women's intuition. I know I'm standing on shaky ground but sometimes, you've got to trust that I know what the hell I'm doing."

Tony and J.J. exhaled and headed toward the park entrance. "Is it too early for a shot of vodka?" she asked.

"For you, yeah. Anytime is too early," Tony replied, his voice between jest and serious as a heart attack.

When they arrived at the car, Russian car had already left, but Jake's car was still in the lot. He hadn't returned.

"Guess they gave up waiting," J.J. said, scanning the lot. "But Jake's still here. We should go get him."

"Just let it go," Tony said to J.J. "We'll see him back at H-Q in a few minutes. Let's get outta here."

J.J. grabbed her cell phone from the glove compartment and checked for Dmitriyev's text.

"Anything yet?"

"Nothing," she glanced at her watch, "but we've still got a little time." She slipped into the passenger seat.

Tony took the driver's seat and started the ignition. "Let's just hope time doesn't run out."

CHAPTER 40

Chris's gut wrenched. Part of him felt relieved the operation was over, yet deep in the conscience he'd longed suppressed, he'd almost wished J.J. was as smart as her reputation purported, that she could've rolled him up and freed him from his hell. He'd grown tired of always looking over his shoulder waiting for his colleagues in raid jackets to corner and arrest him. But he'd gotten away. He'd made another drop. His fear shifted to the hope that the information was valuable, some of the most damaging he'd ever provided. The Russians would pay him handsomely enough to set up him and Koshechka for a long time.

He pulled into the parking lot adjacent to the FBI's offsite polygraph location off Pennsylvania Avenue, stepped onto the cobbled sidewalk. The jitters kicked in. He couldn't pull his nerves together. Sweat poured as from a hooker in church on communion Sunday. Too late to confess his sins now. His throat tightened. But he swallowed hard and proceeded with the plan. They told him he could beat it, evidenced by the test runs he passed with flying colors. But he started to talk himself out of success, told himself he couldn't beat the polygraph unless Jesus himself sat in the chair and took the test in his place.

The closer he got to the entrance door, the more his pores rained. He appeared as if he'd just stepped out of hell's sauna—the fiery furnace in which his conscienceless soul may be destined to rest by the time the day was over. But his Koshechka depended on him, and the new baby too.

So he dug somewhere down deep in his core and scrounged the courage to man up and move forward with the plan. She was right, they had a lot of money, but not nearly enough. Certainly too little to last them the rest of their lives and they'd be on the run for at least that long. Another cool million and they could sever their ties to the area, move to where they could live modestly, without fear of arrest.

He checked in at the receptionist's desk and asked for the bathroom key. At the sink moments later, he splashed cool water on his reddened face to reduce his temperature and glared at himself in the mirror. The reflection sickened him. He'd sacrificed his life, his entire being, for the love of Koshechka. After all was said and done, he wondered if she'd ever be worth the steep price he'd paid.

Chris yanked a paper towel from the dispenser and dabbed it under each arm. It soaked in seconds. He was desperate for a shot of something 80-proof or higher. But ingesting anything except water would all but ensure his failure. He wouldn't make it past the pretest questioning. No, if he was going to fail, he wanted to do so going down in a blaze of duplicitous fire.

"Mr. Johnson?" Mike said as he re-entered the reception area.

Chris nodded his head and offered his damp hand. "Yes. I'm Chris. I'm here for the test this morning."

Mike clasped and shook hands with Chris, then wiped the dampness on his pant leg. "Everybody's always nervous, but this should go smoothly. You've got nothing to be worried about, unless, of course, you've been spying for the Russians. In that case, this will feel just south of hell," he joked.

Chris longingly eyed the exit as his mouth exposed a sheepish grin. "Ha, ha!" he chuckled. "That's a good one."

"Polygraph humor," Mike said. "Right this way."

During the hour-long pretest interview, Chris answered everything as Koshechka taught him. Then Mike escorted him into a small room. Beside the table with the polygraph laptop sat a disturbing chair, the electric chair's baby cousin. Once seated, Mike strapped the larger of the white belts around Chris's torso to monitor his heart rate. The blood pressure monitor placed on his arm tightened moments later. A pair metal sensors resting on the table's edge were attached to his fingers. They monitored his perspiration levels. Soaked from the start, Chris thanked the heavens that sweat alone did not determine one's guilt or innocence. He would've failed the test before they flipped the switch. A second polygrapher, an observer, sat cloaked behind one-way glass. Chris stared at his reflection and allowed his mind to drift off, which relaxed him for a few moments. Then he shook his head to bring himself back to reality.

After taking a moment to explain testing procedures, Mike stepped out of the room, warning Chris that the exam would begin when he returned. His hands trembled on the chair arms as he stared blankly, trying to calm himself, clear his mind. Eventually, he fixed his mind on the vision of his Koshechka, imagined laying his head against her round belly as the baby pressed his little feet against Chris's cheek.

When Mike re-entered the room, Chris faced the ceiling as if waiting for the answer to his prayers to drop out of the light fixture.

"Are you ready?" Mike asked.

Chris was too tense to speak, so he nodded.

"Great. Let's get started."

Don and Mike sat in a state of utter confusion. They examined the result charts, four hours' worth, periodically glancing at Chris through the one-way glass and then again at one another.

"I'm curious to hear your thoughts, Mike," Don said. "I don't mind telling you, something isn't adding up."

"I agree," Mike said, scanning the readings. "Look here at the control questions. These are the readings for all of the counterintelligence issues," he said pointing to the specific areas of concern. "But look at him," Mike said as they watched Chris crumble over the edge of his seat. "And did you see his heart rate? It was almost off the charts...but consistently so."

"I know," Don said. "I mean, the results are obvious."

"Yes, they are," Mike added. "He passed. His readings are high, but he passed."

"But something's definitely off."

"Before we give him his results, I say we just talk to him for a minute and see what he has to say."

"Yeah, that's a good idea. And if I were you, I'd take the minimalist approach," Don said. "The less said, the better."

They returned to the room, solemn and bearing emotionless expressions. Each had perfected the poker face. Don leaned against the wall while Mike returned to his seat behind the laptop.

Overheated, Chris's gaze ping-ponged, shifting back and forth between the two. His face reddened as he stared down at his feet. He grew quiet, lost in his guilt. Their expressions told him everything he needed to know. He'd nailed his coffin. He rubbed his hands up and down his pant legs and broke eye contact.

"Is there anything you'd like to tell us before we provide you some feedback on your results?"

"I failed, right?" He grabbed his forehead, hunched his shoulders and mumbled, "I told her it wouldn't work."

Don folded his arms across his chest and shot a glance at Mike, acknowledging both of their suspicions. "Uhhh...you told *who what* wouldn't work?"

Chapter 41

Early Thursday Morning…

"Comrade Aleksey!" Igor barked. "Come with us!"

Dmitriyev stayed close to his desk the entire morning, waiting for Golikov's people to return with the drop. As the line chief, he knew they'd need his assistance in verifying the information as they were more thug than sophisticated operatives. They'd have little idea how to gauge the value of the source's intelligence. But their stark, cold expressions concerned him. Perhaps, J.J. had not made the drop. Maybe the operation had been compromised.

Even though he feared he was walking to his death, he gravely followed them down the long darkened corridor which led to the secure facility, thinking of all the people he wished he could say goodbye to, wondering what his final words would be. They occupied the "interview" room, the same room where they had only days ago interrogated Vorobyev, the floor was still stained with the remnants of Stan's beating. They allowed Dmitriyev to enter first.

He balled his fists tight, prepared to defend himself if attacked from behind and determined to go down fighting until the end. The sound of blood coursing through his veins loudened. He quickly scuttled to the back of the room and took a seat within close proximity to a fire extinguisher hanging in the corner.

The door slammed shut. Igor and Aleksey took their seats. They stared at him, malice colored every expression.

"You understand why we've asked you here today, right?" Vasiliy asked, his scowl unflinching.

Dmitriyev nodded and said nothing.

Igor reached beneath the table.

This is it! Dmitriyev thought to himself. The faint sound of plastic rumbled beneath. Maybe they'd planned to suffocate him. That was well within the KGB's stable of execution methods.

Dmitriyev watched and prayed, bracing himself for their wrath.

Igor's hand emerged, finally. Dmitriyev gasped before he noticed the duct taped package in his hand. Igor stripped the tape from the edges and removed the contents, a stack of papers.

"We need you to take a look at this information and assess its worth," Igor said as he pushed the papers across the table.

Aleksey steadied his trembling hand as he reached across the table to grab the contents. He slowly and deliberately thumbed through each page, examining each page for information that would save his brother and friend. Several minutes passed before he spoke.

"Hmph. A wide variety of material, similar to what the source usually provides, but this Karat case is interesting. If I'm not mistaken, he has provided the entire FBI file from the case's inception until a few days ago—this is rare, very rare. Based on the latest communication, it appears as if the FBI was unaware that Plotnikov was a code clerk. They thought he was a clean diplomat working the missile defense problem."

"Stupid Americans!" Igor said, laughing from his belly.

Vasiliy sat pensively and listened.

"And you see the dates on these cables?" he said, holding them up to face his colleagues. "These cannot be falsified. They are system generated, so these appear to be valid documents."

Igor looked at Vasiliy who frowned.

On the underside of the stack he found an envelope, a letter…the letter.

"Did you see this?" Dmitriyev said, holding the typewritten envelope up for both to view. "This appears to be some kind of communication from *the asset*."

Aleksey carefully slipped his thumb into the gap at the opening and tore through the seam. He removed the lone sheet of paper and read it to himself.

After a moment passed, he cocked his head to the side as he handed the envelope's contents to Vasiliy. "It seems we have two new developments," Aleksey said.

Vasiliy quickly reviewed the letter, which indicated the mole had, in fact, been mistaken in implicating Vorobyev. He scratched his head, as his brow furrowed. "This is indeed a…*development* as you say. Could this be true?"

"I don't know," Aleksey said, trying not to oversell. "What I can offer is that this letter is written in a manner consistent with the others we've received from him in the past."

"I see." Vasiliy passed the contents to Igor, who glazed over the document. Then they eyed each other as the significance sunk in.

"I can't tell you how to act in this situation, as that is between you and your boss," Aleksey said. "But it seems to me, if we had enough confidence in the source to condemn Comrades Vorobyev and Plotnikov, we must be equally resolute in exonerating them. Wouldn't you agree?"

Igor and Vasiliy glanced at each other again, both knowing.

"Go." Vasiliy said to Igor. "I will call Golikov and inform him of this Karat case. He will be anxious to know."

Dmitriyev's gaze followed Igor out the door, the tension released in his shoulders. He could finally relax, at least for the moment. He only hoped J.J. would be successful in identifying the mole before he himself became the next victim of Golikov's heavy-handed justice.

· · ·

"That's the last one," Vorobyev said to himself, sealing the envelope containing his final letter to his wife and children. He hoped someday they would understand why such drastic measures were necessary.

He'd spent the entire night reviewing his personal papers to ensure there was nothing Golikov's people could twist into their sadistic lies or exploit in a smear campaign to damage his post mortem reputation. His family would suffer enough. He couldn't bear to leave any business unfinished that might cause them additional pain.

Vorobyev dressed himself in his favorite black suit, the one his wife had picked out for him during his tour in Italy many years ago. Told him he was too good for the cheap suits he usually bought for work; his position required a proper suit fit for a man representing his country. And he felt like a king every time he dressed in her gift to him. His life, his love, his dearest, his Marina.

He meandered around until he reached his bedroom, then collapsed onto his mattress back first and stared at the ceiling.

Within seconds, he realized he didn't want a cold, blank wall to be his last memory.

On his dresser stood the photos of all his family and friends in happier times. He collected each, arranged them on his nightstand, and then reached under the pillow and wrapped his hand around the cool, steel grip. He fixed his finger on the trigger and rolled his feet onto the bed, facing everyone he held near and dear. Tears trickled down his cheeks as he pressed the barrel hard against his temple. He took one last look and slowly pulled the trigger.

"God . . . have mercy on my soul."

Bam! Bam! Bam!

The loud knock startled him. He bolted upright, slipped the gun underneath his pillow, and eased toward the door. Had to be Golikov's people. No one else would be allowed to consort with an accused and, for all intents and purposes, convicted spy.

"Yeeees?" Vorobyev called out from the end of the hall.

"It's Igor. Open the door!"

"Just a moment," Vorobyev yelled, scrambling to get out of his suit. "One minute. I'm not properly dressed."

He dashed back into the bedroom and threw off his clothes until down to his T-shirt and slacks. Pulling the sheets back, he messed up the bed as if he'd been sleeping, just in case Igor decided to nose around. Then he paced to the door and turned the doorknob.

"Igor?" Vorobyev asked, leaving only a slight opening.

"I need to speak with you for a moment. It's urgent. Let me inside."

Vorobyev nodded, stepped back, and allowed Igor to push his way through. He could do nothing but shake his head in disgust at the disrespect from this younger generation.

"What is it? What have you to accuse me of now? Or is high treason insufficient?"

Igor made himself comfortable on the couch. "Well, it seems today is your lucky day."

"My lucky day? What do you mean?" he said, his mind flashing back to moments ago when he held a gun to his head, preparing to pull the trigger.

"Turns out our source was fed some bad information. It was a provocation. As a result, you have been cleared of all charges."

"What? I...I don't understand." Vorobyev gasped and his knees wavered as the reality set in. He'd lost all hope for any kind of miracle. He caught his balance and then stood erect.

"You will return home a free man," Igor said as if he had any idea about what freedom was.

Vorobyev smirked. "Free you say? You falsely accuse me. You beat me like a dog. You imprison me in my own home," he growled, jabbing his fist into the air. "After everything you have put me through. What is free? No. I'm *innocent*. I'm not *free*."

Igor, stunned by Vorobyev's insolence, could not find the words to retort, so he stood to leave. "I've said what I came to say." He made his way to the door and gripped the doorknob. He and Vorobyev never broke eye contact.

"Mhm hmm. You be careful." Vorobyev offered his final words. "If Golikov did this to me, he could do it to anyone, including you."

• • •

Back at FBI Headquarters

"Hey Sam, where's Sunnie?" J.J. asked Samantha Monroe, one of the newer agents in her office and the only other female apart from Lana. She certainly looked the agent part in her pin-sharp pantsuits, but J.J. hadn't worked with her long enough to form any real opinion of her professionalism.

"She was just here a minute ago," she said, craning her neck around Sunnie's partition which was adjacent to her own. "She may have run up to the cafeteria. I think it's snack time."

J.J. glanced at her watch and then turned to Tony. "Yeah, she's right. We should probably head upstairs."

Sunnie, one of the best analysts in the Bureau's cadre, was the color of a milk chocolate Lindor truffle, and with her short crop, silky weave, or swaying braids, every day was a hair adventure. Her flamboyant, colorful dress was equally creative. She fed her not-quite-plus-sized curves frequently, never met a snack she didn't like. Neither J.J. nor Tony had ever seen her eat a full meal; she just grazed all day.

They entered Sunnie's happy place and saw her hovering around the salad bar, carefully scrutinizing every piece of fruit before loading them into her Styrofoam container. Sunnie peered up in time to see J.J. and Tony approaching and appeared none too pleased.

"Is it too late to run?" she deadpanned. "What do you two want?"

"There's our favorite analyst!" Tony said with almost too much enthusiasm. Sunnie's bullshit detector rivaled J.J.'s and she could spot it coming a mile away.

"Save it for your partner," Sunnie said. "Now what can I do you for?"

J.J. eyed Tony askance. "Anyway. We need you to run down some information for us."

"What information?" she asked, holding up a piece of fruit in tongs. "Does this pineapple look okay to you? I think I saw it here last week." She threw it back into the container and continued to dig.

"We need you to work your magic and get us access to the personnel files for everyone on the bigot list...except us and Lana."

"Personnel files, huh? You know you aren't allowed to review such information without AD authorization. For me to do so would be breaking Bureau regulations."

"Bella!" Tony said, laying on the Italian as thick as frozen molasses. The lilt in his voice nearly lulled Sunnie into a hypnotic state. "Ho bisogno di andare in bagna prego," he pleaded, batting his lashes as he begged like a puppy dog.

Sunnie's mouth fell open. She nearly salivated, while J.J. stared blankly at them both.

"What did he say?" she asked, still swooning, dazed by the sound of his voice.

J.J. cranked her neck. "Does it matter?"

Tony narrowed his eyes at J.J. then shifted them toward Sunnie. He needed her help, not her attitude.

"I said you are so beautiful and begged for your help. We thought you could . . . you know, pull some strings with Wendell." Wendell was the pocket-protector wearing Chief of Filedom—better known as the senior file clerk. He defended his turf as if he was guarding the crown jewels. A recent graduate of Brigham Young University, Wendell was a black Mormon and still a virgin, a regretful state he hoped Sunnie would rescue him from. "You know he's got a 'thing' for you," Tony said, creating air quotes with his fingers.

She rolled her eyes and resumed her quest. "So, what are you now, my pimp?" Her face was void of expression.

"No . . . no, it's not even like that. I just—"

"I'm kidding." She laughed. "Had you going, didn't I?"

Tony exhaled as J.J. got a chuckle at his expense.

"Of course I'll help my favorite agent. You too, Tony," she said. "You're the only ones in this place who don't treat me as if I put my brain on layaway."

"We owe you big time," J.J. said.

"Yes, you do. And I'll need a full briefing so I'll know what the hell I'm looking for," she said. "But for starters, who's paying for my snack?"

She jammed her hand in Tony's face, palm side up.

Tony pulled a twenty dollar bill from his wallet. Before he could hand it to her, Sunnie snatched it and headed to the cashier line.

"All right," J.J. whispered. "I know your Italian sucks. What did you really say?"

"I'm not sure." Tony chuckled. "But I think I told her I had to go to the bathroom."

"Good one," she patted him on the back. Then her face contorted. She appeared uneasy. "We should get back to the office."

"What's a matta with you?" Tony asked.

"You ever get the feeling you've forgotten something important?"

CHAPTER 42

As Sunnie entered the Special File Room, she took a deep breath and sashayed to the customer service counter. Personnel files and the most sensitive codename cases were stored under heavy security there.

"There's my man, Wendell!" Sunnie prepared to put on yet another Academy Award winning performance. Wendell, with his nerdy style and *resistible* charm, was shunned by his colleagues for his unsophisticated manner and pathetic crush on Sunnie. He'd been begging her for a date for too long and gave in to her every demand with ease, mere putty in her uninterested hands.

She leaned over the counter and fanned herself. Gave him a glimpse of what he wanted to see. He was always more pliable staring down at her distractions.

"Is the air on? It's quite warm in here, don't you think?"

"Quite," he said. He couldn't tell you the color of her eyes, but he could tell you the number of the dye that was used to create the thread holding the cleavage area of her sweater together. He licked his ChapStick-deprived lips and peered shamelessly at the divide between her breasts.

"So, when you gonna take me to dinner?" she asked.

He snorted and blushed. "Every time I ask, you tell me you have a boyfriend."

"You're not going to give up that easily, are you?" She smiled flirtatiously. "Anyway, I need a teeny tiny favor."

"Yeah? What's that?"

She handed him her file request form. "I need to look at these personnel files. Can you pull them for me?"

He scanned the sheet then looked at her over the top of his glasses. "Wow. These must be pretty popular employees. This is the second request today."

"Second?"

He glanced over both shoulders, checked to ensure no one else was listening to their conversation. Of course, the room was empty except them, but he seemed excited by the intrigue. He whispered, "Director Freeman's secretary submitted an earlier request. It's part of some big investigation."

"Is that right?" she replied.

"Yeah. So, I can't let you take them."

She released a woeful sigh. "Wendell, this is really important. Life and death."

"I dunno," he said, hemming and hawing.

She moved close to him and traced her finger around his ear to his lips. "Please, Wendell."

His body trembled. "Woo!" he screeched, wiping his brow. "O-O-Okay. But you can't leave the room. Grab a seat at a booth and review them here. Please make it fast. They're coming in an hour."

"You're a life saver! I owe you one," she choked out.

Sunnie didn't hate Wendell. In fact, with some new glasses, clothes, and a decent haircut, he wouldn't be half bad. Still not her type, but not half bad.

He lifted the heavy stack and placed them in the booth closest to the service desk, no doubt by design. He gave her cleavage one last glance. "Just let me know when you're done."

Sunnie took a seat, removed the file from the stack, and flipped the first page open when she felt Wendell's eyes on her. She whipped her head toward him. "Okaaay, you can go now. Run along."

When she turned her attention back to the file contents, she noticed Lana's name. She hadn't planned to review it, but she couldn't resist the urge to peek. After all, that's why the Bureau paid her the big bucks, for her inquisitiveness.

She thumbed through page after page, scrutinizing each sheet. The more she read, the faster her pulse raced. All of a sudden, her mouth felt dry. J.J. and Tony were missing a big piece of their puzzle.

The first page contained Lana's polygraph examination report. *I'll be damned.* Sunnie's eyes widened as she scanned Lana's biographical information. Full name. Date of birth. Place of birth.

Sunnie fell back onto her seat, vowing to take a moment to pause for her conniption later. She snapped herself out of the shock. No time for that. She had to skim through each of the files as quickly as possible. Jack, Chris, everyone. In just a few short minutes, J.J. and Tony would have the information that might change the course of their entire investigation.

"Tony, this is it!" J.J. scrolled through her cell phone after the text ringtone sounded. Dmitriyev finally sent the text message they'd been waiting for—the location for the money pickup.

"About time! What did he say?"

"He says the drop is going down at noon in Rock Creek park's location 5, right off of Beech drive."

"But Chris is still at his poly exam. Do we need to go?"

"Yeah, we better cover our bases and get some coverage, just in case." She glanced down at her watch and held it up to Tony's face. "Damn, there's no way we can get into position in time."

"Yeah, you're right," Tony said. "Let's radio Jake and get him up there."

J.J.'s eyebrows scrunched. Ever since she returned from the morning operation she had a feeling something was missing. She finally realized what it was. "Wait a minute. Jake's supposed to be here . . . with the package. Is he back yet?"

"I was in the cafeteria with you, remember?"

"Oh . . . right." She stood up from the guest chair in Tony's cubicle. Hurriedly, she tromped around poking her head in partitions elsewhere in the office. As she headed back toward Tony's desk, her skin tingled as if warning her that the shit was but a breeze away from the fan.

"Don't panic. You know how Jake is," Tony said. "He probably stopped off to get a burger or something. I mean we've been at it since five this morning."

"Hmmmm." Overcome with regret, she wished she hadn't ignored her earlier intuition, her gift. But this was Jake, a man she'd worked with for the past five years. A man she'd treated to lunch and attended basketball games with. A man who'd learned as much about her cases as Tony. A man who'd...her stomach sank. "You may be right, but I'm seriously not getting the warm and fuzzies about this. Get him on the radio. Now!"

"His radio's down, remember?"

She pressed her eyelids closed. "How convenient." An almost sickening sensation permeated her. "We need Jiggy on this. He should still be in the area."

"Roger that," Tony said.

"In the meantime, I'm going to try and reach Jake on his cell phone."

"Jiggy," Tony said after grabbing the radio. "This is Blue Leader One. What's your twenty? We need you."

Static poured through the speaker for a moment just long enough to make J.J. nervous.

"Copy that Blue Leader," Jiggy said, to Tony's relief. "I'm about fifteen minutes from location one."

"Okay, we need you to break every traffic law possible and get to location five! The drop's going down in less than a half hour and we'll never make it in time."

"All right. I'm on my way. I'll radio in when I arrive."

Tony laid the handset on his desk and ran to find J.J. at her cubicle. She looked up, her face tense with distress.

"I just called Jake's phone. His cell's no longer in service."

"What!" Tony said. "What the hell is going on?"

J.J. knew, the way she knew Santa didn't exist. He'd gotten away clean with the contents of the real drop intended for the Russians, which they would pay a boat load of money to get their hands on. And he could pretty much name his price. She regretted that she had not been firmer with Tony. If they didn't get the package back, they'd have hell to pay when Director Freeman found out.

• • •

"Blue Leader, it's Jiggy. Do you copy?" He pulled into the small cul-de-sac. If J.J. and Tony's source got his information right, the drop would take place in minutes. Maybe seconds.

"We copy," Tony said. "See anything yet?"

Jiggy scanned the park. "No, nothing so far. There are a couple of cars here. I'm going to park in the rear of the lot so I'll have a better view. Hang tight."

"Don't forget to turn on your dash cam," Tony said.

Jiggy turned his head to the rear, backing into a spot parallel to the parked cars. By the time he turned around to stop the ignition and turn on the camera, he noticed someone, a man maybe, throw a garbage bag into the back seat of the vehicle. An oversized hoodie and sunglasses shrouded his hair and face.

"Blue Leader, I think we've got something. Maybe a male five-feet, eight inches. Dark clothing, a hoodie. Can't get any more of a physical description but I saw them throwing an object wrapped in a garbage bag into the back seat. Looks like a white male from what I can see."

"All right. You stay on him. What's the plate number? We'll go ahead and run it while we wait for your next update."

"Roger that. Looks like we've got D.C. plates Juliet Charlie, five-zero five-zero."

Tony and J.J. snapped their heads toward each other. J.J. remembered the mole wrote a letter signed as "Juliet Charles" and snatched the radio out of Tony's hand.

"I'm sorry," J.J. said. "Did you say Juliet Charlie?"

CHAPTER 43

When Mike turned to Don with his eyebrows raised, Chris folded like a broken beach chair under a Sumo wrestler. They had him, and Chris knew it. And from the expression on Mike's and Don's faces, they knew it too. "Uhhh...why don't you pull up a chair and make yourself comfortable," Mike said to Don. "I think we may be here a while."

Chris's voice trembled as much as his hands. He gripped the arm of the chair to suppress the obvious shaking.

"Would you like something to drink? Some water?" Mike asked.

Chris nodded. The profuse sweating had left him parched, apparent from his dry, cracking lips. He struggled to find some semblance of comfort or calm. Koshechka's voice echoed in his mind; he envisioned her scorn-filled glare, watching him literally dissolve into a puddle of perspiration and fear. He thought he'd be strong enough to withstand the stress of the examination, but his body told him what his mind wouldn't allow him to believe.

He no longer wished to try.

For so long he'd struggled with his own deception, and the shame from the lives and careers he'd destroyed as a result of his constant treachery; it haunted him. Sitting across from his soon-to-be interrogators, he realized it would require more strength to tell another lie than to tell the truth. Still, he'd keep them off Koshechka's scent for as long as possible. When she eventually realized he wouldn't be returning home from his examination, she'd run away with their child and never look back. His only regret was the thought that his only child would grow up without knowing the sacrifice he'd made to keep him (or her) free.

"Since this is no longer a polygraph interview, we must read you your rights. We'd also like to record our conversation with your consent."

Chris tightened his grip on the chair arms and nodded yes. Then Don cited Miranda.

"Do you understand these rights as I've explained them to you?"

"I'm still an agent. I'm vaguely familiar with this part," Chris retorted.

"Now," Don said, "let's take this from the beginning. This Koshechka you mentioned earlier. What's her birth name?"

He hesitated still trying to concoct a way to tell a deceitful truth. He finally conceded to tell them something they wanted to know, even if not everything they *needed* to know. "Svetlana. Her name is Svetlana Aleksandrovna Mikhaylova."

"Is she a diplomat at the Russian Embassy?"

"No. As far as I know she has no affiliation with the Embassy, at least no direct affiliation."

"Hmph," Don said. "Except that she spies for them, *right?*"

Spies, Chris said to himself. For the first time, Chris had begun to separate his love for Koshechka from the evil he'd done. He and she were spies, traitors against his country if not hers. Guilt overcame him like a biblical plague, God's curse for his wrongdoing. The feeling was only compounded by the devastation he'd bring upon his father and grandfather when the truth about his cooperation with the Russians hit the press.

Mike piped in. "Does she have a residence in D.C.?"

He hesitated again but said nothing.

"Come on, Chris. I see you're trying to protect her, but you must realize by now that she was just using you," Mike said.

"This is her job," Don interjected. "She lies and steals for a living. She doesn't love you. You were nothing more than a middleman, a fall guy, the first line of defense in case the worst happened. And the worst has happened. Where are you? And where is she?"

Chris squirmed in his seat, avoiding their judgmental glares.

"If you're gonna be a fool, don't be *her* fool," Don continued. "She's playing you. Correction, she played you before you ever knew you were in the game. Her plan was always to put *you* in the hot seat."

Don's speech stung Chris as his mind flashed back to the moment he caught her in Jack's office. The mere memory filled his heart with the kind of rage that made weak men cause their women to disappear in darkened woods or off river banks. Truth was he didn't even know if the baby belonged to him. For all he knew, it could've been Jack's baby. With little effort, his tongue loosened.

"She lives in Northwest. 7700 Kalorama Road."

Don jotted down the information. "Uhhhh, could you excuse us for one minute? Mike, if I could see you outside for a quick second?"

Don led Mike into the hall and closed the door behind them, returning moments later. He took a deep breath, his eyes filled with pity. Chris dropped his chin to his chest. He wasn't the first man beguiled by the charms of a beautiful Russian spy and certainly wouldn't be the last. Many men had done much more for less.

"Sorry about that. We just need to run a quick check on the name to make sure you're being truthful with us. Now where were we?"

Mike stepped into an adjacent interview room to make a call. Tony could pass the information to his analyst and let her run the checks. Since he was in the middle of an operation, the information might be of immediate use. He dialed Tony's cell.

No answer.

Dialed again.

No answer...again.

Determined to keep trying until he got through, he dialed again. "Where the hell is he?"

• • •

J.J. waited for Jiggy's response. *Juliet Charlie.* Couldn't be sheer coincidence.

"Do you understand the words that are coming out of my mouth?" Jiggy said. He tapped on the radio, causing it to squelch. "Yes. Juliet Charlie, five zero five zero."

"Jiggy. Listen to me carefully. Don't let that car out of your sight! I don't care if you have to hitch your car to the bumper, don't lose 'em this time," J.J. pressed.

The backup lights on the suspect's vehicle lit up and he was set to trail him from the park. "Okay . . . looks like we're *buggin'* out!" Jiggy said. "Puttin' both hands on the wheel and I'll radio in when I've got something to report."

"All right," J.J. said. "We're gonna call NCIC to run the plate and get back to you. Let us know as soon as you can get a better physical description."

Tony hurriedly pressed the numbers on his desk phone.

"Hey, this is Special Agent Tony Donato in the CI Division. I need you to run a plate for me. We're in the middle of a surveillance and we need this information A-S-A—," he said. "Sure, I'll hold."

Incredulous, he crossed his eyes at J.J. A needed laugh in a tense moment. "Yeah, I'm here. The plate—," Tony said, cut off again. "Sure, I'll—"

Moments later, he read off the plate number and stuck up his middle finger at the phone. Nothing happened fast in the FBI. Everything in Bureau time, which was too often ten minutes past late.

"Yeah?" he said. His jaw dropped as he jotted notes on a pad. "Son of a bitch!"

J.J. snapped her head toward him. "What is it? What is it?"

"Sorry, ma'am. Not you."

"What is it?"

"Shhhh!" Tony said to J.J. as he handed her the paper. "Okay, thank you."

J.J.'s nose scrunched as she skimmed the paper. "Jacob fucking McGee!" The note confirmed her deepest suspicion. First heartbroken, then incensed, her mind swam as she struggled to grasp the gravity of the information, literally sending her into shock. She'd trusted him. He'd never given her a moment's pause or an ill-timed itch. But it was clear she hadn't been asking the right questions to the right people. "But . . . Chris and Jake working together? I mean, they barely speak, and I don't believe that's an act. No way they're collaborating."

"Jake bolted with the real drop and probably picked up the cash. Pretty hard to dispute no matter how you slice it."

"I know how it appears, but think about this for a minute. Jiggy and Jake are best friends. He would've recognized Jiggy's car. And if he saw Jiggy's car he would've reacted, don't you think?"

"I dunno. I mean Jake could have more than one car. As for not spotting Jiggy, it's strange, I'll give you that. But maybe he just wasn't paying attention."

"Not paying attention? In the middle of an operation?" J.J. pursed her lips. "*Please.* I get so wired during ops I've heard bees shit. I don't think so."

J.J. ran her fingers through her hair in frustration. They were still digging up more questions than they could answer, and time was running out.

No sooner than the thought crossed her mind, Sunnie burst through the door and ran straight to Tony's desk. "Oooooooh! You guys are gonna love me . . . well, more than you already do. Have I got some intel for you!"

CHAPTER 44

S unnie rolled an office chair between J.J. and Tony and laid the file on her lap. "Okay, you guys, you may want to sit down for this!" Sunnie said, pausing when Tony's phone rang. "You need to get that?"

"No, go ahead. I'll call 'em back in a minute."

"Whatcha got for us?" J.J. folded her arms across her chest and listened intently.

"Hmmm...where to begin, where to begin?" She flipped through the few pages of chicken scratch she'd written in the file room. "Where's the information on Jack? Jack...Jack...Oh, here it is!"

Tony and J.J. stared expressionless.

"What? I'm a researcher, not an organizer," Sunnie snapped. "*Anyway* . . . did you know Jack was on a medication called Paxil?"

Tony straightened his back. "No...but I've seen the commercials." He turned to J.J. "See, I told you he was taking crazy pills."

Sunnie chuckled. "Actually it's a drug for panic, depression, obsessive-compulsive disorders, etc. You know he's got that thing with the arranging stuff on his desk *just so*. I always thought he was a little *off*," she said, spinning her index finger around her temple, speaking at a frantic pace. "Anyway, I Googled the side effects of the drug and it appears that Paxil—if taken in excessive doses—can cause a rapid heartbeat."

"Excessive doses, huh?" J.J. remembered her jailhouse meeting with Jack when he confessed his rapid heartbeat and sweating episode during the poly. She assumed his poor dieting caught up with him. Could it be the medication? "Well, that may explain why he tanked the polygraph. But why would he take an excessive dose right before his test? They expressly tell you not to take anything the night before."

"Maybe he was feeling anxious and couldn't deal with it," Tony said.

"Of course, then again we're assuming he knew he was taking it," J.J. added. "Jack is a creature of habits, eats the same thing, every day, at the same time. Wouldn't be hard for someone to slip something in on him if they were trying to set him up. But we'll come back to this. What else ya got?"

"Well, I know you didn't ask me to check any information on Lana...," Sunnie said sheepishly, "...but Wendell accidentally gave me her file . . . and you know I'm naturally *inquisitive.*"

"Nosy!" J.J. and Tony said in unison.

"You two an act now?" she said, rolling her neck. "Anyway, seems Miss Lana didn't do as well on her polygraph exam as she led on."

She reached into a folder and pulled out three sheets of paper from Lana's polygraph results. Sunnie handed them both to J.J., who scanned them until she came to the polygraphist's notes about the retests. Tony looked over her shoulder.

"Whaaaaat?" J.J. said.

"I know. Surprising, huh?" Sunnie responded. "Turns out Lana had trouble with her polygraph—both of them!"

Tony's phone rang again. J.J. eyed him, waiting on him to answer his call. But he turned his index finger in circles, gesturing Sunnie to go ahead and wrap it up.

"I see the notes here but what happened?" Tony said, anxiously awaiting her response.

"Seems she passed on all the counterintelligence issues," Sunnie began.

J.J. and Tony eyed one another then turned to Sunnie. It didn't make sense. The counterintelligence issues, those questions related to cooperation with a foreign intelligence service, were the entire reason for taking an examination.

"I don't understand, if she passed on the counterintelligence issues, then she passed the test. Everything else is moot."

Sunnie shook her head. "No, look at the notes more carefully. She failed miserably on one of the control questions...you know, the baseline questions they ask to differentiate which readings represent a lie versus the truth."

"How in hell do you fail a control question?" J.J. asked.

Tony's phone rang again. Sunnie and J.J. exchanged looks before staring down Tony. He shrugged it off again and gestured to Sunnie to continue.

"Good question. I'll tell you how. To determine Lana's truthfulness, they asked 'Are you a U.S. Citizen?' The answer should've been 'Yes' and shown no deception."

"Okay. And?"

"When Lana replied 'Yes' the readings registered deceptive. Significantly so."

"Deceptive? To the citizenship question?" J.J. asked, incredulous at the possibility.

That couldn't be. J.J. wracked her brain until it struck her that the only way to fail the question was that Lana believed she was not a U.S. citizen.

"Get outta here," Tony said. "How'd she end up passing the test?"

"They changed the control question, asked whether her age was thirty-two," Sunnie said. "But hold the phone, there's more..."

• • •

Jiggy followed the unknown subject's car at a safe distance. Although the subject had checked his rear view mirror several times, Jiggy felt certain he hadn't been spotted. Jiggy parked a short distance from the driveway and watched him pull up to the house, then waited for them to enter before moving any closer. As soon as he crossed the threshold, he moved to a closer space.

Scanning the area and absorbing his surroundings, the location seemed eerily familiar, but he couldn't recall why. He seemed to remember visiting the street with Jake after a night of heavy drinking. Yes, that was it. Jake.

About a year before, Jake had gone over the deep end, obsessed with his new girlfriend. He droned on about how beautiful and sexy she was, wouldn't introduce her to anyone on the team, which Jiggy found odd. He (if not the rest of the team) had met all of Jake's ladies. The team was like family...before her.

Over time, Jake grew distant, started behaving jealous and possessive, paranoid even. One game night, he'd cajoled Jiggy into riding by the house two or three times, checking her driveway for cars belonging to potential late night visitors. But Jake's suspicions were never satisfied, so he fell deeper and deeper in love with this mystery woman.

Why would surveillance of an espionage suspect lead him to Jake's girlfriend's house, unless...

Jiggy covered his face and threw his head back in disbelief.

Shit! Maybe she was a honey trap set by the Russians. But no way in hell would Jake ever turn. *He'd never volunteer*, Jiggy thought, shaking off his suspicions as ludicrous. She must've manipulated him. Blackmailed him. Drugged him. Something. Anything. Jake was a lot of things—a player, a jerk, and an occasional jackass—but he was no traitor. Perhaps he'd been more pissed about getting rejected from Quantico than Jiggy suspected. Failing the medical exam over an old collarbone injury he sustained during a college football game, obliterating his childhood dream, had to be a significant blow. But he wouldn't be vengeful enough to spy for the Russians...

Would he?

Jiggy pursed his lips as he lifted the radio. "Blue Leader. This is Jiggy. You copy?"

• • •

"I checked Lana's biographical information," Sunnie said. "Turns out she's a naturalized citizen; she wasn't born here. Her name was Madeleine Bouchard. She came to the U.S. as a student from Canada, got a job after she graduated. After applying for and eventually gaining citizenship, she legally changed her name to Lana Michaels. A little sexier I guess. Cartwright, who was up to his ears in debt at the time, helped get her hired. Coincidentally, or perhaps not so coincidentally, Cartwright was debt free a year later."

J.J. collapsed in a chair while she collected her thoughts. Lana a foreigner? Jesus Christ! She'd spent so much of her career trying to identify Russian spies at the embassy, she never thought she'd find one in FBI Headquarters. The more her mind churned, the more the scenario made sense. And the more it made sense, the more sickened J.J. felt.

"So, what are you getting at?" Tony asked.

J.J. spoke up. "I know exactly what she's getting at. Don't you see Tony? She failed the citizenship question. So whatever words she spews from her mouth, in her mind—and dare I say *heart* if she actually has one—her true allegiance is not to the United States."

"Are you suggesting she's spying for Canada?" Tony said, shaking his head. "Because Canadians don't even spy for Canada. When's the last time you saw the Canadian Service at the top of a hard target list?" he joked.

"No, Ton'," J.J. chuckled and shook her head. "Try a little further *east.*"

Tony stood stunned as his phone rang for the hundredth time. J.J. was fed up with the interruptions.

"Tony, please answer that friggin' phone! I can't take anymore. We'll wait."

He expelled a frustrated breath and pressed the answer button. "Donato."

"It's Mike…sorry, *Mike.*" Tony said his name aloud for J.J.'s sake. "We were getting a briefing from our star analyst," he said, winking at Sunnie. "What's up?"

There was a few minutes of silence before Tony yelled, "Fucking rat!" He placed his hand over the receiver and whispered, "Chris confessed and gave up the handler's name."

J.J. and Sunnie sat at attention.

"Svetlana *Aleksandrovna* Mikhaylova," Tony repeated. "7700 Kalorama Road."

Sunnie bolted upright. "Hold up! I've seen that address before," Sunnie flipped through her notes. "Where have I seen that before? Where have I seen it before?" she muttered more times than J.J. cared to hear.

J.J. almost wanted to ask Sunnie to quit while she was behind. *Her mind churned. Svetlana. Aleksandrovna Mikhaylova. Svetlana. Svet. Lana. Lana Mikhaylova. Mikhaylova. Michaels. Lana Michaels?*

"That's Lana's home address!" Sunnie yelled.

J.J. fell back against her chair, buried her face in her hands and shook her head. *No. No. No.*

"You sure?" Tony asked.

"Yeah. I'm positive. I got a photocopy of her bio . . . see here?"

"Mother flying fu—" J.J. yelled, glaring at Tony. "Do you understand what this means? Svetlana Aleksandrovna Mikhaylova. Lana fucking Michaels. I'll be damned."

"Thanks, Mike. I gotta go."

Tony sunk into his chair and checked his email for the NCIC report. "You're really not gonna believe this shit. It's also the address to which Jake registered his car."

"Jake too? She gets *around*. I'm just sayin'," Sunnie said.

J.J. nodded in agreement.

"Wait!" Tony yelled, experiencing an epiphany of his own. "J.J., did you hear what you just said? Svetlana *Aleksandrovna*. Her patronymic is *Aleksandrovna*. That means her father's name is . . ."

"Aleksandr. As in Aleksandr Mikhaylov—the fucking illegals support officer at the Russian Embassy!"

"Get Jiggy on the radio!" J.J. ordered.

No sooner than Tony lifted the radio did Jiggy's voice sound through wave of static. *Cheap ass radios*, Tony cursed to himself.

"This is Blue Leader. We copy. What's your twenty?"

"Uhhh, looks like I'm on Kalorama road at…I'm squinting to see the house numbers, but I can barely make them out. The house is set back forty feet from the curb. I can't really . . ."

"Let me help you out," J.J. said. "Seventy-seven hundred."

There was a long silence before he said, "How'd you guess?"

Another silence.

"Wait a minute, guys. You won't believe who's leaving the house right now . . . with two very large suitcases," Jiggy said.

"Who is it?" J.J. asked, expecting him to respond *Jake*.

Instead, he gasped. "She's got blond hair!"

"Who?" J.J. yelled nearly falling from her seat. "Who is it?"

CHAPTER 45

"Jiggy? Jiggy? Do you read me Jiggy who is it?"

His radio fell silent for seconds that felt like hours. Tony and J.J. had no idea what happened. Had he been spotted and identified? Had Russian counter-surveillance jammed his radio signal? Did he have a heart attack? Nobody had a clue.

Then at once, they heard static.

"It's...a...na,"

"Anna?" Sunnie said.

J.J. and Tony both snapped their heads toward her and rolled their eyes.

"It's Lana!" Jiggy yelled. Finally, they had a clear signal.

"You don't say!" Tony exclaimed.

"She's packing up the car. Just went back inside the house. What do you want me to do?"

'She's gonna defect!" *J.J.* yelled. "You just stay with her. She's probably heading to Dulles!"

"We've got to get somebody out there now! Sunnie, check and see what time the flights are leaving for Moscow today. And call Mike back and let him know we're in pursuit. It might help him loosen Chris's tongue."

"I'm on it!" she said, scampering toward her desk.

Tony got back on the radio. "This is Blue Leader calling all available units. I repeat all available units. What's your twenty?!"

Money T was the first to respond. "We copy. We were leaving from our lunch location when we ran into a sinkhole from a water main break at S and Wisconsin—a one-way street. We're stuck in a sea of traffic, no pun intended. It's probably gonna be a minute before they let us through."

"Tony, grab your stuff," J.J. said. "We're outta here! We'll call Washington Field and get some support units to meet us at Dulles while we're on the way. Neither Lana nor Jake will go quietly, and we'll need back up."

"Uhhh...Blue Leader," Jiggy interrupts. "She's got a couple of moving boxes. Looks like she's not planning to return for some time. I'll keep her in my sights."

"We're on the way," J.J. said "Just stick close.

"Roger that."

• • •

Tony pushed the pedal to the floor, hoping to arrive at Dulles Airport ahead of Lana and Jiggy. Meanwhile, Jiggy trailed Lana through the city. He kept a respectable distance, fairly certain she hadn't yet detected his presence. He'd never worked with her before, by Jake's design, and had only seen her in passing now and again at headquarters. She wouldn't recognize him or his car, not right away.

She picked up speed on the 14th Street bridge, doing seventy-five in a fifty-five, snaking through traffic while Jiggy accelerated to keep pace. His car shadowed hers, moving closer and closer. But her surveillance detection maneuvers were too aggressive and drew him out of cover. He couldn't afford to lose her. Not now.

At once, they were bumper to bumper. She glanced at Jiggy several times in her rear view mirror. Then Lana floored the gas, driving 95 from Route 95 to Route 66. She took off, zigzagging through packed lanes, barely missing the rear bumpers of the vehicles in front of her.

"Blue Leader. I've been spotted! I've been spotted!" Jiggy yelled. Adrenaline coursed through his veins, heightening every sense. "I'm still with—Oh shit!" It appeared in his rear view mirror. A car. Someone was gaining on him, nearly on his bumper. Jiggy glimpsed a male wearing sunglasses, driving a dark sedan. The man pulled up to Jiggy's passenger side about half way to the rear passenger door, boxing Jiggy between the sedan and the concrete barrier. He couldn't be sure, but if he didn't know better he'd swear the man was—

"Jiggy! Jiggy! You okay?" J.J. called through the radio.

Just as he pressed the button to respond.

CRASH!

Their cars smashed together in an explosive-sounding collision. The car rammed Jiggy into the concrete barrier. He pulled away and rammed him again. The sound of shattered glass and metal scraped and grated against the rail, emitting deafening screeches. Jiggy struggled to steer and reach his radio in the passenger seat slid just beyond his reach. He leaned over and managed to grip it; then he hit transmit button. "I've been hit! I've been hit! He's ramming me off—!"

"Who?" J.J. yelled. "Who is it?"

He snapped his head toward the passenger window and slammed on the breaks, immediately recognized the face scowling back at him.

"Jesus! It's Jake!" Jiggy said as his car began to tilt. "My car's leaning. I think he flattened one of my tires!" He craned his head back feeling rush of air against his face. "And I lost a window!"

"Where is he now?" J.J. yelled.

Jiggy watched Jake speed up to catch Lana as he put the car in park and prepared to step out and survey the damage. Jiggy had been driving rim to asphalt, couldn't go any further if he wanted to. And God knows he wanted to. He wanted nothing more than to take Jake to school—the school of hard knocks...and jabs...and uppercuts.

"About a mile ahead now. Joke's on him, though," Jiggy smirked. "Looks like there's a pocket of bumper-to-bumper construction traffic up ahead. Hope you guys aren't taking 66. Traffic's tight."

"No, we're on 395 South and we've got nothing but clear roads ahead. You need us to call emergency?"

"No, I can do it. Good luck. And tell Tony to bash that sucker's face in when he catches him. For all of us."

J.J. held the radio to Tony's mouth. He needed to keep his hands on the steering wheel and eyes on the road. "I've got your back, Jig. Get yourself some help and we'll check on you later."

Her heart thumped through her ribcage as she exhaled. "Man, I'm gonna kick the crap out of Lana when I get my hands around her neck. Gettin' my pressure up."

No sooner than the words left their mouths—*Whoop Whoop!* A Virginia State Police cruiser turned on his takedown lights, signaling for them to pull over. Both grunted in frustration when a text from Sunnie buzzed J.J.'s cell phone.

The next flight to Moscow departs at 2:07 pm.

She checked her watch. "Damn it! The flight leaves at 2:07. It's 1:15! We don't have time for this shit!!"

"Calm down, J.J. We'll show him our creds and we're outta here. We are the F-B-motherfuckin'-I!" Tony joked.

J.J. chuckled and shook her head.

The officer, a 12-year-old with the smell of fresh-out-of-training on his breath, leaned down toward the window. "Afternoon. You were going 75 in a 55. License and registration, please."

"Afternoon officer, we're FBI," Tony said. Both he and J.J. flashed their credentials. "We're in the middle of an operation and we need to get to Dulles."

"FBI, huh?" the cop said, lowering his sunglasses to the edge of his nose. "Hmph. I applied to be an agent and they rejected me, said I was psychologically unfit. License and registration, please!"

"But—"

"License and registration, please!"

His attitude set J.J. on fire. "Excuse me, what is your badge nu—"

Tony hushed her before she could finish. Then he scoured his glove compartment for his registration and pulled his license from his wallet. "Here you go, sir," he choked out.

"I'll be just a moment!" he said, dragging his feet.

J.J. looked down at her watch again—1:22.

Son of a bitch!

• • •

Chris eyed Mike as he re-entered the interview room and returned to his seat. "I cleared all of the dead drops. I marked the signals. She used Jack and Jim to gain access to files."

Chris's voice trembled as he struggled to lift his gaze from the table. Not because he'd lied during the interview, rather, for the first time in a long time, he had to face his own ugly truth.

"Jim knew her true identity and even helped get her hired, but Jack… I'm sure he wasn't aware of her activities. I kept telling her she'd pushed the envelope too far."

"Did she coerce you in any way? Threaten or blackmail you?" Mike asked.

His chin dropped to his chest, his shoulders hunched. "I wish I could say yes, but no. No, she didn't. I fell in love with her, would've done anything to hold onto her."

"Including sell your soul to the devil—or the Russians as it were."

"You can think what you want about me. I tried to confess a dozen times, but she told me if one of us went down we'd all go down."

"All?"

"Me, her, Cartwright…" he said. "So she trained me to beat the polygraph."

Mike and Don glanced at each other, eyebrows raised. "Hold up. You're telling us she *trained* you to defeat the poly?"

"Yeah, she did. But, we see how well that worked out, right?" he said, wiping his brow. "After I passed the test today, we'd planned to pick up the cash and make arrangements to defect. We tried to get enough to raise the baby."

"Baby?" Mike laughed.

"Leave the country?" Don said.

"She said her handler gave her passports for both of us. All we needed to do was make it to Dulles airport and they'd put us on the first available Aeroflot flight out—the government still owns the airline so…"

Mike sat back in his seat. At that point, Don stepped in and took over.

"Can you tell us about your, uhhh, Koshechka's relationship with Jake McGee?" Mike asked.

Chris's eyes protruded from their sockets. "How'd you figure it out?" Chris asked, disappointed he couldn't hold out longer. She'd probably realized by now that his polygraph hadn't proceeded well and was preparing to leave. But he couldn't be certain. Maybe they'd shed some light.

Don's eyes darted between them, as he was not yet privy to the information Sunnie had shared with Mike.

"Never mind that. You just tell me what you can about her relationship with Jake."

Chris shrugged. "They didn't have one as far as I know, nothing outside of work. I'm positive of that."

"You sure you're positive?"

He hesitated. "Yeah . . . I'm positive. Why do you ask?"

Mike leaned forward, elbows resting on his knees. "Hate to break this to you Chris," he began, "but your darling Koshechka is on her way to Moscow if my instincts serve me well . . . and they usually do."

His eyes widened and the corners of his mouth lifted slightly. She knew. She'd made her escape. "Now?"

"Yep. Right now," Mike said. "With Jake McGee."

Chris sucked in a hard breath as if his lungs had collapsed, and he struggled for air, shaking his head furiously.

"No, she wouldn't. She loves me. We're having a baby . . . she loves me." He tried to convince himself more than Mike and Don. Then, on the edge of tears, he buried his face in his hands, conceding his fight to believe in her. He'd been played like Monopoly set. And before the day's end, he'd be resting on a cot in the Alexandria Detention Center.

"That bitch!" he screamed. He slammed his fist against the chair arm, his eyes empty, those of a man possessed. "That two-timing slut bitch!"

Don kicked in, "No, I think she was more like a *three*-timing slut bitch."

"Now we're cooking with gas!" Chris's anger pleased Mike. "Wondered when your balls were gonna drop. Are you ready to tell us everything and stop protecting her now?"

Chris nodded yes.

Mike rubbed his hands together rapidly, getting warmed up for the next phase of the interview. "Your former colleagues are probably trying to head them off at Dulles as we speak. Let's just hope they catch them in time."

CHAPTER 46

Later Thursday Afternoon…

"**A**eroflot Flight 3-0-2-5 to Sheremetyevo will board in ten minutes at Gate B41," an attendant announced over the airport intercom system. Dulles Airport was bustling with afternoon travelers.

Lana, dressed down from her more revealing wardrobe, wore dark-colored Dockers and a reversible navy/red hoodie to help her blend in with the crowd. She scanned the security checkpoint, watching for unusual movements, listening for hurried footsteps pacing toward her. She heard nothing, nothing except the sound of freedom, her escape merely a few feet ahead. She turned her head over her shoulder to look at her darling Jake. He was just a few families behind. He'd taken an extended bathroom break, so she stayed in line.

She emptied her pockets into the plastic X-ray container, sat her purse inside. Her most current weapon was in the holster on her back—she'd left the others, the ones she reported missing, inside her house. Once J.J. figured out Lana's true identity, once Chris realized she had defected and inevitably blabbed their extent of their activities, the Bureau could search her former residence and retrieve them. They'd no doubt comb every square inch of her Cape Cod before sunset. In the meantime, she'd be long gone, back to a place where she'd have no use for them, a place where she'd be a hero to her country and once again the sunlight in her father's eyes.

She reached in her purse for the leather case, the one containing her FBI credentials. She'd flash them one last time to clear the checkpoint, then chuck them in the trash where they belonged. Almost seven years under their noses and they couldn't find her, not if she wore a sign on her back. She laughed to herself. She and her darling Jake had made fools of them all—J.J., Tony, Chris and the rest of the FBI. *Idiots*, she thought to herself. In just a few short hours, she'd be back in Moscow, ready to move into her government-furnished flat. She'd assume her well-earned desk job at the Center during the day. And at night—Jake.

"Remove your weapon, please," the TSA officer directed. "Place it on the X-ray machine."

Hmph. Odd, she thought. They usually didn't ask her to remove it. Just allowed her to pass through metal detectors. A new rule? No matter. She only had a few more steps. Her new life waited, so there was no need to argue with these overpaid peons now.

"All clear," the TSA agent said as she stepped through the scanner.

She reached for her weapon. It wasn't there. She panicked. Her head flitted around the area until she identified the problem.

"Surprised to see me?" J.J. said, smiling at the shock on Lana's face. A large, scowling Italian stood behind her as J.J. dangled Lana's weapon from her index finger. J.J.'s Glock was trained on the traitor's head.

Lana shriveled in her momentary daze, her eyes darting to the X-ray machine where the TSA agent stood, his hands the size of baseball mitts and her shoes and purse in his hands. She had no creds, no gun, no passport, and no boarding pass.

"Where the hell did you think you were going?" Tony said, grabbing Lana's gun from J.J. and zipping it into his jacket pocket.

Lana gasped, her surprise at J.J.'s appearance evident. Her face turned ghostly pale as she took a step back. But she'd never give up without a fight. Where there was a will, there was a way. And she'd find a way.

• • •

"Where's the fucking drop, Lana?" J.J. eased toward Lana, her 9-mm still aimed and ready to fire. At the worst time, her hand began to tremble again. The numbness, it dulled the feeling in her fingers. Her grip weakened against the handle.

No. No. Not now!

"You all right, J.J.?" Tony said. He eased up slowly behind her. She could feel his body heat against her back.

"I'm okay!" she barked.

"Jake, run!" Lana screamed before launching a kick to J.J.'s firing arm, her foot slamming into the bone in J.J.'s wrist. She stepped back hard into Tony and threw them both off balance. Meanwhile, J.J.'s gun fell and slid a short distance, slamming against the base of the X-ray machine. J.J. and Lana dove, scrambled toward the weapon. Lana edged out J.J. out by inches, seconds.

J.J. gritted her teeth and continued to tug and pull Lana's clothes. If Lana grabbed her gun, she was dead. And she'd have no one but herself to blame. Her denials could've gotten her and Tony—the man she respected, the man she adored, the man she loved—killed. She desperately stretched her arm, willed the feeling back into her fingers. But Tony's size fourteen foot landed against Lana's ribcage, sending her reeling onto her side. She rolled onto her hands and knees, and scrambled through the metal detector as startled passengers screamed and backed out of the way.

Dazed for only a few seconds, Lana sprinted down the walkway in trouser socks toward the escalators. J.J. could see Jake running with a saddle bag in the distance. He'd taken the intel but had waited long enough to ensure Lana broke free.

Tony pulled J.J to her feet and both returned their guns to their holsters and took off after their targets, pursuing them with incensed abandon. If Jake and Lana made it to the Aerotrain on the next level down, they were both as good as gone.

TSA called for back-up, but the agents present couldn't leave the checkpoint.

"I won't let you down again!" J.J. yelled to Tony, who was on her heels. "Where the hell is Washington Field?"

"I don't know but Jake's getting away!" Tony said, kicking in the jets. "Catch up with you ahead."

The moment he passed her, fatigue set in. Her Belvedere binge began to drag her down, and she sucked wind as she chugged down the passenger walkway too many steps behind Lana. The vodka leaded her limbs, slowed her sprint. Exhausted, hung-over she wanted to give up, but she couldn't. She had promises to keep, to Viktor, to Tony, to herself.

"I'll never drink again," she thought to herself. "I'll never drink again." She took a deep breath and picked up the pace.

Jake was the farthest ahead and had managed to dissolve into the crowd. Lana, slowed by the dense crowds and the slippery linoleum, was still in view a few meters ahead. Lana was clueless, had no idea J.J. still had an eye on her. When at last J.J....tripped. Over a child's stray duffle bag.

Shit!

She'd fallen in the middle of a chase like the inept TV agents she mocked. She wanted to kick herself, but the kick would have to wait. She dragged herself to her feet, trying to find a way through the crowd, trying to make up the few feet of distance she'd lost. The announcer made the last call for the flight to Moscow. Lana was too far away from the gate to catch a flight, but she put more distance between them. Step by step. Getting too close to the Aerotrain escalator for J.J.'s comfort.

J.J. scanned the area for anything that would help her.

Where to go? What to do? Then she spotted it.

The people mover!

She sprinted up the grated moving walkway. Left nothing behind but the scent of Tony's favorite cologne. She concealed herself behind travelers as she hurdled baggage, apologizing profusely along the way. She was close. She could make it. She'd catch Lana before they reached the train exit.

Then it happened, she closed the distance. Lana was back within her reach, only a few steps ahead on the down escalator. J.J. shrouded herself behind the tall gentlemen in front of her, two linebacker-sized hulks. She watched below as Jake and Lana slowed their pace. Tony was nowhere to be found. He was well hidden. J.J. had no idea where.

She saw Jake looking behind him, the saddlebag strap running diagonally across his chest. He was near the Aerotrain exit. As another flight was called and a crowd headed toward baggage check area, a space opened up and Lana appeared. She had reversed her jacket from navy to red, her head concealed beneath the hood; J.J. knew the trick.

Lana appeared jittery and scanned the travelers desperately seeking Jake.

Jake slowed to allow her to spot him. They closed the distance between them as J.J. looked on, concealing herself everywhere she could, checking around to spot Tony. She wanted to nab them together, at the same time.

Finally, she'd made it. A few steps behind Lana.

With their arms outstretched, Jake held out his hand for Lana to grab. As she neared Jake, increasing the speed of her paces, she didn't see the man, the one in the power wheelchair rolling from her blind spot. They collided in an instant and Lana lost her grip and fell to her knees.

"Jake!" she yelled her voice heavy with desperation.

The slip and Jake's hard stare distracted Lana just long enough to put J.J. in reaching distance. As Lana returned to her feet, J.J. lurched forward, caught Lana by her natural blond tresses, and dragged her screaming to the floor, the weight of her body throwing J.J. off balance. Jake was stunned, easing toward the door, seemingly trying to decide whether to jump in or make a run for it on the Aerotrain she heard approaching.

"Run Jake, run!" Lana yelled.

His face reddened, and he froze, just froze.

J.J. and Lana tussled before Lana jerked away, breaking free of J.J.'s weakened grip. She stood firm to her feet, both eye to eye. Neither noticed the curious crowd that had begun to form or the security personnel charging toward the area. They wanted to kill each other. Both exchanged bone shaking slaps to the face. Lana lunged for J.J.'s weapon, determined to end the life of the witch who stood between freedom and death. In one swift motion, J.J. grabbed Lana's arm and twisted behind her back until she submitted and fell to the floor on her knees. Then a loud thud sounded as J.J. drove her knee into Lana's back, a force powerful enough to dent a steel enforced door. Lana's chest slammed against the tile, her body limp, her mind barely conscious. She gasped for air—breathless and disoriented.

"That's for making me run," J.J. snarled, baring her teeth. Her nostrils flared as she pressed her knee deep into Lana's spine.

Lana made a feeble attempt to squirm her weakened body free. "Get off of me...bitch!" she yelled.

Incensed, J.J. raised her balled hand to the heavens. Then she dropped a blow to the visible side of Lana's face, the force of which emptied Lana's tear ducts, knocking Lana out for the count. "The only bitch you need to worry about is your cellmate at Supermax." J.J. said. She quickly put handcuffs on Lana and exhaled. *It's over!* J.J. said to herself. She hardly had a moment to catch her breath. Everything happened so fast. Only minutes had passed since they'd arrived at Dulles, but Lana was in custody.

J.J. stood up, hovering over Lana's limp body. She scanned the area to find Tony. As security personnel approached with guns drawn, she reached to pull her creds from her pocket and open them. Then she spotted Jake. His face was reddened, his expression screamed revenge. He reached his hand in the small of his back, inside his jacket, and pulled out an object. The silver caught a ray of sun and glimmered. J.J. realized what he was holding—a .22 caliber gun small enough to conceal in his palm, big enough to kill at short range.

Of course, he's armed. He had credentials which differed little from those of an FBI agent. He could get through the security checkpoint with a quick flash.

With his arm outstretched, he aimed it at Tony's head, waiting to get a clear shot.

After ensuring Lana was still out, J.J. opened her credentials and removed the gun from her holster. "FBI! FBI! Everybody down! Everybody down!" she yelled at the stunned crowd. Security stopped their pursuit toward her and began to secure the innocent bystanders when they noticed Jake. "Tony! Behind you!"

Jake stood statue still until Tony spun around to see him.

Within a moment too short to blink, the crowd cleared. Some hit the floor, protecting their heads; a few rubberneckers stood in the background, watching, waiting for the events to unfold. Only she, Tony and Jake were left standing—and Tony's gun was still in its holster.

 She dropped her credentials on the floor and grasped her weapon, this time with both hands.

Jake didn't shift his eyes from Tony for a moment. Seemed he'd never intended to shoot J.J., maybe out of their friendship, or perhaps because he knew shooting Tony would hurt her far worse than any wound he could inflict on her. At that moment, J.J. knew. Tony was the love of her life and she'd move heaven, earth, and a hollow point to protect him.

J.J.'s gaze volleyed back and forth between them as she willed her hand steady and outstretched her arms. Her mind swam; her heart raced. She didn't want hurt Jake, but she'd die before watching him kill Tony.

And she had no plans to die.

A wicked smirk edged the corners of Jake's lips upward. He had the drop on Tony. J.J. had the drop on Jake. She dreaded her choice. Did she have enough heart to pull the trigger? Could she kill him if she needed to? She prayed he would just give up.

"Drop the gun, Jake! Drop it!" she pleaded. She eased around to get a clean shot at his torso. "Give this up, Jake. You don't want to do this! Tony's your friend."

He didn't respond. His arms shook as tears rolled down his eyes.

"I don't give a shit who he is. You know me, J.J. And you know my philosophy," he said, his voice trembling. He lifted the gun to his face and pressed it into his temple. Then seconds later turned it back to Tony. "When all hell breaks loose…"

At once, Jake's finger flinched.

J.J. pumped the trigger twice, delivering two bullets, sending Jake reeling backward. She mumbled, "Only the devil takes one in the neck and one in the chest."

Her trusted colleague for nearly a decade died before he collided against the floor. It was her first kill shot—she'd never taken another man's life. And she never dreamed she'd have to kill a man she once called friend.

Lana regained consciousness, saw Jake lying in a pool of his own blood, and cried out. "Jaaaaake! Noooooooooooooo!"

• • •

Adrenaline pumped through J.J.'s veins, erasing the ill effects of the previous night's binge. The day's events blurred together. Moments passed before she spotted the herd of TSA agents approaching them at a rapid pace. Jake lie in a pool of blood, and Lana lie in a pool of tears. J.J.

glimpsed the flashes of light from camera phones, the crowd of onlookers filming the entire incident like a gang of paparazzi. Suddenly she felt ill. She had no doubt the incident would wind up on the evening news. Director Freeman wouldn't be happy about this unexpected development. More inquiries, more explanations. At least now she and Tony could answer the most important questions, and her feelings for Tony were as resolute as they'd ever been.

After a brief discussion with TSA personnel, the threesome was escorted through the automatic main entrance doors. Lana was greeted by a slew of FBI agents wearing raid jackets.

An ambulance arrived for Jake's corpse.

"What the hell took you guys so long?" Tony said. "It's all over but the shoutin'."

"Traffic on 66 is a bitch!" one of the arresting agents replied.

J.J. and Tony handed over custody of their battered, bruised, and disheveled detainee and the saddlebag full of intel. "Lana would second that emotion, wouldn't you?"

Lana glared at J.J., blood dripping from the corner of her mouth, the side of her face a rainbow of red, black, and blue. "Laugh now but this isn't over. It's only just begun," she snarled with a sinister laugh.

J.J. rolled her eyes. "Got that right. I'll see your ass at sentencing!"

"I'll see *you* in hell!" Lana growled.

"Ha! Joke's on you, baby! I'm already there!" J.J. turned to her Washington Field colleagues. "Now, please get this wench out of my face before I bash her face in...*again*."

Tony and J.J. stood stoically as they watched the cavalcade of squad cars leave the terminal loading area. She exhaled long and deep, running her fingers through her hair.

"You, okay?" Tony said, carefully watching J.J.'s expression for what her mouth wouldn't say.

"Is that a trick question?" She forced a smile.

"You put up a good front but I know that must've been rough on you, with Jake and all. I know how much he meant to you."

"You mean more," she said. "Besides, I made the tough choice, right? Pulled the trigger. I proved...*something*, to *someone*."

An uncomfortable silence settled between them. He shoved his hands in his pockets. "You saved my life."

"I swore I wouldn't let you down again, and I meant it. Every minute of every day I mean it." She leaned toward him and playfully bumped him with her elbow. "But you *so* owe me."

A seductive grin sliced through his lips. "Anything you want. Just name it."

"Well, I could use a drink!" J.J. said as she turned to Tony and held his gaze. "Except...you know what? I don't *want* one. Give me a little time though, I'm sure I'll think of something else."

His cheeks blushed red. "Anyway, we probably should get out of here and brief Director Freeman before he sees us on the five o'clock news. This scene has lead story written all over it."

Back at headquarters in the Director's office, Mrs. Whitehouse appeared flustered. She was engrossed in an intense phone conversation when J.J. and Tony entered the reception area.

"Ahhhh, here they are. I'll speak with you later," she said, hanging up the phone, no doubt spinning up the rumor mill. "Director Freeman's been waiting. Please go straight inside, he's quite eager to speak with you."

They hesitated for a moment, then plodded inside. Director Freeman faced the television screen, his eyes peeled on the image of J.J. yanking Lana to the ground by her golden locks, captured via bystander cam and now the third story on the six o'clock news.

"Sir, we were told you wanted to see us," Tony said to Director Freeman, uneasy about his reaction. Neither J.J. nor he had accounted for nosy onlookers sending a video of the incident to Channel 4. Everything happened so quickly.

"Well, well, well, if it isn't the Bonnie and Clyde of the FBI. Have a seat." He turned back toward the screen. "See that? Every channel."

Tony and J.J. sat statue still waiting to be admonished.

"You okay, Agent McCall? That must've been a tough shot to take. You've worked with Jake for a number of years, I understand."

"Well, I did what I had to do," J.J. said. "He was on the wrong side of the law and my Glock."

Freeman eyed her closely, searching her expression for vulnerability. He found none. "Obviously, when an FBI agent gets arrested, a G gets killed at Dulles for attempting to defect to Moscow, and the arrest makes the six o'clock news, the FBI director is going to have a few questions to answer."

"We understand, sir," Tony said.

"Not to mention a second agent's arrest and an assistant director's death. The damage assessment on this one will take years if it takes a minute. I've been responding to calls from the Hill and the DNI for the last hour."

As Tony sat paralyzed, J.J. surveyed the room, searching for escape routes. Unfortunately, apart from the office door, her only other option was to leap from the Director's seventh-floor window into the headquarters stone-floored courtyard. Suddenly, the temperature in the room stifled her attempts to catch a breath.

"You're not here to get your hands slapped if that's what you're concerned about," Freeman said.

They both exhaled, the tension releasing from their shoulders.

"But I need the elevator version of what happened," he said, wielding his pen over a notebook. "You can save the minutia for the report you're turning in tomorrow." He glanced up and waited for their nods of acknowledgment; they obliged.

J.J. glared at Tony before he bowed his head toward her, conceding control of the floor.

"Long story short. Lana Michaels is a really Svetlana Aleksandrovna Mikhaylova, a Russian illegal who used sex and blackmail to recruit two agents and one G . . . that we're aware of so far anyway. We also believe she's the daughter of Aleksandr Mikhaylov, the illegals support officer posted at the embassy."

"What about Jim Cartwright's involvement, if any?"

"Mr. Cartwright hired Lana and we also believe he knew her true identity. He had major financial issues and had engaged in some apparent homosexual activity. His family was unaware of his *leanings*, and he tried to conceal it. She probably blackmailed him and paid him big money to keep him on the hook."

"Okay . . . Okay . . ." he continued to jot down notes. "In your professional opinion, what was Jack's involvement?"

Once again, an opportunity presented itself to J.J, a new chance to put the screws to the bane of her professional existence, and to the most senior executive in the FBI no less. Despite his apparent remorse, she knew the asshole still dwelled just beneath the surface. But she suppressed her unquenched longing for revenge and cleared his name.

"Well, sir, in my professional opinion…," she said before pausing to glance at Tony. His expression begged her to ignore everything that was good and holy, slather on the Vaseline, and screw that racist bastard to the wall for everything he was worth and then some. "…Lana and Chris framed Jack. I don't believe he knowingly or directly provided classified information to the Russians."

Tony coughed, the break no doubt intended to allow J.J. to reverse course. She reluctantly parked on the high road.

"However! I do believe he knowingly and willingly committed countless security violations. I believe the investigation will reveal that he gave a professional advantage to the woman he was sleeping with. There is more than sufficient evidence to support that."

Tony's smile said, "Good girl!"

"I see. Interesting," the director said. "So if I recommended that the U.S. Attorney drop the espionage charges and release him from jail immediately, you would support this decision?"

She paused in a lengthy pregnant silence. With a shaky voice, she answered, "*Legally*, there is no reason to hold him. Personally? That's another story."

The corners of his mouth rolled up into a smile. He almost appeared to take some warped enjoyment in J.J.'s reluctant honor. "Is there anything else I should be aware of?"

"I think there's one more thing we should tell you." Tony glanced at J.J. "We can't discount the possibility of a larger network of illegals operating throughout the community."

"Yeah," he said. "Unfortunately, I share the same concern. It's one of the issues I'm scheduled to discuss with the DNI at the briefing in the morning."

"We can't link all the compromises to Lana, particularly some of the CIA and NSA information," Tony continued.

"I agree," he said. "I'll be sure to convey your opinions."

He stood up from his seat and stacked his notes in a pile.

"I think I have everything I need. I've listened to Chris Johnson's interview with the polygraphist, and let's just say it's entirely too gripping for my comfort. I should survive the first round of meetings." He stood and gestured for them to do the same, then led them to the door. "I'll expect full reports on my desk by noon. Sharp."

"Sir, what about our polygraphs in the morning?" Tony asked.

"They've been canceled. Obviously you have more important work to do. Your vault access has already been fully restored as well. Keep up the good work."

Tony and J.J. smiled as they left the office. Once safely out of sight, they bumped fists to celebrate.

"Well, looks like my work is done. You're going to be on your own after we turn in our reports tomorrow."

"Quit talkin' crazy. No way in hell am I gonna let you quit." Tony turned to J.J. and smiled. "Besides, Ms. McCall, you and I have some very important unfinished business to discuss, remember?"

"How could I forget?" Her eyes were tired and her body ached. "But it's been a long day. Let's table this discussion until tomorrow evening, okay? Scouts honor."

CHAPTER 47

Late Thursday Night…

All night long, J.J. tossed and turned between her new 800-count sheets thinking about Tony and his proposition. Thinking about the problems she'd tried to deny about her future with the FBI, she snatched back the duvet and made her way into the family room, straight to the shelf which housed "his" picture. That's the first thing she needed to get rid of.

She lifted Six's photo and traced his profile with her index finger. Oh, the passion she'd shared with this man. He had the eyes of an angel, the soul of Satan himself. Her time to move one was well overdue, and she knew it. She could choose to dwell on what was, what could've been. Or focus her heart and mind on the future, a future with the man who never made her itch, as her mother had done more than 40 years before. She'd never find another like Tony, and a rejection would send his frail ego in the arms of another, the thought of which made her sick to her stomach. No, she refused to lose him. Besides, Six had never been one to take refuge on the sidelines, not for long. By now, he was probably preparing to depart for Zimbabwe, where he'd shop for goats to woo some chief's daughter, no more thinking about J.J. than the man on the moon.

When she arrived in the kitchen, picture frame in hand, J.J. reached into the cabinet, removed three bottles of Belvedere and poured the contents of each into the sink. She'd wanted to begin her new life without a crutch, face life on her own two feet. She stepped on the pedal at the base of the trashcan which flipped the top open and, when the lid popped up, she slammed the frame and bottles inside with a loud crash, left nothing but the sound of broken glass and the memories of shattered outdated dreams. She had new dreams now. It took a year, but she'd done it, cleaned house. Mr. Six...and the booze were gone for good.

After shaking off the final remnants of her emotional crutches, she sat down at the dining room table and drafted her resignation memo. With each word written, she felt the weight of the world lift from her shoulders. It was brief but would serve its purpose.

Dear Mr. Nixon,

I quit. Effectively immediately.

Sincerely,

Former Special Agent J.J. McCall

She returned to her bed moments later and sat on the edge. At once, her emotions flooded into tears; she heaved sobs for everything and everyone she'd lost that day. It was a much-needed cleansing that would allow her to welcome with open heart everything and everyone she was about to gain.

• • •

Early Friday Morning…

Director Freeman's secretary, Mrs. Whitehouse, called at the crack of dawn. He had good news to convey to J.J. that couldn't wait for regular business hours. And J.J. was mighty glad he didn't. She rolled over and palmed the alarm clock on the nightstand. It read five a.m.

Ugh! she grunted as she ascended from the bed and felt her way to the bathroom. In the mirror, the dark circles and red cracked eyeballs divulged openly what her body concealed. She was damn exhausted. Professionally fulfilled but exhausted. Romantically on the verge of a new adventure with the man of her dreams but exhausted. Vindicated. But exhausted. She slogged through the house, pulled herself together.

She'd waited patiently for the day to arrive, and in a twist that could only be part of a larger Karmic plan, J.J. would deliver the news alongside her new man. After their early morning appointment and their mid-morning meeting with the Director later on, they could grab some lunch, maybe an early dinner at their favorite watering hole. There she'd break the news to him—he was stuck with her forever. *If* he behaved as a good boy should.

She checked herself in the mirror just before she grabbed her keys to head out the door.

Her lips curled upward when her caller ID lit up.

"Donato! What's shakin' bacon?"

"You on the way? We've gotta hurry. He's gonna be released in less than an hour and traffic's a beast."

"Yeah, I just opened the door."

"So, uhhh....I know our morning's full, but do you think we'll get a chance to have that talk later today?"

"Absolutely, and let me just say, I think you're going to be very pleased with the conversation."

"Very pleased? Or just sorta pleased."

"Very."

She listened closely to hear his smile. *There it is.*

"You don't know how happy I am to hear that. I'll see you in a few."

She slipped the letter in her pocket and took another look around her apartment. Indeed, her world would change forever—and for the better. When she returned home, she'd be a self-employed girlfriend of an Italian FBI agent, a surprising turn of events indeed.

• • •

The exit gate at the Alexandria jail opened, and Jack, stepped beyond the barbed-wire fence. He looked to the heavens, as if speaking to God, the same god he'd probably ignored for the sum total of his miserable life. He was wearing his typical tired polyester slacks and cotton button-down he'd worn to work on his last free day. When he spotted Tony and J.J. leaning against the passenger door of her car, he stutter-stepped and then moved toward them. The corners of his mouth lifted with each step until roughly 30 of his 32 teeth became visible. He bowed his head forward to greet Tony and then turned to J.J.

"You did it! You cleared my name." He extended his hand to her. In the almost seven years that she'd worked for him, she'd never felt his greasy skin next to hers, and there was little cause to break that stellar record then.

But she did.

"I did my job."

Although she'd never sought vengeance, she'd relish it.

He tugged the unbelted waist of his pants and pulled it over his beer gut. Then he smirked as if the fresh life lesson had already begun to fade from his memory. "You're a good agent McCall, a lot like your mother."

Her body stiffened; she stood erect. "My mother?" J.J. said almost breathless. "You mean, *you* knew her?"

Tony snapped his head toward J.J., baffled and confused.

"Yeah...I knew her," he said. "I've been an agent for 33 years, of course I knew her."

"Then you know what happened."

He nodded. "Maybe we'll talk...when I get back to the office."

"I'm afraid there might be a problem with that." J.J. glanced up at Tony and then back at him.

Jack's eyebrows scrunched. He looked at them both repeatedly.

"Well," J.J. said. "Director Freeman has authorized me to inform you that your clearances have been revoked due to excessive security violations. You can no longer work at headquarters. Security will, however, escort you to your desk long enough for you to pack up your belongings."

His mouth fell open. "This is ridiculous! I'm innocent!"

"Yeah, well . . .the Director doesn't seem to think so," Tony chimed in.

Jack jerked his head back, shaking his head in denial.

"He's giving you the option to accept an early retirement or face termination," J.J. said. "It's your choice."

Jack tipped his head to the side, turned on his heel, and his chin dropped to his chest as he walked away.

"Jack, what about my mother. What happened to her?"

He started to speak then stopped himself. "You should ask your father," he said and never looked back again.

"My father?"

"What's 'at all about?" Tony asked.

She shrugged. "I don't know, but I'm going to find out at Sunday brunch."

J.J. walked around to the driver's side to slip into the car. Just as she poked the key in the ignition and they prepared to pull out, Tony's phone rang.

"Donato," Tony answered.

"Hi. This is Mrs. Whitehouse. The Director would like to see you immediately."

"Us?" he asked.

"Yes sir," she said. "Immediately. As in five minutes ago."

"All right. We're on the way."

He turned to J.J. "We gotta get back to Headquarters. The director needs to meet with us now."

"What's going on? We were supposed to meet with him in a couple of hours anyway."

He sighed. "Guess we'll find out soon enough."

• • •

"Sir, you wanted to see us?" Tony asked as he and J.J. blocked the doorway.

"Good! You're just in time," he said. "Follow me."

Tony and J.J. parted like the Red Sea and Freeman led them out of the office. Their heels clacked against the tile as he guided them down nearly empty corridor, not a word spoken as to their destination.

"Again, I want to commend you both on a job well done," Freeman said. "This compromise issue has been plaguing the Bureau for far too long. Somehow, you managed to solve the problem in less than a week."

"Thank you, sir," J.J. and Tony now flanked him on either side.

"You've been in the Bureau long enough to know that no good deed goes unpunished."

J.J. and Tony chuckled as they continued on.

"First, we've had a few developments that I need to make you both aware of," he said, his expression one of concern. "We got a call from the coroner's office. Based on the angle of the entry and exit wounds, they don't believe Cartwright committed suicide. He was murdered."

"What!" both yelled. J.J. and Tony literally froze in their tracks.

"Lana?" J.J. asked.

Freeman nodded.

Tony inhaled a deep frustrated breath. "Glad she's locked up."

"Afraid not. Lana escaped from sheriff's custody this morning. She claimed she was suffering from severe abdominal pains, apparently put on quite a performance. Let's just say there was a failure to do a thorough body search. She picked the lock on her restraints at the hospital and escaped."

"No freakin' way!" Tony yelled.

J.J. stood in stunned silence.

"According to the sheriff, she made nice with one of the guards watching her room, had a little help."

"Get the fu…heck outta here!" Tony said before he caught himself. "Sorry, sir, but I bet that idiot's feeling like a piece of shit right now."

"Don't worry," Freeman said. "I believe I used those exact words when I found out. We've got every law enforcement agency in D.C., Northern Virginia, and Prince George's County looking for her. We've got her house, the airports, and the embassy under surveillance. If a Russian intelligence officer so much as passes gas, a G will be there to smell it. She won't get far."

"I'm stunned. Absolutely stunned," J.J. said. She shook her head incessantly. Lana was shifty and a threat to J.J. as long as she remained free. She'd get caught, all right...if J.J. had to hunt her down on her own.

They all took deep breaths, as Freeman continued to lead them down the hall.

"In the meantime, I need to personally enlist your assistance," Freeman said. "CIA, NSA, and Defense Intelligence have each provided the DNI with information that corroborates our theory that Lana was part of a tight network of Russian illegals. They've infiltrated the entire Intelligence Community."

J.J. and Tony glanced at each other then turned forward, still trying to figure out where he was taking them. "We suspected as much," Tony said.

"So, I want you both to head up an inter-agency task force to flush them out of the cracks and crevices in which they hide."

"I'm sorry, sir," J.J. said. "Did you say *'head up'*?"

She placed her hand on her pant pocket, containing her resignation letter. Finally, a chance to prove she could lead, to prove Sabinski, Cartwright...perhaps even Tony they'd been wrong about her. She not only had heart—she also had balls. But with her fingers on the precipice of her new life, her freedom, did she have anything left to prove?

They rounded corner at the end of the corridor, which led to an executive conference room. J.J. could see human shadows behind the frosted glass. This was her last chance to back out. Once she stepped in, she'd be committed until they caught the moles.

She stopped walking before they reached the door, her silence awkward and unexpected.

Director Freeman asked, "Everything okay Agent McCall?"

CHAPTER 48

"All the great things are simple, and many can be expressed in a single word: freedom; justice; honor; duty; mercy; hope…" Winston Churchill

J.J. touched her pocket again and looked at Tony, her eyes confessing her intentions before she spoke. Tony shook his head, his eyes pleading, begging her not to go through with it. She could refuse, walk away, and her life would be better. Problem was, J.J. had a realization at that moment. She wanted something else, something better than…*better*.

She sighed deeply, then responded. "Oh no, I'm fine," she said. "I forgot where I put my key. It's in my purse. Getting forgetful in my old age."

Freeman nodded and smiled. "Ohhh, I understand. Anyway, to continue our discussion, yes, head up. Each agency involved is providing one representative. The FBI has lead on all domestic issues. The Agency has lead on overseas activities, with the exception of those directly involving military personnel, which will be handled by DIA. Are we understood?"

"Yes, sir. But the Agency doesn't really play well with others," J.J. said as they neared the conference room door.

Freeman stopped and turned to them as he placed his hand on the door knob. He whispered, "I know. But you've got find a way to work it out." He locked his gaze on J.J. "If you're capable of clearing Jack, you're capable of cooperating with the CIA for the good of this country."

Her lips parted in surprise.

"Now let's get inside. Everyone is waiting."

"Everyone?" Tony said.

Freeman turned the knob and pushed the door open.

"Come in so I can introduce you to your new team. Everyone meet Special Agents Antonio Donato and J.J. McCall."

Tony led the duo across the threshold, and her eyes circled the room absorbing all the unfamiliar faces until her gaze locked on his. She'd plunged straight into her own personal and professional hell.

J.J. gasped as her heart plummeted through the seven floors beneath them; she felt woozy.

Tony caught her arm to stabilize her. "You okay?" he whispered.

"Yeah, yeah. I'm fine," she replied in an equally hushed tone.

Meanwhile, as she got her bearings, Freeman moved to the head of the conference room, inviting Tony and J.J. to take the two seats flanking his. He remained standing to speak.

"If you saw the six o'clock news last night, I'm sure these two need no introduction."

Everyone laughed as the two culprits smiled sheepishly.

"Welcome to Task Force PHANTOM HUNTER" Freeman said. "Now, if we can go around the room so everyone can introduce themselves?"

The first to respond was a dark-haired, doe-eyed, Italian-to-Greek bombshell sitting to Tony's right. "Hello everyone. Gianna Campioni. I'm with DIA and have been working counterintelligence and force protection issues for the past ten years."

Tony's entire face lit up when he heard her name, which did not escape J.J.'s notice.

"La vostra famiglia Siciliana?" he asked her, his Italian sounding better than it had since she'd met him.

"Si, mio padre," she responded, her voice floating as if on a cloud. When Tony finally remembered J.J. was sitting across the table eyeing him with a lethal stare, he mouthed, "She's Sicilian. Her father."

J.J. rolled her eyes.

"Glad to be part of the team. Looking forward to working with all of you," she said, eying Tony as if to direct her message toward him and him only.

In the seat next to Gianna sat the next team member. NSA, J.J. guessed. He looked like the child Steve Urkel and Pee Wee Herman would produce if men could mate and bear children. He ran his hand across his moussed-back mane and pushed his oversized frames securely onto the bridge of his nose.

"I'm Walter Lowenstein . . . with No Such Agency," he joked, nearly snorting himself into a coma. More sound funneled through his nose than his mouth. "I've been with NSA's Cyber Counterintelligence Unit for the past eight years."

Last but not least—*him*. His smug smile spread half way across the room as he stood to introduce himself and ensure everyone could absorb the essence of him in all of his chocolate glory. No sooner than he reached the full upright position did Tony's jaw drop. It appeared that he finally recognized the man from the picture in J.J.'s living room. He snapped his head toward J.J., who could only shake hers and shrug. *It's not as if I could've planned it*, she thought. *And you have your nerve after making goo-goo eyes with Missa Thanga over there.* From what J.J. could see, Gianna had nearly exploded with orgasm at the sight of Tony.

J.J. gripped her chair and braced herself as the sound of his voice had been known to transform her to mush, and J.J. mush would not be professional for an agent leading a task force.

"Hello, all. My name is Grayson Chance," he announced, his voice oozing a velvet tenor. Then he stared at the object of his affection. "But you can call me Six."

Her skin tingled but did not itch, warning her more was at work than her lie detector capabilities.

"I'm CEG—Counterespionage Group. I've been working counterintelligence and CE issues for fifteen years, including a couple of tours at Moscow station. And this will be my second chance with Agent McCall," he said, feigning a Freudian slip. "I mean...my second time *working* with Agent McCall."

She surveyed the floor for any sign of a hole she might be able to dive into head first.

"Okaaaay," said Director Freeman, eying J.J. with his eyebrows raised. "I have a meeting to attend on the Hill. I'm sure you can all take it from here. I expect great work."

He walked out of the room and closed the door behind him.

"Hmmm...carry on! Best idea I've heard all day, right Agent McCall?"

Every eye in the room turned toward her, waiting for her reaction to the not-subtle flirt. "He's such a...kidder," she replied.

Translation: asshole.

She stood to make an announcement that would end her misery, at least for the day. "As you can all imagine, Agent Donato and I have a fair bit of paperwork to submit before the day's end. So let's say we adjourn this meeting until 9:00 a.m. Monday?"

Everyone looked around the room, shrugged, and then nodded their heads in agreement.

"Great! We'll meet here first thing Monday. We have a difficult task ahead of us. Please come prepared to discuss your agency's reporting."

Gianna and Walter led the pack out the door with Tony and J.J. straggling behind. Perhaps out of a desire to take one last look, J.J. had the fool notion to glance back at Six. He hung back in his cocky stance, his hungry eyes feasting on J.J. as if she was seasoned and seared au jus.

"Agent McCall, may I speak to you for a sec?" Six asked in the sexy way he asked for shit.

J.J. paused before questioning what harm a quick word or two could do. It would give her the perfect opportunity to tell Six there was a new sheriff—or FBI agent—in town. Tony wouldn't go far with Six in the room, at least she hoped he wouldn't.

J.J. turned to Tony. "I'll be out in a minute. And just a minute," she emphasized.

"All right," Tony said, hesitant to leave the room. "I'll be waiting for you. *Out here.*" He pointed at his watch. "Don't forget we have a deadline."

"I'm on it!" she said, comforted by his concern. When the door shut, she snapped her head toward Six and hissed, "What is it, Six? I've got work to do!"

"Awww, why you gotta be like that, J.J.?" he sang in his usual sexy serenade. "Why haven't you returned my calls? Didn't you miss me?"

She replied with stone silence; he could take her quiet defiance however he chose to. Her glare shanked him with jagged daggers if he needed a clue.

"Well," he said, invading her body bubble, standing so close she could tell him the day and hour he bought her favorite hypnotic scent, which he no doubt wore for the sole purpose of tormenting her. "I think it's only fair to warn you that I don't really give a damn about this case, although you know I'll excel at my job. I can't help it."

J.J. rolled her eyes.

"I came back for one thing and only one thing—you."

She waited for the itch, any sensation to remind her of the liar she knew him to be.

Nothing.

No matter. Just because he came back for her didn't mean his intentions were honorable. This was Six after all.

"Well, I'm sorry to disappoint you but I'm not avail—"

At once, his mouth lunged into hers, dancing a slow and easy drag. She struggled to fight him off, but her lips and body waved the white flag about five seconds after they touched. By the time she regained consciousness and pressed her hand against his chest to force him backward, the door had opened.

"J.J. you about . . ." Tony froze, paralyzed by the sight of J.J. in Six's arms, his lips parting from hers. "Uhhhh . . . I can see you're not...ready yet. I'm just gonna head back to the office and get started," he said, storming away in a huff.

"Six! What the hell's wrong with you?" She pointed to the door as if she was kicking him out of her house . . . again. "Get out!"

"Hmph. I see you have some unfinished business to take care of," he said coolly as he pimped toward the door. He glanced over his shoulder and winked. "I'll leave for now, but baby, handle your business, so I can handle mine. Because I'm back—for good."

J.J. groaned as she watched him leave, wondering how he could create so much chaos in a little less than five minutes. It was Six's way, bursting into J.J.'s life like a human tornado, powerful and equally destructive. She collapsed in a chair, threw her head back, and looked to the heavens. Then she slipped the gold-plated badge from her leather belt and eyed that powerful yet graceful eagle once again.

"God," she said. "I love your sense of humor...but this is so not funny."

Her mouth began to salivate as she thought about the drink she wanted but couldn't have. She reached into her purse to get a couple sticks of Trident to relieve the urge when she felt an old mini-fridge bottle of Smirnov left from a trip to the New York office several months ago. She preferred the mini bottles. They were just enough to soothe the nerves, never enough to get fall-out-of-the-chair intoxicated. That's all she needed.

She exhaled and mumbled under her breath. "Why Six? Why now?"

Sunnie, who just happened to be passing on her way to drop off some files to Wendell, stuck her head in the door a minute later. She noticed J.J. sitting alone. "Hey! Is everything okay in here?"

J.J. choked past the heat in her throat and turned to Sunnie with a pasted on smile. "I'm...fine, Sunnie. Just fine."

One step forward. Two steps back.

Now available, the next exciting installment in this series...

Winner! 2014 Next Generation Indie Book Award for Multicultural Fiction

★★★★★

" If you like a brilliantly executed, thrilling, and addictive suspense novel, [Situation Critical] is for you. S. D. Skye can flat write her butt off, I was sold, and tagged. This is a great series and
J.J. is Jack Ryan with a [lady part]."—Sebella Blue

This award-winning follow up to *The Bigot List* takes J.J. and her counterintelligence task force on the hunt for Russian moles who breached the nerve center of U.S. national security.

CHAPTER 1

Friday, November 6th – Irving Street NW

M ist crawled through the darkness as the sound of revenge echoed with Lana Michaels' every step along the quiet residential street. It was lined with a mix of neglected and pristine darkened row houses. Her body teetered on the edge of collapse since she'd broken free from the hospital. She'd grown tired of riding the metro, looking over her shoulder, flinching at each splashed puddle, paranoid that police cars stalked her in the darkened side streets. Still, she kept her pace swift and determined, pressed into the fog, ready for battle. She tightened her paper-thin jacket around her neck as the wind wrapped her in a shivering blanket. Nothing could quell her insatiable thirst...nothing except that bitch's tears.

She had no doubt J.J. McCall was now a hard target. FBI protocol demanded it. Lana suspected the Bureau had already retrieved her personal files from her laptop. The director had probably assigned a detail of Special Surveillance Group personnel to tail J.J. and ensure Lana didn't get within five feet. That's the reason Lana selected a softer target, one easier to kill. And Lana planned to savor his death and the untold pain inflicted on her nemesis.

For too many years, Lana had labored tirelessly in virtual isolation, sacrificed her body, and risked her freedom, all to end up with nothing.

No small thanks to that meddling so-called star FBI agent and her bitter ex-lovers.

When Jack Sabinski, Lana's lump of a boyfriend, was freed from Alexandria jail, he went into seclusion and hadn't been seen in public since. According to *The Washington Post* clenched beneath her arm, Chris Johnson, her moronic stooge, was now keeping Jack's cot warm. He sang like the Harlem Boys' Choir during his Bureau interrogations and confessed each and every one of their sins, still angry the baby she claimed to be carrying had never spawned. She had no one to rely on except the Service—which was stifled by diplomatic protocols and bound by the Embassy compound gates.

Then her mind flashed to *him*, and tears for Jake McGee's spilled blood flooded her eyes. She tightened her lids and saw him laying in a scarlet pool, murdered by the merciless bullet fired from J.J.'s Glock.

Lana's TV photo, the one in which she played the blond FBI agent, now fueled intensive manhunts for the so-called Red Honeytrap across six states. Her treachery had been splashed over headlines from LA to Moscow, and the FBI had issued every all-points bulletin, short of the Amber alert, dangling a million dollar bounty to sweeten the pot for greedy hunters. Her dyed black hair and green contact lenses couldn't conceal her for long. But by the time they figured out her location, the deed would be done. Her work would be complete. And she wouldn't be the only one left suffering a crippling loss.

Head down, shrouded in her hoodie, she rounded the corner onto Irving Street and pulled the folded newspaper from beneath her arm. She glanced at the address, then strained to see house numbers through the night fog. Halfway up the block she'd finally arrived.

"Here it is." She opened the rickety gate to the three-story duplex, trotted up the steps, and rang the doorbell. A tall, older gentleman with cotton-colored hair answered moments later. He stretched inches above her head, but his frame was thin, frail.

She peered up at him and noticed the hearing aid and thick bifocals. "Hi. I'm here about the room? I called earlier."

He inspected her, squinting his eyes and leering skeptically. The dead air gave Lana pause. For a moment, she believed his expression revealed a glint of recognition. How she hoped she was wrong. Exhausted, she grimaced at the thought of using her last shred of energy to slaughter the old man. Her right hand tensed when she imagined tightening her grip around his neck until his motionless body slammed against his pristine wood floors. An easier feat than convincing him she wasn't Lana Michaels when, in fact, she was.

"You don't remember? I told you…my apartment caught fire and I need a temporary place to stay." She flashed a sheepish smile and nervously swiped her bangs from her forehead. Then she glanced down at the newspaper where she'd scribbled the name beside the advertisement. "I believe I spoke with a Mr. O'Leary? I'm Katherine."

He hesitated for another moment then patted his chest. "Katherine, ahhh yes, yes. Come in." He stepped aside and his smile warmed. She scanned the foyer and waved to the matronly woman poking her head out from the kitchen. "I'm sorry, but I've been getting so many calls, it's hard to keep all the names straight."

She exhaled and the rigidness in her body released. "No problem, I understand. The room is still available, right?"

"Yes, yes. Do you have the deposit?"

Lana pulled a wrinkled white envelope from her pant pocket and counted out five one-hundred dollar bills. "This should do it."

He held a bill up to the light and stretched it at the ends. "Can't be too careful. You'd be surprised by how much counterfeit money is floating around D.C. these days."

He pulled a key from the drawer of the side table near the door and led her outside.

"My wife and I live in this half. We rent out the rooms on the other side. There is a gentleman sharing the home with you. Nice guy. Respectful. Very quiet. You'll be perfectly safe. We've got bolts on both bedroom doors so no one can get inside." He escorted her back outside, opened the door, and led her up the wooden steps. "You two will share the kitchen, but you each have a bathroom. Yours is here," he said pointing to a water closet-sized room containing an old-fashioned pedestal sink and footed bathtub with a shower.

"Here's where you'll be staying. Rent's due by the fifth of the month. All utilities included." The cramped space was clean, old fashioned, contained the basics. A bed, dresser with mirror, and a nightstand were positioned against the longest wall. Lace curtains hung from the windows which covered the venetian blinds.

She walked over and peered out. "I like it. You've saved my life."

"You're welcome," he said, easing toward the doorway. "Will that be all?"

"What about the neighborhood? It's not dangerous, is it? I mean, you know, I'm single. I'll probably be alone a lot, sometimes at night."

"Oh yes, yes, perfectly safe. Most of the residents have lived here for twenty years or more. Except one. Max McCall. He lives in the red-brick house right across the street. He's been here longer than any of us."

"Is that right?"

"Yeah, keeps to himself mostly. Doesn't go out much except to check on his business."

"Oh?"

"Yes, he owns a corner store a three blocks down 7th street. You can pick up eggs, bread, milk, and the basics there. A Giant grocery store is located near the metro," Mr. O'Leary said. "Now, if that's about all, I'll be getting back to the house. Time for Law & Order."

He grasped the rail and descended down the stairs. "Oh, by the way, not that I'm rushing you out or anything but how long do you think you'll be staying? The wife and I are going on Caribbean cruise for two weeks starting tomorrow."

Lana smirked as she once more peered at the house across the street. "Not much longer than a week or two. The minute I finish my business, I'm going home."

And her business was sinking hot lead into the skull of J.J.'s father—Max McCall.

About the Author

S.D. Skye is a former FBI Russian Counterintelligence Program Intelligence Analyst and supported cases during her 12-year tenure at the Bureau. She has personally witnessed the blowback the Intelligence Community suffered due to the most significant compromises in U.S. history, including the arrests of former CIA Case Officer Aldrich Ames and two of the Bureau's own—FBI Agents Earl Pitts and Robert Hansen. She has spent 20 years in the U.S. Intelligence Community.

Skye is a member of the Maryland Writer's Association, Romance Writers of America, and International Thriller Writers. She's addicted to writing and chocolate—not necessarily in that order—and currently lives in the Washington D.C. area with her son. Skye is hard at work on several projects, including the next installment of the series.

www.ingramcontent.com/pod-product-compliance
Lightning Source LLC
Chambersburg PA
CBHW060821120726
47909CB00006B/2021